Praise for JAY... P9-CFS-454
"One of the Hottest Writers on Romance Today,"*
and Her Marvelous Bestsellers

GRAND PASSION

"Filled with the kind of intelligent, offbeat characters . . .
[who] are so fun to get to know that it's hard to close the
book on them."

—*USA Today**

ABSOLUTELY, POSITIVELY

"[A] cheerful escapist package combining sex and
mystery. . . ."

—*Cosmopolitan*

WILDEST HEARTS

"The phenomenal Jayne Ann Krentz once again delivers
one of her patented storytelling gems. . . . Another guaran-
teed top-notch read!"

—*Romantic Times*

EYE OF THE BEHOLDER

"[A] well-paced thriller fraught with tension—both
sexual and suspenseful. . . ."

—*Publishers Weekly*

THE GOLDEN CHANCE

"Irresistible romance and high-powered corporate
intrigue. . . . Splendid."

—*Romantic Times*

SILVER LININGS

"Krentz entertains to the hilt. . . . The excitement and
adventure don't stop."

—*Catherine Coulter*

Published by POCKET BOOKS

JAYNE
ANN
KRENTZ

PERFECT
PARTNERS

POCKET BOOKS
New York   London   Toronto   Sydney   Singapore

The sale of this book without its cover is unauthorized. If you purchased this book without a cover, you should be aware that it was reported to the publisher as "unsold and destroyed." Neither the author nor the publisher has received payment for the sale of this "stripped book."

This book is a work of fiction. Names, characters, places and incidents are products of the author's imagination or are used fictitiously. Any resemblance to actual events or locales or persons, living or dead, is entirely coincidental.

An *Original* Publication of POCKET BOOKS

POCKET BOOKS, a division of Simon & Schuster, Inc.
1230 Avenue of the Americas, New York, NY 10020

Copyright © 1992 by Jayne Ann Krentz

All rights reserved, including the right to reproduce
this book or portions thereof in any form whatsoever.
For information address Pocket Books, 1230 Avenue
of the Americas, New York, NY 10020

ISBN: 0-671-72855-5

First Pocket Books printing April 1992

18 17 16 15 14 13 12 11 10 9

POCKET and colophon are registered trademarks of
Simon & Schuster, Inc.

For information regarding special discounts for bulk purchases,
please contact Simon & Schuster Special Sales at 1-800-456-6798
or business@simonandschuster.com

Front cover illustration by Lisa Litwack

Printed in the U.S.A.

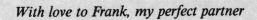

With love to Frank, my perfect partner

PERFECT
PARTNERS

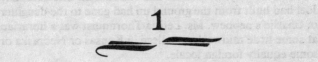

Charlie, you son of a bitch, you always did have a warped sense of humor. How the hell could you do this to me?

Joel Blackstone stood at the back of the tiny church and surveyed the cluster of mourners gathered in the front pews. September sunlight filtered down through the stained-glass windows illuminating the inside of the A-frame structure with a glow. The minister's voice was strong and surprisingly cheerful, given the fact that he was officiating at a memorial service.

"Charlie Thornquist was the most dedicated fisherman I ever knew," the minister said. "And that's saying something, because God knows I've done a pretty fair job of dedicating myself to that noble pursuit. But for me it was an avocation. A hobby. For Charlie it was nothing less than a true vocation. A calling."

At the minister's right, an urn rested on a wooden stand. The small brass plaque that hung on it was engraved with the words GONE FISHING. Inside the urn were the last earthly

1

remains of Joel's eighty-five-year-old boss, Charlie Thornquist. Several photographs of Charlie with some of his prize catches were displayed around the urn. The most impressive was the one of Charlie with a marlin he'd landed off the coast of Mexico.

Joel still could not believe that the old bastard had ripped him off in the end. After all that talk of letting Joel buy him out in another year, Charlie had stiffed him. The company Joel had built from the ground up had gone to the daughter of Charlie's nephew. Ms. Letitia Thornquist was a librarian at some little midwestern college in Kansas or Nebraska or some equally foreign locale.

The hell with it. Thornquist Gear belonged to him, Joel Blackstone, and he was damn well not going to allow it to fall into the grubby little palm of some ivory tower type who didn't know a balance sheet from an unabridged dictionary. Joel's insides tightened with anger. He had been so close to owning Thornquist free and clear.

The company was his in every way that really counted. It was Joel who had poured everything he had into the firm for the past ten years, Joel who had single-handedly turned it into a major player in the marketplace. And it was Joel who had spent the past eight months plotting a long-awaited vengeance. But to carry out his revenge, he needed to retain complete control of Thornquist Gear.

One way or another, Joel thought, he was going to maintain his hold on the company. The little librarian from Iowa or wherever could go screw herself.

"We have gathered here today to bid Charlie Thornquist farewell," the minister said. "In some ways it is a sad moment. But in truth we are sending him into the loving hands of the master fisherman."

We had a deal, Charlie. I trusted you. Thornquist was supposed to be mine. Why the hell did you have to go and die on me?

Joel was willing to concede that Charlie probably had not intentionally collapsed from a heart attack before changing his will as he had promised to do. It was just that Charlie had a way of letting business slide in favor of fishing. He had always been good at that. This time good old Charlie had let things slide a little too far.

Now, instead of owning Thornquist Gear, the rapidly expanding Seattle-based company that specialized in camping and sporting equipment, Joel had himself a new boss. The thought was enough to make him grind his back teeth. A librarian, for God's sake. He was working for a librarian.

"For most of his adult life Charlie Thornquist enjoyed one driving passion." The minister smiled benignly on the small group. "And that passion was fishing. For Charlie Thornquist, it was not the actual catch that counted, but the communion with nature that accompanied each and every fishing trip. Charlie was happiest when he was sitting in a boat with a pole in his hand."

That was true enough, Joel reflected. And while Charlie had gone off to fish, Joel had sweated blood to transform Thornquist Gear from a two-bit storefront operation into a cash-rich empire, a young and hungry shark that was on the verge of swallowing whole its first live prey. Charlie would have appreciated the analogy.

Joel narrowed his eyes against the golden glow filtering through the colorful windows. He studied the trio in the front pew.

He had already met Dr. Morgan Thornquist, thanks to Charlie. Morgan was a full professor in the department of philosophy and logic at Ridgemore College, a small private institution in Seattle. Morgan had been raised on a midwestern farm, and some of his past still showed in his sturdy frame and broad shoulders.

But nothing else about Morgan reflected his early years as a farm boy. He was in his early fifties and, according to Charlie, had lost his first wife five years earlier. With his bushy brows, a neatly trimmed gray beard and an air of academic pomposity, Morgan perfectly suited Joel's image of a college professor. Joel had nothing against Morgan. On the couple of occasions when they had met, the man had been gracious and civil. Joel respected intelligence, and there was no denying Morgan Thornquist was highly intelligent.

The same could be said of his current wife, the tall, ice-cool, very pregnant blonde seated on Morgan's right. Stephanie Thornquist was, by all accounts, just as brilliant as her husband. Forty years old, she was a professor in the department of linguistics at Ridgemore College.

There was no denying Stephanie was a striking woman. Her features were patrician, her figure tall and elegant, even in pregnancy. Her silver-blond hair was cut in a very short, very sleek, very angular style that was at once modern and timeless. Her cool blue eyes reflected the same serene intelligence one noticed in her husband.

Having at least made the acquaintance of Morgan and Stephanie, Joel had a fair idea of what to expect from them. They were neither a direct threat nor a mystery. His new boss, on the other hand, was both.

Joel's gaze slid almost reluctantly to the young woman seated on Morgan Thornquist's left. He had not yet met Letitia Thornquist, and he was not looking forward to the experience.

From where he was standing he could not see her face very clearly, mostly because she kept sniffling into a huge hankie. Ms. Thornquist was the only one in the small crowd who was crying. She did so with some enthusiasm, Joel noticed.

Joel's first impression of the new owner of Thornquist Gear was that she bore no resemblance whatsoever to her stepmother. Instead of being tall, elegant, and blond, she appeared to be short, rumpled, and definitely not blond.

In fact, the thick, wild mane of honeyed brown hair was the first thing Joel really noticed about her. She had made an obvious effort to anchor the unruly mass in a severe topknot, but the entire affair was already slipping its moorings. Tendrils of hair had wriggled free of the gold clip and gone exploring on their own. Some dangled down the soft nape of her neck; others were darting playfully over her brows and curled down her cheeks.

Charlie had told him once in passing that Letty was twenty-nine years old. Charlie had also mentioned the name of the college where she worked as a librarian, but Joel had since forgotten. He tried to recall the name of the institution —Valmont or Vellcourt, something like that.

At that instant Letitia Thornquist turned around and saw him watching her. Joel did not look away as she peered at him through a pair of round tortoiseshell frames. Her eyes were large and curious. The little round glasses and the high arch of her dark brows combined to give her a look of wide-eyed innocence. It reminded Joel of the expression on the face of an inquisitive young kitten.

She frowned thoughtfully at Joel, apparently trying to figure out who he was and what he was doing there.

He realized with a small shock of interest that she had a nice full mouth. He also noticed that the jacket of her suit appeared to be rumpled, at least in part, due to a certain roundness of her figure. She was not the least bit heavy, he saw, just pleasantly curved in all the right places. There was a certain earthy sensuality about her. This was the kind of woman men secretly pictured in their minds when they thought of home and hearth and babies.

Joel groaned inwardly. As if he did not have enough problems on his hands. Now he had to figure out how to do business with a bright-eyed innocent who looked as if she should be toiling over a hot stove with a couple of toddlers playing around her feet.

On the other hand, he told himself encouragingly, if Letitia Thornquist was what she appeared to be—a naive midwestern librarian—he should be able to handle her. He would make her the same offer he had made Charlie.

With any luck Ms. Thornquist would jump at the chance to get rich in a few months and hop the next plane back to Kansas, or wherever it was she came from. There was supposed to be a fiancé in the picture somewhere, Joel belatedly recalled. He was sure Charlie had mentioned her recent engagement.

Joel was checking out her slender fingers in search of a ring when Letitia Thornquist turned her attention back to the minister, who was concluding the service.

"Charlie left this world while engaged in the activity he loved best," the minister concluded. "Not all of us are thus privileged. His family and friends will miss him, but they can take satisfaction in knowing that Charlie lived his life the way he wished."

Joel gazed at the urn. *I'm going to miss you, you old son of a gun, even if you did throw a monkey wrench into everything at the end.*

Joel watched with interest as Letitia opened her black bag, removed another large hankie, and blew her nose. She shoved the handkerchief back into her purse and tried to straighten her suit jacket with an unobtrusive movement. It was a useless effort, Joel concluded as he watched. It was obvious Letty was one of those people who could not put on a suit without having it look rumpled inside of five minutes.

As if again aware of his gaze, Letty turned around. With an odd rush of prurient interest that came straight out of the blue, Joel found himself wondering if she wore that same expression of intent curiosity when she was in bed with a man. He could just imagine her surprise when she reached her climax. The thought made him smile. He realized it was the first time he had done so in days.

"Let us all observe a moment of silence as we wish Charlie Thornquist an endless fishing trip." The minister bowed his head, and everyone else followed suit.

When Joel looked up again, he saw the minister hand the urn to Morgan Thornquist. The small group in the pews rose and started down the aisle toward the front of the small church.

Morgan and Stephanie paused to talk to a couple of the other mourners. Joel kept his eye on Letitia, who was reaching for another hankie. When she opened her purse, two of the large pile of used handkerchiefs popped out and fell to the floor. Letitia bent over to retrieve them from under the pew. The action exposed the curves of a sweetly rounded derriere. The movement also tugged her blouse free of her skirt band in back.

It was then that he decided Ms. Letitia Thornquist was going to be merely an inconvenience, not a major problem. On impulse he started down the aisle toward the pew where Letitia was on her hands and knees searching for the lost hankies.

"I'll get that for you, Ms. Thornquist." Joel came to a halt, bent down, and scooped up the damp handkerchiefs. He handed them both to Letitia, who was still crouched between pews. She looked up in astonishment and Joel found himself gazing down into a pair of huge, intelligent sea green eyes.

"Thank you," she murmured, struggling to get to her feet and straighten her skirt and jacket at the same time.

Joel stifled a sigh. He grasped her arm and hoisted her up. He realized she felt light but surprisingly strong. There was a healthy, vibrant quality about her.

"Are you all right?" he asked.

"Yes, of course. I always cry at funerals."

Morgan Thornquist ambled over, smiling. "Hello, Joel. Glad you could make it."

"I wouldn't have missed Charlie's funeral for the world," Joel said dryly.

"I understand. Have you met my daughter?" Morgan inquired. "Letty, this is Joel Blackstone, Charlie's chief executive officer at Thornquist Gear."

Letty's eyes were brilliant with curiosity and a hint of excitement. "How do you do?"

"Fine," Joel said shortly. "Just great."

Morgan looked at him. "You'll come out to the cabin with us, won't you? We're going to have a couple of drinks and dinner in honor of Charlie."

7

"Thanks," Joel said, "but I had planned on driving back to Seattle tonight."

Stephanie walked over to join the small group. "Why don't you spend the night with us, Joel? We have plenty of room. That way you can join us for drinks and dinner."

What the hell, Joel thought. It would give him a chance to see just what he was going to be up against in the form of Ms. Letitia Thornquist. "All right. Thanks."

Letty was frowning thoughtfully. "You're my uncle's chief executive officer?"

"Right."

Her eyes skimmed somewhat disapprovingly over his black windbreaker, jeans, and running shoes. He knew the precise instant when she noted the absence of a tie.

"Were you in a hurry to get here, Mr. Blackstone?" she asked politely.

"No." He smiled faintly. "I dressed for the occasion with Charlie in mind. I worked for him for nearly ten years, and I never once saw him with a tie."

Morgan chuckled. "Good man. Charlie was always telling us how useful you were. He claimed it was solely because of you that he got to spend the past ten years fishing full-time."

"I did my best to take the day-to-day problems of running Thornquist off his shoulders," Joel murmured.

"I know you did. I'm sure you and Letty are going to work very well together, too," Morgan announced. "You two have obviously got a great deal to discuss."

"Dad, please," Letty said, "this is hardly the time or place to talk about business."

"Nonsense," Morgan retorted. "Uncle Charlie would not have wanted us to get maudlin. And you and Joel need an opportunity to get to know each other. The sooner the better. Letty, why don't you come on back to the cabin in Joel's car? You can give him directions, and the two of you can introduce yourselves properly."

Joel saw the uncertainty in Letty's eyes as she considered that proposition. He decided then and there that the best way to handle his new boss was to save her the difficulty of having to make challenging decisions all by herself.

"Good idea," Joel said easily. He took a firm grip on Letty's arm and started toward the church steps. "My Jeep is parked right outside."

"Well . . ." Letty's eyes darted quickly back and forth between her father and Joel. "If you're sure you don't mind?"

"I don't mind at all."

Just as Joel had anticipated, his own decisiveness seemed to make up Letty's mind for her. Clutching her black shoulder bag, she allowed him to draw her along in his wake.

No sweat, Joel thought. This was going to be like taking candy from a baby. Charlie had been just as easy to handle in his way.

Right up until the end, that is, when good old Charlie had screwed him over royally.

"Ouch," said Letty. "You're hurting my arm."

"Sorry." Joel forced himself to relax his fingers.

Charlie, you bastard, how could you do this to me?

Letty sat uneasily in the passenger seat as Joel drove the Jeep through the tiny mountain community and onto the blacktop road that ran along the small river gorge. She gripped her purse firmly in her lap and slanted her new CEO an assessing sidelong glance. She was puzzled by the tension she sensed in Joel Blackstone.

Granted, funerals were emotional occasions, but this was more than the somber mood one would have expected at the loss of a boss. There was a restless impatience in Joel Blackstone. Letty could feel it. It burned in his tawny gold eyes and vibrated along every line of his lean, hard body.

He seethed with it, although he was masking it well beneath a layer of cool self-control. There was anger burning in him, too. Letty could feel it, and it sent a shiver down her spine.

Angry men were dangerous.

The sense of potentially explosive power in Joel was underlined by the fiercely molded planes and angles of his face. It was a savage face, Letty thought, a face that reflected the ancient hunting instincts that by rights should have lain deeply buried in a modern, civilized man. They were clearly much too close to the surface in Joel Blackstone. She guessed he was in his mid-thirties, thirty-six or thirty-seven, perhaps. Something about him looked and felt far older, however.

Letty was torn between a nearly overwhelming curiosity and an equally strong sense of caution. She had never met a man who managed to make her wary in quite this manner. It was a primitive sensation.

"How long did you work for my great-uncle, Mr. Blackstone?" she finally asked politely when the silence got to be oppressive.

"Nearly ten years."

"I see." Letty moistened her lips. "He, uh, spoke highly of you. Said you were very sharp. He thought you had a certain instinct for business."

"Yeah. I had an instinct instead of an M.B.A." Joel flashed her a brief amused glance. "He spoke highly of you, too, Ms. Thornquist. Said you were a bright little thing."

Letty winced. "I don't think Great-Uncle Charlie was very much impressed by academia. He always treated it with a sort of indulgent condescension."

"He was a self-made man. He didn't think too much of the ivory tower life."

"And neither do you, I take it?" With effort, Letty kept her tone polite.

"Charlie and I had a few things in common. That was one of them."

Letty pursed her lips. "Not exactly. I think you feel actual disdain for it. Charlie was not disdainful."

"Is that right?" Joel did not sound particularly interested.

"Charlie raised my father after my grandparents died. It was Charlie who financed Dad's education all the way through graduate school, you know. So you see, he couldn't have been completely disdainful of the academic life."

Joel shrugged. "Charlie believed in letting people do what they wanted with their lives. All he asked was that they leave him alone so that he could go fishing as often as possible."

"Yes, I guess that's true, isn't it?" So much for trying to ease the tension with idle conversation, Letty thought. She wondered what sort of woman Joel Blackstone dated. Surely if he had a wife he would have brought her to the funeral.

Whoever his woman was, she would have to be a very sensual creature, Letty decided. A man like Joel would want a woman who could respond to him in a very physical way.

Of course, she reminded herself, most men wanted that sort of woman. Even Philip, whom she'd thought would not be quite so demanding, had needed a more responsive woman. It was fortunate for all concerned that she had discovered that fact during their engagement rather than after the marriage had taken place.

"How long will you be out here on the Coast, Ms. Thornquist?"

"You may call me Letty."

"Sure. Right. Letty. How long?"

"I don't know yet."

Some of Joel's superficial control dissolved for an instant, revealing a hint of the restless impatience Letty sensed churning inside him. "What do you mean, you don't know?" Joel glowered at the narrow, winding road through the Jeep's windshield. "Don't you have to get back to that college where you work?"

"Vellacott?"

"Yeah, Vellacott, or whatever. Don't you have to get back to your job?"

"No."

"But Charlie said you worked in the library there."

"I did. Reference desk. Nearly six years." Letty gripped the dashboard. "Would you mind slowing down a little?"

"What?" Joel threw her a scowl.

11

"I said, would you mind slowing the car a little," Letty repeated carefully.

"Your father's already pulling ahead of us. Nice car, by the way."

Letty glanced at the red Porsche convertible. It was moving swiftly, clinging to the twisting road like a limpet. Morgan had the top down, and Stephanie's silver-gold hair was secured beneath a white scarf. Stephanie looked good in white, Letty reflected. It suited her ice-maiden beauty.

"The Porsche belongs to Stephanie," Letty said. "My father drives a BMW."

Joel cocked a brow. "You sound as if you disapprove. Got something against nice cars?"

"No. It's just that it's a little odd to have a stepmother who drives a candy red Porsche," Letty admitted, "when the most exciting thing I've ever driven is a Buick. Please slow down. You don't have to worry about getting lost. I know how to get to their house."

Joel eased his foot off the accelerator. "You're the boss."

Letty smiled, pleased at the sound of that. "Yes, I am, aren't I? It feels very strange, you know."

"Inheriting a company the size of Thornquist out of the clear blue sky? Yeah, I can see where that might feel a little weird." Joel's hands tightened around the steering wheel. "Tell me, Letty, do you have any experience in the business world?"

"No, but I've read a great many books and articles on the subject since I learned that Great-Uncle Charlie left me Thornquist Gear."

"Books and articles, huh? You know, Letty, there's quite a difference between the business world and an academic environment."

"Is there?" She studied the scenery. Twilight came early in the Cascades, she noticed. The heavily forested terrain was already turning dark and mysterious as the last of the sun disappeared. She was accustomed to wide open spaces and gentle rolling hills. These wild, aggressive mountains were a bit overpowering. Just like Joel Blackstone.

"A world of difference," Joel said pointedly. "I don't know if Charlie ever mentioned it to you, but he and I had a sort of unofficial understanding."

"Did you?"

"I was going to buy him out in another year."

"Were you?"

Joel flicked her another quick sidelong glance. "That's right. Look, I know it's a little too soon to talk about it, but I want you to know I'm still prepared to go through with the deal. I'll continue to run the company for the next year, just as I have for the past ten years. Then, when I've got the financing in place, I'll cash you out. How does that sound?"

"The turnoff is up ahead on the right."

Joel's jaw tightened. "Thanks."

He slowed the Jeep and obediently turned off the river road onto an even tinier one that led into the trees. The structure of glass and wood at the end of the lane was a cabin in name only. By anyone's standards it was a lovely and expensive home.

"You can park behind the Porsche," Letty said.

"Nice place," Joel said, casting a knowledgeable eye over the sleek lines of the house. "I didn't know professors got paid enough to afford Porsches and weekend cabins like this."

"My father is one of the country's leading experts on medieval philosophy. By temperament and training, he is himself a fine logician. My stepmother has written some of the most important papers being published today on syntactic and semantic analysis."

"So?"

Letty was amused. "So they are both brilliant analytical thinkers. It gives them an edge when it comes to making financial investments."

"I'll keep that in mind the next time I want some advice

13

on the stock market," Joel said. He opened the Jeep door and got out. Then he started around the hood to open Letty's door.

Letty saw what was happening and scrambled out on her own. She did not want Joel getting the impression that just because he worked for her, he was expected to wait on her hand and foot. She had a feeling things were going to be difficult enough as it was between herself and Joel Blackstone.

Letty walked hesitantly into the gleaming kitchen and saw Stephanie at the sink. "Can I help?" she offered, already knowing what the answer would be.

"No, thank you, Letty." Stephanie smiled her cool, serene smile as she peeled shrimp. "Everything's under control in here. Why don't you go out and visit with your father and Joel?"

Everything was always under control with Stephanie. Letty wondered what it would take to ruffle the glassy smooth surface of her stepmother's glacial poise. "All right. If you're certain there's nothing I can do."

"I'll call you if I need you," Stephanie promised.

"Well, if you insist. What are you preparing?"

"Black linguini with shrimp and mussels."

Letty blinked. "I don't believe I've ever had black linguini. Do they use food coloring to make it black?"

"Heavens no." Stephanie looked startled. "Squid ink."

"Oh." Letty retreated from the kitchen.

Stephanie would not call for assistance, Letty knew, because she would not want anyone else in her pristine, orderly world. Too much risk of a mess, no doubt.

Stephanie was a gourmet cook. This did not surprise Letty, because she had learned very quickly that everything Stephanie did, she did with a high level of expertise. What amazed Letty about Stephanie's cooking was that she turned out truly exotic fare without creating so much as a

14

ripple of disorder on the surfaces of her steel and white tile kitchen.

Morgan was talking to Joel near the seven-foot windows when Letty entered the living room. He glanced at his daughter.

"Ah, there, you are, my dear. We were just about to open a bottle of Yakima Valley sauvignon blanc. I think you'll like it." He turned to Joel. "Letty hasn't spent much time out here in the Northwest yet. We're trying to educate her palate."

"I am told Seattle is a foodie town," Letty said dryly.

Joel shrugged. "I don't know about that, but we like to eat. And we like to eat well."

"So I have been given to understand. All right, Dad. I'm ready to try your latest discovery." Letty sat down on one of the white leather sofas. She noticed Joel stayed near the window, gazing out over the night-darkened forest.

"This one is a genuine find, I'm pleased to say." Morgan went to work at the small bar built into the far end of the living room. "Great depth and finesse. Very subtle. Quite sophisticated, actually."

"Sophisticated" was a word Professor Morgan Thornquist would never have applied to a bottle of wine in the old days. Letty was still coming to terms with the changes she was witnessing in her father.

Some of them were good, she conceded. He had shed the extra twenty pounds he had carried for as long as Letty could remember, and he'd given up his pipe. He looked healthy and happy, and there was a new spring in his step. There was no denying he was thriving out here in the Pacific Northwest.

For the most part Letty was happy for him. But as far as she was concerned, the decision to start a second family at Morgan's age was taking things too far. She still could not believe she was going to have a baby brother soon.

"Here we go." Morgan drew the cork from the bottle with

a flourish. "Excellent color, don't you think, Joel? Letty, let me have your glass."

Letty got up and handed her father the long-stemmed wineglass. Morgan filled it before setting it down on the lacquered Art Deco coffee table in front of the sofa.

"None for Stephanie, of course," Morgan said. "She won't touch alcohol again until after Matthew Christopher is born. How about you, Joel?"

Joel, who was standing near the window, studying the magnificent view, glanced at the wine bottle. "Any beer in the kitchen?"

Morgan smiled. "Of course. I kept the refrigerator stocked with Charlie's favorites. You know how he liked his Northwest-brewed beer and ale." He raised his voice. "Stephanie my dear, would you bring Joel a bottle of that good ale we picked up last month at that new brewery in north Seattle?"

Stephanie appeared almost immediately in the doorway with a bottle and a glass. "Here you are, Joel."

"Thanks." Joel ignored the glass and accepted the bottle. "To Charlie." He took a long swallow.

"To Charlie."

"To Charlie."

"To Charlie."

Letty took a sip of the sauvignon blanc and surveyed the platter of vegetables that sat in the center of the lacquered table. She was familiar with most of them, although she noticed one or two odd-looking items. She dunked a peapod in the dip.

"What is this?" she asked politely. "I don't recognize the flavor."

"That's a tahini- and tofu-based dip I whipped together," Stephanie said. "Do you like it?"

"Very interesting," Letty said. She moved on to a little dish of deep red spread surrounded by crackers. "And this?"

"Just a little something I make using sun-dried tomatoes. I'll give you the recipe if you like."

"Thank you," Letty said formally, aware that everyone was watching her with varying degrees of amusement.

"Do you like sashimi?" Joel asked a little too politely.

"Back home we bait fish hooks with sashimi," Letty said.

Morgan laughed indulgently. "Everyone eats sushi and sashimi out here on the Coast. Isn't that right, Joel?"

Joel nodded slowly, his eyes on Letty. "There are sushi bars on every third corner from here to Vancouver. And the corners that don't have sushi bars usually have Thai restaurants. But I imagine Letty prefers beef."

Stephanie looked immediately concerned. "Oh, dear, Letty, you aren't still eating red meat, are you? Nobody eats red meat anymore."

"Well, we don't eat a lot of raw fish back in Indiana, either. I read an article that said there's a risk of worms in raw fish. They cause a very unpleasant illness that can be extremely difficult to cure."

"Nonsense," Stephanie said as she started back into the kitchen. "Statistically, the chances of getting contaminated fish are extremely small if one is careful to eat in good-quality restaurants."

Morgan looked at Letty. "Why don't you tell us what your plans are now that you have your own business?"

"Actually, I've been giving that a lot of thought." Letty paused to take another sip of wine. She could literally feel the seething tension vibrating close to the surface again in Joel. He had clearly gone on high alert. She realized with a trickle of dread that she had never been more aware of a man in her life. It was a very disconcerting sensation.

"Go on, Letty. Tell us what you've been thinking," Joel said softly, his eyes intent.

"I've come to the conclusion that I need to make a few changes in my life," Letty murmured. "This inheritance from Great-Uncle Charlie could not have come at a better time. It might almost have been fate. On the plane trip out here I decided not to go back to Vellacott."

Morgan looked astonished, but vastly pleased. "Well,

well, well. I'm glad to hear it. You're not normally the impulsive type, my dear. What were these changes in your life that you made on the spur of the moment?"

Letty munched a sliver of toast slathered with sun-dried tomato spread. "I've broken off my engagement to Philip, I've quit my job, and I've decided to move to Seattle and take over the reins of Thornquist Gear."

The sharp crack of glass exploding on hard tile drew everyone's attention. Letty glanced across the room to where Joel had been standing by the window and saw that he had dropped his bottle of ale.

Joel looked up from the shards that glittered at his feet. His eyes burned like those of a tiger in the night as he stared straight at Letty.

"Sorry," Joel said very softly, his tone devoid of any emotion. "An accident. Don't worry. I'll clean it up."

2

Joel came awake in a cold sweat, fragments of the dream still far too clear in his head. He could see the car going over the cliff and sinking into the sea. His father's face appeared, as it always did, at the window on the driver's side, fingers clawing at the glass, eyes staring wildly at his son. Joel could see him screaming as the car sank below the surface. There was no sound, but Joel could hear the words in his head as his father shouted at him.

"This is all your fault," he had yelled.

All your fault.

Joel lay still for a moment, orienting himself to his strange surroundings. The sighing of the wind in the trees outside the window brought him back quickly to reality. He threw aside the covers and sat up on the edge of the bed.

He was having the dream more often these days. He did not need a shrink to tell him why. He was on the verge of taking revenge after fifteen years of waiting, and all the old feelings were awakening and starting to churn inside him.

With any luck he would stop having the damn dream when everything was finally finished. Only a few more weeks and it would all be over.

In the meantime, he knew from experience that he was not going to get back to sleep until he had worked off some of the adrenaline. Back home in his own apartment in Seattle, he would have worked out on the equipment he kept in the spare bedroom. Unfortunately there was no treadmill, stationary bike, or weights here at the Thornquists' mountain place.

There was, however, plenty of room to run. Joel put on his jeans and running shoes, picked up a towel from his private bathroom, and headed down the hall.

He sensed that Letty was awake when he went past her bedroom, but he paid no attention until he realized she had gotten out of bed and followed him into the living room. Her soft, startled voice caught him just as he was unlocking the sliding glass doors.

"Where in heaven's name are you going? It's one o'clock in the morning."

He glanced back over his shoulder and saw a wild-maned ghost in a long white cotton nightgown. Letty's glasses were perched on her nose, making her look like a very serious, very intellectual sort of ghost. As she moved out into the weak moonlight, Joel saw that the long flounced nightgown was trimmed with a jaunty sailor collar and a red ribbon tied in a bow. The streamers of the ribbon drifted down the front of the gown.

The blue-white moonlight glinted on the lenses of her little round glasses and revealed the frowning disapproval on her face. Her gaze raked him from head to toe, taking in the fact that he was wearing nothing but a pair of jeans. Joel wondered if she was about to rap his knuckles with a ruler.

"Don't worry. I'm not making off with the family silver," he said. "I'm just going to take a run."

"You're going running?" She stared at his bare chest as if

she had never seen one before. "But it's the middle of the night. You can't be serious."

"Trust me. I'm serious." He slid open the glass door. The crisp air flowed over him like clear, cold water rinsing away the last images from the nightmare.

"Joel, wait. You can't go out there alone at this time of night."

The patter of her bare feet on the hardwood floor stopped him. Joel reluctantly turned his head again. "What the hell's the matter, Letty? I'm just going to run. Go on back to bed and get some sleep."

"I won't have it." She scurried forward and came to a halt directly in front of him. "I can't let you do this, Joel."

He studied her with growing curiosity. "Okay, I give up. Why can't you let me do this?"

Her eyes widened behind the lenses of her glasses. "Because it's dangerous, of course. What's the matter with you? Are you out of your mind? You can't go dashing about in an isolated area at this time of night. Anything could happen. Why, just the other day I saw an article about a series of murders in mountain campgrounds."

Joel folded his arms across his chest, half amused in spite of his foul mood. "Did the article specify which campgrounds and where they were located?"

"Somewhere down in California, I think," she mumbled. "But it hardly matters where it happened. The point is, it's dangerous to run around alone at night. There are a lot of crazy people in the world."

"I can outrun them."

"What about bears?" she shot back, undaunted. "Can you outrun a bear?"

"I don't know. I've never tried."

"It's quite chilly out there," Letty said.

"It's not that cold. I'll be warm enough once I start moving."

"I read an article about some sort of horrible creature that

lives in the mountains out here in the Pacific Northwest."
She looked a bit desperate now.

Joel nearly laughed. "You don't believe in Bigfoot, do
you?"

"No, of course not. All the same, I think this is a very bad
idea."

Joel felt another wave of cold night air flow through the
open door. "Your reservations on the subject are duly noted,
Ms. Thornquist. Now, if you'll excuse me, I'm going to
run."

She touched his arm, her fingers light and gentle. "I really
wish you wouldn't. It's going to make me very uneasy."

He shook his head, losing patience with her. He stepped
out onto the deck and draped the towel over the railing.
Letty came as far as the door. He scowled at her. "Damn it, I
don't want to hear any more about this. Go on back to bed."

Her chin came up at a stubborn angle. "No, I will not."

He sighed. "What do you intend to do?"

"If you're going to insist on this foolishness, I'll keep
watch from here. I can see a good portion of the road, and
there's a full moon. I'll be able to keep an eye on you."

Joel gazed at her in disbelief. "You're going to wait up for
me?"

"I don't have much choice, do I? I couldn't possibly go
back to bed and get any sleep knowing you're running
around out there like a moving target in a shooting gallery."

Joel gave up. "Suit yourself. I'm going to run."

He loped down the steps without a backward glance. The
crisp, clean night called to him, offering to blow away some
of the anger and frustration that had been threatening to
consume him all day.

He looked back once as he moved out in a long, easy
stride. He could just barely make her out behind the sliding
door. Her nose seemed pressed anxiously to the glass. For
some reason she did not look like a prim little midwestern
librarian in that moment. Instead, with her ghostly pale
nightgown and her wild, tangled mane she seemed more like

some fey creature of the night. There was an intriguing, sweet, rather innocent sensuality about her that Joel was finding increasingly disturbing.

Hell of a time to be thinking about sex.

He jerked his attention back to his running. What was the matter with him? he wondered grimly. Letty Thornquist was a major thorn in his side at the moment. He did not need to complicate an already difficult situation with sex.

Ms. Thornquist probably did not approve of sex, anyway. She had undoubtedly read an article that detailed the myriad dangers involved these days.

Hell, even he had read a few of those articles.

Joel ran easily on the edge of the blacktop road that paralleled the twisting river. When he looked down the steep embankment of the small gorge he could just barely make out the sheen of moving water. Charlie Thornquist had come up here often to fish in that river.

Joel gave himself over to the running, channeling his frustration into energy with a directed purpose. He could handle it as long as he did that. It was an old tactic, one he used whenever the restlessness deep within him reached the boiling point. Nights were always the worst times.

On the other hand, he reminded himself, nights were often the times when he saw things most clearly. Ideas that had been whirling around in the back of his mind for weeks would suddenly crystallize into a clear vision at night. Problems that appeared incredibly tangled during the day often unraveled at night.

Joel knew he did some of his best work at night. He had learned that some things, such as revenge, were best plotted in the dark hours before dawn.

And wouldn't the fact that he intended to use her company to destroy an old enemy shock the hell out of sweet, innocent little Ms. Letitia Thornquist? Joel grinned savagely to himself and ran harder.

By the time he turned and started back toward the house, he could feel the satisfying film of sweat on his shoulders and chest. His breathing was deep and strong and steady. The night air had acted like a sponge, soaking the remnants of the dream out of his mind. His brain began to function in a more disciplined manner.

All right, so there had been a minor setback in his plans. So Letty was coming to Seattle to take over Thornquist Gear. How long could it last? She would realize within a month that it was a lousy idea.

Letty knew nothing about business. He could arrange to keep her isolated and removed from the important stuff until she grew bored or confused. If he kept tabs on things, she would not be much more than a minor nuisance. She was bound to realize in short order that the best thing she could do was head back to her nice safe ivory tower job at Vellacott College.

No doubt about it. Within a month she would understand that she was out of her league. Within a month she would see that the smart thing to do was let Joel continue to run the company for the next year and then cash her out. She would end up with lots of money, and he would end up with Thornquist Gear.

Which was exactly how it should be.

In the meantime there was no reason why he could not proceed with his plans to crush Victor Copeland. No reason at all. Hell, Letty would never even have a clue to what was going on, and even if she did guess, Joel would simply tell her it was nothing out of the ordinary. Just a simple business maneuver. Companies like Thornquist took over outfits like Copeland Marine Industries every day and then liquidated them. Right down to the last outboard engine.

No big deal, Ms. Thornquist. This is known as business as usual. Welcome to the real world. If you don't like it, go on back to your ivory tower. Maybe if you ask very nicely, that fiancé of yours will take you back.

Joel frowned at that last thought. He wondered what sort of man Letty would welcome into her bed. The fiancé she had mentioned earlier was no doubt some stodgy, absent-

minded English lit professor. Joel tried to imagine the guy
fumbling around politely under the covers while mentally
reviewing his notes for the next day's lecture on the nine-
teenth-century novel.

Maybe Letty enjoyed discussing Austen or Thackeray
while reaching orgasm.

That brought up the very interesting question of whether
or not Ms. Thornquist had ever *had* an orgasm—a real
climax, not some wimpy little release but the kind that
would make her scream right out loud. The kind that would
make her clutch at the man who was giving it to her and dig
her little nails into his skin. That aura of innocence about
her made him doubt it.

Joel groaned and pounded along the road with every bit of
energy left in him.

The sweat was streaming off him in rivulets when he
finally stopped running. He glanced ahead at the house as he
slowed to a walk to cool down. Letty was no longer standing
at the window. Perhaps she had decided to abandon him to
his fate out here in the wilderness.

When his breathing had returned to normal and his pulse
had slowed, Joel climbed the steps to the deck and picked up
the towel he had left there. He felt in control again. With any
luck he would be able to sleep for the rest of the night.

Wiping himself off with the towel, Joel opened the sliding
glass door and stepped inside.

Letty was curled up on one of the white sofas. She stirred
when Joel loomed over her.

"Oh, you're back." Letty opened her eyes, yawning.

"Safe and sound, no thanks to you. Some guardian you
turned out to be." Joel found himself smiling. "I could have
been violated and murdered out there and you would have
slept through the whole thing."

Letty considered that and then shook her head swiftly. "I
might have slept through the murder part, but I doubt if I
would have missed the sound of you being violated. Something tells me you would have made a lot of noise."

Joel narrowed his eyes slightly in surprise. "Well, well, well. Are you always this witty in the middle of the night?"

"I wouldn't know. I'm rarely up at this hour." She stared at him, unmoving. "How come you are?"

He shrugged. "I don't need a lot of sleep."

"Everybody needs a good night's sleep. I read an article somewhere that said persistent insomnia should be investigated to rule out the possibility of a health problem."

Joel grinned slowly. "Believe me, I am very healthy."

She frowned. "All the same, it could be a psychological problem, you know. I mean, you might feel perfectly fit physically and still have some sort of neurosis that's keeping you awake."

"I've got better things to do than waste my time being neurotic."

Joel studied her intently in the silence that followed. He was grimly aware that he was getting hard. She looked very soft and vulnerable lying there in the moonlight. The nightgown was hiked up around her knees and he could see that she had beautifully arched feet.

This was insane, he told himself. The last thing he needed. Where the hell was his common sense? He had to keep his mind on the big picture. He was going to be juggling a lot of firecrackers during the next couple of months. He could not afford to let himself get distracted.

But curiosity was riding him now, Joel realized. There was a mystery lying right in front of him, and he had a thing about solving dangerous puzzles before they exploded in his face. If he had learned one thing over the years, it was to be prepared. The more he knew about Letty Thornquist, the safer his plans would be, he told himself.

"You mentioned earlier this evening that in addition to quitting your job, you broke off your engagement to somebody named Philip," Joel said carefully.

"Dr. Philip Dixon, associate professor in the department of business administration back at Vellacott College. Several publications in notable journals to his credit, consultant to

industry and chairman of important faculty committees."
Letty was not looking at him now. She had her arms behind
her head and was staring out the window with half-closed
eyes.

So the guy was not in the English lit department, after all.
"Sorry to hear it didn't work out."

"Thank you."

Joel could see the gentle curves of Letty's breasts outlined
against the cotton gown. "Maybe you'll change your mind.
Give things another chance or something."

"I can't see that happening."

"Who broke it off?"

"I did."

Joel absorbed that. Now he was more than curious. He
had to know what would make Letty break off an engagement to a man who should have been perfect for her. "A
misunderstanding?"

"You could say that."

This was like pulling teeth, Joel decided. He kept prodding. "Did you find yourself interested in someone else?"

"No."

"Did he, uh, get involved with someone?"

Letty turned her head to look at him. Her eyes were
drowsy as she focused on his face. "You want to know what
actually happened?"

Joel sensed victory at last. He kept his voice even,
noncommittal. "If you feel like talking about it, I don't
mind listening."

"I haven't told a single soul. It was too embarrassing."
Letty switched her gaze back to the moonlit deck. "We were
engaged about six weeks. I went to see Philip in his office
about ten days ago. He wasn't expecting me. I knocked once
and then opened the door. He had someone with him. A
pretty graduate student named Gloria."

"They were in what might be called a compromising
position, I take it?"

"Philip was sitting in his chair, his legs spread, his pants

27

unzipped. She was on her knees in front of him, and there was a rather appalling sucking noise. It was"—Letty paused —"quite amazing, really."

Joel drew a deep breath. "Yeah, I can see where that would have been a little upsetting."

Letty's shoulders started to shake. She put her hand over her mouth and made a tiny, muffled sound. Joel stared at her, alarmed. Hell, she was going to start crying. He was no good with crying women. He had no idea what to do. "Letty, don't. Christ, I'm sorry I brought up the subject. Look . . ."

"No, you don't understand." She glanced at him, but her eyes slid quickly away before Joel could read the expression in them. There was another choked squeak, and then the giggles spilled forth.

Joel realized with a jolt of surprise that she was laughing.

"Oh, I was shocked at first," Letty admitted as she struggled to catch her breath. " 'Stunned' would be a better word. But then I realized I had never seen anything so ludicrous in my entire life. He looked so *silly* with his, uh, you-know-what . . ." She broke off again as words failed her.

"Male member?" Joel suggested dryly.

Letty succumbed to a fresh burst of giggles. She nodded wildly, springy hair bouncing around her shoulders. "Yes, perfect. With his *male member* stuck in her, I mean, inserted between her . . . her . . ."

"With his male member inserted between her scarlet-tinted lips?"

"Exactly. It was the most ridiculous thing you can imagine."

"I get the picture."

"Disgusting, actually."

"Probably depends on your point of view," Joel temporized.

She finally stopped giggling and gave him an embarrassed smile. "I guess you had to be there."

"On the whole, I'm glad I missed it."

"Yes, well, you have to know Philip to really understand just how ludicrous he looked," Letty confided. "You see, he's so incredibly *professorial*. Tweed jackets, tasseled loafers, button-down oxford shirts, paisley ties, the works. He looks a lot like—" She stopped abruptly.

"A lot like what?" Joel asked.

She made a small, dismissing motion with her hand. "Nothing. It just occurred to me that in some ways Philip dresses and acts a bit like Dad. I wonder if that's why I . . . Never mind."

Joel realized that avenue of conversation had just been shut down. "Yeah, well, it doesn't sound like you're carrying a torch for Dixon."

"No." Letty sighed. "It was horribly humiliating at the time, of course. But when it was all over, I knew it was for the best. I thought Philip and I had a lot in common. But I guess it was all rather superficial in a way. And he did have the most annoying habit of pontificating about things."

"Pontificating?"

Letty smiled wryly. "If we went to a film, he'd analyze it to death afterward. If we attended a play, he evaluated each actor's performance. It was embarrassing to go out to a restaurant with him because he always sent something back to the kitchen. And his opinion was always the deciding one. He assumed that because he had more degrees than I did, he was always right. I think it would have gotten to me after about six months of marriage."

"I'd figure six weeks at the most."

"You may be right." She glanced at him. "There was something missing in my relationship with Philip. I think I knew it from the first, but I tried to pretend it didn't matter. Maybe I hoped he just wouldn't notice."

"What do you think was missing?" Joel asked, curious again.

She scowled intently. "I don't know. Some spark. A feeling of passion. An underlying sizzle. I'm not sure how to describe it. All I know is, never in my wildest dreams could I

29

even conceive of getting on my knees in front of Philip Dixon when he had his pants unzipped."

"Ah."

"It seems to me that if there had been a shot of genuine passion in the relationship, I would at least have been able to imagine doing that. I'm not saying I would have actually done it, of course. I mean it is rather . . ." She floundered.

"Wanton?" Joel supplied helpfully.

"Yes. Wanton." She appeared relieved by the word. "As I said, if there had been a lot of real passion in our relationship I think I should have at least been able to visualize it. Don't you think so?"

Joel tried valiantly to squash the picture he had conjured up in his own head. He failed. "Yeah. Sure." Damn. At this rate he was going to need another long run before he would be able to sleep.

"What I have come to realize lately, Joel," she continued with a burst of earnest intensity, "is that passion is exactly what's been missing in my life. It's missing in every area of my life. My career, my past, my future. Everything seems to have gotten into a rut. I want out."

"Out. I see."

"Lately I've begun to feel as though I'm sitting on the sidelines of my own life. Normally I'm a very goal-directed person, but I feel as though I've lost my way or something. I need to revitalize and redirect myself. Great-Uncle Charlie has given me the perfect opportunity to do just that, and I'm going to grab the chance. Thornquist Gear is going to change my life."

Joel was torn between wanting to insert his male member between her scarlet-tinted lips and the equally strong desire to throttle her. *Thornquist Gear was his.*

"Letty, have you really thought this out? I know the idea of being president of your own company probably sounds exciting, but it's not that easy. You have no background in retailing, let alone in the sporting goods business. Hell, I'll bet you haven't even done much camping."

30

She wrinkled her nose. "So?"

"Letty, camping equipment is one of our staple product lines. We cater to campers. We sold over a million and a half dollars' worth of tents alone last year."

Her eyes widened. "I don't see why I have to be an expert with the product in order to sell it. I'm interested in management and growth and the creation of a thriving enterprise. I'm excited about running a big business, not setting up my own tent."

Joel swore under his breath. "You don't know what you're getting into, lady. Running a growing corporation is not a game. It's not even a good way to amuse yourself while you get over a broken engagement."

Her mouth tightened into a mutinous line. "I am fully aware that I am about to embark on a major career change, and I am prepared to devote myself completely to learning everything I need to know to be successful. I am a very fast learner, Joel."

"You think you can just sit down behind the president's desk tomorrow or the next day and start running things? You think it's going to come naturally?"

"Of course not." She smiled. "I told you I've done a great deal of research."

"Oh, great. Research."

"I am a librarian, you know."

"Don't remind me."

"Now, Joel, there's no need to get so intense over this," she said soothingly. "I think that may be one of your problems, you know. You're very intense. As it happens, I have read several articles on the subject of women in business, and they all point to one component that seems to be crucial to success."

"What the hell is that?" he demanded.

"A mentor."

That stopped him in his tracks for an instant. "A mentor? Jesus Christ, what are you talking about?"

"A mentor. You know, a teacher. Someone who takes you

31

under his wing and shows you the ropes. That's how most people make it up the ladder in the corporate world, Joel. They have mentors who guide them and bring them along."

"I never had a mentor," he snarled.

"Of course you did. Great-Uncle Charlie was yours. You just didn't think of him that way because you weren't familiar with modern corporate jargon."

"*Shit.* You think Charlie was a mentor?" Joel's hand clenched into a fist around the towel. "Let me tell you how it was with me and Charlie Thornquist. Ten years ago I walked in off the street looking for a job. He hired me to run the little shop he had on First Avenue in downtown Seattle because he wanted to go fishing more often. He showed me how to work the cash register and how to lock up at night, and then he left town for two weeks."

Letty fixed him with a fascinated gaze. "Really? What happened next?"

"When he came back to town to check up on me, I told him I thought we ought to start stocking a couple of different lines of sleeping bags. He said fine and took off for a deep-sea fishing trip. I didn't see him for a month."

"Then what happened?"

"When he got back from that trip, I said the new tents were selling like hotcakes and maybe we should look into renting ski equipment for the season. He told me to do whatever I wanted. After that, I did. I made Thornquist Gear what it is today, damn it."

Letty gave him a pleased look. "Which makes you the perfect mentor for me."

"*Me.* Your mentor? Are you out of your mind?" He thought about picking Letty up by one slender ankle and dangling her over the railing. He'd be damned before he'd teach her how to run his company.

"I think it's going to be a perfect partnership, Joel."

"I think I am going to take a shower and go back to bed." Joel swung around and stalked down the hall to the bedroom. He knew for a fact he was not going to get any sleep tonight.

Letty awoke the next morning with a sense of well-being that she had not felt in a long time. She lay quietly for a while, gazing out the bedroom window as a clear dawn broke over the mountains.

She still could not believe she had conducted such an intimate conversation with Joel Blackstone last night, but in retrospect she was glad she had done so. What she had confided in him was nothing less than the truth.

She was going to find whatever it was that had been missing in her life, and she was going to find it in Seattle running Thornquist Gear.

Letty jumped out of bed and burst into the white tile bathroom. She was feeling so exuberant this morning that she thought she could even find it in herself to be a little more tolerant of Stephanie.

Not that she had much choice, Letty thought. She had a baby brother on the way, whether she approved of it or not.

Matthew Christopher. It seemed strange to know the baby's name and sex before it had even arrived. But, as Stephanie had explained, she'd had certain tests done because of her age. In addition to assuring herself that the baby was healthy, she had also learned it was a boy. Stephanie was thrilled and so was Morgan.

Letty could not imagine either her father or Stephanie changing diapers, but she knew she was going to have to accept reality.

In the meantime, she was going to be busy reshaping her own life.

A few minutes later, dressed in neatly pleated gray tweed trousers, a pale yellow button-down shirt, and her trusty penny loafers, Letty went down the hall. She stepped into the kitchen and blinked as the morning sunlight bounced off the gleaming stainless-steel and tile surfaces.

"'Morning," Joel said from the corner. He sounded surly.

Letty frowned in concern as she took in his brooding, haggard expression. "Didn't you get any sleep last night after all?"

"I'll live." He was halfway through a cup of coffee. He sat hunched over the mug as if preparing to do battle for it. His tawny eyes glittered with the restless intensity Letty was beginning to associate with him. He was watching her as if she were a bug in a jar.

Letty remembered the intimate things she had told him in the middle of the night, and she felt herself flushing. "You really should try to find out what's causing your insomnia."

"I know what caused my insomnia last night."

"Oh."

She was saved from having to think of a more intelligent response when Stephanie breezed into the kitchen looking cool and poised in a black and white maternity dress. Her deftly applied makeup was flawless.

"Good morning, everyone." Stephanie paused, frowning. "Oh, I see you found the coffee machine, Joel. I usually make the coffee. But since it's already done, you may as well help yourself, Letty."

"Thank you." Letty reached for a mug, aware that although Stephanie was putting on a polite front, she was a little irritated that Joel had dared to invade her kitchen. Letty wished she could think of something soothing to say, but she rarely knew quite what to say to Stephanie. It was like dealing with a woman from another planet. They had nothing in common. "Would you like me to pour you a cup, Stephanie?"

"Absolutely not," Stephanie said. "I'm not taking any caffeine during my pregnancy. I'll have fruit juice."

"Yes, of course. Fruit juice." Letty felt like an idiot because she didn't know the latest rules. Out of the corner of her eye she caught Joel watching her with a sardonic expression. She ignored him as she tried a sip of the coffee.

"Something wrong?" Joel asked when she made a face.

"I think it's burned. Shall I make a fresh pot?"

"I'll make a fresh pot if it's necessary," Stephanie said quickly.

"It's not burned," Joel said. "It's a dark roast. Letty probably isn't used to the flavor. That's the way we like our coffee to taste out here, isn't it, Stephanie?"

"Yes, of course." Stephanie smiled condescendingly. "You'll get accustomed to it, Letty."

Morgan appeared in the doorway. "Good morning, everyone."

Everyone murmured a response. Stephanie busied herself preparing breakfast with her usual awesome efficiency and skill. Letty was wondering if she would be allowed to at least set the table when the white wall phone buzzed.

Stephanie closed the refrigerator door and reached for the phone. "Hello?" Her eyes flew to Letty. "Yes, she's here. Just a moment, please."

Letty glanced up, alarmed. "Who is it?" she mouthed.

"He's says he's Philip Dixon," Stephanie murmured, holding the phone out to Letty.

Letty took a step back and frantically waved away the phone. "Tell him I'm not here," she whispered. "Tell him I've gone for a walk or something. Please, I really don't want to talk to him."

Joel stood up. "I'll handle this." He took the phone from Stephanie's hand. "This is Joel Blackstone. I'm Ms. Thornquist's CEO. What can I do for you, Dixon?"

Letty stared at Joel in astonishment. Her father and Stephanie did the same. The kitchen was suddenly very quiet until Joel spoke again.

"No, I'm afraid that's not possible, Dixon. It's an image thing. I'm sure you understand. Ms. Thornquist is now the president of Thornquist Gear. In her position she can't take calls from some asshole who's dumb enough to get caught with his dick stuck in the mouth of a grad student who's trying to suck her way to an A."

Joel hung up the phone without waiting for a reply and

returned to the table. He seemed oblivious to the stunned silence in the room. He sat down and picked up his mug of coffee.

Letty finally managed to find her voice. She cleared her throat weakly. "'Asshole'? 'Dick'? What happened to a 'compromising situation' in which a certain 'male member' was inserted between 'scarlet-tinted lips'?"

"You said you wanted me to be your mentor," Joel muttered. "That makes me the teacher and you the student, right?"

"Well, yes. Right."

"So listen up and pay attention as we go along, because I won't repeat this stuff and there will definitely be a quiz. That was lesson number one. It was called How to Avoid Unwanted Phone Calls."

"I think," said Letty, "that I had better take notes."

3

Excuse me," Letty said, as she came into the living room. "I didn't mean to interrupt you."

Stephanie looked up. She was sitting cross-legged on the floor, hands resting gracefully on her knees, obviously meditating. The afternoon sun was streaming in through the windows. "It's all right. I'm through. I meditate for half an hour every afternoon. It's very soothing for Matthew Christopher."

"I see." Letty was at a loss. She struggled for a way to keep the conversation going. Joel had left for Seattle early that morning, and Letty was restless. "How are you feeling?"

"Very well, thank you." Stephanie was obviously going to take the question literally. "I saw the doctor last week for my regular monthly checkup. She said all indicators were completely normal."

"That must be reassuring to hear."

Stephanie nodded seriously. "She's an excellent doctor.

One of the best obstetricians in the state. Board certified in two specialties, of course."

"Of course."

"She's administered all the latest tests. Ultrasound, alpha-fetoprotein screening, and amniocentesis. They revealed no problems or abnormalities."

"I see," Letty said.

"Morgan and I have toured the neonatal facilities at the hospital we chose. All the equipment is first class and state-of-the-art. They are fully prepared to deal with any complication that might arise."

"I take it you're not going to have Matthew Christopher delivered by a midwife at home?" Letty regretted the small joke instantly.

Stephanie looked horrified. "Good Lord, no. This baby will have the best and most advanced care available."

That did not surprise Letty. She wondered if Matthew Christopher realized how much money, time, and attention were being spent to ensure that he arrived first class.

Morgan came into the room, a mug of coffee in his hand. "Finished with your meditation, my dear?"

"Yes, I am." Stephanie allowed Morgan to assist her to her feet. "It's three o'clock, time for my afternoon protein allotment."

Morgan glanced at Letty. "Why don't we take a walk while Stephanie is having her snack?"

Letty smiled, relieved at the excuse to get out of the house. Stephanie's emphasis on control and order was getting to her. "Great."

It was the first time Letty had had an opportunity to be alone with her father since she arrived for Great-Uncle Charlie's funeral service. It felt good to have him to herself for a while. It brought back memories of how things had been before Morgan made that fateful trip to Seattle two years ago.

He had flown out to attend an academic conference

dealing with the uses of logic in the study of linguistics. Letty had been delighted to see him go. She'd been worrying about the fact that, since the death of her mother, her father was turning into an old man much too quickly. The spark had gone out of him.

The spark had definitely been reignited in Seattle. Letty had been pleased at his renewed enthusiasm and animation. But she had been stunned when he announced he was accepting a position at Ridgemore College.

Three months later she had been even more astonished to get a phone call from Morgan in which he told her he planned to be married.

And now there was a baby on the way.

It would have been a lot easier to handle, Letty decided, if she had been able to find some common ground with Stephanie. But Stephanie was as remote as an Amazon queen. She certainly bore no resemblance to Letty's mother, who had been the perfect faculty wife.

Mary Thornquist had been warm, open, and charming. She had not held a doctorate, and she had not written any impressive papers, but she'd had a knack for creating a home. She'd also known how to deal with Morgan when he grew too stuffy or pompous. There had been a lot of laughter in the Thornquist household.

"How do you like Ridgemore?" Letty asked as she and Morgan strolled along the blacktop where Joel had taken his late night run.

"Very much. My lecture load is light. Got an office with a window. Plenty of time to write my papers. And no Friday afternoon faculty sherry hours, thank God."

Letty winced. "I know you never enjoyed attending those."

Morgan smiled at her. "I've had enough of ivy-covered halls and moribund traditions. And so have you, I think. I'm sorry Dixon proved to be a bastard. But I'm glad you found out before the marriage."

"So am I."

Morgan paused. "Did you really walk into his office and find him with his—"

"Don't say it, please," Letty muttered.

"His you-know-what in some grad student's mouth?" Morgan amended.

Letty felt herself turning a bright red. "Yes, and I wish to heaven I had not confided that little snippet of information to Joel Blackstone. I don't know what got into me last night."

"Maybe you just needed to talk. Knowing you, you probably didn't confide the details to anyone at Vellacott."

"No, it's not something one wants to discuss with one's co-workers. Lord knows why I chose Joel Blackstone as my confidant. I guess I was just tired because it was the middle of the night and my common sense was half asleep. At any rate, I certainly learned my lesson."

"What lesson?"

Letty glared at her father. "You know what I'm talking about. I could not believe what Joel said to Philip on the phone this morning. Last night when I made the mistake of pouring out my heart and soul to him, Mr. Blackstone seemed quite gentlemanly. Very understanding. I had no idea he could be so crude."

Morgan chuckled. "His tactics may strike you as crude, but something tells me he's effective. Charlie said everything Thornquist Gear is today was the direct result of his putting Blackstone in charge ten years ago."

"I'm not questioning Joel's executive ability. It's obvious he's got plenty of it." Letty straightened her shoulders. "And I intend to learn everything I can from him."

"Everything?"

Letty nodded enthusiastically. "Everything. He's going to be my mentor while I learn how to run Thornquist Gear."

"This should be interesting."

"What's that supposed to mean?"

"Just what I said." Morgan's bushy brows came together in a thoughtful frown. "Interesting. Blackstone isn't like any other man you've ever known, Letty. He's no ivory tower type. He doesn't deal in theory; he deals in hard facts."

"I realize that."

"I seriously doubt he's had any sensitivity training," Morgan said dryly."

Letty smiled ruefully. "I'm sure you're right."

"He doesn't play the game by the book. He's the kind of man who makes up his own rules."

Letty was alarmed. "Are you saying he's probably unethical in his business dealings?"

"No. I'm just warning you that his idea of fair play will probably be considerably different from your own."

"If I find out that he's dishonest or underhanded, I'll fire him immediately."

"That," Morgan said slowly, "might be quite a trick."

"Dad, he works for me, remember? I can get rid of him at any time."

"Don't bet on it, my dear."

"I own Thornquist Gear, darn it," Letty retorted. "I can do as I wish."

Morgan grinned. "Spoken like a born corporate leader."

Letty was starting to feel insulted. "What's the matter, Dad? Don't you think I can learn to handle the company? As head of the reference department I've been managing people for several years."

"Running Thornquist Gear will not bear much of a resemblance to running the reference desk at Vellacott Library. Letty, you're as smart as they come. You can do anything you want. I always told you that and I meant it. All I'm trying to do is warn you that you've never come up against anyone quite like Blackstone before. Tread carefully around him until you know what you're doing."

Letty relaxed. "Okay."

"On the whole," Morgan said, "I'm glad you've decided to give it a whirl. You need a major change in your life even more than I did, my dear. If nothing else, the move to Seattle will shake you out of your routine, expose you to new influences, and open up your world. If running Thornquist Gear doesn't suit you, you can always sell it to Blackstone in a year or so. In the meantime, the experience will be good for you. Just be careful."

"You're a fine one to talk. The changes I'm making are petty compared to the ones you've made, Dad." Letty bit her lip. "I still can't quite believe I'm going to have a little brother."

Morgan raised his brows. "I knew we were going to get around to that sooner or later. You still haven't gotten over the shock of my marriage to Stephanie, either, have you?"

"That's not true. I've adjusted to the idea," Letty said, picking her words carefully. "But I'll admit that at times it still seems strange. Everything has happened so fast."

"At my age I can't afford to waste a lot of time," Morgan said gently.

"You're only fifty-three, Dad."

"Stephanie makes me feel thirty again."

Letty sighed. "I guess that says it all, doesn't it?"

"Yes, my dear, it does."

"She's so unlike mother."

"Letty, your mother was a wonderful woman, and I loved her for nearly thirty good years. But she's gone, and I know she would have wanted me to be happy again."

"Yes, but with someone like *Stephanie?*" Letty broke off, horrified that she had gone too far.

Morgan's brows drew together, forming a solid line above his sea green eyes. "Stephanie is my wife now, Letty. She is about to become the mother of my son. I can't force you to develop any real affection for her, but I can and will make certain you treat her with respect."

Guilt swamped Letty. "I'm sorry, Dad. You know I would

never be rude to her. For your sake, I'm trying to think of her as a member of the family."

"Do that. Because she *is* a member of the family."

Letty lifted her chin. "You know what the real problem between Stephanie and me is?"

"You think she's trying to take your mother's place."

"No, not at all. The truth is, she intimidates me."

Morgan narrowed his eyes in astonishment. "Intimidates you? What do you mean by that?"

"It's hard to explain," Letty admitted, wishing she had not even tried. "She's only eleven years older than me."

"You're not going to lecture me for having married a woman you think is too young for me, are you?"

Letty shook her head. Stephanie *was* too young for her father, of course, but there was no sense pointing that out now. The deed was done. "No. What I'm trying to say is that although she's only a few years older than I am, she makes me feel unsophisticated."

"Unsophisticated?"

Letty scowled. "Maybe that's not quite the right word. Unworldly. Gauche. Dad, she makes me feel like a small-town hick. Now do you understand?"

Morgan's face softened. "I think so. If it's any consolation, she made me feel the same way at first. But underneath that glossy exterior is a charming, very genuine person. I want you to get to know the real Stephanie. I want you to be friends with her."

"I'm trying, Dad."

"I want you to try a little harder."

Letty eyed him. "How am I supposed to do that?"

"I want to ask a favor of you, Letty. Stephanie has signed up for a series of seminars dealing with pregnancy and infancy. I'd appreciate it if you'd accompany her to some of the classes. I think it would help if the two of you spent some time together."

Letty stared at him. "You want me to take a bunch of baby classes?"

"For my sake, Letty. And for the sake of Matthew Christopher."

Two days later Letty found herself back in Seattle sitting next to Stephanie in a roomful of pregnant ladies. The speaker, Professor Harold Blanchford, was an expert on fetal development, and his subject was not without some interest. Letty noticed that Stephanie was sitting very erect in her chair, her attention focused completely on the talk. She was taking notes with military precision.

"There is ample evidence," Professor Blanchford said, "that the third trimester fetus hears and responds to auditory stimuli. There is also a great deal of data supporting the fact that newborns have a strong preference for their mothers' voices. This raises the interesting possibility that newborns respond to their mothers' voices for the simple reason that they have been listening to them for several weeks in the womb. Listening and remembering."

Being surrounded by pregnant ladies was making Letty feel strange. It was forcing her to deal with an issue she had spent a lot of time pushing aside lately. But the truth was, it was difficult to go on pretending that she would someday have a home and family of her own when confronted with this kind of reality.

Letty knew that sooner or later she would have to face a few disturbing facts about her own prospects for marriage and children. The recent fiasco with Philip had brought home the realization that she might not ever be able to respond properly to a man.

"Tests on newborns who have been exposed in utero to the sound of their mothers reading a story prove that the infant is capable of remembering the story after birth. The responses in our tests were conclusive."

Letty leaned over to whisper in Stephanie's ear. "Maybe you could read Matthew Christopher a cookbook before he's born. Turn him into a trained chef. Just think, he'd have a marketable skill before he can even walk. We'll make a fortune on him."

Stephanie's pen never stopped moving, and she did not look up. "Please be quiet, Letty. I'm trying to concentrate."

"Sorry." Letty slouched uncomfortably in her chair and gazed at Professor Blanchford. Something told her it was going to be a long afternoon. She was glad she'd be starting work at Thornquist Gear tomorrow. At least she would have an excuse for avoiding these afternoon classes with Stephanie.

Unfortunately that still left all the evening classes Stephanie had scheduled.

"Now, then," Professor Blanchford intoned. "You will no doubt want to consider carefully what you read to your infants while they are in the womb. One must keep in mind that memory is functioning even at this early stage and it's up to you, the mother, to determine what your baby will recall after birth."

"Talk about putting pressure on poor Mom," Letty murmured. "As if there isn't already enough at this point."

"Letty, please." Stephanie scowled at her.

Letty shut up.

Fifteen minutes later the seminar was dismissed, much to Letty's relief. She watched Stephanie buy Professor Blanchford's book and set of tapes. There was clearly money in this baby class business.

"What did you think of it?" Stephanie put on her sunglasses as she led the way back out to the car.

"Very impressive research." Letty searched for something more to add. "Are you going to read to Matthew Christopher?"

"Definitely. We'll start with Shakespeare."

"I bet he would prefer *Road and Track.*"

Stephanie was not amused. "And I think we'll try music, too. Mozart or Vivaldi would probably be best."

Letty managed to restrain herself from suggesting a heavy metal group. "Should be interesting to see if he hums at birth," she muttered under her breath.

Fortunately Stephanie didn't overhear the remark. "I can't wait to tell Morgan how well it went today." She slid behind the wheel of her red Porsche. "He'll be pleased."

Letty climbed into the passenger seat and carefully fastened her belt. "I imagine so."

"Your father is as happy about this pregnancy as I am, Letty." Stephanie eased the Porsche out of the parking slot.

"Yes." Letty wished desperately for some light, intelligent conversation. Her mind went blank. "Yes, he certainly seems to be thrilled."

"I feel extraordinarily lucky to have met Morgan."

Letty nodded, her eyes on the street as Stephanie zipped the Porsche out of the parking lot. It would be nice to be able to handle a racy car like this with Stephanie's skill, she thought wistfully.

"Are you quite certain things are over between you and this Philip Dixon?" Stephanie asked.

"Yes."

"I don't blame you," Stephanie continued, pitching her voice to be heard above the sounds of the street. "I divorced my first husband because I found out he was having an affair with his secretary. I knew then and there I did not want him to father any child of mine. A marriage must be founded on trust."

"I agree."

"Morgan is so very different from Grayson," Stephanie said. "I knew the minute I met him that he would make an excellent father."

"Is that the reason you married him?" As soon as the words were out of her mouth, Letty was appalled. She closed her eyes, wishing desperately she could recall the question. "I'm sorry. I shouldn't have said that."

"It's all right." Stephanie sounded amused rather than

affronted. "To be perfectly truthful with you, the fact that Morgan was good father material was far more important to me than any other single factor. At least in the beginning. But now that I've gotten to know him better, I've come to realize that he has any number of other wonderful qualities."

Letty's hands clenched in her lap. She glanced across the seat, unable to read Stephanie's expression because of her blue-mirrored sunglasses. "Stephanie, I know I have no business asking this, but do you really love my father?"

"Of course." Stephanie smiled serenely and tooled the Porsche into the parking lot of a supermarket. "But I would not be surprised if your definition of love is somewhat different from my own. I hope you don't mind if we stop here for a minute. I'm out of feta cheese and salsa."

"No, I don't mind."

Much later that night Letty lay in bed and listened to the murmur of voices drifting in through the open window. Her father and Stephanie had not yet retired for the night. They were still sitting out on the glass-enclosed deck overlooking the city lights and Elliott Bay. Letty could not see them, but she could hear their low-voiced conversation.

"Do you think she'll stay in Seattle, Morgan?"

"I don't know. But she needs the change. The worst thing she could do right now is go back to Vellacott."

"You may be right. I feel sorry for her. She seems a little lost, if you know what I mean. Maybe breaking off her engagement bothered her more than she's willing to admit."

"She's strong. She'll bounce back fast enough. It's nice of you to be so concerned about her, Stephanie."

"She's your daughter. Naturally I'm concerned about her." There was a short silence, and then Stephanie added, "I don't think she fully accepts or understands our relationship yet, though."

"Give her time."

There was another period of silence. Letty turned onto her side and curled up. Then she heard Stephanie's voice again.

"The class was wonderful today, Morgan. I'll be starting a new auditory stimulation routine for Matthew Christopher tomorrow."

Morgan chuckled. "It won't be much longer and you'll be able to talk to him face to face."

"Two more months."

Letty heard the expectant hope and satisfaction in Stephanie's voice, but she also detected something else, a note of tension. She thought of the intense way Stephanie had taken down everything Professor Blanchford had said that afternoon. It was as if she had been afraid of missing a single word.

Afraid. Yes, Letty suddenly realized. That was the right word. *Afraid.* But that conclusion made no sense. Stephanie was the most unflappable, most coolly controlled woman she had ever met.

"I'll have to check on that Italian crib we ordered," Morgan said. "It should be in by now."

"I called the artist who's doing the mobile that will hang over the crib. He said it was almost ready. He chose botanical subjects as his motif."

Letty listened to the soft voices for a while longer. The bottom line, she decided, was that she felt like an outsider in her father's home.

It was definitely time to move out. She would start looking for an apartment right away.

Tomorrow she would be sitting in the president's office at Thornquist Gear. That thought sent a jolt of euphoria through Letty. Her new life was waiting for her to take command.

Joel studied the printout that lay on his desk. Everything looked solid. All the little ducks were lined up in a row waiting for him to fire the howitzers. Copeland Marine

Industries was so much dead meat ready to start rotting in the fields.

He should have felt more of a sense of satisfaction, he thought. He had waited long enough to bring down Victor Copeland. Fifteen years, to be exact. In another month the business would be over and done.

So why was he feeling edgy today? Joel got up and went to stand at his office window. His problem was the impending arrival of Letty Thornquist, and he knew it. She would be here tomorrow, expecting to take over the presidential suite.

Presidential suite—the term was a joke. Thornquist Gear had never had much use for a president's office. It had never had a president who spent any time at his desk. The only thing Charlie had ever done while seated at his desk was tie flies.

Four stories below Joel the sales floor of the downtown branch of Thornquist Gear hummed with activity. The summer camping season was over and the ski season was about to begin. The annual run on ski boots was already starting.

Ten years ago Thornquist Gear had occupied one tiny shop on First Avenue. Today the company leased half a block of office space and had retail outlets on the east side and down in Portland.

The first two floors of the downtown store were retail, and the two upper floors housed Accounting, Marketing and other operations. Joel still got a surge of pride and deep satisfaction every time he walked through the front door of Thornquist Gear.

First Avenue was busy, as usual. From his window Joel could see one Thai restaurant, a sexy lingerie shop, a take-out deli that featured Mediterranean cuisine, one adult theater, and a pawnshop. Facing the building that housed Thornquist was a fine old hotel that dated back to the turn of the century. It had recently been gutted and converted into upscale condominiums.

Joel watched as a plane came in over Elliott Bay. The slice of water he could see from his window was the color of steel under a gray sky. There was rain on the way, according to the forecast. Some people had a tough time with the continual gloom of Seattle. They moved to the city and ended up leaving six months later because they couldn't take the clouds and endless mist.

Joel wondered hopefully if Letty would be driven off by long periods of overcast skies. It would certainly make the task of persuading her to sell out to him easier if she was.

With his luck she would find the rain romantic.

Behind him his secretary's firm, no-nonsense voice sounded on the intercom.

"Mr. Blackstone, there's a call for you on line two. Manford from Marketing. He says it's important."

Joel turned toward the desk. "Thanks, Mrs. Sedgewick. I've got it. By the way, Mrs. Sedgewick?"

"Yes, Mr. Blackstone?"

"How is Ms. Thornquist's office coming along?"

"Should be ready by tomorrow, sir. And I've finally lined up a secretary for her. Arthur Bigley from Accounting." Mrs. Sedgewick paused meaningfully. "I believe he is exactly what you were looking for. And he is thrilled with his sudden and unexpected promotion."

"Good. Send him in here for a few minutes, will you? I want to brief him personally on his new responsibilities."

"I understand, Mr. Blackstone."

"Fine." Joel punched a button. "Blackstone here. What's the problem, Cal?"

"We've got to make some decisions on the thrust of the new ad campaign before we get the agency on line. I can't hold things up much longer or we'll start missing some deadlines. We need your approval on the contract, Joel."

"All right. Let me take one more look at it this weekend. Schedule a meeting for Monday morning."

"Right." Cal cleared his throat. "Uh, shall I include Ms. Thornquist?"

"There's no need to bother her with this kind of thing during her first week here," Joel said smoothly. "She'll have enough on her hands just getting the feel of the place."

"Sure. Monday morning, then. I'll talk to your secretary."

Joel hung up the phone and sat fiddling with a pen for a few minutes. He was normally much more decisive about things than he had been on the matter of this new ad campaign. The trouble was that while he knew what he wanted to accomplish, he was unsure of how to reach the goal.

During the past ten years he had built up Thornquist Gear using traditional approaches in the marketplace. He understood the kind of people who lived in the Pacific Northwest. His family had lived in Washington for three generations. Joel knew instinctively how to target the basic market.

With the new campaign he would be taking some chances. The idea was to appeal to people who had no more than a nodding acquaintance with the wonders of the magnificent countryside that surrounded them.

With the influx of enthusiastic new residents into Oregon and Washington, a whole new market was taking shape for companies such as Thornquist Gear. The way Joel saw it, that new market, which had yet to be firmly targeted and defined, was basically composed of people who liked the idea of being northwesterners but who did not know quite how to go about it. Joel intended to teach them with a new line called Pack Up and Go camping equipment.

But he was not yet absolutely certain how to grab the attention of that new market. His small marketing department had come up with several ideas, but Joel had not felt solid about any of them. Now time was running out, and he had to make some decisions soon.

He got up and moved restlessly back to the window. Too many firecrackers in the air. Charlie's death, the impending

51

arrival of Letty Thornquist, the new ad campaign, the carefully planned slaughter of Copeland Marine Industries —it all added up to a volatile situation.

The buzz of the intercom caught his attention. "Arthur Bigley is here, sir."

"Send him in, Mrs. Sedgewick."

The door opened. A very nervous looking young man with close-cropped curly brown hair and wire-rimmed glasses walked into the office.

"You wanted to brief me on my new position, Mr. Blackstone?" Arthur adjusted his tie with anxious fingers.

Joel leaned back in his chair. "Sit down, Bigley. You'll be working for Ms. Thornquist when she arrives tomorrow."

"Yes, sir." Bigley sat down. "I'm very excited about that, sir. This is a wonderful promotion for me, sir, and I'm very grateful."

Joel smiled grimly. "I'm glad to hear it. Now, then, the most important thing you need to know in your new position is that I do not want Ms. Thornquist bothered by routine matters. Is that clear?"

"I guess so, sir." Arthur looked skeptical. "Uh, how exactly do I keep her from being bothered by them?"

"You keep Mrs. Sedgewick informed of everything that happens in Ms. Thornquist's office. Mrs. Sedgewick will keep me informed. I'll monitor the situation and step in when I'm needed. That's how the chain of command works, Bigley. Do you think you can follow those simple instructions?"

"Yes, sir. Definitely, sir."

"Excellent. I want to know everything that goes on in the president's office. You'll check with this office before putting through any calls to Ms. Thornquist, and you'll notify me of all visitors. You will be advised as to how to handle such matters."

"Yes, sir."

"Mrs. Sedgewick will give you further instruction about your day-to-day office routine. You may go now."

"Yes, sir." Arthur shot to his feet and turned to leave.

The toe of his shoe caught on the edge of the carpet, and he lost his balance. His arm swept out, groping for something to keep him from falling. He grabbed the arm of the chair, and it toppled over.

"I think you'll do very well for Ms. Thornquist," Joel said as Arthur Bigley picked himself up off the carpet and darted from the room.

4

Two weeks later Joel came to a halt in the doorway of the new suite of offices that had been assigned to the president of Thornquist Gear. The inner door was standing wide open, and he could see at a glance that Letty was nowhere around.

He scowled at Arthur Bigley, who was seated behind the desk in the small outer room. Arthur, attired in a white shirt and tie, had been typing briskly. But he visibly flinched when he realized Joel was in the doorway. He looked up with an anxious expression. Joel noticed Arthur was not wearing his wire-rimmed spectacles and that he was blinking frequently. Apparently Bigley had decided to try contacts.

"Where is Ms. Thornquist, Bigley? I was under the impression she was here in her office."

Arthur's rate of nervous blinking increased swiftly. It was clear he was alarmed to discover that he was being held responsible for the fact that Letty was not where she was supposed to be. "I believe she went down to the conference room on the third floor, Mr. Blackstone."

"There's no conference scheduled down there, Bigley." Joel's patience was wearing thin and Arthur knew it, as did the rest of the staff. The past two weeks had not been easy on anyone, except possibly Letty. As far as Joel could ascertain, the new president of Thornquist Gear was thoroughly enjoying herself.

"Yes, sir, I know that, sir. She said she had a special project going on down there this afternoon."

"What special project?"

Arthur froze in his chair and blinked frantically. "I wouldn't know, sir. She didn't say what it was."

Joel gave up. You could not get information out of a turnip. It was clear Bigley was in the dark. "The hell with it. I'll go see what she's doing myself."

"Yes, sir." Arthur was enormously relieved to be off the hook. "Oh, I almost forgot, sir. There have been a couple more calls from that Philip Dixon person. I informed Mrs. Sedgewick."

Joel, who was already turning away, paused. "You told him what I told you to tell him?"

"Yes, Mr. Blackstone." Arthur risked an anxious smile. "I told him that Ms. Thornquist could not come to the phone, just as you said."

"And you didn't mention the calls to Ms. Thornquist?"

"No, sir. Absolutely not. You said not to bother her with them, and I've been very careful to follow your instructions."

"Very good, Bigley. Ms. Thornquist has enough on her mind these days without having to deal with annoying phone calls." Joel inclined his head in a brisk, brief nod of approval. "You're doing a fine job. Keep up the good work."

"Yes, sir. Thank you, sir." Arthur appeared on the verge of collapsing from sheer relief. He reached for a fresh sheet of typing paper and started to insert it into his machine. Then he abruptly leaped to his feet as if he had been stung. "Oh, no."

Joel frowned. "What the hell's the matter, Bigley?"

"Nothing, sir. My contact lens just popped out, sir. I'll find it right away, sir." Arthur dropped to his knees and began sweeping the rug with a cautious hand.

Satisfied that damage control operations were in effect and functioning in the president's office, Joel headed down the hall to the stairs. He never took the elevator. You had to wait forever for the damn thing. At least it seemed to Joel that he had to wait forever. He noticed a lot of other people did not mind the short delays. At any given time he could find a large percentage of his staff standing around in the hall, wasting time while they waited for an elevator.

He opened the stairwell door and started down, frowning in anticipation of what he might find in the conference room. During the past two weeks Letty had turned out to be energetic, unpredictable, and potentially the most explosive of the incendiary devices Joel was trying to juggle these days.

She had thrown herself wholeheartedly into the business of learning all she could about Thornquist Gear. She was spending twelve hours a day in the building, working on the sales floor, out on the loading dock, and in the accounting department.

Three days ago he'd found her trying on down jackets in the clothing department. The memory made him smile faintly. The thick, voluminous coats had swamped her small frame. The added layers of padding over her already pleasantly rounded bosom and hips had done amusing things to her figure. She had looked like a plump little pigeon with feathers fluffed against the cold.

Joel, who had started to grin, had stopped immediately when she blithely informed him she thought Thornquist Gear needed to add a line of petite-sized down jackets.

"These things look great if you're six feet tall," Letty said.

"But for those of us who are five feet four or under, they're a bit much."

"We'll talk about it later, Ms. Thornquist," Joel cut in before the floor manager could add his two cents to the discussion.

She nodded, temporarily satisfied. "I also want to talk about widening the color range. Look at these jackets. Rows and rows of dull blue, flat green, and off-red. Not very exciting."

That observation annoyed Joel. "Those colors happen to be called midnight, khaki, and burgundy. They're the most popular colors in down jackets."

"Well, I think we should consider carrying jackets in yellow, bright red, and turquoise," Letty said, waxing enthusiastic. "At least in the women's styles. Women like bright colors."

The floor manager started to nod in agreement.

"I think we should discuss this at another time also, Ms. Thornquist," Joel said very politely through his teeth.

"Certainly. I'll just make a note." Letty whipped out a pen and jotted a few words down on a clipboard she carried with her everywhere.

Joel had given strict orders that Ms. Thornquist was to be treated with the respect due the president and owner of the firm, but that she was not to be bothered with petty details. Unfortunately, Letty had a way of prying details out of people. Just last Wednesday, Joel had walked into her office and found her immersed in a printout of extensive data about last quarter's sales figures. He was stunned to discover that she had been asking questions all over the building, and that by noon she had a disconcertingly thorough grasp of Thornquist Gear's current financial picture. It was sheer blind luck that she had not stumbled into information that would clue her into the Copeland Marine Industries takeover.

Joel had gone straight down to Accounting that afternoon and instituted tighter controls on all computer printouts ordered from the president's office. Henceforth the requested printouts were to be sent to his office first. He would personally go over them with the new president.

Sooner or later, Joel thought as he reached the third floor, he was going to have to deal with the Copeland Marine situation. After all, once he made his final moves, there would be no way to keep the takeover a secret. He had to have his explanations ready. They had to sound like good business and nothing more.

Problems. Firecrackers waiting to explode.

And the most potentially explosive factor of all, Joel now realized, was his own personal fascination with Letty Thornquist. It was dawning on him with increasing pressure that he wanted her. Badly. And he was not altogether sure why.

The acute awareness he had experienced that night at her father's house in the mountains had not been a fleeting attraction fed by exercise endorphins, moonlight, and the proximity of a lady in a nightgown. He still wanted her.

He had tried telling himself it was the novelty. Letty was very different from any other woman he knew. It was not just her oddly innocent enthusiasm or even her unusual, rather fey looks. Nor was it the vibrancy of her features, which more than made up for whatever she lacked in conventional beauty.

It was something else that drew him, and it worried him. Letty was sweet, even endearing in some ways. She called forth a protective response in him that was ludicrous under the circumstances. He was the one who needed protection, Joel thought ruefully. As long as she owned Thornquist Gear, she was dangerous.

Unfortunately that knowledge did not alter the surge of desire he felt whenever he was near her or the sense of possessiveness that was beginning to pulse just below the surface.

In the past few days Joel had begun to realize that he was

not only trying to keep a lot of firecrackers in the air, he was also trying to walk a tightrope.

Maybe he should have gone to work for a circus instead of Thornquist Gear. Lately it was hard to distinguish between the two.

Joel heard Letty's voice as soon as he opened the stairwell door and started toward the large conference room. Either she was talking to herself or there was someone else in the room with her.

"That can't be right," Letty called out. "Read that one again, Cal."

Cal Manford's voice droned in response. "'Insert brace pole into section B of number three upright pole.'"

"That's ridiculous. It doesn't fit. Are you sure?"

"That's what it says, Ms. Thornquist."

"Who wrote that manual, anyway?"

Cal hesitated, apparently thinking. "Someone in the manufacturing design division, I imagine."

Joel reached the doorway of the conference room and beheld a small scene of chaos. One of the new tents that had been manufactured to Thornquist specifications and carried the new Thornquist Gear Pack Up and Go label was in a state of partial erection.

Not unlike his own condition these days, Joel thought. And for the same reason: Letty was in the vicinity.

To be more accurate she was somewhere inside the precariously tilting tent. He could see one small, beautifully arched, nylon-clad foot peeping out from where the zippered door flapped open. A trim little ankle and a few inches of nicely curved leg were also visible.

Cal Manford, the head of Marketing, stood nearby. He looked harried and useless with the instruction manual in his hand. He had taken off his jacket and was in his shirtsleeves.

Manford was in his mid-fifties and sported a fringe of gray hair and a definite paunch. The paunch was the reason he was rarely seen without a jacket. Apparently the tension of trying to help Letty pitch a tent had overcome Cal's concern about the way his stomach hung out over his belt. Joel noticed there were damp stains under Manford's arms.

Joel also noticed with a sense of irritation that Cal was staring at Letty's foot instead of the loose-leaf instruction manual.

"Well," Letty declared from inside the wavering tent, "if this is any example of how the rest of the manual is written, we'll just have to insist that the entire thing be revised. Nobody who was not already an expert could get one of these tents up in less than two hours. And even then I'm not sure it would stay up."

"I'll, uh, mention the problem to Mr. Blackstone, if you like," Cal volunteered uneasily. He was still staring at Letty's foot and still unaware of Joel's presence. "He approved the new line of tents, himself."

"Never mind. I'll talk to him about it. In the meantime we might as well keep going. Read the next instruction."

Joel propped one shoulder against the frame of the door and folded his arms across his chest. "Forget the next instruction. You're going to have to start all over again. You haven't got the ridgepole in place."

There was a sudden commotion inside the tent. "What are you talking about? Is that you, Mr. Blackstone?"

Joel had found her insistence on office formality humorous at first. Now it was getting to be irritating. "Right. It's me, Ms. Thornquist."

Cal Manford swung around, startled. Joel could have sworn he looked both relieved and disappointed. "I was just helping Ms. Thornquist field-test one of the new tents."

"So I see." Joel eyed the listing tent. "I take it there's a problem with the instructions?"

"You can say that again," Letty called out. The side of the tent bulged as she shifted position and in the process apparently rammed her elbow into the strong nylon. "Mr.

Manford says this new line is designed to sell to novice campers. I asked him if it had been tested on any novice campers and he said no. So I thought I'd run an experiment. It's been a very educational experience."

"Obviously." Joel shook his head and gave Manford a wry man-to-man, what-can-you-do-with-'em smile. It was the sort of smile men had exchanged among themselves when discussing female mechanical competency for several thousand generations. Cal returned it fleetingly, but he still looked worried.

"I want to see how far I can get following the instructions. It's best to document the problems with them as we go along," Letty said. She changed position inside the tent once more. Her foot vanished.

Joel eyed the wobbling upright pole. "Come on out, Ms. Thornquist. I'll show you how to pitch a tent, if you really want to learn."

"No, no, no. That's the whole point. If I, a typical novice camper, can't do it myself using the manual, we've got a major problem with the new line. Don't you understand?"

The rebuke took Joel completely by surprise. For one single, exceedingly unpleasant instant, he felt a wave of embarrassed heat singe his cheekbones. He was aware of Cal Manford watching him with an expression of uncertainty.

Anger flashed through Joel, driving out the embarrassment. It was bad policy for the company's chief executive officer to be taken to task by the president of the firm in front of another member of the staff. Manford, like everyone else around the place, had to be reminded of just who was in charge.

"If you'll get yourself out of that tent, Ms. Thornquist," Joel said evenly, "I'll go over the manual personally with you. Step by step, if you like. We can see if there are any major problems with it. If so, they can be taken care of easily enough. Isn't that right, Manford?"

Cal coughed and swallowed. "Yes, sir."

At that moment one of the wavering aluminum poles fell over. There was a small scream from inside the tent as the entire structure collapsed.

"Oh, my God," yelled Letty. "Joel, do something. Get this thing off me!"

So much for office formality.

Joel eyed the writhing mass of yellow nylon. Letty was neatly trapped beneath it, floundering about like a netted fish. Cal Manford looked horrified and baffled by this new development.

"Uh, Ms. Thornquist? Are you all right, Ms. Thornquist?" Cal called anxiously.

"No, I am not all right." Letty's voice was muffled by the tent fabric.

Joel straightened and held out his hand. "I'll handle this, Manford. Give me that manual. I'll help Ms. Thornquist complete her *field test.*"

"Yes, sir." Cal shoved the manual into Joel's fingers. He summoned up a nervous smile. "If you don't need me any longer, I'll get back to my office."

"Do that." Joel dismissed him with a glance and walked across the room to the churning tent. He reached down, took hold of the lightweight fabric and several loose poles, and hauled it all upward.

Glasses askew on her nose, topknot in complete disarray, Letty crawled out of the tent door on her hands and knees.

Wispy tendrils of hair hung in her face. The skirt of her conservative gray business suit was more than normally rumpled. It was hiked up well above her knees and twisted back to front. Her peach silk blouse had been tugged free of the skirt's waistband.

Joel caught a tantalizing glimpse of bare skin at the base of her spine and was immediately intrigued. He noticed there was an elegant dip at the small of her back that promised a full, plump derriere.

All indications were that Letty Thornquist had a very nice ass.

Joel had just been surprised to discover that he could be aroused by the shape of Letty's foot. But the interest he took in the design of her rear came as no surprise at all. He had always found the unique curves of the lower portion of the female anatomy aesthetically appealing. Letty, he saw, was designed very lushly indeed in that area.

For a few seconds he almost forgot how annoyed he was with his new boss. He reached down to grasp her arm and assist her to her feet. "You okay?"

"Yes, of course. Thanks, Joel. I mean, Mr. Blackstone."

"There's no one around to hear if you slip up and call me by my first name."

"Mustn't get into the habit while we're in the office." Letty pushed her glasses more firmly onto her nose. She yanked at her skirt and shoved the hem of the blouse back inside the waistband. "That manual is a disaster. Totally incomprehensible to the novice."

"This is the simplest tent in the entire line."

"There is nothing simple about pitching that tent. I can't even imagine trying to do it in a high wind or a driving rain. It would be a totally frustrating experience."

Joel took a grip on his own frustration and on his temper. "Why don't we go back to your office and I'll explain the instructions to you?"

"Don't you understand? This new line of camping gear is supposed to be designed for beginners, right?"

"Right."

"I'm a beginner and I'm intelligent and I'm highly motivated. Yet I could not get it up on my own. That says it all."

"It does?" He quirked a brow.

"Certainly. That stupid manual needs to be rewritten. Either that, or the basic design of the tent is bad."

Joel sucked in his breath. "Letty, we've taken delivery on the first shipment of five hundred of those damn tents. They're in the warehouse. They'll be on the sales floor in another two months when we start the new ad campaign. *There is nothing wrong with the design of that product."*

She frowned and took a step back. "There is no need to raise your voice."

"I am not raising my voice."

She gave him a placating smile, which only annoyed Joel further. "Tell you what. Let's go to my office and go over the manual together. I'll show you where I had problems. If the tent design is all right, then the difficulty must lie in the way the instructions are written."

"Christ," Joel muttered under his breath. He forced himself to calm down. This was a juggling act, he reminded himself. He had to keep all the firecrackers in the air while he maintained his balance on the tightrope. The last thing he could afford to do was lose his self-control.

"Joel? I mean, Mr. Blackstone?" Letty's sea green eyes were widening with concern. "Is something wrong?"

"No. Nothing is wrong. Let's go back to your office and discuss the manual."

"It's loose-leaf," she said brightly. "It wouldn't be all that difficult to fix. We only have to correct the pages that are badly written and reprint them."

"Thank you. I'll keep that in mind." He took her arm and started toward the door.

"Wait. My shoes. And my jacket." Letty tugged free of Joel's grip and darted across the room to grab her jacket and slide her feet into her shoes. She picked up her clipboard and started toward him again with another cheery smile. "Okay. I'm ready."

Joel took hold of her again and steered her through the door and down the hall. "You know, Letty, this manual was written by experts."

"That was probably the problem. But don't worry, Joel. This is an area where I can really be of assistance. I used to be a librarian, remember?"

"Only too well. I think about your real career quite a lot."

64

"My former career," she corrected neatly. "At any rate, one of the things I'm very good at is locating, analyzing, and summarizing information. I think I'll call in one of the tent designers and . . . Oh, are we going to take the stairs?"

"Yes."

"Fine. Well, as I was saying, I'm going to call in one of the tent designers and have him tell me exactly what he was going for in this particular model."

"I can tell you exactly what the designers were going for in this particular model. And I will be happy to do so as soon as we get to your office."

Joel shoved open the stairwell door and hauled Letty through the entrance. He hurried her up the steps to the next floor. When they reached it, he set such a swift pace down the hallway that she was forced to skip once or twice to keep up with him.

She never once stopped talking about her plans for the manual revisions during the entire trip. Joel was ready to gag her by the time they walked through her office door.

Arthur, apparently having located his missing contact lens, looked up. His eyes darted from Joel to Letty. When he got a good look at his new boss, his eyes widened in shock. "Ms. Thornquist, are you all right? Did something happen?"

"A tent collapsed on me," Letty said. "Think nothing of it. I expect that sort of thing is just one of the job hazards around here. Any messages, Arthur?"

"Yes, ma'am. A Mr. Rosemont called and said to tell you that your new apartment is ready. You can pick up the keys today."

Letty smiled with obvious delight. "Wonderful. I am more than ready for a place of my own." She started toward the inner office. "Come in, Mr. Blackstone. Let's get to work on that manual."

Joel gritted his teeth. He was not accustomed to taking orders from anyone, let alone an interfering, unpredictable librarian who thought she could run Thornquist Gear. He stalked past Arthur's desk, aware of the secretary's barely concealed curiosity. Bigley's expression reminded him of Cal Manford's a few minutes earlier.

He could see in Bigley's eyes the same question he had seen in Manford's: Who's in charge around here?

Joel knew if he did not get things back on track quickly the entire staff would begin questioning the chain of command.

He closed Letty's office door with a solid thud and paced across the room to the window. Letty sat down at her desk and opened the manual.

"Let's start at the beginning," Letty said, turning pages swiftly.

"Yeah, I think maybe we'd better." Joel turned and walked back toward her desk. He planted both hands on the polished wood surface and leaned forward. "Ms. Thornquist, I don't think you quite understand the command structure here at Thornquist Gear."

She raised her head and pushed her hair out of the way so that she could gaze at him with owlish concern. "I don't?"

"Let me spell it out for you. This is a corporation. I don't know how things are handled in an academic library, but around here the chief executive officer is in charge."

"I realize that a CEO's function is to see to the day-to-day operation of the company and make the executive decisions."

"Good. I'm glad you've got that. Now, then, it is crucial that the president of the company not undermine her CEO's authority in the presence of others. She must appear to place her entire trust and confidence in him. Is that clear?"

Letty began to look uneasy. "Of course. Are you trying to tell me that I'm undermining your position here at Thornquist Gear?"

"Not yet, but it could happen if you continue to treat me like a very expensive executive assistant. I am not a gofer,

Ms. Thornquist. I am the one who's supposed to run this company."

"Oh, dear. I never meant to treat you like an *assistant*, for heaven's sake."

He saw the appalled guilt in her eyes and barely controlled a smile of satisfaction. Much better. "People are starting to wonder who's in charge. That question must never crop up around here. Do you understand that, Ms. Thornquist?"

"Yes. Yes, of course." She looked suitably subdued now.

Joel took his hands off the desk. "This is your company," he said gravely. "You have a right to learn as much or as little as you wish about it. But if you start casually counter-manding my decisions or criticizing my actions in front of others, we're all going to be in big trouble. People can sense a power struggle going on at the top the same way sharks smell blood in the water."

"But there is no power struggle." Letty watched him anxiously. "I fully respect the fact that you're in charge and that you've been doing an excellent job with this company for the past ten years."

"Thanks. Then do us both a favor and don't interfere with the day-to-day operations. You'll only confuse people and make them question my authority. Do you understand that, Ms. Thornquist?"

"Yes."

Joel relented when he saw the genuine apology in her eyes. He gave her an encouraging smile. "Now that we under-stand each other, what do you say we go over this manual?"

She nodded quickly. "All right. I'll tell you where I first started running into problems."

Joel listened to her with half of his attention at first. It had worked, he thought. He had controlled her without losing command of the situation. The firecrackers were all up in the air again. Like taking candy from a baby. He just had to be cautious, he warned himself. Letty Thornquist was a bright little thing, just as Charlie had once told him.

An hour later Letty leaned back in her chair and stretched her arms high over her head. The action pulled her blouse free from her skirt again and added intriguing new wrinkles to her gray jacket. "So what do you think about my ideas for the manual revisions?"

Joel drummed his fingers on the desk, frowning intently at the loose-leaf page of instructions in front of him. His business instincts were now at war with his need to keep Letty's inquisitive little nose out of company affairs.

His business instincts won out. She had a valid point, he was forced to admit. Damn it, he should have field-tested the new tent and its manual on a couple of amateurs.

"Okay, I can see where we might have a couple of problems with the instructions." A thought occurred to him. He looked up expectantly. "So why don't I put you in charge of getting the manual corrected?"

She glowed with enthusiasm. "Sounds like a good idea."

"Might as well take advantage of your talents." The assignment would keep her busy and out of trouble for a while. Idle hands were dangerous hands.

"Mr. Blackstone?" She cleared her throat, glanced over at the door to be certain it was closed, and then lowered her voice. "I mean, Joel?"

"Yeah?" He flipped a page in the manual, wondering why he had not paid more attention to it right from the beginning. Novice campers would want the simplest step-by-step instructions.

"I was just wondering." Letty tapped a pencil on the desk. "You know I'm moving into my new apartment this evening."

"So I heard. Congratulations." He turned another page.

"Well, I was, uh, wondering if you'd like to come over for a drink and dinner tomorrow night. To help me christen the place."

Joel raised his head swiftly. "What?"

She blushed, but her earnest eyes held his. "A drink. Or

something. A few hors d'oeuvres. Dinner, maybe? Look, if you're busy, I'll understand."

"No. I'm not busy tomorrow night." Joel felt his insides clench. He closed the manual with great care. "I'll bring the champagne."

She hadn't invited Joel over to help her celebrate moving into the new apartment on a whim. She had been thinking about it for days but had almost chickened out after he read her that polite little riot act in her office.

Letty winced in recollection as she opened the oven door to check on the lasagne. She was mortified to think she had been accidentally stepping on Joel's toes during the past two weeks.

He had been running things for ten years. He no doubt felt somewhat proprietary toward Thornquist Gear, and he had every right to feel that way. And she certainly understood the importance of a clear chain of command in any organization.

But she owned the company, she reminded herself. She had every right to become familiar with its operation. It was her responsibility to do so.

The buzz of her new phone interrupted Letty's contemplation of the lasagne. She closed the oven door and snatched up the receiver. Her heart sank as she realized it might be Joel phoning at the last minute to tell her he couldn't make it.

"Hello?"

"Letty, is that you?"

The cultivated masculine voice was unmistakable.

Letty frowned. "Yes. Yes, it's me, Philip."

"It's about time," Philip Dixon observed. "I've been trying to get through to you for days. Do you realize your secretary has been refusing my calls? I've been checking Directory Assistance every day for a week. I knew that sooner or later you'd get an apartment and your own phone. What is going on out there? Are you all right?"

"Of course, I'm all right." Letty struggled to follow what he was saying. "What do you want, Philip?" Another thought struck her. "And what do you mean, my secretary has been refusing your calls?"

"What I want is to talk to you, Letty my dear. I've been trying to get hold of you since you disappeared. I called your father's mountain cabin on one occasion, and a rather rude individual named Blackstone hung up on me. Were you aware of that? He actually had the nerve to claim he was your CEO."

"He is."

"Well, you'd better start thinking about getting rid of him," Philip said. "I can tell from the one short conversation we had that he's not the kind of man you want working for you at Thornquist Gear. Very blue-collar. Letty, my dear, what is going on out there? I was told you'd quit your job here at Vellacott without even giving notice."

"I did."

"Darling, that's so unlike you. You never used to be so rash." Philip's voice softened. "It was because of us, wasn't it? Letty, you must believe me when I tell you I regret what happened in my office that day more than I can say. I assure you, it meant nothing. Absolutely nothing."

"It meant something to me."

"Darling, she was just a grad student. It wasn't serious."

"It was serious, Philip."

"Letty, I did not want to have to say this, but I'm afraid I must."

Letty cringed. Philip was moving into his lecturing mode now. "What is it you feel you have to say?"

"That unfortunate incident in my office would never have occurred if our relationship had been normal."

That stung. "I didn't realize you thought our engagement was abnormal."

But with a flash of guilt, Letty admitted to herself that it *had* been abnormal and she was the one who had made it that way. The engagement had lasted only a month and a half and during the last two weeks of it, Letty had been pulling back emotionally. And as for the physical side of things, she knew only too well that she had never really given much at all.

On the surface, Philip had all the qualities Letty had been searching for in a husband, plus a couple of extras. He was strikingly good looking, for one thing—tall, urbane, and golden-haired. More importantly, however, he was from her world. They had a great deal in common, or at least Letty had thought they had a lot in common. Philip was intelligent and well educated, and he seemed eager to undertake the responsibilities of a husband.

He had started pressing her for sex the minute his engagement ring was on her finger. She had held him off until that point because of her deep-seated, old-fashioned need for a firm commitment. Once she had the commitment, Letty told herself she had no more excuses for resisting his requests for sex.

With hindsight she realized that the fact that she had been searching for excuses in the first place should have been ample warning.

A few short, unfulfilling bouts in bed with Philip Dixon had confirmed Letty's secret fears. Her limited sexual experience before Philip had made her wonder if she was truly unresponsive but she had told herself it was simply that she had not yet met the right man.

After Philip, however, Letty had been forced to face facts. There was a growing possibility that she was not a very sensual woman.

At twenty-nine she was old enough and well read enough to know that some women were not able to have orgasms easily. Some never had them at all. According to one article, estimates of the number of women who never experienced a genuine climax were shockingly high.

Before Philip, Letty had told herself she could live with that unpleasant reality. It did not mean that she could not have a reasonably happy marriage and children.

After Philip, though, she had to wonder if it might very well mean just that. If she could not fake enough of a response or work up sufficient enthusiasm in bed to hold Philip's attention, she probably would not be able to do a good enough acting job to fool any man.

No one was more self-centered than Philip, and even he had noticed her unresponsiveness.

When she went to bed with Philip the first time, Letty had been realistic enough not to expect the earth to move. But she had been hoping for some increased sense of intimacy, a feeling of developing a stronger bonding with him.

Tonight Letty realized that her most clear-cut memories of those few sputtering occasions in bed with Philip were mostly of his muffled grunts and groans. He had reminded her of a certain familiar barnyard animal at the feeding trough.

For her part, she recalled only being grateful the entire process did not take very long.

In reality the engagement had already ended in Letty's mind even before she walked into Philip's office a few weeks ago and found Gloria the grad student on her knees in front of him.

"Philip, I don't know why you're calling, but I really wish you would hang up. I have things to do."

"We were having problems in our relationship," Philip said, ignoring her protest with typical arrogance. "We should have faced those problems together. I should have helped you deal with them in a reasonable, mature fashion. I've been giving our situation a great deal of thought, and I've come to the conclusion that you need professional help, my dear."

"Professional help?"

"Therapy," Philip explained gently.

"I don't think counseling would do me much good, Philip."

"Nonsense. It's just what you need to help you deal with

your inability to respond sexually and your failure to achieve a climax."

Letty felt herself turning red with humiliation and anger. "Philip, *please.*"

"I'd be happy to attend therapy sessions with you, of course. As I said, we're a couple. We need to face these things together. In a way, I suppose one could say it's my fault we're in this situation. I should have insisted on the counseling right at the beginning when I first realized you needed help. Instead, I foolishly allowed my own frustration to build up to a flash point."

"I'm going to hang up now, Philip."

"Out of desperation, I took consolation where I could."

"Good-bye, Philip."

"Letty, in a way I did it for us."

"Good grief, Philip. You expect me to buy that?"

"You must not hang up."

"Why?"

"I told you, we've got to talk."

"I don't like talking about our relationship, Philip. It's too depressing."

"I understand that," he said soothingly. "We'll deal with it slowly. I realize you're under a lot of stress at the moment because of your inheritance. Your friend Connie at the reference desk told me all about your great-uncle leaving you his company. She said you actually plan to run it personally." Philip chuckled. "That's quite a responsibility, Letty."

"Yes, it is, isn't it? I'm hoping to use my new responsibilities as a form of sublimation. It's cheaper than therapy."

Letty hung up the phone. She frowned, wondering what Philip had meant about her secretary failing to put through his calls. There had to be some mistake. She would worry about it tomorrow. Joel would be arriving at any minute.

The doorbell chimed. Letty hurried out of the kitchen. She went down the short hall and opened the door to find

Joel waiting with a bottle of champagne in his hand. The label was that of a Northwest winery that was unfamiliar to her.

"Doesn't smell like sushi," Joel said.

Letty relaxed and smiled back. It was going to be all right. He was here, and he was no longer annoyed with her. She felt inexplicably giddy and unaccountably nervous.

"Just a little something I whipped up using green gelatin and lima beans," she said glibly. "You can do the most amazing things with green gelatin. Add marshmallows and you've got dessert. Add some of that bacon-flavored cheese that comes in a tube and you've got hors d'oeuvres. And of course there's just no limit to what you can do once you start working with hamburger and green gelatin."

Joel's eyes narrowed. "I do believe you're pulling my leg, Ms. Thornquist."

"I do believe I am, Mr. Blackstone. What I've actually got in the oven is lasagne made with some wonderful fresh spinach I found in the Pike Place Market on the way home."

"Sounds terrific. Why don't I come on in and open the champagne?" Joel suggested gently.

Letty realized she was blocking the doorway. She stepped back quickly. "Yes. Please. Come in."

"Nice place." Joel's eyes swept over the interior of the apartment, taking in the sweeping view of Elliott Bay.

"Thanks." Letty closed the door behind him. All of a sudden her new abode, which had seemed so spacious earlier this afternoon, felt small and very crowded. She started for the kitchen. "I'm still unpacking, of course, but I should be completely settled in another couple of days. I got the phone connected this afternoon."

"Is the rain bothering you?" Joel followed her into the kitchen and set the champagne on the counter. "We've had a lot of it lately."

"Heavens, no." She opened the oven door again and bent over to double-check the lasagne. "I love rain."

Joel laughed softly behind her, as if at some private joke that only he understood. "I had a hunch you'd say that." There was a muffled explosion as the cork came out of the bottle of champagne. "Got a couple of glasses?"

"Here." Letty closed the oven door and handed him two stemmed glasses from the nearest cupboard.

Joel poured the champagne and picked up the glasses. He handed one to her, his eyes steady. Letty shivered under the raw energy she sensed in his gaze.

"You know," Joel said thoughtfully as his fingers grazed hers, "if I had any sense, I wouldn't start this." He bent his head and brushed his mouth lightly, teasingly, across hers. "God knows things are complicated enough as it is."

Letty's mouth fell open. *He had kissed her.* As casually as you please. He had just up and kissed her. She stared at him from under her lashes, half afraid of what she would see. The energy in his eyes was not only raw, it was sexual. That was why it was sending these chills of anticipation through her.

Letty knew she was out of her league. A man like this would expect so much more from a woman than she could give. It was time for a dose of good old-fashioned midwestern common sense.

"You're right. Things are complicated," she said breathlessly. "If you think it would be best for us not to get involved in a social friendship outside of business hours, I'll certainly understand. I know it probably isn't a very good idea. I wasn't sure if you would even come here tonight."

"Letty . . ."

"I hope you didn't accept the invitation because you thought you had to, what with me being the boss and all. I mean, I consider you a friend as well as a co-worker, but I wouldn't want you to feel compelled to socialize with the boss."

He silenced her by the simple expedient of putting his

fingers against her lips. "Letty, have you ever done any juggling?"

"No."

"Then we're both going to have to hope I know what I'm doing." He took his fingers away from her mouth and kissed her again.

Hard.

5

Letty set down her glass of champagne with shaking fingers. She took a deep breath and put her arms around Joel's neck. She kissed him back.

Hard.

It was glorious. It was unlike anything she had ever experienced. She felt wild, unchained, *free*. A jolt of unfamiliar energy swept through her. She recognized it instantly as pure, undiluted passion.

Her glasses fogged up. That had never happened when Philip had kissed her. It had never happened when *anyone* had kissed her.

"I'll be damned," Joel said against her mouth. His voice was hoarse. "I was afraid of this." There was a clink as he set his champagne glass down beside hers.

Letty felt herself being crowded back against the counter. One of Joel's hands was cradling the nape of her neck. His other hand was braced against the tile behind her, supporting both of them as he leaned into her. Letty was amazed at how heavy he was. He enveloped her the way a Thornquist Gear down jacket did. The warmth was astonishing. She felt hot all over.

Letty gasped when she felt Joel's leg slide between hers. He brought his knee up slowly and deliberately so that she was, for all intents and purposes, riding his muscled thigh. The fiery intimacy of the contact left her dazed and disoriented.

Her neat camel-colored flannel trousers proved to be totally inadequate protection against the heat of Joel's thigh. It burned through the denim of his jeans, through the wool fabric of her pants, and scorched the vulnerable softness between her thighs.

Letty knew she was still fully clothed, but she felt as if Joel had stripped her naked.

Joel's thumb moved along her jawbone, tracing the shape of her as if he intended to sculpt her face. Letty heard him groan deep in his chest. His thigh pressed more firmly against her, forcing her legs wider apart, lifting her up off the floor. She clutched at his shoulders, and his tongue slid into her mouth.

Panic seized her.

"Oh, my God, *Joel.* Joel, wait. *Stop.*" Panting for breath, she used the grip on his broad shoulders to force her head up and away from his. She opened her eyes and stared at him through tilted, steamed-up lenses. She found herself gazing straight into the heart of a blast furnace.

Everything was happening too quickly. She knew she had started this with her invitation to dinner, but it was all moving far too fast. She had to get a grip on herself and the situation. Time to slow down and let her glasses unfog.

"Letty?"

"The lasagne." She gave Joel a shaky smile, aware that her breathing was much too quick and shallow. "It's done. Got to get it out of the oven. Now."

"Sure. Wouldn't want dinner to burn." Joel smiled slowly

and eased her down so that she was standing on her own two feet again. He lowered his lashes, briefly shielding his gleaming tawny gaze. When he lifted them again, the fire in the furnace had been banked.

Letty nearly collapsed when he took his hand away from her neck. Excitement pounded through her. She felt as if she had just had a very close call, and part of her was disappointed that disaster had been narrowly averted.

There was plenty of time for things to happen between her and Joel, Letty thought as she grabbed two pot holders out of a drawer. If it was truly meant to be, then it would happen. No need to rush.

She noticed she could see clearly again.

Letty staggered to the oven and jerked open the door. A cloud of aromatic steam refogged the lenses of her glasses.

"Letty?"

"Yes?" She busied herself hauling the lasagne out of the oven. The pan weighed a ton. She wondered if doubling the recipe had been a mistake. But Joel was a large man who obviously needed a lot of fuel to maintain his phenomenal energy level. She had not wanted to run out of food tonight of all nights.

"I think I'm going to like being a mentor," Joel said softly.

She set the pan down with a clatter and turned to face him. He was watching her with an intensity that both alarmed and thrilled her. "I want to make something clear, Joel."

"Let me take a wild guess." His mouth kicked up at the corner. "You don't want to rush things, right?"

She laughed with relief. "Right. I wasn't sure how you felt. I wasn't certain if you were as interested in me as I was in you. I wondered if my imagination had gone wild or something."

"Now you know, don't you?"

She searched his eyes. "Do I?"

"I'm interested." He picked up his glass of champagne and leaned back against the counter. "Very."

Letty drew a deep breath and took the plunge. "Yes, well, so am I. But where I come from we do things a little more slowly."

Joel flashed her a grin. "You're not in Kansas anymore."

"I'm not from Kansas," she retorted. "I'm from Indiana."

He held up a palm. "Fair enough. I'll try to remember that and make allowances."

"There's something else I think you should know right up front," Letty continued firmly.

"I'm listening."

"I'm not interested in any one-night stands or short-term affairs."

"Neither am I. Too messy and too dangerous."

She toyed with a pot holder. "If we—you and I, that is—if we start something, I want it to be because we both believe we've got a future together. Joel, this is very awkward. Do you understand what I'm trying to say?"

"Yeah, I understand all right, Letty. You want to know if my intentions are honorable. It's a little early to ask me that, isn't it?"

She winced at the note of laughter in his voice. "It's a little too early for a lot of things."

"I thought you came out here looking for passion and adventure."

"Yes, well, somehow I wasn't expecting to find it quite so quickly," she admitted.

Joel laughed and put her glass of champagne back in her hand. "Don't worry, we'll do this on your schedule. After all, you're the boss."

That thought soothed her frazzled nerves. She *was* the boss, Letty repeated to herself. She had started this, and she would control it. She would test the waters cautiously. She would learn in due course if this man really was the one.

"To us and to Thornquist Gear." Letty raised the champagne glass to her lips.

"Right. You, me, and Thornquist Gear."

She sent him home early that night, and he went reluctantly but without a fight. Letty was smiling as she crawled into bed. She lay gazing happily at the neon-lit rain coming down outside her window.

Everything was going to work out beautifully here in Seattle. She had made the right move. She was going to find all the things that had been missing back in Indiana.

The next morning Letty sat at her desk on the fourth floor of Thornquist Gear and gazed out the window. Her thoughts went back to the phone call she had received from Philip.

Not just his call but something he had said during the call bothered her. Something about trying to reach her for several days. Letty made up her mind. It was time to confront her secretary.

She reached out and punched the button on the intercom. "Arthur, will you come in here for a moment, please?"

"Yes, Ms. Thornquist."

The door opened a moment later, and Arthur hurried into the room. He nervously adjusted his tie and blinked frantically. "What is it, Ms. Thornquist? Is something wrong?"

"Sit down, please, Arthur. I want to talk to you."

Arthur's eyes widened as he sank into the nearest chair. He clutched a notepad in one hand and a pen in the other. "Please, Ms. Thornquist, you're not going to send me back to Accounting, are you? I know I was promoted to executive secretary too quickly. I did warn Mr. Blackstone that I didn't have all the skills you would expect, but he said it would be all right. And I am trying very hard. Honest, I am."

Letty smiled reassuringly. "I believe you, Arthur. I have no complaints about your skills."

"Thanks. That's a relief. I thought maybe you were mad or something."

"I'm not angry, but I do have a couple of questions. First, have you been receiving phone calls from a Professor Philip Dixon?"

Arthur brightened. "Yes, ma'am. Several of them. And I've been handling them just the way Mr. Blackstone told me to. I've explained to Mr. Dixon that you could not take the calls. Mr. Blackstone said you didn't want to be bothered."

"I see." Letty tapped her pen on the desk, thinking swiftly. "Did Mr. Blackstone give you any other specific instructions about how to handle your work in this office?"

Arthur began to look alarmed again. His blinking speed increased rapidly. "Yes, but I've been doing exactly what he said when he briefed me on my duties for you, Ms. Thornquist. I swear it. When in doubt I always check with Mrs. Sedgewick."

"What, exactly, did Mr. Blackstone tell you to do?"

"He said I was to route all requests to see you through his office. He said he would deal with them until you were settled in here at Thornquist Gear. He also said I was to let his secretary know if there were any problems. In addition, he made it clear he wants to be kept informed of everything that happens here in your office."

"Does he really? How thoughtful of him." Letty grimly recalled Joel's short lecture on making certain the staff knew who was in charge around Thornquist Gear. Apparently he had gone out of his way to ensure that.

"Did I do anything wrong, Ms. Thornquist?"

"No, Arthur. You followed Mr. Blackstone's orders very well." Letty forced a smile. "But it will no longer be necessary to shield me from routine matters such as phone calls and requests from the staff. I'm quite settled in now. You may consider Mr. Blackstone's orders rescinded."

"What does that mean?" Arthur gave her a cautious look. "Rescinded?"

"It means they are no longer in effect."

Arthur coughed discreetly. "Does, uh, Mr. Blackstone know that?"

"I shall inform him myself," Letty said grimly. "In fact, I will do so immediately."

Arthur appeared only partially relieved by that information. "All right. Could you also tell Mrs. Sedgewick?"

"Mrs. Sedgewick?"

"She's a very forceful woman," Arthur explained uneasily. "I just want to be certain she understands I no longer have to get everything approved through her."

"I will explain matters to Mrs. Sedgewick," Letty assured him.

Arthur relaxed a little more. "What about those calls from Mr. Dixon?"

"Let me know whenever Professor Dixon calls, and I'll decide for myself whether or not I have time to talk to him."

"Yes, ma'am." Arthur got to his feet, blinking. "Is that all?"

"That's all for now, Arthur."

Letty sat back in her chair and waited for the door to close behind him. Then she picked up one of the computer printouts that littered her desk. She had not requested this particular printout. It had apparently been mistakenly attached to the last stack of data she'd managed to get from one of the computer operators in Accounting. She studied the figures for a long time before she got to her feet.

Carrying the printout under her arm, she left her office and went down the hall to Joel's lair.

"Is Mr. Blackstone around, Mrs. Sedgewick?"

Mrs. Sedgewick, the imposing dragon who guarded Joel's outer office, looked up. She was a strong-boned woman of indeterminate years whose gray hair was permanently frozen into a bouffant curve. "He's in his office, Ms. Thornquist. I'll let him know you're here."

"Do that," Letty murmured.

Mrs. Sedgewick spoke into the intercom. "Ms. Thornquist is here to see you, Mr. Blackstone."

"Send her in."

"Thank you, Mrs. Sedgewick." Letty paused, her hand on the doorknob, "Oh, by the way . . . ."

"Yes, Ms. Thornquist?"

"Arthur Bigley is now fully trained, and he and I are starting to function together as a team. He will no longer require assistance from you, and you need not concern yourself with directing his activities. Do I make myself clear, Mrs. Sedgewick?"

Mrs. Sedgewick pursed her lips disapprovingly. "I don't understand, Ms. Thornquist. Arthur is very new at his duties, and I was told to give him detailed instructions and guidance."

"Forget the detailed instructions and guidance. Arthur will get them directly from me from now on."

Without waiting for a response, Letty pushed open the inner door and walked into Joel's office.

Joel looked up from a file that sat amid the chaos of his desk. He was dressed for work in his usual manner. Letty had not really minded his habit of wearing running shoes, jeans, and long-sleeved, open-throated shirts to the office until now. This morning his overly casual attire annoyed her.

"Good morning, Mr. Blackstone."

He grinned at her slowly, his gaze deliberate and blatantly sensual. "You're looking good this morning, Madam President. I like that suit."

"Thank you." Letty immediately tried to straighten her blouse, which had bunched up beneath the jacket. She caught herself and stopped. She must not allow herself to become flustered by that look in his eyes. This was a serious matter. She had to face the possibility that his apparent interest in her was all a sham. Last night he had been testing the waters, trying to discover whether or not he could use sex to manipulate her. What had made her believe, even for a moment, that he was genuinely attracted to her?

She sat down across from him and fixed him with the sort of smile she usually reserved for the more obnoxious members of the Vellacott faculty. "How about intelligent? Do I look reasonably intelligent this morning, Mr. Blackstone?"

Joel narrowed his eyes. "I doubt if you could look any other way."

"How gallant. And would you also say I appear competent to handle the pesky little details of life? Do I appear able to deal with minor stuff like phone calls and appointments, for example? Do you think I might just manage to get myself to a meeting on time if I tried real hard? *If* someone bothered to inform me about that meeting in the first place?"

Joel tossed aside the pen he had been using to mark up the file. He sat back in his chair. "Okay, I give up. What game are we playing?"

"Good question." She smiled with chilly approval. "I was under the impression it was a game you had invented. I know for certain we've been playing it by your rules thus far."

"You're in a weird mood this morning, Letty. Why don't you stop fooling around and tell me what the problem is? Are you upset about last night? Because, if so, you've got no cause. I thought we had an understanding."

"I thought we did, too." She slapped the printout down on his desk. "I talked to my ex-fiancé last night."

"Dixon called you?"

"That's right. At home. You can imagine my surprise when I found out he had been trying to get through to me for several days here at Thornquist Gear. Apparently my secretary had been instructed not to put the calls through to me."

Joel shrugged, looking unrepentant. "I told Bigley not to bother you with them."

"You also gave him a few other instructions," Letty said evenly. "Instructions that effectively keep me out of the loop here at Thornquist."

"You *are* out of the loop. You may own Thornquist, but you don't run it. That seems to be a distinction you haven't quite grasped. I told you yesterday that the staff has to have a clear idea of just who is in charge around here."

"You've certainly taken pains to make it clear to everyone, haven't you?"

"Letty, you make terrific lasagne, and I think you're sexy as hell, but you do not run this company. I do. Around here, things get done my way or they don't get done at all."

Sexy as hell? Letty refused to examine that remark too closely. She would deal with it later. "I told you yesterday that I respect the fact that you are the CEO, Mr. Blackstone. But you keep forgetting that I own Thornquist Gear."

"Believe me, I haven't forgotten that fact for one minute."

"I insist on being kept informed. I insist that my secretary, at least, take orders from me and me alone. I insist that I be allowed to make my own decisions on whom I talk to, and I insist on being included in important meetings. Stop trying to pretend good old Great-Uncle Charlie still owns the place. Because he doesn't. I do."

Joel sat forward suddenly, his eyes igniting with temper. "Goddamn it, Letty—"

"Ms. Thornquist in the office, if you please."

"Goddamn it, *Ms. Thornquist,* if Charlie were still around, he'd be making arrangements to sell Thornquist Gear to me right now. Today. That was the plan. That was the way it was supposed to go down. Thornquist was supposed to be mine."

"Well, it's not. It's mine."

"Don't you think I damn well know that?"

Letty realized her fingers were trembling. All the ferocious restless energy she had sensed the first time she met Joel was blazing in him now. "Look, I don't like confrontations. I don't want to argue with you."

"Then don't. Get the hell back to your own office and rewrite tent instruction manuals. Let me run Thornquist Gear."

"I want us to work together."

"We will, just as long as you stay out of my way and let me do my job."

She sucked in her breath. "You don't want me here at all, do you?"

"I've told you what I want. I want you to sell the company to me."

"I'm not prepared to do that."

"I realize that. You want to use Thornquist to *find* yourself, don't you?" He surged to his feet and stalked to the window. "You want to use the business I've sweated blood to build up over the past ten years to put a little pizzazz in your life. You want to find passion and adventure. You want to amuse yourself with my company."

Letty was horrified. "Joel, that's not true."

"It is true, damn it. Don't bother denying it. We both know you decided to take up the reins of Thornquist only because you were bored with life back in Indiana."

Letty suddenly felt queasy. "Joel, I have to ask you something."

"Go right ahead. You're the boss."

She winced under his heavy sarcasm, but forced herself to ask the question she desperately needed answered. She moistened her lips. "I have to know if the reason you came to dinner last night—" She broke off and went straight to the point. "If you kissed me and let me think you were interested in a relationship with me because you thought you could control me with sex."

"Jesus," he muttered, not turning around.

"I have to know, Joel. Was it just one more control tactic, like manipulating my office procedures and giving orders to my secretary? Because, if so, I can save you a lot of trouble by telling you up front that it wouldn't have worked."

"Is that so?" He slanted her a chilling glance over his shoulder.

"Yes, it's so. Just ask Philip." Letty got to her feet, afraid that she was about to burst into tears. She refused to lose control of her emotions in front of him.

Joel swung around and caught hold of her arm as she started for the door. "What the hell is that supposed to mean?"

"Never mind." She wished she had kept her mouth shut.

"Lady, you are not getting out of here until you tell me what you meant by that remark."

She looked up, saw his expression, and she believed him. She pushed her glasses up on her nose and glared at him. Her cheeks were burning. "I meant what I said. I am not vulnerable to that particular approach. Sex is not high on my list of priorities."

He looked incredulous. "You expect me to believe that after that kiss last night?"

"I'm not saying I'm totally uninterested," she informed him stiffly. "But to be perfectly blunt, I find it vastly overrated. In short, sleeping with the boss is not going to get you anywhere in your career, Mr. Blackstone. I just thought you ought to know."

"Thanks for the tip. I'll keep that in mind."

"You do that." Letty felt better now. Stronger. She was definitely not going to cry. "I think you should also know that things are going to be run a little differently around here."

"Is that right?"

"Yes." She straightened her shoulders and freed herself from his grasp. She walked back to the desk and picked up the printout she had brought with her. "From now on, I want to be kept in the loop. And for starters, you can tell me why Thornquist Gear owns fifty-one percent of a failing company called Copeland Marine Industries."

Christ, he really hated this town. He had not realized just how much until tonight.

He had left Echo Cove fifteen years ago. Today was the first time he had been back. From what he could tell this afternoon during the drive through the small downtown section, little had changed.

Echo Cove was still Victor Copeland's personal kingdom by the sea.

Joel concentrated on knotting his tie as he listened to the wind in the trees outside the motel room window. He could hear Letty moving about in the room next door. She was probably putting on one of her staid little business suits, the kind with the patented automatic wrinkling device built right in.

It was her fault he was in this damn motel room dressing for dinner with Victor Copeland tonight. The fuse on the firecracker that was Letty had been lit. Joel knew he was going to have to work very hard to make certain it did not explode in his hands. Joel grimaced as he recalled the scene in his office.

"Why does Thornquist Gear own fifty-one percent of a company called Copeland Marine Industries?" she'd wanted to know.

He had been expecting the question. It was inevitable the deal would eventually surface and equally inevitable that Letty would be curious about it. Her curiosity, it seemed, knew few boundaries.

The problem with Letty's inevitable question was that Joel had not been expecting it that morning two days ago. She had hurled it at him after all that other garbage about not giving orders to her secretary and not thinking he could use sex to control her.

His brain had still been working on the interesting notion of manipulating Letty with passion when she had dropped the little bomb about Copeland Marine.

Joel had scrambled for his prepared answer: "Copeland Marine is a small company that specializes in boat outfitting and repair. They handle marine engines, deck layout, custom work. That kind of thing. They have a yard out on the coast in Echo Cove."

"So why do we own a controlling interest?"

Joel had picked his words carefully. "The company has been sliding into financial hot water for some time. A year ago they approached Thornquist about a possible buyout. They needed an infusion of cash and in exchange were willing to sell us fifty-one percent of the company."

"And we went for the deal? Just like that? But Copeland Marine has nothing to do with camping gear or sporting goods."

"Charlie didn't see it that way," Joel had explained carefully. "You know your great-uncle. He was a sucker for anything that had to do with fishing. He did the deal over my objections. It was one of the few times in the past ten years that he overrode me." Lies, all lies. Charlie had known nothing and cared less. He had simply signed whatever Joel told him to sign.

Letty scowled. "But Copeland is still in trouble, according to the figures in this file."

"Unfortunately, yes. In fact, they're worse off than they were a year ago when they came to us."

"So what are we going to do?"

"Only one thing we can do under the circumstances. We're going to have to take over Copeland Marine and liquidate the assets."

"Liquidate? That's pretty drastic, isn't it? I've read some articles on this type of maneuver. A lot of people will be put out of work."

"That's the way it goes," Joel said coolly. "Business is business."

"Does Copeland Marine know we're planning to move in and liquidate their assets?"

"No. Copeland hasn't been told yet. When the time is right I'll let them know what's happening."

Joel had been planning to handle that detail personally. He wanted to see Victor Copeland's face when the older man realized who was really behind Thornquist Gear and what fate had in store for him.

Joel wanted to look straight into Copeland's eyes when he found out that his little kingdom was about to be sacked and destroyed.

What Joel had not figured into his calculations was Letty's response to the whole thing. Yesterday morning, after apparently dwelling on the matter for a full day, she had marched back into his office and told him she wanted to take a look at Copeland Marine Industries herself before making a final decision to liquidate.

Before Joel could think of a way to stop her, she had told her secretary to call Victor Copeland and tell him that the new president of Thornquist Gear was on her way to Echo Cove to review the situation.

Joel barely had time to order Mrs. Sedgewick to make reservations for two at the Marina Motel.

He convinced Letty he should accompany her and told her they might as well drive out to the coast together. Joel spent the two-hour trip talking. Fast. He went into great detail about the hard realities of the business world. He carefully explained that Thornquist Gear could not pour good money after bad. Copeland Marine had to be liquidated.

He was not sure if Letty had been paying attention to his lecture, however. She'd had a rather vague, distracted, faraway look in her eyes. She appeared to be lost in thought somewhere deep inside herself.

The invitation to join Victor Copeland for dinner had been waiting for Letty when she checked into the motel with Joel an hour earlier.

"You might as well come along, Joel," Letty had said as she picked up her key. "I hope you brought a jacket and tie. This is a business dinner, you know."

What the hell. He didn't mind wearing a tie when he told Victor Copeland it was all over.

He finished adjusting the knot on the tie and picked his jacket up off the bed. It had gotten a little crushed in the back seat of the Jeep, but he was willing to bet he would look less rumpled than Letty did. Joel hooked the jacket over his shoulder as he went to the connecting door and rapped loudly.

"Just a minute," Letty called.

The door opened a moment later, and Letty peered up at him, scowling thoughtfully. Joel hid a grim smile. Letty's heavy tweed suit already looked as if she had slept in it. Her hair was in its usual feisty state, already struggling to break free of the clip at the nape of her neck.

Joel was annoyed with her and uneasy about the recent turn of events, but he could not help thinking that she looked remarkably cuddly. He had to keep reminding himself just how dangerous the lady was.

Letty pushed her glasses up on her nose and gave him a brisk nod of approval. "You look very nice."

"What did you think I was going to wear? Jeans?"

"From what I've seen of your normal business attire, I couldn't be certain how you would dress for a formal business dinner." Letty turned away and stepped into her high heels. "Are you ready? We're due at the restaurant in twenty minutes."

"Don't worry. The restaurant is on the other side of the marina. We can walk to it in ten."

Letty brightened. "Good. I'd like to see more of the town. I want to get a feel for the place."

"Why?"

She gave him an unreadable glance. "I just do, that's all."

"Suit yourself."

She smiled a little too sweetly. "I will. After all, I am the boss, right?"

"You're the boss," Joel agreed softly. "Just remember that a lot of money is at stake here. Don't go making any rash statements tonight, Letty."

"I told you, I just want to meet Copeland and talk to him personally before Thornquist Gear makes a final decision on liquidation."

"The final decision has been made," Joel told her. "It's too late to change it. I explained that to you on the way down here. I went over all the figures with you. The only thing left to do is inform Copeland that there will be no extension on his loan and no further investment cash from us."

"Well, for heaven's sake, don't tell him over dinner."

"All right. I can wait," Joel said.

But there would be no waiting. The instant Victor Copeland saw Joel at Letty's side, he would know it was all over for him.

Letty surveyed the lights of the Echo Cove marina as she and Joel made their way along the waterfront. Only a handful of brightly painted private yachts and cruisers were tied up at the docks. The vast majority of the boats were clearly working craft. Fishing vessels of all sizes made up most of the small fleet.

Everything from small aluminum outboards to large commercial trawlers bobbed in the water. Many of them needed paint, but all of them appeared neat and orderly. Nets and lines and a variety of gear were stacked on the decks. Letty wrinkled her nose at the smell of fish that hung in the air.

"So this is Echo Cove," she said into the heavy silence that had persisted between Joel and her since they left the motel.

"Yeah."

"It's not a very large town."

"No, it's not large."

"Copeland Marine must be one of the main industries."

"Biggest company in town. There's a commercial fishing outfit that works out of here, but it's small compared to Copeland."

Letty thought about that. "Then Copeland is the largest employer in town."

Joel slanted her an unreadable glance. "Yeah."

Letty said nothing more as they walked the rest of the way to the restaurant. She did not know what to make of Joel tonight. He had seemed to change this afternoon when they had driven through town.

Tonight she was aware more than ever of the tension deep within him. It seemed to be growing and coiling, drawing him as dangerously taut as a nocked bow. She had a hunch this would be one of the nights when he would want to run at one o'clock in the morning.

But from what she could see, there was no place to run here in Echo Cove.

Five minutes later Joel opened the door of the Echo Cove Sea Grill. The restaurant sported a huge neon fish on the roof and boasted a marina view. A large roaring fire blazed on the stone hearth that dominated the entrance area.

Letty smiled at the hostess. "The Thornquist party. I believe Mr. Victor Copeland is expecting us."

The hostess, a heavily made up woman in her early forties, was wearing a dress that was a size too small for her ripe figure. Her hair was the color of straw and had been teased to a fare-thee-well. She glanced at Letty, but her gaze skipped immediately to Joel.

"Mr. Copeland said he was expecting only one guest," the hostess said, still staring at Joel.

"There's been a last-minute change. I hope that won't be a problem." Letty watched the hostess with some irritation. The woman obviously could not take her eyes off Joel. For his part, Joel had lost interest after a short nod of greeting. He was scanning the dimly lit lounge, which was just off to the right.

"Uh, sure. Sure. No problem." The hostess plucked a second menu out of the stack. "I'll have one of the busboys grab an extra chair." She stared at Joel again. "Excuse me, sir. Do I know you? You look awfully familiar."

"Blackstone," Joel said calmly. "Joel Blackstone."

The hostess's eyes widened in surprise. "Well, I'll be darned. I thought it was you, Joel. Marcy Stovall. Remember me? I worked at the bowling alley when you were in high school."

"I remember."

"What in the world are you doing back here—" Marcy broke off abruptly. When she continued, her voice started to rise. "Wait a second. You're here with Ms. Thornquist? You're going to have dinner with the Copelands tonight?"

Joel smiled without any warmth. "Looks like it."

"Holy shit," Marcy breathed. "This should be interesting." She jerked her gaze back to Letty. "This way, please." She led the way into the dimly lit eating area.

Letty shot Joel an angry, baffled glance. "What is going on here?" she whispered.

"I used to live here in Echo Cove. Guess I forgot to mention it."

"I guess you did," she snapped. "What in the world . . . ?"

But it was too late to grill him further. Marcy came to a halt beside a table for six that had been set for only four. Two men and a woman were already seated.

The older man dominated the table by virtue of sheer bulk. He was a mountain of a man who seemed to be composed of equal parts muscle and fat. His gray suit strained across his huge midsection and was equally tight across his massive shoulders. He had pale eyes that were nearly lost in his florid, heavily jowled face. As Letty approached, he lumbered to his feet, smiled genially, and held out a hand the size of a side of beef.

"Miss Thornquist? Victor Copeland. I was sorry to hear about Charlie Thornquist's death. Never met him personally, but we did business together."

"Thank you," Letty murmured as she briefly lost her fingers inside his massive grasp. "Do you know my CEO, Joel Blackstone?"

"We've met," Joel said. He stepped out of the shadows so that those at the table could see him clearly for the first time.

Somehow, Letty thought, she was not at all surprised by the stunned expressions on the faces of Copeland and the lovely woman who sat beside him as they turned to stare at Joel. The other man at the table, however, merely nodded with the normal response one expected between strangers.

"Jesus H. Christ," Victor Copeland muttered, eyes narrowing. "What the hell are you doing here?"

"*Joel.*" The woman looked as if she were seeing a ghost. "My God. What on earth is going on?"

"Business." Joel held Letty's chair for her. He smiled

coldly as he sat down beside her. "Nothing personal. Just business. How have you been, Diana?"

The sandy-haired man seated next to Diana spoke up quietly. "Excuse me. I don't think we finished the introductions." He turned to Letty. "I'm Keith Escott. This is my wife, Diana. Diana is Victor's daughter, in case you didn't know."

"I see. How do you do?" Letty smiled at the attractive woman, but Diana was staring at Joel.

Keith glanced at his wife, looking uneasy. Then he smiled at Letty. "I hope you don't mind the crowd. Victor said he thought we should all come, since we're all involved in Copeland Marine in one way or another. If that's a problem, let me know."

"Of course not." Letty smiled, liking Keith at once.

Keith Escott appeared to be in his mid-thirties. He was a good looking man with an open, mobile face and neatly trimmed sandy hair. There was an air of quiet intelligence about him. He reminded her of some of the earnest young faculty members she had known back at Vellacott. He had that same look in his eyes, the one that said he was just beginning to understand how greasy the ladder of success really was, but he was ready to climb it anyway.

Diana Escott smiled coolly across the table. "I'm sorry. Seeing Joel again after all this time was a surprise. How do you do, Ms. Thornquist?"

"Fine, thank you."

Diana looked to be thirty-one or thirty-two, but it was hard to tell. She was a striking woman with creamy white skin and raven black hair. Her eyes were huge and dark. The natural contrasts of her own coloring had been expertly highlighted with a judicious touch of eyeshadow and blusher. But the makeup did not hide the strained, unhappy look that lay like a mask over her beautiful features.

Letty noticed that Diana favored a bright, vivid shade of lipstick.

A fine pair of scarlet-tinted lips.

The mocking words popped into her brain for no apparent reason. She suppressed them immediately along with a disturbing image of a certain CEO's male member inserted between said scarlet-tinted lips.

But even as she squelched the image, Letty knew her instinct was correct: Joel and Diana had been more than friends at one time. That realization was as glaring as the neon sign on top of the Echo Cove Sea Grill.

"We had no idea Joel was with Thornquist Gear." Diana's sultry eyes filled with a hard mockery as they swung to Victor Copeland. "Did we, Daddy?"

"No," Copeland said brusquely. "We didn't." He looked straight at Letty, ignoring Joel. "Mind telling us just what's going on here, Ms. Thornquist? We had a deal with your uncle. Things have been going real well. I'd like to know what your intentions are now that you've inherited his company."

Letty glanced at Joel. He reminded her of a lion waiting for the perfect moment to rip open a gazelle's soft throat. She swiftly made an executive decision.

"I'd rather not get into specifics tonight, Mr. Copeland," Letty said smoothly. "We both know that Copeland Marine is in trouble, but I'd rather discuss it tomorrow after I've looked around your boatyard and seen something of your operation."

Victor snorted. "You want to look around? Now, see here, Ms. Thornquist—"

"Please call me Letty."

He grinned, pleased at the invitation. "Why, sure. Now, the thing is, Letty, all I need is a little more time and a little more cash. I can pull Copeland Marine out of the red if I just have a little bit more of each. I figure I can get it back into the black in another year. Did you take a look at last quarter's figures? Definitely up from the previous quarter's."

"But still drowning in red ink, Daddy." Diana smiled tauntingly. Her eyes were on Joel. "And I'll bet Joel knows that, don't you, Joel?"

"It's no secret," Joel said. "Last quarter's figures look slightly better than those of the previous quarter only because of the usual seasonal variation in the business. They'll drop like a stone again next quarter."

"Goddamn it, what the hell do you know about my business?" Copeland hissed.

"As Charlie's CEO, it was part of my job to keep track of Copeland Marine. I set up the original deal, of course, and worked out the details, and I've kept tabs on things ever since." Joel's smile was carved in ice. "We have a lot of cash tied up in the Copeland Marine yard. And we own fifty-one percent of the business."

Letty gave Joel a repressive look followed by a meaningful smile. "I said I would prefer to discuss specifics tomorrow. Do I make myself quite clear?"

The fury of the predator that has been temporarily deprived of its legitimate prey leaped in Joel's eyes. In the next moment Letty saw that he had himself back under control.

"Sure, boss. Whatever you say."

"Thank you." Letty picked up her menu.

"I love it," Diana murmured. " 'Sure, boss. Whatever you say.' Oh, God, that's rich." She swirled the wine in her glass and took a long swallow. "Tell me something, Letty. How does it feel to own your own company?"

"I'm enjoying it," Letty answered with a polite smile.

"It must be fun to be able to order someone like Joel around," Diana observed with a throaty chuckle. "I know exactly what I'd have him do if he worked for me."

Letty did not look at Joel to get his reaction to that barb. It was not necessary. She could feel his anger lapping at her in waves.

"I think you've said enough, Diana," Keith muttered.

Diana smiled brilliantly at him. "Keith darling, I haven't even begun."

"Shut up, Diana. You've already had too much to drink." Victor threw a warning glare at his daughter and then turned his attention back to Letty. "What do you say we get you a drink, Letty?"

"Thank you." She looked up at the young woman who was hovering nearby. "I'll have a glass of white wine, please."

"We've got a sauvignon blanc, a chardonnay, and a Riesling by the glass," the waitress said.

"She'll have the chardonnay," Joel said before Letty could make a choice. "And I'll have whatever you've got on draft."

Out of the corner of her eye, Letty saw Diana arching one elegant dark brow as she watched Joel place the order.

"So you're now the sole owner of Thornquist Gear," Victor said to Letty in a hearty tone as the drinks were brought to the table. "Big responsibility for a little lady."

"So I'm told." Letty hid her reaction to Copeland's patronizing tone and slid Joel a laconic glance. "Some people think I'm in over my head."

Keith glanced at her with genuine interest. "What were you doing before you inherited Thornquist?"

"I was a librarian at a college back in Indiana."

Diana sputtered on a swallow of wine. "A librarian? This get's better and better. That's wonderful. A *librarian* is going to tear Copeland Marine to shreds." Her eyes narrowed and her smile became malicious. "With the help, of course, of a dirty no-good upstart bastard who can't keep his jeans zipped." She turned her brilliant smile on her father. "Wasn't that how you described Joel fifteen years ago, Daddy?"

Letty was not the only one who was momentarily stunned by Diana's savagery. Only Joel looked amused.

Keith was staring at his wife as if he had not seen her

before. "Christ, Diana. What the hell's the matter with you tonight?"

Victor was turning a mottled red. "Get her out of here, Escott. Get her out of here right now."

Keith got to his feet and reached down to grip Diana's arm.

"That won't be necessary." Letty was already on her feet. "I think we had better postpone our get-acquainted conversation until tomorrow. I'll call on you at your office at nine, if I may, Victor."

Victor struggled to regain some control of the situation. "Look, I'm sorry about this. My daughter has been going through a bad patch lately. Depression or something, the doctor says. I thought it would do her good to get out tonight, but obviously I was wrong. Let Escott take her home, and get rid of Blackstone, here. No reason you and I can't have dinner."

"I'm not going anywhere," Diana declared, taking another deep swallow of wine. "I wouldn't miss this for the world."

"I am afraid you'll have to miss it, Mrs. Escott." Letty adjusted her glasses on her nose and shouldered her purse. "As president of Thornquist Gear, I cannot allow my employees to be insulted in public. Image, you know. I'm sure you understand. Let's go, Joel."

"I'm right behind you, boss." Joel took a swallow of his beer, put the glass down on the table, and got to his feet. He smiled humorlessly at the three people left at the table. "So long, everyone. It was a real pleasure. Nothing like coming back to your hometown and renewing old acquaintances. Enjoy your dinner."

Letty was aware of him trailing obediently after her as they walked through the restaurant, but she did not look back. When they stepped out into the chilly night, Joel paced beside her in silence. The air around him was almost crackling with the energy he was generating.

Letty shoved her hands deep into the pockets of her suit jacket. She felt as if she were walking through a minefield. "You want to tell me what that was all about?"

"Old friends," Joel said softly.

"Who? The Copelands?"

"Yeah."

Letty came to a halt and stepped straight into his path, forcing him to stop. "Damn it, Joel, what is happening here?"

His eyes gleamed in the shadows. "No big deal, boss. Just business as usual. We're taking over Copeland Marine, and we're going to liquidate the assets. Real simple."

Letty had never in her life felt such an overpowering desire to slap a man's face. She barely restrained herself. "Tell me what this is all about," she ordered tightly.

"You've read the file. You know what it's about. It's just business, Letty."

"It is not just business. It is very clear that whatever is going on here is extremely personal. Explain it to me."

"I don't see why I should. It's personal for me, but not for you or the company. All you have to worry about is the business side of things, boss. And as far as the business angle is concerned, all the decisions have already been made. It's a cut-and-dried situation. Copeland Marine is dead meat. The only option is to liquidate."

Joel started moving again, obliging Letty to fairly leap out of his way.

"Joel, wait a minute, damn you." Letty hurried to catch up with him. "I want some answers."

"And I want some dinner. I'm starving. There used to be an old drive-in a couple of blocks past the motel. Let's go see if it's still there."

Letty started to protest, realized the futility of it, and closed her mouth again. Instead, she trotted along beside Joel, wincing at the punishment her feet were taking in the high heels.

Joel came to a halt two blocks later and nodded his head

at the familiar neon logo that blazed forth over the restaurant. "I should have known. Old Ed sold out to a fast-food chain. Figures. Come on, Letty, you can buy."

"Gee, thanks." Grumbling, Letty dug into her purse.

"Only fair," Joel said as he ordered two sacks of french fries and two fish sandwiches. "You deprived me of my first meal this evening, the one Victor Copeland was going to buy."

"Somehow, I doubt that anyone would have enjoyed eating in that atmosphere."

"I would have enjoyed it. A lot."

"I don't see how." Letty took her sack of french fries from him. They walked toward a plastic booth. "Not after what Mrs. Escott said. Did Victor Copeland once say all those things about you?"

"He said a lot more than that." Joel slid into the booth and opened the carton containing his sandwich. "But what the hell. All water under the bridge, as far as I'm concerned. I'm a real forgiving sort of guy."

Letty went still. "Joel, let me tell you something. You don't do Magnanimous well, so don't try to make me think that whatever happened here fifteen years ago is water under the bridge."

"As I said, you don't have to worry about it. It doesn't concern you." Joel ripped a huge bite out of the sandwich with his teeth.

"You wanted to come here to Echo Cove so we're here," he said a few moments later. "But there's no point to this little exercise. Complete waste of time and money. If you've got any sense, you'll decide we can go home in the morning."

"I had planned to spend two days here. You know that."

"We've got a company to run back in Seattle."

"It can survive without us for two days."

There was no use arguing with him. Letty could see that. She could also tell that it was highly unlikely he would confide in her right now. He was throbbing with anger, and it was all focused on that little trio they had left behind in the restaurant.

Tomorrow morning she would try to find out exactly what the bad blood was that ran between Joel and the Copelands. The inquisitive librarian in her would not rest until she knew what had happened fifteen years ago.

Several hours later, Letty came awake with a start. She sat straight up in bed and listened to the sounds from Joel's room. He was moving about on the other side of the wall.

Letty reached for her glasses on the bedside table and peered at the clock. It was one in the morning. She threw back the covers and got out of bed. She padded over to the connecting door, put her ear to the wood, and listened carefully.

He was definitely getting dressed; she could hear the zipper of his carryall sliding open. Letty rapped softly on the door.

"Joel? What are you doing?" she called through the door.

The connecting door opened, and Joel, dressed in jeans and nothing else, scowled down at her. "What the hell are you doing up?"

Letty stared at him, ignoring the question. "Oh, my God. You're going to run, aren't you?"

"Yeah. Go back to bed, Letty."

"Joel, it's one o'clock in the morning, and there is no private road anywhere near this motel. I will not have the CEO of Thornquist Gear dashing up and down the main street of Echo Cove at this hour. Anyone who sees you will think you're crazy. You'll probably get picked up by the police."

"Don't worry about it, Letty."

"Think of the company image," she insisted. "Think of your personal image as a representative of Thornquist Gear."

"Right. Image. That's a real big issue with me, all right. Believe me, Letty, the good people of Echo Cove couldn't think any worse of me now than they did when I left town fifteen years ago. Now go back to bed."

"No." She pushed past him and stalked into his room. The cotton skirt of her prim white nightgown flounced around her bare ankles. "We're going to talk about this."

"The hell we are." Joel took two strides toward her, put his hands on her shoulders, and yanked her up against him.

"Joel."

He kissed her roughly and then raised his head, eyes glittering with menace. "If you don't want me to run down the main street of Echo Cove tonight, you'd better think of some other way for me to burn off a little energy. Got any ideas?"

Letty stared mutely up at him through fogged glasses. She touched her mouth with curious, wondering fingertips, and then she touched his bare chest. "No. No, I don't actually have any alternative suggestions."

"Well, I sure as hell do." He started to lower his mouth to hers once more.

Letty was suddenly finding it very difficult to catch her breath. She fumbled awkwardly with her glasses. "Uh, Joel, I'm not at all certain you want to do this."

"I'm certain." He brushed his mouth across hers. His mood was altering with blazing speed from anger to passion. The kiss was not at all rough this time. It was slow and full of exciting promise. "Real certain."

Letty put her arms slowly around his neck. She shook her head slightly. "It won't work, you know. You can't control me this way."

"I've got a better plan."

"What's that?"

"Why don't you try to control *me* with sex?"

The thought of wielding that kind of sensual power over

him or any other man was so ludicrous that Letty started to laugh. It was a nervous, giggly kind of laughter that, to her horror, she could not seem to stop once it had gotten started.

But Joel knew how to stop her. He covered her mouth with his own.

7

Joel eventually raised his head. When he did he was breathing heavily. Letty opened her eyes and looked up at him through tilted, steamed lenses. His face was a foggy blur. But then, she felt a little blurred herself.

"Joel?"

"Let's try it without these." Joel gently removed her glasses and set them on a nearby table. He cradled her face in one hand and lowered his mouth once more to hers.

His mouth felt good, Letty decided. Very good. Not wet and sloppy like Philip's. She sighed softly and wrapped her arms more tightly around Joel's neck. Craving more of his wonderful warmth, she instinctively pressed herself closer. His broad chest was as solid as the face of a granite cliff.

"Can I take this to mean that you are not totally opposed to the idea of going to bed with me?" Joel asked against her mouth.

"Yes. I mean, no. I'm not totally opposed." Letty opened

her eyes and looked up. Even without her glasses she could see the lambent fire in his gaze. "I just didn't want you to get the wrong idea."

"I know. I got the point." He raked his fingers slowly through her wild, thick hair. "I can't control you with sex."

"That's right."

"Why not?" he asked with a whimsical tilt to his mouth.

"Why not?" She frowned, feeling she owed him an explanation of some sort. "I suppose it's because I'm not a particularly sensual person, if you know what I mean."

"You don't like sex?" He ran his palms over her shoulders and down her forearms.

"I like being kissed and held as much as the next woman." Letty shivered a little as his warm palms slid back up to her shoulders. She felt his strong fingers flex gently. "I like the feeling of closeness. But I think the rest of the business is overrated. I'm not alone, you know," she added defensively. "I read an article—several articles, actually—that said a lot of women feel that way."

He nodded, looking very serious. "Ah. An article. Let me see if I've got this right. You're not real wild about sex, so I can't use it to manipulate you. And the thought of being able to control me with it gives you the giggles."

She smiled tremulously. "Well, it *is* kind of amusing, in a way. I doubt that anyone could control you with sex or anything else."

"You think I'm so damn tough?"

"I think you're very tough," she said honestly.

"Why don't you try it?" he invited softly.

She eyed him uncertainly. "Try what?"

"Controlling me with sex." His hands tightened on her shoulders. "You're the boss around here, right?"

Letty licked her lips. "Right."

"So why don't you try calling the shots tonight and we'll see what happens?"

"I don't understand."

"It's simple." Joel brushed his mouth lingeringly across

hers and then carefully took her earlobe between his teeth. "You give the orders, Madam President. I'll follow them, just like a good, respectful, well-trained employee."

Letty's mouth went dry. "I'm supposed to give you orders? For *this?*"

"Tell me exactly what you want and how you want it done." He kissed the tip of her nose. "My only goal is to please."

A wave of heat washed over Letty. "Joel, this is embarrassing. If this is your idea of teasing me, forget it."

"I've never been more serious in my life. Tell me what you want me to do, Letty."

She stared at his bare chest, refusing to meet his eyes. "How am I supposed to tell you stuff like that?"

"Don't you know what you like and what you don't like?"

"Not exactly," she muttered.

"You must have read a couple of articles on the subject," Joel said.

Letty gave a muffled groan and dropped her forehead down onto his rock-hard shoulder. "Well, yes. I have read a couple of articles on the subject. Whole books, in fact."

"I figured you probably had. You being a librarian and all." His hand moved lightly in her hair.

"Oh, my God, Joel, this is too much."

"Was there anything in those articles or books that sounded particularly interesting?"

She nodded her head against his shoulder, unable to speak. She could not believe this was happening.

"Give me an example of something that sounded really fascinating." Joel trailed his forefinger just inside the neckline of her nightgown.

Letty gripped his shoulders and took a deep breath. "Kiss me."

"Where? Here?" He kissed her cheek, just under her eye.

"No. On the mouth. The way you did a minute ago." She raised her face.

"Whatever you say." Joel brought his lips down on hers.

He kissed her slowly, lightly. He used no real force, and he seemed to be asking nothing in return.

"Harder," Letty whispered, standing on tiptoe so that she could get closer.

"Sure, boss."

Joel obligingly deepened the kiss. His mouth moved a little more roughly on hers. Letty strained upward on her toes, seeking a better angle. She put her hand on the back of his head and tried to force him even closer.

"Now what?" Joel whispered invitingly against her lips. "Tell me, Letty."

"Open your mouth," she breathed, feeling bolder by the minute.

He did as she instructed and opened his mouth against hers. Letty parted her own lips at the same time and then waited on tenterhooks for the feel of his tongue.

Nothing happened.

Tentatively Letty ran the tip of her tongue along Joel's lower lip. He groaned in instant response, and his arms tightened around her. A curl of fire sizzled through her at the realization that she had elicited such a reaction from him.

"Now you do it to me," she managed.

"Do what?"

"You know. What I just did to you." She dug her nails into his scalp. "Do it."

"You got it, boss."

Letty held her breath as she felt his tongue slip warmly across her lips, teasing her. It wasn't enough. She gripped him harder, not minding the wetness of the kiss at all.

"Inside," Letty commanded urgently.

His tongue moved obediently into her mouth. She touched it with her own and was astounded at the sense of intimacy. A shiver went through her.

"You like that, boss?" Joel's voice was low and husky.

"Yes. *Yes.* I like it very much."

"Good."

For a long while Letty was content just to explore the full

potential of the deep kiss. Joel seemed prepared to oblige her until the end of time. She leaned against his chest, aware that the feeling of damp heat that was filling her mouth was beginning to flow in her lower body.

After another minute or two of the intimate kiss, Letty pulled away just far enough to speak.

"Joel?"

"Yeah?" His voice was darker, harsher, almost raw. "What next, boss?"

"Touch me."

He went still for an instant. "Where?"

"My . . ." She hesitated, losing her nerve at the last second. "My waist. Put your hands on my waist."

"Right. Your waist." His fingers settled just above her hips and squeezed gently. "Like that?"

"Maybe a little higher?"

"You don't sound sure."

"Try it," she murmured, frustrated.

"Anything you say, boss." His hands slid up her sides until his thumbs were resting just below the weight of her breasts. "Now what?"

Letty mentally flipped through the articles and books she had read on the subject of sex. She stopped scanning when she recalled one particular discussion on erogenous zones.

"My nipple," she got out in a tight little voice.

"What about it?"

"Touch it."

"Like this?" Joel's thumb grazed it through the fabric of her nightgown.

"Oh, God, yes. Just like that. Do it again."

He did it a second time. "How about the other one?"

"Yes, please. That one, too."

"My pleasure." Joel lightly scraped her other nipple.

It was not enough. Not nearly enough. "Take off my nightgown," The instant the words were out of her mouth, Letty was appalled. She could not believe she had given such an instruction.

But it was too late to recall it. Joel was already undoing the buttons. Letty closed her eyes and held herself very still as he peeled the nightgown off her shoulders and let it fall to the floor at her feet.

"Oh, my God," Letty muttered.

"How am I doing so far, boss?"

"Oh, my God." Letty did not open her eyes. The thought of herself naked in front of him was simply too much. She clung to him, afraid she would collapse if she let go. "Do what you did that night in my apartment."

"What did I do?"

"You know, that thing you did with your leg. Between mine."

"Oh, yeah. Right. You liked that, huh?"

"Yes," she breathed. "Do it. Please."

"Yes, ma'am." Joel eased her back against the wall, bracing himself with one hand behind her head. His bare foot slid between hers, edging her legs apart.

Letty kept her eyes squeezed shut as she felt his denim-clad leg move upward. The jeans were excitingly rough on her bare skin. Slowly his thigh slid along hers, easing her legs farther apart, opening her.

It was too outrageous for words.

It was too erotic for words.

The damp heat within her began to feel like a river of lava. Her nails dug into his shoulders, and her head fell back against the wall.

And then he was there—or rather, his knee was—pushing against her softness, lifting her up onto her toes and then off the floor entirely. Panic seized her for an instant. She felt so vulnerable.

"Joel."

"Change your mind?" His leg started to slide back down, lowering her to the floor.

"No, no, I haven't changed my mind. Do it again, please." She grabbed at his shoulders.

Then he was letting her ride the heat of his leg once more.

It was the most incredibly erotic thing Letty had ever experienced.

"Oh, my God." She was dimly aware that her vocabulary had become extremely limited.

"Anything else, boss?" Joel kissed her throat.

"The bed," she gasped.

"What about it?"

"I want to be on it. I'm going crazy. I must be out of my mind. Put me on the bed."

Without a word, he eased her down so that her feet touched the floor. Then he scooped her up and carried her over to the bed. He settled her lightly on the rumpled sheets.

When he started to pull away, Letty opened her eyes at last and clutched at him. "No, wait. Come here."

Joel grinned faintly. "I take it I'm not finished yet?"

"No, you are not finished. I want to try some other things." She licked her lips, willing him to come closer again.

"Why am I not surprised?" He came down onto the bed beside her. He propped himself up on his elbow and moved one jeaned leg lightly against hers. "So what else did you learn in those articles and books that you want to try now?"

"Touch me."

"Here?" His fingertips moved over her breasts again. "You have beautiful breasts, Letty."

"Thank you," she said breathlessly, not knowing how else to respond to such a compliment. Philip had never told her she had beautiful breasts. God, she felt beautiful all over right now. "Lower, please."

"Hmm?" His tongue was on her nipple.

Letty swallowed, summoning up her courage. She had gone too far to stop now. She had to see if it would work. "Move your hand lower."

"Here?" Joel's hand moved down to rest on her belly. His fingers splayed across her skin, heavy and warm.

"Lower," she ordered in a desperate, tiny voice.

His fingers slipped through the triangle of honey brown

curls until they found the dampening folds of flesh between her legs. "Here?"

"Yes." Letty lay stunned under the sensual impact of his touch. Her fingers dug into the sheet beneath her. Her toes flexed and pointed, and then her knees lifted. She could barely speak when she tried her next command.

"A little higher, please."

"Like this?"

Joel's finger drifted upward with tantalizing slowness, and suddenly he was touching a part of her that Letty had read a great deal about in the past few years. A part that had never seemed to function according to specifications until now.

She thought she would go through the roof. "Yes. Right *there*. Right *there*."

"Do you like circles or long, slow strokes?"

"I don't know. Try both." She was breathing quickly, as if she were jogging or working out.

"Circles." Joel's fingers moved lightly.

"Oh, my God."

"Strokes." Joel altered the pattern.

"Oh, my *God*."

"Which do you want, boss?"

"I don't know. Either. Both. Just keep doing it."

"Whatever you say."

For long, glorious minutes Letty gave herself up to the incredible sensations that were budding swiftly within her. Occasionally Joel asked for further instructions. She gave them eagerly, trying different patterns until she found the ones that seemed to have been designed precisely for her body.

"Joel, it feels so good. So good. I can't believe it."

"Neither can I," he muttered. His fingers were wet and slick with her essence. He whispered something else, but Letty did not catch it.

"What?" she asked.

"Nothing, honey. Anything else you want to try?"

"I don't know. This is good enough. Better than anything

I've ever felt before. Wonderful. Joel, I don't think I can stand much more." Letty arched her hips up off the bed, pushing against his fingers. One of them slid just inside her. *"Joel."*

"I'm still here, babe. I'm not going anywhere. Are you sure there isn't anything else you want to try? No other commands you want to give me tonight?"

There *was* something else about which she was extremely curious, but there was no way on earth she could ask him to do *that*. Not this first time, at any rate. Not until she knew him a lot better. Not until she'd had a chance to feel him out on the subject.

"I'm fine, Joel. This is wonderful. Oh, my God."

"You ever read any articles on this?" Joel kissed her stomach, and then she felt his breath fanning the curls of hair that shielded her softness.

"Joel."

"Did you?"

"Well, yes. Yes, I read something about it, but I wouldn't ask you to do that. I couldn't."

"You're giving the orders tonight, remember? You have to be very specific."

"Good grief, Joel, this is hardly the kind of thing a woman orders a man to do."

"Try it."

She could not stand it any longer. His breath was so warm, and his fingers felt so good. "All right, *do it.*"

"You got it, boss."

And then his mouth was on her in the most intimate, the most exotic, the most passionate caress Letty had ever known. It robbed her of breath for a single, exquisitely painful moment.

It was too much. It was all far too much.

"Oh, my God, Joel!" Letty screamed as everything inside her came undone and shattered into a thousand bright shards. The world fell away.

When it was over, she collapsed like a rag doll.

She wanted to laugh.

She almost burst into tears.

She did not have the energy to do either, so she closed her eyes and floated.

At some point Letty realized that Joel was sliding up alongside her and pulling the covers up over her. She turned on her side and nestled into his warmth, utterly exhausted. A part of her registered the fact that he was still wearing his jeans.

"Joel?"

"Go to sleep, Letty."

"Philip thinks I need therapy."

"What kind of therapy?"

"For this kind of thing. You know. To improve my sexual responsiveness."

"Lady, if you were any hotter or more responsive, we would have set the damn motel on fire. Now go to sleep."

She relaxed blissfully. Then she belatedly realized what the fact that he was still wearing his jeans meant. "Joel, you didn't . . ."

"Yes," Joel growled. "I did. I'll admit the last time I came in my jeans was when I was sixteen, but what the hell. I'm only a man, and you are pure dynamite."

Letty smiled. She felt suddenly content and sure of herself in a way she had never been before. A heady sense of feminine power swept through her. "You really think so?"

"I know so. I've got the singed fingers to prove it." It was Joel's turn to fall silent for a moment. Then he stirred slightly, pulling her more firmly into the cradle of his thighs. "Letty?"

"Hmm?"

"I didn't thank you for what you did tonight."

She yawned. "What are you talking about?"

"I'm talking about you walking out on Victor Copeland because you wouldn't tolerate your CEO being insulted in public."

"Oh, that."

"Yeah, that. Thanks. I doubt if anyone has ever walked out on Victor Copeland. And as for me, I've never had anybody try to protect me like that."

"Noblesse oblige," Letty said grandly. Then she started to giggle.

Joel gave her a small admonishing squeeze. "Shut up and go to sleep, boss."

This time she did as he said.

The ringing of the bedside telephone awakened Letty the next morning. She groped for it without opening her eyes.

"Hello?" A dial tone was the only response.

"Wrong phone," Joel muttered into the pillow. He was sprawled on his stomach beside her, taking up three-quarters of the available space.

When the phone rang again, Letty realized what was happening. "It's my phone."

"Don't worry about it."

But Letty was already scrambling out of bed. She blinked as she caught sight of herself in the mirror and realized she was stark naked.

The phone rang again.

Letty found her glasses and pushed them onto her nose. Then she grabbed her nightgown up off the floor and pulled it on over her head as she hurried through the connecting door into her own room.

"Hello?"

"'Morning, Letty. Victor Copeland here. Hope I'm not calling too early?"

"No." Letty sat down on the edge of her bed and tried to blink herself awake. "No, this is fine. What can I do for you?"

"I'd like to buy you breakfast if I may. I want to apologize for my daughter's behavior last night."

"That's not necessary, really."

"Please." Victor sighed wearily into the phone. "Look. We both know there's a hell of a lot at stake here. To be real

117

blunt, I don't think there's any way I can do business with you as long as you've got Blackstone hovering over your shoulder. In case you don't know it by now, he hates my guts."

"Look, Mr. Copeland—"

"Victor. I have to talk to you, Letty. You're the president of Thornquist Gear, and I'm in charge of Copeland Marine. Let's do business together like a couple of normal, rational human beings. You owe me that much, don't you think?"

Letty looked up and saw that Joel was filling the doorway between the two rooms. He was still wearing his jeans. His face was harsh in the watery morning light. She knew that Copeland was right about one thing: it would be difficult to talk business in any normal fashion with Joel nearby.

"All right, Victor. I'll have breakfast with you. Forty minutes?"

"Forty minutes is fine. There's a café one block down from your motel. I'll meet you there." Victor paused. "Thanks, Letty. I appreciate this."

"Good-bye, Victor." Letty hung up the phone.

"That son of a bitch thinks he can charm you into letting him off the hook," Joel said quietly.

"He just wants to talk."

"Bullshit."

"I owe him a chance to present his side of the situation before I make any final decisions, Joel."

"The final decision has already been made, and you don't owe Victor Copeland a damn thing. Don't meet him for breakfast, Letty."

She crossed her arms tightly beneath her breasts. "I'm going to hear what he has to say. It's only fair. It's why I came down here. If I were in his shoes, I'd want to talk, too."

"I'll come with you."

"I'm sorry, but I don't think that's such a good idea, Joel. I'm afraid your presence will make it difficult to get a clear picture of the situation."

"You've already seen the spread sheets. The picture is clear enough, and you know it."

Letty drew herself up proudly, wondering where all the sweet, hot passion of last night had gone. "I'm going to talk to him, Joel."

The room was suddenly alive with a menacing silence.

"Suit yourself, *boss.*" Joel closed the door between the two rooms with a soft, dangerous thud.

Letty barely resisted the impulse to dash across the room, fling open the door, and hurl herself into his arms. She wanted to say she was sorry. She wanted to beg him to explain the messy situation in Echo Cove to her so that she could understand and side with him. She wanted to plead with him to hold her close and touch her the way he had last night.

Letty stared at herself in the mirror. Her eyes grew round with shock as she realized just where her thoughts were heading. She was not going to let Joel Blackstone use sex to gain her cooperation. She was not that much of a twit.

If he thought for one minute that she was under his thumb now because of what had happened last night, he could damn well think again.

Letty leaped to her feet and stalked into the bathroom.

So what if it had been good? So what if it had been terrific? So what if she felt like a new woman this morning?

She had called the shots last night. She had given the orders. All Joel had done was follow instructions.

Who was she kidding?

Letty groaned and stepped under the full blast of the shower.

Forty minutes later Victor Copeland picked up his mug of coffee and studied Letty across the small table. The café was busy at this hour, but Copeland had told the waitress he wanted privacy, and she had hurried to provide it.

Nearly everyone in the restaurant had looked up and

nodded in respectful greeting when Copeland lumbered heavily down the aisle between the rows of booths.

The effect was not lost on Letty. Victor Copeland was definitely an important man in Echo Cove.

"I reckon you've probably figured out by now that me and Joel Blackstone go back a long way," Victor said gruffly.

"Yes, I got that impression." Letty noticed that Victor's color did not appear any better in the morning light than it had last night. She wondered if he had recently been ill or if his obvious weight problem was the cause of his florid skin.

"I'll be the first to admit that our association ain't exactly been what you'd call real pleasant," Victor allowed with a deep sigh. "He used to work for me in the yard, you know."

"No, I didn't know."

"Him and his pa, both." Victor shook his head at some old memory. "Hank Blackstone worked for me his entire adult life, until he got drunk one night and drove off a cliff just outside of town."

Letty absorbed that information. "Joel's father is dead?"

"Yeah. Been gone some fifteen years."

"I see."

"I liked Hank. Good man. Hard worker. Always gave an honest day's labor for an honest day's pay. Too bad his son didn't cotton to the same values. But young Joel, he was always looking for the fast way, you know what I mean?"

Letty thought about the ten years Joel had sweated to turn Thornquist Gear from a tiny storefront business into a major corporation. "No, not exactly. And I don't see that it matters. I'm not interested in your opinion of Joel."

Victor gave her an injured look. "I just wanted you to understand the reason for all the bad blood between us. Old Hank was a good solid, honest-as-the-day-is-long kind of guy, but that boy of his was trouble right from the start. Just ask anyone who remembers him. And that's a lot of people in town, I guarantee you."

"Mr. Copeland, I think we should confine our conversation to business, don't you?"

He shook his head slowly, small eyes almost disappearing as he narrowed them. "The thing is, you got to understand why me and him can't ever do business together. He's out for revenge, Letty. Pure and simple."

"Revenge?"

"Yep. That's the way it looks to me. Knew it as soon as I saw him walk into the restaurant last night. Now that Charlie Thornquist is gone, Blackstone wants to use his position to try to screw me out of Copeland Marine Industries. What's more, it don't matter none to him that in wiping out my company he's going to wipe out this whole town."

"You think that's what will happen if your boatyard closes?"

Victor eyed her speculatively, obviously sensing a weak point. "I know so. Hell, Echo Cove wouldn't even exist without Copeland Marine, and that's a fact. Just ask anyone. Whole damn town will go down the tubes if the Copeland boatyard closes."

Letty had been afraid of that. She took a swallow of the bad coffee. A few weeks ago she would have said the brew tasted fine. But today she found it weak and totally lacking in character. She had apparently become addicted to Seattle-style coffee.

"Maybe you'd better tell me just why Joel wants to destroy your company," Letty suggested after a moment.

Copeland's eyes gleamed with satisfaction. "I thought after last night you might have figured it out for yourself."

"I'm afraid not." She'd had a lot of other things on her mind last night, Letty thought wryly.

"I told you Joel Blackstone was the kind that was always looking for the easy way. Fifteen years ago that bastard——"

Letty held up a palm to silence him. "Please watch your language when you refer to my employee."

Victor scowled. "Fifteen years ago Joel Blackstone decided he could cushion his life real nice by marrying my daughter, Diana."

Letty stared at him, her heart sinking. "I see."

Victor nodded sadly. "Yes, sir, thought he'd set himself up real nice. Thought if he was my son-in-law I'd just naturally turn Copeland Marine over to him, and he could sit back and prop his feet up on my desk for the rest of his natural life."

Letty decided to put her coffee mug down before it slipped from her trembling fingers. But her voice was very steady when she spoke. "I take it you did not approve of the marriage?"

"Hell, Blackstone knew I'd never approve of Diana throwin' herself away on a no-good troublemaker like him. So he seduced her." Victor's eyes flashed with old anger, and the color in his jowls darkened. "The s.o.b. dared to put his hands on my daughter. Sorry, Letty, but that's what he was. Probably thought that if he got her pregnant, I'd agree to let him marry her. I caught 'em together red-handed, myself."

"Then what happened?" Letty asked carefully.

Copeland shrugged and gave her a wry grimace. "I did what any father would have done in those circumstances. Told him if he ever touched my girl again, I'd get my gun and I'd use it. Told him to get out of town. He left a couple of days later."

"Just like that?"

Copeland sighed heavily. "No, it wasn't quite that simple. The next day he came by my office at the yard. Made some threats. Tried to take me apart. I had a couple of the men toss him out. Then he left town. I haven't seen him since. Until last night, that is."

"It must have been quite a shock to find out he was the one who had set up Copeland Marine for a takeover."

"Hell of a shock, Letty. Hell of a shock." Victor gave her an odd look. "You want to know the real pisser?"

"What's that?"

"After Diana married that namby-pamby Escott three years ago, I started wondering if I'd made a mistake runnin'

Blackstone off fifteen years back. At least Blackstone had balls. Gotta give him that."

Letty stopped in front of the small brick building she had passed earlier on her way to the café. The name Echo Cove Public Library was chiseled in stone over the entrance. She went up the steps and opened the door.

Inside she instantly felt at home. There was something very civilized about a library, she thought, even a tiny small-town library such as this. Since the days of ancient Alexandria libraries had stood for all the best that mankind could achieve.

The very existence of libraries held out hope for the future of the human race, as far as Letty was concerned. If people had enough sense to collect and store information and make it available to everyone, perhaps they would someday have enough sense to use that wisdom to stop wars and find a cure for cancer.

Being a corporate president was interesting work, but Letty knew that a part of her would always be a librarian.

"Can I help you?" The pleasant middle-aged woman behind the circulation desk asked when Letty approached.

"Do you keep your local newspaper on file?"

"Of course. We send the copies out to be microfilmed every six months. What dates do you want to see?"

"I just want to browse," Letty said, not wanting to give out too much information.

"Certainly." The woman came out from behind the desk and led the way toward a single microfilm reader machine housed in a corner. "The film is stored by year in those drawers. Help yourself."

"Thank you." Letty opened one of the drawers.

The librarian cleared her throat discreetly. "You're Ms. Thornquist, aren't you? You're here in town with Joel Blackstone?"

Letty arched her brows. "Word travels fast."

The librarian grinned ruefully. "You know small towns. I'm Angie Taylor. My husband and I were having dinner in the Sea Grill last night when you arrived. I have to say it was a rare sight to see someone walk out on Victor Copeland. He was not pleased, I can tell you."

"It was an awkward moment for all of us," Letty murmured.

"I don't know about that. Joel Blackstone looked pleased with himself. But, then, it's no secret he hates Copeland. Look, I know this isn't any of my business, but my husband works down at the yard and we've lived in this town most of our lives. Is it true Copeland's in trouble financially?"

"I'm afraid I really can't discuss it, Mrs. Taylor."

Angie sighed morosely. "I was afraid of that." She shook her head. "All of us in that restaurant knew there was trouble brewing when we realized Joel Blackstone was in town. There's only one reason he would come back to Echo Cove, and that's to get revenge on Victor Copeland."

"Did you know Joel well?" Letty asked carefully.

"No, I don't think anyone ever knew Joel well. He was always a very private person, even when he was a teenager. I started working here in the library when he was in high school."

"Did he come in here often?" Letty asked.

Angie nodded. "He spent a lot of time in here after his mother died. His father started drinking after her death. He couldn't handle his sorrow. Her death was hard on Joel, too. He was left to cope with his grief on his own. He went to work in the Copeland yard that summer. Worked every hour he could and buried himself in books the rest of the time."

Letty pictured a lonely young man trying to lose his pain in books here in this room. She understood completely. Books had been her secret refuge all her life. "I imagine this library was very important to him."

"I think so. He certainly spent enough time here." Angie smiled ruefully. "I don't imagine the town will be able to keep this place open for long if Copeland Marine goes under. Be a real shame to close this library. Joel wasn't the only kid who ever needed it."

Half an hour later Letty found what she was looking for on the microfilm. There was not much to the story. Just a few short paragraphs stating that one Harold Blackstone, known as Hank, had been killed the previous evening in a car accident outside of town. He was survived by his son, Joel.

....
....
....
....
....

8

Joel paced the motel room, feeling like a caged lion. Make that a caged gerbil, he thought. Nobody except an idiot with the brains of a gerbil would have gotten himself into this mess.

Firecrackers. He was losing control of all the damned firecrackers.

Every time he turned at the window and started back toward the far side of the room, he had to walk straight past the bed. The maid had not been in yet, and the sight of the rumpled sheets was making him crazy. It brought back memories of Letty lying there last night.

He altered his course to walk over to the bed. Reaching down, he grabbed a handful of the sheet and brought it up to his face. He inhaled deeply.

Hell, he could still smell her. He would never forget her unique scent as long as he lived. It was making him hard right now.

Christ, he had been a fool to let her go off alone to have breakfast with Copeland.

He dropped the sheet and stalked back to the window. There was no way he could have stopped her. She was the boss.

"You're the boss. You tell me what you want, Letty."

"Oh, my God. Joel, it feels so good. I can't believe it."

Her first real climax. He'd lay odds on it. And he'd been the one to give it to her. Joel hoped she would remember that.

She was so incredibly responsive. Joel had never had a woman react that way. Wild, gloriously wild. She was a hot, sweet treasure waiting to be opened up and explored and enjoyed. All she needed was a little experience with the right man.

All she needed was a little experience with him. Better yet, a lot of experience.

Next time, Joel promised himself, next time he was going to be deep inside her when he came. He had to know what it was like being inside when her whole body tightened and then gave itself up to such a shuddering release. He wanted to feel her nails in his skin and find out how tightly she could hold him.

Most of all he wanted to look into her eyes when he buried himself in her. He wanted her to know it would work like this only with him.

He hoped it would work only with him.

He prayed it would work only with him.

Fat chance. Letty was a very sensual woman. He had known that from the start.

He jerked his gaze away from the bed and looked down on the marina. It did not matter what Copeland said to her this morning. It did not matter how the bastard pleaded his case. It was too late to change anything. Letty had to realize that. Copeland Marine had to be liquidated. She could not justify pouring another penny into the failing boatyard.

The knock on the door had the galvanizing effect of a fire alarm. *She was back.* He whirled around and crossed the room in four long strides.

He yanked open the door. "It's about time you got back." Then he realized who was standing on the other side of the door. "Diana. What the hell do you want?"

She looked up at him, uncertainty pooling in her dark eyes. "I wanted to talk to you, Joel. Don't you think you owe me that much?"

He forced himself to calm down. This was business. He had to control the raging frustration, had to make himself think and act coolly. "I don't believe I owe you a damn thing, Diana, but go ahead and talk, if that's what you want to do." He glanced at his watch. "I've got a few minutes to spare."

"You must really hate me," she whispered.

He scowled. "I don't hate you."

"I'm glad."

She smiled at him with a wistful sadness that fifteen years ago would have shredded his heart. Christ, had he really been that stupid?

"Look, Diana . . ."

"Can I come in?" The sunlight gleamed on her ebony hair. The glossy black mane was parted in the middle and fell straight to her delicate jaw, where it curved gently inward. Fifteen years ago she had worn it in a feathery cut that had had an equally dramatic effect on her eyes. But this style was far more sophisticated, Joel decided. It suited her classic profile. Her black sweater and close-fitting black pants heightened the impact of her striking looks.

The prettiest girl in town. Just ask anyone.

"Yeah, sure. Come on in." Joel scanned the sidewalk below as he stood aside. There was no sign of Letty returning from breakfast. "The maid hasn't been in yet. The place is a mess. You want to go downstairs?"

"I don't think we need an audience, do you, Joel? We had enough of one last night."

He shrugged as he closed the door. "The show didn't last

long, did it? My boss got me out of there when things turned nasty. She's kind of softhearted about some things."

"A regular little guardian angel." Diana walked slowly over to the window.

Joel saw her eyes slide across the bed. "Yeah. She calls it noblesse oblige."

Diana ignored that cryptic comment. She halted and stood gazing out over the small harbor. "So you finally came back."

"Don't worry, it'll be a short visit."

"Just long enough to let us know that you're the one who engineered the destruction of Copeland Marine."

"I didn't exactly engineer it, Diana. Your father had already started to sink it. I just gave him enough rope so that he could hang it and himself."

"Very clever." Diana blinked but not quickly enough to stop two crystalline tears from coursing down her high-boned cheeks. "You're going to destroy Daddy because he wouldn't let you have me all those years ago."

"Diana, I really am not in the mood for a lot of drama, okay? I lost my taste for that kind of thing about fifteen years back. But while we're on the subject, let's try a little honesty. We both know it wasn't your father who kept us from getting married. It was you. I asked you to leave town with me. You refused."

"Joel, I was nineteen and I was scared."

"Sure you were scared. Scared to make your father mad by running off with me. Scared you'd lose the Copeland money. Scared you'd lose everything that went with being Victor Copeland's daughter in Echo Cove. Believe me, Diana, I understand exactly what you went through."

"Oh, Joel, I'm so sorry. You'll never know how sorry I am." She swung around, the tears spilling from her eyes in earnest now. "When I looked up and saw you last night in the restaurant, I thought I was seeing a ghost. It's as if you've been haunting me all these years and now you've come back."

"Not from the grave," he assured her.

"Joel, please don't torment me like this. I know you've come back because of me. Because of us. I know you want vengeance for what happened. But you have to understand why I couldn't run off with you fifteen years ago. I was too young to handle the situation between us. Too young to make such a serious decision. I was afraid. Surely you can make allowances for that?"

"Sure. Why not?" Joel dropped into the nearest chair and leaned back, legs spread. He wondered what lies Copeland was feeding to Letty at that moment. "You were a kid. I was only twenty-one myself, and I didn't have more than fifty bucks left from my last paycheck at Copeland Marine. Hardly enough to put you up for one night at the kind of hotel you expected, was it?"

Her eyes filled with tears. "You're so bitter. So angry. I can't blame you." She started across the room.

Joel realized her intention about three seconds too late to get out of the chair. Before he could move, Diana was right in front of him. She threw herself down on her knees between his legs, grasped his thighs, and lifted an imploring face.

"Joel, please, listen to me. I want you to know that if I had it to do over again, I would have run off with you all those years ago. You have no idea how much I've regretted making the wrong decision."

At that moment the connecting door between the two rooms opened without warning. Letty stood there, staring at the scene in front of her.

Joel looked up and saw her eyes widen in shock as she took in the sight of Diana on her knees between his spread legs. He knew what was going through Letty's mind just as surely as if she'd spoken aloud. She was remembering how she had walked in on her ex-fiancé and found him with a grad student between his legs.

"Jesus." Joel shot to his feet as if he'd been burned. The sudden action tumbled Diana to one side.

"Joel, no, wait. You must listen to me." Diana stretched out a hand in a beseeching gesture. "I'm begging you on my knees. I want you to understand."

Joel reached down and yanked her unceremoniously to her feet. "Damn it, Diana, stop acting as if you're on a stage," he snapped.

"Excuse me." Letty's voice was ice. "I didn't mean to interrupt. I just wanted to tell Joel that we've been invited to tour the Copeland Marine facilities this afternoon."

Diana glanced at her and then apparently lost interest in the new arrival. She turned back to Joel. Her small hands doubled into fists. The tears pooling in her eyes started to fall.

"You were supposed to come back, Joel," Diana whispered. She raised her clenched hands and struck his chest. "Damn you, you were supposed to come back and rescue me. I waited for you."

She rushed past him to the door, jerked it open, and fled.

The sound of Diana's receding footsteps echoed in the sudden silence that filled the motel room.

Letty glanced at her watch. "I told Victor we'd be there at one-thirty. I hope that fits in with your busy schedule." She stepped back into her own room and started to close the connecting door.

Joel leaped forward and shoved the door open again. "Damn it to hell, Letty, that was not what you think it was."

"Your private life is no concern of mine, Joel."

"Bull. After last night we both have a hell of a lot of interest in each other's private lives."

"I'd rather not discuss last night," she said primly.

"Yeah, I'll just bet you don't want to talk about it." Joel strode forward, driving her back until she was trapped by the bed. He loomed over her, not touching her.

"Now, Joel . . ."

"You don't want to admit how good it was, do you?

What's the matter, Letty? Can't you deal with the fact that it was me who made it good for you? *Me,* not that damned professor back at Vellacott? What's the matter? Did you think a man had to have a Ph.D. after his name in order to know how to make a woman like you have a climax?"

"Stop it, Joel. What are you yelling at me for? It's not my fault I walked into your room a minute ago and found Diana kneeling in front of you like some sort of acolyte."

"Acolyte?" He stared at her.

"Yes, acolyte. A very admiring, very devoted acolyte. And it was quite obvious just what portion of your anatomy she found worthy of devotion and admiration."

"Maybe you'd be interested in that portion of my anatomy, too, if you gave me a chance to get my jeans off," Joel shot back before he could stop himself. He groaned and closed his eyes while he got a grip on his raging temper. "Damn. I can't believe this."

"Neither can I. Would you please get out of my way, Joel?" Letty pushed at him.

Joel took a step back, freeing her. She sprang away from the bed and stood glowering at him, arms folded tightly beneath her breasts. He forced himself to take a deep, steadying breath. "Okay, okay, let's call a truce here and take it from the top. I'll go first and explain what you saw."

"It doesn't need any explanations."

"Yes," Joel said grimly, "it does. Diana was staging a scene."

"That much was obvious."

"She came here for a little drama, and she got it. She always did like to be the center of attention. She's convinced herself that I set up Copeland Marine because of something that happened between us fifteen years ago."

Letty studied a small painting on the wall just past Joel's shoulder. She rubbed her palms up and down her forearms. "Victor told me that you and Diana were lovers," she murmured. "He told me everything."

Joel watched her closely, eyes cold. "Everything?"

She nodded brusquely, her expressive face turning an embarrassed shade of scarlet. "Yes. Everything. How he found you and Diana together and how he ordered you never to see her again. He admitted he virtually ran you out of town."

"Is that all he told you?" Joel asked.

"Not quite." Her eyes, serious and questioning now, met his. "He said he realizes he may have made a mistake all those years ago. He wonders if you would have made him a better son-in-law than Keith Escott has. That should give you some satisfaction."

"I don't give a damn how I compare with Escott."

"Joel, I don't see any point in pursuing this conversation. We both know you're using my company to get your revenge against the Copelands."

"Your company?" Hearing her say the words aloud was more than enough to trigger Joel's anger all over again.

"Yes. Whether you like it or not, Joel, Thornquist Gear belongs to me. One of these days you're going to have to accept that."

"The hell with trying to explain things to you. You're right. There's no point in rehashing the past. Tell me what Copeland said at breakfast."

"I just told you what he said."

Joel waved that aside with an impatient gesture. "Not about what happened fifteen years ago. Tell me what he said to convince you that we shouldn't shut down Copeland Marine. I want to hear the sob story."

Letty slanted him a repressive glance. "It is a sob story. A true sob story. And I'm sure you're well aware of just what's at stake here. It's clear that if we close Copeland Marine, we'll be shutting down a major portion of the town's economy, just as I suspected."

"Business is business. What's this crap about touring the yard this afternoon?"

"He offered to show us around, that's all."

"You going?" Joel asked.

"Of course. Don't you want to come with me?"

"Shit. I guess I'd better. If I don't, Copeland will probably play a few more violins for you."

Letty's chin came up. "And I just might listen."

"Listen all you want. You can't stop this thing, Letty. It's too damn late. You can't risk Thornquist Gear just to save Copeland Marine, and that's what trying to keep Copeland afloat would do. It would jeopardize Thornquist. Kill off your own company and you'll put three times as many people out of work as you will here in Echo Cove. That's the bottom line, boss."

"Don't call me boss," she shouted.

He was startled by her burst of fury. She had been so cool and controlled until now. "Okay, okay. Take it easy, Letty."

"I am going to take a walk along the waterfront and have a look around Echo Cove before our tour of Copeland Marine. I need some fresh air." She went over to the closet and found a pair of trousers. Then she turned to glower at him. "If you will excuse me, I would like to change."

Joel did not trust her mood. "I'll come with you. I can show you around the place."

"No, thanks. I'll find my own way around town. Don't worry, I won't get lost."

He squelched an uneasy sense of disappointment. Something told him he was not doing a good job of handling the boss today. Maybe she just needed time to cool down. "All right. Suit yourself." He walked reluctantly toward the connecting door.

"Joel?"

He stopped at once and turned his head. "Yeah?"

"Diana said you were supposed to rescue her fifteen years ago. From whom did she need rescuing?"

"Diana did not need rescuing," Joel said. "Believe me, she was the town princess fifteen years ago. She had everything she wanted. The best clothes, a new convertible, admission to an exclusive private college, everything. All she had to do was ask her daddy for something one day and the next day it was hers."

"Except you. Victor wouldn't let her have you."

"No." Joel walked into his own room. He started to close the door.

"Joel?"

"Now what?"

"It's becoming fairly obvious that you're back in Echo Cove because of what happened between you and Diana fifteen years ago. You apparently failed to rescue her then. Are you thinking of doing it now?"

Joel shook his head in disgust. "You aren't getting the picture here, boss. I am no longer in the rescue business."

Half an hour later Letty stood in Echo Cove's tiny shorefront park and gazed out over the water. The sun was shining, but there were clouds moving toward the land. A brisk breeze was toying with her hair and making her jacket flap.

She felt restless and disheartened for the first time since she had left Indiana. Everything had seemed so clear a few weeks ago when she made the decision to quit her job and move to Seattle. Thornquist Gear and a new life had been waiting for her. She had seized the opportunity with both hands, sensing the rightness of it. It had seemed so easy, so perfect.

She recalled Great-Uncle Charlie telling her once during a rare philosophical moment between fishing trips that there was no such thing as a free lunch.

Letty realized she was only just beginning to understand what an enormous glitch Joel Blackstone was causing in her new life-style.

Nothing went right around Joel. Nothing happened the way it was supposed to happen. Nothing was quite what it seemed.

Except last night, Letty thought wistfully. For a while last night everything had gone perfectly.

How odd for Joel to say he was no longer in the rescue business. Last night he had rescued her from her secret, growing fear that she would never experience the full power of her own body.

Letty told herself with some satisfaction that she had known all along she just needed to meet the right man.

Too bad the right man was so hell-bent on vengeance and destruction.

Letty knew that, for her, the possibility of love was beginning to loom very large.

At two-thirty that afternoon, Victor Copeland led Letty and Joel into his upstairs office. A window on one wall provided a view of the boatyard they had just toured.

In spite of the financial problems of Copeland Marine, the facilities were active. Dozens of men in hard hats and work clothes moved about among the assortment of yachts, cruisers, and fishing boats that had been dry-docked for repair or outfitting.

Coiled lines, winches, and chains were everywhere. The sound of high-powered construction machinery rumbled through the walls. The smell of varnish and tar seemed to seep through the office window.

Copeland's office was littered with blueprints and marine supply catalogs. The old steel desk was stacked with papers and file folders.

"You see what I'm saying, Letty? Copeland Marine is getting the work. My reputation is rock solid. Always has been. We got into a bind a few years ago when the economy took a downturn. I'll admit I was a little overextended at the time because of some modifications I made to the yard."

"You were ass-deep in debt, Copeland." Joel stuck his hands in his back pockets and smiled coldly. "The interest rate on the bank loans you had taken out were eating you alive. Another six months and you'd have lost everything. It was plain bad management that got you into that mess."

Victor ignored him, just as he had during the tour. He looked at Letty. "Like I said, I was a little overextended, and when Thornquist made its offer, I jumped at it. I didn't know I was being set up. But things are working out the way I planned. And if you'll just give me a little extra time I can pull this company out of the red."

"You've had all the time you're going to get, Copeland." Joel glanced at Letty. "We've seen enough. Nothing's changed around here in the past fifteen years. Copeland's still running his yard like it was some five-and-dime operation he had going out in his garage. He couldn't save it even if we gave him an extra hundred years."

Copeland's face turned a violent red. He swung around, confronting Joel for the first time that afternoon. "You shut up, goddamn it. I'm trying to talk to the owner of Thornquist Gear. And that sure as hell ain't you, Blackstone."

Joel looked steadily at Letty. "There's no point in hanging around here any longer."

"Now, just a damn minute," Copeland yelled. "I got a right to tell her how it is. This is business, damn it."

Letty frowned as she realized the superficial calm that had existed during the tour was fading fast. "Excuse me," she said briskly. "I would like to see the rest of the offices."

Victor swung his large head back to her. He glowered. "Huh? What are you talking about?"

She smiled. "If you don't mind. I just want to get a feel for the administrative structure of Copeland Marine."

"Administrative structure? I am the administrative structure of Copeland Marine. Always have been. This yard is mine."

"I understand. But you must have some support facilities —an accounting department, a payroll office, secretarial help. That sort of thing," Letty said gently.

"Well, yeah. Sure." Victor walked past Joel without looking at him. He opened the door. "This way."

Letty stepped out into the hall and promptly collided with Keith Escott.

"Excuse me, Ms. Thornquist." Keith caught her arm to steady her. He had a file folder in his other hand. He frowned in concern. "Didn't mean to run you down. You okay?"

"She's fine," Joel muttered.

Keith looked at him without expression. "I'm glad to hear it." He glanced back at Letty. "How did the tour go?"

"It was very interesting," Letty said quietly. Memories of Diana on her knees in front of Joel filled her with a rush of sympathy for Keith. She wondered if he was aware that his wife had visited Joel in a motel room that morning. She sincerely hoped he never found out. Keith appeared to be a sensitive man. Letty would have hated to see him hurt.

"We're in a hurry here," Victor said impatiently. "I'll talk to you later, Escott."

Letty saw Keith's eyes narrow briefly at the peremptory tone but his voice was mild when he spoke.

"I thought you might want to show Ms. Thornquist some of the numbers I came up with when I did a long-range plan for Copeland Marine," Keith said. He offered Victor the file he had under his arm. "I think she might find it interesting."

Victor knocked the file out of Keith's hand. It fell to the floor, and the papers slid out. "You and your goddamn long-range planning. Get out of the way, Escott. Go play with your fancy little computer. I said I'd talk to you later. Come on, Letty."

But Letty was already kneeling down to help Keith gather up the papers. "Here, let me help you."

"Thanks, I've got them." Keith stood up and nodded stiffly. "See you later, Letty."

Joel had watched the entire exchange with a grim expression, but he said nothing.

Letty smiled coolly at Victor. "Shall we continue with the tour?"

"Sure. Might as well get it over with," Victor said, striding down the hall. "Not that much to see."

At midnight Letty awoke with the nagging sensation that something was wrong. She lay quietly in bed for a moment, listening for the sound that had awakened her.

It came again and she identified it instantly. It was the rattle of the knob on the connecting door. Joel was trying to get into her room.

The man had real nerve, Letty thought furiously. After the way he had behaved today he actually expected to be allowed to take up where he had left off last night.

She pushed aside the covers, snatched up her glasses from the nightstand, and got out of bed, glad that she had thought to lock the door on her side earlier.

The knob stopped rattling. Letty stood in the middle of the floor, wondering if she should let him know what she thought of his arrogance or if it would be best to pretend she had not heard him try the door.

Before she could make up her mind, she heard other muffled sounds. A closet door opened and closed. A chair squeaked as Joel sat down. There was a short silence, and then it squeaked again as Joel rose. Letty heard him walk across the room and open the outside door. She suddenly realized what was happening.

She dashed across the room and fumbled quickly with the lock on her own outside door. She got it open and stepped barefoot out onto the cold concrete walkway that ran in front of all the rooms on the second floor.

The chilly night air hit her full force, making her cotton gown ripple around her feet. She caught sight of Joel as he finished locking his door and started toward the stairs. She knew he must have heard her door open, but he did not look back. He was dressed in jeans and a gray windbreaker.

"Joel?" Letty hissed.

He finally condescended to stop and look back at her over one shoulder. "What the hell do you want now?"

She scowled at him. His face was grim in the harsh light cast by the outside lamps. He looked like a warrior ready for battle. It was clear all he lacked was a suitable victim. "Where do you think you're going?"

"Out."

She winced at his tone. "I've told you before, I do not want you running around downtown Echo Cove in the middle of the night. It will look strange, Joel."

"I'm not going running, Madam President," he said with awful politeness.

She blinked and pushed her glasses up on her nose. "You're not? Well, where are you going at this hour, for heaven's sake?"

"I'm going to a tavern called the Anchor." Each word was chipped off a glacier. "It's one block from here. Fifteen years ago it was the place the local men went to escape nagging women and difficult bosses."

Letty drew herself up angrily. "Really, Joel."

"Yes, really. I passed the place earlier today, and it looks as if nothing has changed. It still appears to be that kind of place, and I seem to be saddled with a two-in-one arrangement lately—a nagging woman *and* a difficult boss. So I'm going to do what generations of Echo Cove men have done: I'm going down the street to the Anchor. Satisfied?"

Letty stared at him, appalled. "You're going to go hang out in some sleazy tavern? At this hour of the night? Joel, you can't do that."

"You got a better suggestion?" He raked her nightgown-clad body with a taunting glance.

Letty was furious now. "Joel, you are not going to go out drinking. I absolutely forbid it."

His answering smile would have done credit to a shark. "Is that a fact?"

Letty abandoned the forceful approach. "Joel, please.

Think of the company image. It won't look good to have the CEO of Thornquist Gear going out to a local tavern to get smashed."

"Screw the company image." Joel took a menacing step forward. "And screw the company president."

Letty retreated hastily into her room and quickly slammed the door. She threw the bolt for good measure. Then she leaned back against the wood panels and closed her eyes as she listened to the sound of Joel's footsteps fade into the distance.

9

The first person Joel saw when he walked into the Anchor was Keith Escott. Which only went to show, Joel supposed, that nagging women were a universal problem that cut across all social boundaries. And the Anchor existed to serve both the high and the low.

In a larger town a man in Escott's position might have found another place to do his serious drinking, but in Echo Cove, there was not much choice.

Escott was sitting on a stool at the end of the bar, hunched over a whiskey in the best traditional style. He was wearing a maroon and white V-necked sweater and cuffed trousers. The outfit did set him apart, sartorially speaking, Joel decided. Most of the rest of the clientele in the Anchor were dressed in heavy work boots, denim pants, and plaid shirts.

Joel felt a brief jolt of pity for Escott. It could not have been easy being married to the princess of Echo Cove. And working for Victor Copeland was probably sheer unadulterated hell. It occurred to Joel that he had had one heck of a narrow escape fifteen years earlier.

It was not the first time that thought had flashed through his mind. Not that the realization changed anything.

Fifteen years ago he'd had some crazy notion of trying to rescue Diana from her golden cage. She'd encouraged him to think she needed him to snatch her away from her domineering father and carry her off on his white horse.

Convinced he was in love and that his love was reciprocated, Joel had vowed to play knight-errant. He could only shake his head in disgust now over his youthful naïveté.

Diana had not needed or wanted rescuing. She had just been looking for a taste of the forbidden, and Joel Blackstone was definitely on her father's list of forbidden things.

Joel was not in a conversational mood tonight. He scanned the row of stools at the bar and chose one at the opposite end from where Keith Escott sat.

"What'll it be?" the stout, balding bartender demanded.

Joel looked at him. "I'll have a beer, Stan. Whatever you've got on draft these days. Not the light stuff."

Stan frowned blankly. "Do I know you?" Then his furrowed brow cleared. "Hell, it's you, Blackstone. Heard you was back in town. Working for that Thornquist woman or something, ain't you?"

Joel set his teeth. "Yeah. Something like that."

"Is it true about Thornquist Gear ownin' a chunk of Copeland Marine?"

"It's true."

Stan rested his elbow on the bar and leaned closer. He kept his voice low as he picked up a glass and started polishing it. "There's a rumor goin' 'round that Thornquist Gear is gonna shut down Copeland's yard."

"I see the rumor mill still works real well here in Echo Cove. You going to get me that beer, Stan, or do I get it myself?"

Stan sighed and pushed himself erect. He shoved the glass

he had been polishing under the nearest spigot and pulled the lever. When the glass was full and foaming, he set it in front of Joel. "So?"

"So what?"

"So is the rumor true or what?"

"It's true."

"Christ Almighty." The whispered words were a fervent prayer. Stan shook his head in despair. "It's gonna kill the town."

Joel scowled into his beer. "Blame Copeland. He's the one who got his yard into a financial mess. Thornquist Gear has kept him afloat for the past year. Can't expect me . . ." Joel cleared his throat with a swallow of beer. "Can't expect us to go on rescuing him forever."

Stan's eyes narrowed in speculation. "You never were too fond of Copeland, were you?"

"You know anyone who is?"

Stan's gaze locked on to Joel's. "So he's an s.o.b. Most guys in his position are, if you ask me. One thing I'll say for him—he's kept a lot of people in this town working for the past thirty-some years."

"He didn't keep everyone working, Stan," Joel said softly. "Some people got fired real easy, as I recall."

Stan was quiet for a moment. "What the hell did you expect after he caught you messing around with his daughter?"

Joel shrugged. "I figured he'd probably try to beat the crap out of me. Run me out of town."

"So you got off light. He didn't beat the crap out of you."

"He tried." Flashes of the grim scene in the old barn went through Joel's head. "Used a length of solid teak that he brought with him from the yard."

Stan eyed Joel thoughtfully. He picked up another glass and started polishing it. "I didn't hear about that part. I take it you survived."

"Mostly because he was almost as big and slow fifteen years ago as he is now," Joel admitted.

"So he fired your ass and ran you out of town. And you didn't get the girl." Stan glanced down the length of the bar to where Escott was sitting. "If you ask me, you were lucky."

"I was just thinking the same thing, myself."

"Tell me something. This business of you workin' for Thornquist and Thornquist gettin' ready to shut down the yard. It ain't all one big coincidence, is it?"

Joel smiled faintly. "You were always smarter than you looked, Stan. No, it isn't a coincidence."

Stan scowled. "You're gonna persuade that Miss Thornquist to close down the yard and a good chunk of this town just because you didn't get the girl fifteen years ago?"

"No," Joel said. "Not because of that."

"Then why in hell you gonna do it?" Stan demanded.

"Business." Joel took another long swallow of beer. "Just good sound business reasons, Stan. Nothing personal."

"Bullshit. There's a lot of good people who are gonna wind up in real trouble if you go through with this."

"Good people, Stan? Nice people like you, maybe? You think I give a damn what happens to folks like you?"

Stan glared at him, looking uneasy. "Now, see here, Blackstone. I had nothing to do with what happened between you and Copeland. And it sure as hell ain't my fault your father got drunk and drove himself off a cliff that night."

"Not your fault, Stan? You were serving the drinks. You knew exactly how drunk he was, didn't you?"

"He was drunk, damn it. I know you don't believe that, but your old man was soused. And you can't blame me for it, neither. Not my job to get in the way of a man's drinkin'," Stan huffed. He looked ready to add to his own defense, but at that moment he glanced past Joel. He nodded brusquely at whoever was standing there and took himself off to the far end of the bar.

Joel glanced over his shoulder and saw Keith Escott. "'Evening, Escott. Buy you a drink?"

"You've got a hell of a lot of nerve, you son of a bitch."

145

Keith's voice was low and tight as he slid somewhat ungracefully onto the neighboring stool. He turned to confront Joel, one arm lying along the bar. His hand was clenched. The smell of alcohol was strong on his breath. "Who the hell do you think you are?"

Joel picked up his beer. "I take it this is not a social call?"

Keith glared at him with angry, glassy eyes. "I know what happened today, you bastard. Damn you, I know all about it."

"Yeah? What happened?"

"Diana went to your motel room. I know she was with you."

Joel lowered his glass carefully onto the bar. "Take it easy, Escott. It wasn't what you think it was," he said quietly.

"Did the two of you think I wouldn't find out? This is a small town, in case you've forgotten."

"I haven't forgotten."

Keith flushed. "She thinks you've come back here to take her away. She thinks you're going to rescue her."

"She knows that's not true." Joel looked at him. "Listen, Escott. I am not interested in Diana. I did not come back here because of her, and I have no intention of taking her away with me. Got that?"

"That's not what she thinks. And that's not what I think. You're here because of what happened fifteen years ago. Admit it, God damn you."

"I'm here because of something that happened fifteen years ago," Joel said quietly. "But it had nothing to do with Diana."

"You wanted to marry her."

"I changed my mind."

Keith braced himself against the edge of the bar and stood up. "You mean *she* changed *her* mind. She came to her senses and wouldn't run off with you. Why should she? You were just some no-account scum who worked in her father's boatyard. Fun to fool around with for a while, maybe, but why in hell would she want to marry you?"

"Right. Why would she want to marry me? I had nothing to offer Diana. She made that real clear."

"But you look different to her now." Keith's voice was getting louder. "You come back here looking like a high-power corporate executive, and she thinks you've turned into her knight in shining armor. The one who's going to take her away from all this." His arm swept out in a broad arc that connected with his whiskey glass.

The glass crashed to the floor, causing the nearest patron to scramble off his stool. A sudden silence descended on the Anchor as heads turned toward Keith and Joel.

"Take it easy, Escott." Joel kept his voice low. "Sit down. I'll buy you another whiskey."

"You won't buy me shit." Keith swayed slightly but stayed upright. "I know what you are, Blackstone. You're the same lowlife Copeland says you were fifteen years ago. Maybe you've got a little more money to throw around these days, but we all know why that is, don't we?"

"Shut up, Escott," Joel advised quietly.

"You got money and a big-time executive title now because you're fucking the owner of Thornquist Gear. *Isn't that right?* How does it feel to sleep your way to the top? How does it feel to be Ms. Letitia Thornquist's private stud? You on call twenty-four hours a day?"

Joel came up off the stool without any warning. In spite of his inebriated condition, Keith was ready for him. He swung wildly.

Joel ducked beneath Keith's arm and went in close just long enough to throw a short, solid punch. Then he stepped back quickly.

Keith doubled over from the blow to his midsection. He staggered backward, but stayed on his feet. "You son of a bitch. I'll teach you to mess around with other men's wives. You can't have Diana." He surged forward.

Chairs scraped along the floor of the Anchor as everyone darted out of the way of the two combatants. A circle formed around Joel and Keith, but no one made any move to get involved. This was no free-for-all. Joel knew why. This was between Copeland's handpicked son-in-law and the man who had come back to shut down Echo Cove.

Keith lashed out with a surprisingly well-aimed blow that caught Joel on the side of his face. Joel saw a few stars as he reeled back. Escott was not as soft as he looked.

Escott pressed his advantage, sidling in close for another solid roundhouse.

Joel threw up his arm to block the punch. "This isn't going to solve anything," he snarled. "I learned that a long time ago."

"If you'd learned anything, you wouldn't have come back here, you bastard." Keith delivered a well-coordinated kick with his left foot.

Joel took the heavy blow on his left thigh. He lost his balance and went down to the hardwood floor. It occurred to him that he was making a complete fool of himself in front of the patrons of the Anchor.

So much for the virtues of sweet reason.

In the distance a siren wailed.

Keith launched another kick at Joel's ribs. Joel managed to catch hold of Escott's ankle. He jerked hard.

Escott fell with a thud. Joel rolled on top of him, pinning him to the floor.

Lights from a police cruiser flashed through the windows of the tavern. An instant later the door flew open.

"Everybody freeze," the young cop roared. "You two on the floor. Don't move."

"Shit," Joel muttered. It struck him then that Letty was not going to be pleased with this new development.

Letty knew she was not going to get to sleep until Joel returned to his room. She gave up the effort and got out of bed to turn on the television.

Fifteen minutes of late-night programming was almost more than she could take. She sat through an interview with a celebrity who had recently completed his fourth therapeutic stay at a fashionable substance-abuse clinic. The actor assured the audience and the show's host that this time he was definitely cured. Then she watched the talk-show host make a lot of incredibly tasteless jokes about a female guest's cleavage. When the host started in on the cleavage of the male guest, Letty got up again and turned off the TV.

She went over to the window and stared out into the darkness. Echo Cove lay shrouded in light fog and heavy silence.

The uneasiness Letty had been feeling since Joel stormed off into the night was growing stronger. When she found herself starting to pace her room, Letty got mad.

He was in some sleazy tavern having a great time, she decided. He was probably guzzling beer, ramming quarters into a jukebox, and dancing with every loose female in the place.

He had never once danced with her, Letty realized. Not once. Oh, he had made love to her, all right, but he had never taken her dancing.

He called her a nagging woman. Accused her of being a difficult boss. All because she was getting in the way of his carefully planned vengeance.

God only knew what sort of trouble Joel might get into tonight, Letty thought anxiously. He was mad enough and wild enough to do something really stupid.

A police siren howled in the distance. It made Letty realize how rare such sounds were in a small town like Echo Cove. She had gotten used to hearing sirens regularly in Seattle.

Letty gnawed on her lower lip for a moment, thinking hard. She decided she'd better go fish him out of the Anchor and bring him back to the motel before he ruined the corporate image. After all, she had her duty as president of the company.

Who the hell was she trying to kid? Letty asked herself grimly as she pulled on slacks and a sweater and slid her feet into her loafers. She was not going off to pull Joel out of some tavern because of the Thornquist Gear corporate image. She was going to find him and bring him back before he got himself into serious trouble. She was worried about him.

Letty slung her purse over her shoulder and went out the door. Joel had said something about the Anchor being only a block away. She hurried down the steps of the silent motel and strode briskly along the sidewalk.

The light fog cast a menacing gloom over downtown Echo Cove. Letty hitched her purse more firmly onto her shoulder and broke into a trot. This was not downtown Seattle, but the realization that she was out alone at night in a strange place had the overall effect of raising her anxiety level.

She spotted a neon anchor in the distance a short time later. Relief flooded through her. She began rehearsing exactly what she would say to Joel. She sincerely hoped he was not too smashed to be reasonable.

Letty noticed the flashing lights on top of the police cruiser as she crossed the deserted street. The vehicle with the logo of the Echo Cove police department painted on the door stood directly in front of the entrance to the tavern.

Alarm shot through her. With a gathering sense of dismay she rushed toward the door.

It slammed open when she was only a yard away. Joel came through first. He had his hands behind his back. Letty realized with horror that he was handcuffed. He was closely followed by a man in a police uniform. The officer's hand was wrapped around Joel's forearm. He was steering Joel in the general direction of the cruiser.

Letty's mouth fell open in shock. *"Joel."*

Joel glanced at her. He looked thoroughly disgusted. His gaze met hers and then he raised his eyes toward heaven. "Somehow I knew you'd turn up at just the right moment, boss."

Letty stepped into the path of the officer, forcing him to halt. She drew herself up the way she was accustomed to doing back at the reference desk when an especially demanding faculty member tried to bulldoze a member of her staff.

"Just one moment, if you please, Officer. I demand to know what is going on here. This man happens to belong to me."

Joel and the officer stared at her as if she had gone crazy.

"What was that, ma'am?" the officer said carefully.

"You heard me. He works for me. I am his employer."

The officer nodded politely as comprehension dawned. "Got it. Well, you may own him, but I'm taking him down to the station on account of he just caused one hell of a disturbance. You want to bail him out, you're welcome to come get him. The station's two blocks over and one block down, on Holt Street."

"Bail him out?" Letty squeaked. "I've never bailed anyone out of jail in my life."

"Don't feel obliged to break a perfect track record by doing it for me," Joel muttered as the officer pushed him into the back seat of the cruiser. "Go on back to the motel."

Letty ignored him. "Officer, please, I'm new at this kind of thing. What's the procedure here? Doesn't somebody have to press charges or something?"

"Yep." The officer, whose name tag read Echler, looked bored. "That'll be Stan. He called in the complaint."

"Who's Stan?"

"Owns the Anchor." Echler slammed the rear door of the cruiser, locking Joel inside. He started around the front of the patrol car.

Letty rapped on the rear window. "Joel? Joel? I'll be right down to get you out of jail. Don't say or do anything stupid. Do you hear me?"

Joel did not bother to respond to that. He leaned back and focused on the mesh screen that separated him from the front seat of the patrol car.

Letty realized with a start that he was probably horribly embarrassed. "As well he should be," she muttered beneath her breath as Officer Echler started the car and drove off.

She would have a few things to say to Joel when she got him out of jail.

But that would have to wait. There were other things that needed doing at the moment.

Letty swung around and eyed the crowd that had trickled out of the Anchor and gathered in front to watch the proceedings. The men were talking and laughing among themselves.

Letty put her hands on her hips. "I'm glad you find this amusing," Letty said in a loud voice. "Because I do not."

The tavern patrons hushed immediately. They stared curiously at Letty.

"Who's she?" someone mumbled in the rear.

"Heard her say she owns Blackstone."

That comment was greeted with a guffaw.

Letty started toward the tavern door, forcing the small crowd to part. "Which one of you is Stan?"

"Stan's inside. Big guy in a white apron. Can't miss him," someone volunteered.

"Thank you," Letty said in her coldest tone.

She pushed open the door and walked into the dimly lit tavern. The first person she saw was Keith Escott. He was sitting by himself at a table. He was holding a cold, wet towel to his jaw.

A big man in a white apron was mopping up spilled drinks on the other side of the room. She ignored him for the moment, concentrating instead on Keith.

Letty's stomach contracted as she surveyed the scene. She knew at once what had happened: Joel and Keith had been fighting, and she knew without being told there was only one thing the two men could have been fighting about. She walked over to the table and sat down.

"Keith? Are you all right?"

Keith groaned. "What does it look like?"

Letty tried again. "I take it you and Joel had a misunderstanding?"

"Bastard had my wife in his motel room this morning. Thinks he can come back here after all this time and just pick up where he left off. *Son of a bitch.* I should have killed him."

Letty tried to calm herself. Keith was obviously drunk and probably severely traumatized from the bar fight. He did not look like the sort of man who got into tavern brawls. She strove to keep her voice crisp and businesslike.

"Keith, are you by any chance making reference to the fact that your wife called on Joel and me this morning to discuss the Copeland Marine situation?"

Keith blinked, apparently having trouble following the question. "She was in his room with him."

"Yes, of course. So was I," Letty said smoothly. "Joel and I have a suite with a connecting door. The three of us had a short business meeting. Your wife is quite naturally concerned that we might be forced to liquidate Copeland Marine. We assured her we will make every effort to find an alternative, but frankly, the situation does not look good."

Keith stared at her, bleary-eyed. "What are you talking about? She went to see him."

"About Copeland Marine. Yes, I know. As I told you, I was there." Letty mentally crossed her fingers. She was not exactly lying. It was more a case of finessing the situation. It was a tactic corporate executives and overworked reference librarians used all the time. "What seems to be the problem here?"

But Keith had finally managed to focus on the crucial point. "You were there?"

"Yes. As I said, Joel and I share a connecting suite."

"I knew it," Keith muttered. "Son of a bitch is sleeping with his boss."

Letty felt herself turning red. She was grateful for the dim lighting. "You may rest assured that I do not share my CEO with anyone. For any purpose whatsoever. Do I make myself quite clear, Mr. Escott?"

"He didn't take my Diana to bed?"

"Absolutely not." Letty stood up. "Just how do you plan to get home tonight, Keith?"

"Got my car out front."

"You're in no condition to drive. I'll call a cab for you."

"Don't have any cabs here in Echo Cove," Keith said.

"Then I'll call your wife."

Keith straightened in the chair, looking slightly more sober. "No. For God's sake, don't do that."

"I don't see why Diana should miss all the excitement," Letty retorted. "What's your phone number?"

Apparently too weary to argue further, Keith subsided in the chair. "Five-five-five-seven-two-three-one."

Letty went over to the bar and called to the big man in the apron. "Stan, where's your phone?"

Stan looked up, startled. "End of the bar. Why?"

"Isn't it obvious? I want to use it." Letty found the phone and dialed swiftly. It was answered on the second ring.

"Hello?" Diana's voice was as sultry over the phone as it was in person. "Who is this? Is that you Keith? Where are you?"

"This is Letty Thornquist," Letty cut in briskly. "Your husband has been in a brawl down at the Anchor. He has severely pummeled my CEO, and I am extremely upset over the matter."

"Joel is hurt?"

"Yes, he is. He has been subjected to a totally unwarranted assault. I am, in fact, seriously considering a lawsuit," Letty said. "I will not have my employees beaten to a pulp by jealous husbands, and I will not tolerate having them thrown into jail without just cause."

"What are you talking about?" Diana whispered, sounding badly shaken.

"Your husband has spent the evening defending your honor, Mrs. Escott. Due to his efforts on your behalf, he is in no condition to drive. I suggest you get down here to the Anchor and pick him up immediately."

"Keith? In a *fight*? Good God," Diana muttered. "This is crazy."

"My sentiments exactly. If you do not get here in the next fifteen minutes, Mrs. Escott, I shall take your husband back to the motel with me. He can spend the rest of the night in Joel's room."

Letty dropped the phone back into the cradle and rounded on Stan, the bartender. He was staring at her in growing consternation.

"Just what the heck is going on here? Are you that Miss Thornquist we've been hearing about?"

"*Ms.* Thornquist to you, Stan. I am the president of Thornquist Gear, and that man who has just been unfairly hauled off to jail is my CEO. I am not a happy camper."

Stan's expression turned mulish. "Me neither. You can see for yourself he tore up my place. Won't hurt him none to spend the night in jail."

"Thornquist Gear will pay for any damages that you may have sustained, Stan. You and I, however, have something to discuss."

"Yeah? And what's that?"

"I am told that you intend to press charges against Mr. Blackstone."

"Damn right I'm gonna press charges."

"You may wish to reconsider your decision after you have taken a couple of things into account, Stan." Letty sat down on one of the barstools and gripped her purse on her lap. "I expect you have heard the rumors of Thornquist Gear's involvement with Copeland Marine."

"Yeah, I heard 'em."

Letty smiled sweetly. "You will no doubt be aware, then, that the entire town of Echo Cove finds itself in a very delicate situation."

"Delicate? Jesus, lady. You are something else."

"Thank you. As I was saying, the situation is"—Letty fluttered a hand in the air—"unstable, to say the least. Grave decisions that will affect the future of this entire town

155

will soon be made. I want you to understand, Stan, that as president of Thornquist Gear, I will be the one making those decisions."

Stan stopped mopping up spilled beer. He eyed her warily. "What are you tryin' to say?"

"Simply put, the situation is so extremely delicate that the least little contingency could shift the balance, as far as I am concerned," Letty said. "At this moment, for example, the balance is shifting quite rapidly in favor of shutting down Copeland Marine tomorrow morning at eight o'clock. Do I make myself clear, Stan?"

"You're threatenin' me, ain't you?" Stan looked scandalized.

"How do you think the Copelands will feel if they discover that they have no time left in which to negotiate—and all because of you, Stan?"

"Goddamn it. This is outright blackmail. You're one tough little broad."

"Thank you."

Stan grabbed the phone from behind the bar. "I'll call Echler right now and tell him I ain't pressin' charges."

"A very wise decision, Stan. Rest assured I will not shut down the yard tomorrow morning at eight. Nor will I mention to Victor Copeland how extremely upset I was to discover that you had my CEO hauled off to jail at midnight. Bygones will be bygones, Stan. I am, however, making no promises concerning the future."

"Damn," Stan said. "Damn." He dialed the police station with trembling fingers.

Letty walked out of the tavern a few minutes later. A pale yellow Mercedes was just pulling up in front. Diana Escott got out and immediately accosted Letty. "What do you want? Haven't you caused enough trouble? Why can't you just get on with the business of shutting down my father's boatyard? Finish it, will you? Just finish it before there's any more violence."

"There will be no more violence," Letty said firmly.

"You don't know what you're talking about. You don't know how bad this could get. Just do what you came here to do and leave, damn you. The sooner it's over, the better off we'll all be."

Diana turned and walked into the tavern.

Letty waited until the tavern door opened again to reveal Keith and Diana emerging. She watched both get into the Mercedes. Neither said a word to the other.

Letty quickly walked the three blocks to the Echo Cove police station.

When she went up the steps and through the front door she found Joel in the process of collecting his wallet and a few other personal items from Officer Echler.

"Well, well, well. If it isn't Madam President." Joel shoved his wallet into his back pocket and sauntered toward Letty. His expression was unreadable. "I hear you've been throwing your weight around town. How does it feel?"

Letty studied the darkening bruise under his left eye. "For the record, you lost tonight."

"Says who?"

"Says me. You were fighting over Keith's wife. That puts you in the wrong, so I am declaring you the loser. Are you ready to leave?"

Joel whistled soundlessly. "You're really pissed, aren't you?"

"Yes, Joel, I am." Letty turned and led the way out into the night.

Joel came swiftly down the steps behind her. "How come you rescued me, Letty?"

"I was merely protecting the corporate image."

"I should have guessed you'd say something like that." Joel was silent for a moment as he walked along beside her. "I don't suppose it will make any difference if I tell you that Escott started it?"

"None whatsoever. The poor man is under a great deal of stress. He knows Diana was in your motel room this morning."

"That wasn't my fault, either. I didn't exactly invite her, you know."

Letty had had enough. She stopped abruptly and whirled around to confront him. "You're back here in Echo Cove because of her. Don't you think poor Keith knows that? How would you feel if you were in his shoes?"

"Damn it, for the last time, I am not here because of Diana," Joel said.

"Then why are you here? Why have you gone to so much trouble to destory Copeland Marine and this town?"

"Because it's Victor Copeland's company and Victor Copeland's town, and I am here to destroy Victor Copeland," Joel shot back.

"Tell me why, damn it."

Joel's eyes blazed. "You want to know why? I'll tell you why. Because that son of a bitch killed my father."

10

Joel's first thought when he awoke the next morning was that at approximately twelve-thirty last night, he had managed to make a complete ass of himself in front of Letty.

His second thought was that when all was said and done, Letty had not pushed him the way he had expected she would. In fact, she had been remarkably cool. He had dropped a bombshell in her lap, but she had not pressed for explanations.

After he had made that wild accusation about Copeland killing his father, Letty had simply put her arm through his and walked back to the motel with him.

"You can tell me about it in the morning," she had said quietly as she let herself into her own room. "Neither of us is in any condition to talk rationally tonight."

Maybe she had concluded he was crazy. Psychotic or paranoid or nuttier than a fruitcake. It might be hard for the president of the company to have a lot of confidence in a psychotic CEO.

Joel lay back against the pillows and watched the rain drip steadily outside the window. One thing was clear as crystal this morning. He owed Letty an explanation. In fact, Joel suddenly realized, he wanted to tell her everything. He wanted to talk about it. He wanted Letty to understand.

It was an odd sensation, this feeling of wanting Letty's sympathy. He had rarely bothered to explain himself to anyone during the greater portion of his adult life. He had certainly never felt the need to justify his actions to anyone.

But Letty was different.

He had never known anyone quite like Letty.

Joel shook his head in amazement as he recalled the events of the night. Little Letty Thornquist, respected member of the staff of Vellacott College, professional librarian and ex-fiancée of some turkey professor, had single-handedly strong-armed the forces of law and order in Echo Cove, Washington.

Translated, that meant Letty had gone up against the Copeland power and won. She had gotten her chief executive officer out of jail. All charges had been dropped.

She was turning out to be an okay executive, Joel decided. As a mentor he must be doing one hell of a good job. The thought made him grin briefly.

The cocky amusement faded as he sat up in bed and became more acutely aware of his assorted bruises. Escott might look like a preppy, but he had managed to get in a few good punches last night.

Joel tossed aside the covers and surveyed the motel room with a sour gaze. No doubt about it, the place was beginning to get to him.

It was time to get out of Echo Cove. He and Letty were scheduled to leave today. But first he wanted to explain things to her. She had a right to know.

Half an hour later Letty walked into the motel coffee shop. Joel glanced up and watched her as she came toward him down the aisle between the vinyl-covered booths. She appeared to be oblivious of the murmured comments and speculative glances she received en route.

This morning Letty was both brisk and rumpled, as only she could look in a businesslike navy blue suit. Her little round glasses were perched firmly on her nose and her wonderful, wild hair was held back over her ears by a pair of gold combs. There was a militant expression in her fine eyes.

Joel sprawled in the booth, gazing at Letty with a pleasant rush of possessiveness. It was getting to be a familiar sensation. He was not certain when he had started thinking of Letty as his woman, but the feeling was entrenched somewhere deep inside him now.

And maybe it wasn't a one-sided feeling, either, he thought.

He remembered what she had said last night when she discovered that he was being hauled off to jail: "This man happens to belong to me."

"I'm certainly glad one of us has something to smile about this morning." Letty sat down across from Joel and gave him a severe glare. "What's so amusing? I'd have thought you would feel quite awful. You certainly look it."

"Sorry, boss. Didn't mean to annoy you. After last night we all know how you kick butt when you get annoyed." Joel saluted her with his coffee cup.

"It's not a joking matter, Joel. I have never been so outraged and so mortified as I was last night when I watched that man put you into a patrol car and take you off to jail."

"Not even when you found Dixon with Gloria the grad student?"

Color stained her cheeks. "If you have an ounce of common sense, you will not make any more stupid remarks like that one this morning."

"Right, boss."

"Don't you dare get sarcastic with me today. I am not in the mood to tolerate it."

Joel held up a palm. "Okay, okay. No sarcasm."

Letty sat back. "What occurred last night was absolutely inexcusable. You are an executive, the CEO of a major company. How could you get into a barroom brawl?"

"Would it help if I told you again that Escott started it?"

"No, it would not. Joel, I will not tolerate that kind of behavior from you in the future. Do I make myself perfectly clear?"

"Yeah."

"It was immature."

"Yeah."

"It was unprofessional."

"Yeah. You know something, boss? It's not a good idea to chew out a subordinate in front of an audience." Joel indicated the crowd of locals hovering over their morning coffee, ears cocked. Conversation in the room was at a minimum. Everyone was straining to listen to Letty. "Just a small management tip from your mentor."

Letty's mouth tightened. Nevertheless, she lowered her voice. "I think you owe me some explanations of your recent conduct. I want to know what you meant when you mentioned your father last night."

Joel put down his coffee and slid out of the booth. "Come on. We can't talk here." He reached down and tugged her up out of the seat.

"Joel, wait. I haven't had any breakfast."

"We'll pick something up at that fast-food place down the street. Then we're going for a drive." Joel cast a disgusted look at the crowd in the restaurant. "There never was much privacy in this one-horse town."

Joel slowed the Jeep as he cruised past the small weather-beaten clapboard house on the outskirts of town. For some reason it was a shock to realize someone was living in it. A pickup truck was parked in the front yard, and there was a basketball sitting on the tiny lawn. Somebody had planted flowers under the windows.

"Why are we stopping?" Letty turned to look at the old house.

"I was raised in that place."

Letty studied the house through the steady gray rain that was still falling. "That was your home?"

"Dad and I lived there after Mom died. Couldn't afford my own place. Took a long time to pay off Mom's medical bills. Copeland Marine didn't provide its workers with much in the way of medical insurance back in those days. Still doesn't for that matter."

"What did your mother die of, Joel?"

"Breast cancer. I was eighteen at the time."

Letty closed her eyes briefly. "How terrible for all of you."

"Her death changed everything. That house isn't much to look at, but when Mom was alive, it seemed different somehow. It was a good place to grow up."

"Your mother made it a home."

"Yeah. Dad was different in those days, too. He used to laugh a lot. We did things together. Talked about the future. He always had plans." Joel paused. "He never talked about the future again after Mom died."

"Oh, Joel, how awful."

Joel shrugged. "Dad and I combined our paychecks for three years and managed to get the hospital off our backs. I had plans to move out the summer Dad was killed. I was free at last and ready to take on the world. I was heading for the bright lights of the big city."

"With Diana." Letty's voice was very soft.

Joel smiled wryly. "Yeah, I thought Diana was going with me. I should have known better." He put his foot back down on the accelerator. "No way was she going to disobey her daddy. And she sure as hell was not going to walk away from everything she had here. Not for some working-class nobody like me."

"You've come a long way, haven't you?" Letty asked dryly. "If it's any consolation, Diana apparently regrets her decision fifteen years ago."

"I don't give a damn whether she regrets it or not. I'm just grateful she made the choice she did."

"Are you certain of that, Joel?"

"Damn certain. I'll say this one last time, Letty: I am not carrying a torch for Diana Copeland Escott. Got that?"

"If you say so."

Joel frowned. She did not sound convinced. He drove in silence for a few minutes, collecting his thoughts, trying to decide where to begin. He thought he was driving aimlessly with no particular destination in mind, until he realized he had taken the turnoff that led to the old gray barn. He eased his foot off the gas.

"Why are we stopping this time?" Letty asked quietly.

"I don't know. I used to come here sometimes." Joel halted the Jeep at the side of the road, switched off the engine, and rested his arms on the steering wheel. He stared at the ramshackle barn through the rain. "I could be alone here. Nobody else ever bothered to come out this far. No reason to. The place was abandoned years ago. I'm surprised it's still standing."

"This was where you headed when you wanted privacy?"

"Yeah."

Letty smiled softly. "I had a special place, too. Not a great old barn like this, just a little potting shed in my mother's garden. I'm sure Mom and Dad knew where I was when I disappeared into it, but they never said anything or bothered me when I was there."

"So maybe you and I have a few things in common," Joel suggested.

"Could be." Letty unbuckled her seat belt. "Come on. Let's go see what's happened to your barn in the past few years."

Memories seared through Joel's head. Diana's screams. Copeland's enraged face. The heavy length of teak crashing down hard enough to break bones.

"Letty, wait." Joel stretched out a hand to catch hold of

her, but it was too late. She was already out of the Jeep, raising her umbrella.

Joel reluctantly got out and stood in the rain. Letty hurried around the front of the Jeep to hold the umbrella over his head.

"Don't you have a hat, Joel?"

"I'm all right."

He started walking toward the dilapidated structure. Letty followed. The place did not look all that much different than it had fifteen years ago, Joel realized. Same barnyard overgrown with weeds. Same broken windows in the loft. Same sagging door.

But the weathered roof was still doing an amazingly effective job of keeping out the rain, Joel discovered as he led the way into the gloom. He halted and stood searching the shadows. They were still filled with bits and pieces of rusted-out farm machinery and empty feed troughs.

Compelled by grim curiosity, Joel walked over to the horse stall on the right. Metal hinges squawked in protest as he opened the door. It was the same sound they had made that night fifteen years ago, a sound that had probably saved his life. It had given him the split-second warning he needed to roll to one side and thereby lessen the impact of the teak board Copeland wielded.

"Someone left some old horse blankets behind," Letty said, looking past Joel into the stall.

Joel glanced down at the blankets where he had been lying with Diana that night. Nothing had changed. Even the damned blankets were still here. A surge of uneasiness rose like bile in his gut.

He should never have come back here today. Not with Letty.

"We've seen enough." Joel grabbed Letty's wrist, intending to start back to the Jeep.

"Wait, Joel. I want to look around some more."

"I don't."

Letty glanced at him, eyes widening with surprise at his tone. "Joel? What's wrong?"

"Nothing, damn it." Joel tried to school his roiling emotions. He could hardly explain that this was where he had brought Diana the night Victor Copeland discovered them. Nor did he want to talk about the peculiar way his stomach was twisting as the memories cascaded through his mind. He should never have come back here, Joel thought again.

Letty was watching him with anxious sympathy. "Maybe it's time you told me what you meant about Copeland killing your father."

"Yeah, maybe it's time I did." Joel looked down at her. "You're probably going to think I'm nuts. I've got no proof. No witnesses. Nothing to go on except my own instincts."

Letty put her fingers gently on his arm. "Tell me everything. Right from the beginning."

"You know most of it. I was seeing Diana Copeland. Her father didn't know about us. She said she wanted to wait to tell him. We both knew he wasn't going to like the idea of his daughter marrying me. I was getting impatient, though. I told her if she wouldn't do it, I'd tell him myself. She got really upset."

Letty frowned. "Upset?"

"She started crying. Made me promise not to say anything to Copeland until after she'd gone back to college in the fall. I don't know what the delay was supposed to accomplish. It was just a stalling tactic as far as I was concerned. Hell, I was trying to get her out from under his thumb. She was always telling me how domineering he was."

"Sounds as if she was simply afraid to tell him about you and was biding her time."

Joel lifted one shoulder in a negligent shrug. "Maybe. More likely she didn't really want to marry me. She just liked the thrill of fooling around with a guy she knew her father would never tolerate. In the end our luck ran out. Copeland caught us together."

"Copeland told me that much. He said he was furious."

"He was. When Victor Copeland loses his temper, he goes kind of crazy. He's a wild man." Joel decided there was no point in going into the details. "He fired me, of course. Told me to get out of town."

"Did you agree to go?"

Joel exhaled slowly. "I was more than happy to leave. I asked Diana one more time to go with me, and she had hysterics. Said she couldn't possibly go with me. Wanted me to understand that this wasn't what she had planned."

"She was scared. Panicked by a choice she was not prepared to make. She was just a young woman at the time."

"Don't kid yourself. She knew what she was doing." Joel realized he was clenching his jaw. His dentist had told him six months ago he had to stop doing that. He forced himself to relax the muscles of his neck and shoulders. "To make a long story short, I went home and went to bed. It was two o'clock in the morning, so I didn't wake Dad to tell him what had happened. I figured the next day would be soon enough to give him the bad news."

"What happened the next day?"

"Dad left for work early that morning, before I got up. I spent the day packing my stuff. When he came home after work, he was very, very angry. I'd never seen him like that. Said Copeland had just fired him. He said that he had lost his job, that he was too old to find another one, and that his life was ruined."

Letty looked at him with an aching sympathy in her eyes. "Copeland fired your father? Because of what you'd done?"

"Right. Or as Dad put it, because I didn't have enough sense to keep my pants zipped around Diana Copeland." Joel ran his fingers through his damp hair. The old tight feeling deep inside was getting bad. He could feel himself growing tense and twisted like a spring. Usually it got like this only late at night. Usually he could run it off.

But today there did not seem to be anyplace to run.

"Joel, that was a terrible thing for Copeland to do. It was

167

so unfair. I can see that in his anger he might have fired you, but he had no right to let your father go."

Joel swore softly at her naïveté. "Fairness had nothing to do with it. Copeland was in one of his rages, and he was determined to punish all Blackstones, not just the one who had transgressed. My father had worked for Copeland Marine for over twenty years, but that didn't matter a damn to Victor Copeland. Copeland killed him."

Letty searched his face intently. "I don't understand. What do you mean he *killed* him?"

"It's real simple, Letty. Getting fired was more than Dad could handle. His job down at the yard was the only thing that kept him going after Mom died."

"He had you."

Joel leaned back against the stall door, remembering the emptiness in his father's eyes. "I don't think he cared too much one way or the other about me after he lost Mom. He just sort of sank into himself. We shared the same house but it was like having a roommate. Something went out of him after Mom was gone."

"It sounds as if he fell into a clinical depression and didn't come out of it."

"Whatever. All I know is that losing his job was the last straw. He went out to the Anchor. Stan swore he drank himself stupid, but a couple of guys who were at the Anchor that night said he wasn't that far gone when he left the place. They told me they would have driven him home if he'd been drunk. They were old friends of his, and I believe them."

"What happened?"

"He drove off a cliff into the sea on the way home. A lot of people said if it wasn't drunk driving it was probably suicide. Everyone knew he had never recovered from Mom's death."

"My God," Letty breathed.

"But I've always had a few other ideas," Joel said slowly. "He took my car that night because his pickup was out of gas. He was driving home alone in the rain. It was late at night. It would have been impossible for anyone to tell who was behind the wheel."

Letty's eyes widened. "Are you saying what I think you're saying?"

Joel clenched his teeth. "I think there's a hell of a good chance that Victor Copeland saw my car on that narrow, winding road above the sea that night. I think it's possible he decided to take advantage of a golden opportunity to get me out of his daughter's life once and for all. I think he might have run Dad off the road with that big old Lincoln he used to drive."

Letty looked shaken. "That's an incredible accusation."

"I know. Also one I can never prove. I went down to the yard after they found Dad. I told Copeland what I thought. He got livid and called a few of his men. They threw me out."

"Copeland told me you went to see him at the yard."

"For all the good it did. But even if that isn't the way it happened, even if it was an accident or suicide, Copeland is guilty as far as I'm concerned. Guilty as hell."

"I understand how you must feel," Letty said softly.

Joel was quiet for a moment. "For some reason the worst part has been never knowing for certain just what did happen that night. I think that's what twists me up and makes me dream about it sometimes. I think it's the uncertainty. Not knowing if it was an accident or murder or suicide."

"There's no sense of closure because you don't know the answer. Too many loose ends and too many questions. You keep going back to it, trying to resolve it."

Joel gripped the side wall of the stall, bracing himself for what he was going to say next. "Do you know what Dad said to me that night before he went down to the Anchor?"

"No."

"The last thing he said was that it was my fault." Joel touched his stomach in fleeting memory. "He took a swing at me. Punched me once, right in the gut, and then he said,

169

'This is all your fault, you goddamn stupid son of a bitch. All your fault. I'm glad your mother died before she found out what kind of a son she had.'"

Letty stepped close and wrapped her arms around him. "Joel, I am so very sorry." She said nothing more, just held him tightly and rested her head on his shoulder.

Joel was unable to respond. He stood stiff and inflexible, like a man made out of stone. It was as if all the circuits that controlled his emotions had simply shorted out. He felt utterly blank. No one had offered him this kind of simple, undemanding comfort since his mother died.

But at least there had been time to say good-bye to his mother, Joel thought. At least he had been able to tell her that he loved her, and she had told him how much she loved him.

There had been no chance to make his peace with his father. "This is all your fault, you goddamn stupid son of a bitch," he had said. "You couldn't pick some girl from your own crowd. Hell no, you had to screw the Copeland girl. Christ, didn't you even think for one minute about what you were doing? Were you so goddamn stupid you couldn't tell she was just playing with you? Did you think for one minute about what would happen to me when Copeland found out you'd dared to go after his daughter? This is all your fault."

All your fault.

Joel was aware of Letty's warmth and softness closing gently around him. The effect was like water on stone for a while. He could feel her, but her warmth just washed off him.

But she continued to hold him as if she would never let him go, and gradually the tension in Joel started to lessen. After a few minutes he found the strength to raise his hand and sink his fingers into the softness of her hair. She stirred against him, hugging him tighter as if determined to let some part of herself meld with a part of him.

Joel had no real idea how long they stood like that. The rain drummed on the barn roof in a steady, soothing pattern. He was thinking about that curious, mesmerizing rhythm when he realized Letty was finally lifting her head from his shoulder.

He looked down into her face and saw the sweet, serious warmth in her eyes. He realized her lips were slightly parted and she still had her arms wrapped around his waist.

Joel did not even stop to think about it. He lowered his head and covered Letty's mouth with his own.

Her lips softened instantly under his, parting for him, inviting him into her heat. A sharp, urgent need shook Joel. It was followed by a desire that was beyond anything he had ever known. The feeling was not so much physical as emotional.

He had to have her. He would be cold and empty for the rest of his life if he did not make love to her in that moment. She was the only one who could save him from the pain that was washing through him in a torrent.

He gripped her waist and dragged his mouth across hers, desperate for the hope and the promise of her. She wrapped her arms more tightly around him, silently offering him whatever he wanted, whatever he needed.

"*Letty*. Oh, God, Letty, I want you."

"It's all right, Joel. It's all right." She was responding feverishly now, clinging to him, kissing his throat.

Joel knew he had lost his self-control. This was not like the other night when he had been determined to find out just how hot Letty would burn for him. The sensations that surged through him now were raw and wild. He needed her right this minute. And she was offering herself.

Joel slid his palms down over her firm, lushly rounded hips, yanked her skirt up to her waist and cupped her buttocks. He lifted her up against his painfully engorged shaft. She whimpered softly and speared her fingers through his hair.

Then Letty wrapped her legs around his waist. Joel staggered slightly and found his balance. He thought he would burst into flames.

He realized his jeans and Letty's panty hose were in the way. Desperate to get rid of the barriers, he lowered her to the floor and eased her down onto the old blankets. A small cloud of dust wafted upward. Joel paid no attention. He was too busy struggling with Letty's panty hose.

Nylon ripped. Letty gasped, but she did not pull away. Instead she reached for the zipper on his jeans.

"I'll get it," Joel muttered, aware that the denim was stretched tautly over that portion of his anatomy. He reached down and lowered the zipper cautiously. An instant later he felt that part of himself thrust free of confinement.

Letty's beautiful, gentle hands were waiting for him. Joel groaned as she stroked the length of him.

"Damn," he muttered thickly as the fierce desire swirled in his veins. "Letty honey, that feels so good. So damn good. I need you."

"Yes." She looked up at him through her lashes. The warmth in her eyes was all-consuming. He could drown in that warmth, and he would be safe in it.

Joel did not take his eyes from hers as he ran his hand up along the inside of her thigh. He found the place where he had torn her panty hose, inserted his fingers inside, and ripped hard to create a wider opening.

He cupped the softness between her legs, awed at the depth of her response. She was hot and ready. He slid one finger into her, and she shivered.

"Joel."

He wanted to savor her reaction, but there was no time. His body was surging toward release.

"I need to be inside you," he rasped, willing her to understand. "I can't wait this time. *I can't wait.*"

"Yes. It's all right." She cradled his head between her palms, kissing his jaw and then his throat. "Come inside."

He could not even take the time to get out of his jeans. He sprawled on top of Letty, crushing her into the filthy blankets. She widened her legs for him. He reached down to part the plump folds that guarded her softness. She was slick and incredibly warm. He positioned himself and then, with a deep groan, drove into her in a single long stroke.

He was startled by the initial resistance of her body. Then she closed around him like a small, clinging glove. Joel nearly went out of his mind with the sensation.

"You're so tight," he muttered. "So hot and tight. Christ it feels good."

He pounded into her, unable to slow down or exert an ounce of finesse. He had to fill her with himself. He needed to lose himself in her forever.

And then he was over the edge, arching himself above her, gritting his teeth against the exquisite pain, exploding inside Letty's softness.

He was lost.

He was free.

He was complete and whole for one single instant in time. He was at last the man he was supposed to be.

Joel shuddered heavily and collapsed on top of Letty. He gulped air into his lungs and luxuriated in the pure satisfaction that engulfed him. He was vaguely aware that Letty's fingers were moving gently through his hair in a soothing motion.

The rain was still pounding on the roof. Perhaps that was why he had little or no warning. Or perhaps he was simply too far gone in the safe, warm world he had discovered.

Joel was jerked back to reality when the stall door creaked on its hinges.

It was the same small noise that had saved his life the last time. Disoriented from the aftereffects of the shattering release, he rolled off Letty and scrambled to his feet. One searing thought burned in his brain: *he had to protect Letty.* Whatever was happening, he had to take care of her.

But it was not an enraged Victor Copeland who stood staring into the stall with angry eyes. It was Diana.

"Couldn't you have taken her somewhere else, Joel?"

Diana raised her tear-filled gaze from Letty's sprawled form to Joel. "Did you have to bring her here? This was our place."

"Damn it, Diana." Fury washed through Joel as he jerked his zipper closed. "Get out of here." He took a step forward.

She whirled and ran from the gloomy barn.

Joel stood staring after her until he heard the distant sound of a car engine. A soft noise behind him made him turn finally to look down at Letty.

She was sitting up, trying vainly to straighten her sadly rumpled clothing. "You brought her here that night, didn't you?"

"I'm sorry, Letty. She must have followed us when we left the motel. She's acting crazy." He reached down to help Letty to her feet. He righted her easily and could not resist an amused, affectionate smile at the sight of her. He felt so much better now, he realized. Even the shock of having Diana appear like a specter from the past could not shake his new mood.

Letty was delicious in a state of disarray. Her glasses were askew on her nose, her hair looked as if it had come in contact with an electrical circuit, and she had discarded her shoes and her torn panty hose.

Joel wanted to pull her back down on the floor and make love to her all over again. He reached for her.

"This time I'll do it right," he promised.

"No, wait, *don't.*" Letty stepped back quickly. Too quickly. Her feet got tangled in her panty hose, which were lying on the floor. "Oh, my God." She tried to grab hold of the side of the stall and missed.

"Take it easy, Letty. It's okay, honey." Joel caught her and held her steady. He pulled her close against him. "Easy, honey. I didn't mean to scare you. I know I rushed things a few minutes ago. I lost control. It won't happen again. I swear it."

"It's not that," Letty whispered, her voice muffled against

his chest. "Tell me the truth, Joel. You were here with her that night when Copeland found you, weren't you?"

He grimaced as he heard the accusing tone in her words. "Well, yeah, I was. But I don't see what that has to do with us."

"Joel Blackstone, when we get back to Seattle I am going to enroll you in a sensitivity-training seminar." Letty jerked away from him. "Damn." She straightened her glasses on her nose and scowled down at her ruined pantyhose. Angrily she yanked them away from her feet and tossed them aside.

"Letty, what the hell is the matter?"

She nodded toward the old blankets on the floor of the stall. "Same blankets? Same stall?"

Joel was outraged at the unfairness of the implied accusation. "It happened fifteen years ago, for God's sake."

"You could at least have picked one of the other stalls." Letty stepped barefoot back into her pumps and stalked past him. "I think it's time we went back to the motel. I need a bath. And then I think it's time to start packing. I've had enough of Echo Cove."

11

"I'm sorry, Letty."

The words were the first Joel had spoken since leaving the barn. Letty slid him a sidelong glance and noticed the way his fingers were clenched around the Jeep's steering wheel. Her gaze traveled upward to the grim set of his jaw. She felt herself soften in spite of her recent embarrassment.

"Forget it." She surveyed the main street of Echo Cove as they drove toward the motel.

"I shouldn't have stopped at that damn barn in the first place."

"I'm glad you told me the full story about what happened here all those years ago. At least I understand now why you're so determined to destroy everything that Victor Copeland has built. Maybe he even deserves it. The problem, Joel, is that you're going to destroy this whole town in the process."

"I don't give a damn about this town. It's Copeland's town." Joel jerked a thumb at a small cluster of people

176

gathered in front of the bank. "Not one of those fine, civic-minded citizens would stand up to Victor Copeland if he took a mind to start chopping off heads at noon in the town square."

"You're being too harsh, Joel."

"I'm telling you how it is, that's all. Don't waste any sympathy on the good folk of Echo Cove. They sure wouldn't waste any on you."

Joel pulled into the motel parking lot, then got out and came around to open Letty's door. "I'll be packed and ready to leave in fifteen minutes."

"Fine." She smiled coolly at his eagerness to be gone. "I'll be ready in about an hour. Probably more like forty-five minutes. I told you I wanted to take a shower. I'm a mess." She reached up and pulled straw from her tangled hair.

His mouth tightened, but he did not argue. They climbed the stairs in silence. When she reached her room, Letty let herself inside and closed the door with a sense of relief.

She was still shaky.

The effects of Joel's incredible lovemaking combined with the shock of being discovered had definitely rattled her nerves. She hoped a hot shower would relax her. It was going to be a long drive back to Seattle.

Kicking off her dusty pumps, Letty started toward the small bathroom. Her hand paused on the jacket of her suit as she caught sight of herself in the mirror.

She was a walking disaster. Everything seemed to be twisted, torn, or creased beyond recognition. Her navy blue suit was so filthy it would have to go directly to the cleaners. The lenses of her glasses were dusty. And her hair looked as if it had been put into a blender. She would have to wash it before the drive to Seattle.

But there was a rosy flush on her cheeks and an unfamiliar brightness in her eyes. She could feel a lingering warmth between her legs.

With a start, Letty realized she was still a little aroused. As she stared at herself in the mirror, she turned an even brighter shade of pink. If Joel had not been in such a frantic hurry back there in that horrible barn, she would have had another of those mind-shattering climaxes that he had introduced her to the other night. She had been on the brink. She was certain of it.

She made a face at herself in the mirror. She was becoming obsessed with sex.

"Oh, my God." The thought sent her reeling into the bathroom. Somewhere she had read an article that claimed women really hit their stride, sexually speaking, in their thirties. And she was, after all, on the verge of turning thirty. Maybe it was all coming together for her at last.

Thanks to Joel Blackstone. No, Joel had told her she was hot. Hot and sexy. She, Letty Thornquist, was normal, after all. Just something of a late bloomer, apparently.

But a part of her knew that if she was the plant, Joel was the gardener.

Half an hour later Letty was feeling much more fit and ready to deal with the world. She had dressed in wool trousers and a pullover sweater and was trying to force her willful hair into a clip when a knock sounded on the motel room door. Letty put down her brush and went to answer it.

Keith Escott stood outside, an earnest if somewhat sheepish expression on his handsome face. He had a black eye, and he was holding a file folder in one hand.

"Sorry to bother you," Keith said. "But I wanted to talk to you in private, and I think this is going to be my only chance. Do you mind if I come in for a few minutes? This won't take long."

Letty glanced uncertainly over her shoulder at the unmade bed and the open door of the closet. The bathroom was filled with steam. It occurred to her that a lot of modern businesswomen must have to face this sort of dilemma. One point in favor of her former career as a librarian was that she had never had to conduct business in a motel room.

"Would you rather go downstairs to the coffee shop?" she offered tentatively.

"There's a crowd down there. Everyone knows me and will recognize you. I'd rather talk to you in private, if you don't mind."

Letty summoned what she hoped was a corporate smile. "Certainly. Please excuse the mess. The maid hasn't been in yet."

"Believe me, it's nothing compared to the mess Copeland Marine is in these days. And that's what I want to talk to you about." Keith walked into the room and headed straight for the table and chairs near the window. He took a seat and opened the file, clearly too intent on business to notice the state of her room.

"What have you got there?" Letty came slowly across the room and sat down on the other side of the table.

Keith looked up. "It's a five-year plan to salvage Copeland Marine. I've been working on it for six months, using computer projections."

"I see."

"All I'm asking is that you look it over and give it fair consideration. I believe we can rescue the company and put it back on its feet if we do some major debt restructuring and if we overhaul the entire management approach."

"Victor Copeland said something about being able to pull the firm out of the red in another couple of quarters."

Keith shook his head impatiently. "Not a chance. Not the way he's going at it. Blackstone is right about that. Copeland Marine is going straight down the tubes, and Victor Copeland doesn't have a clue as to how to stop it. He's locked into too many old patterns."

"You mean he won't listen to new ideas?"

"Copeland hasn't moved with the times, and now he's paying the price. I've been telling him that for three years." Keith grimaced. "But of course I'm the last person he wants to hear it from."

"But he's given you a key position in the company."

"In name only," Keith said bitterly. "Oh, sure, I get to crunch numbers and handle a lot of the routine work. I even waste a lot of time on my computer trying to put together operating assessments that will persuade Copeland to change his methods. But the truth is, my father-in-law thinks I'm about half an inch below pond scum."

Letty tilted her head while she considered that. "Something tells me Victor Copeland doesn't respect too many people."

"I've learned the hard way that the only thing Copeland respects is someone bigger and stronger and more ruthless than he is."

"A real old-fashioned kind of guy," Letty murmured. "Why do you stay at Copeland Marine if you don't like working for your father-in-law?"

"Isn't it obvious? I'm married to the boss's daughter. Diana insists we stay here in town, and as long as her father wants me working at Copeland Marine, that's what she wants, too. I've tried to make the best of things for the past three years."

"Anything for Daddy, right?" Letty asked curiously.

Keith's eyes narrowed. "Diana has her reasons for wanting us to stay here. I suppose that, in the beginning, she thought Copeland would actually turn the yard over to me. After all, he was the one who introduced me to her in the first place, and he gave his full approval to the marriage."

"I take it he no longer shows any indication of being willing to turn the management of Copeland Marine over to you?"

Keith smiled ruefully. "I was beginning to think the only way I'd get anywhere at Copeland Marine was if Victor Copeland died. But having the yard get taken over by Thornquist Gear a year ago put a whole new light on things."

"You want a chance to run the yard?" Letty watched him intently.

Keith shrugged. "I don't mean to sound arrogant, but the fact is, I'm the only one who can save it. With your help and that of Thornquist Gear, of course. And I think it's worth saving. The town's entire economy is dependent on that yard. A lot of good people will be badly hurt if Copeland Marine closes."

"I'm beginning to realize that."

Keith looked at her. "I realize Thornquist Gear is not a charitable institution. I don't expect you to keep Copeland Marine going out of sympathy for the people of Echo Cove. But I think I can offer you a plan that will work."

"A plan that will effectively put you in charge?"

Keith nodded. "Copeland is a bullheaded, stubborn old man who thinks he can continue to run his company and his town the way he has for the past thirty years. He won't change voluntarily, but Thornquist Gear has the power to make him change. You can set up a new management system, Letty. You can restructure things the way I've outlined in this file. You can save the company and this town."

"Now just why in hell would she want to do that?" Joel asked, his voice deadly and quiet.

Keith spun around in the chair and saw Joel lounging in the doorway between the two rooms. "Hello, Blackstone."

Letty glowered at Joel. "I didn't hear you open that door, Joel. You should have knocked."

Joel ignored her. "You didn't answer my question, Escott. Why would Letty want to save Copeland Marine?"

"Because there's a lot more at stake here than your personal vendetta with Victor Copeland." Keith got to his feet. "I came to see Letty because I had a hunch she'd be a lot more reasonable about this than you are."

"You came to see Letty because you had a hunch she'd be a soft touch."

"That's not true. I said reasonable and I meant reasonable," Keith retorted.

"Don't you think I'm reasonable?" Joel murmured.

"No, frankly, I don't. I think your judgment is skewed by

what happened between you and Copeland fifteen years ago."

"And I think your judgment is warped by the fact that you're Victor Copeland's son-in-law."

Keith's shoulders bunched. "You want another chance at the job, Blackstone? Is that the real reason you're back in town?"

"If you believe that, you'd believe anything," Joel muttered. "Including the possibility that Copeland Marine can be saved."

"Gentlemen." Letty surged to her feet. "Quiet, both of you. I will not tolerate this kind of bickering. You have both been involved in one disgusting brawl already, and you both look very much the worse for it. I will not permit any further violence. Is that clear?"

Joel and Keith turned to stare at her as if she had just materialized out of thin air.

Joel shoved his hands into his back pockets. "Christ, Letty, you're not back at Vellacott College telling a couple of sophomores to be quiet, you know."

"Is that right? It's hard to tell the difference."

Keith had the grace to look embarrassed. "Sorry, Ms. Thornquist. I've been a little on edge lately."

"So has Joel." Letty glanced from one to the other. "I understand that this is a highly charged situation, but I nevertheless expect you gentlemen to conduct yourselves in a civilized manner. At least I will insist upon it while you are in my presence. Now, I want you to shake hands."

"I said this wasn't the reference desk at the Vellacott Library," Joel growled. "For the record, it's not kindergarten, either. We don't shake hands and make up just because teacher says so."

Letty swallowed and pushed her glasses more firmly onto her nose. "I insist, Joel."

"You insist," Joel repeated softly.

Letty gathered herself and straightened her shoulders,

realizing that she had painted herself into a corner. Joel was watching her with gleaming eyes. He was well aware of her dilemma. She had, in her role as president of Thornquist Gear, just issued a direct order to her CEO in front of a member of the enemy camp. But she was powerless to enforce it.

She had a sudden, vivid recollection of Joel's short lecture on the importance of not undermining the corporate chain of authority in front of others. So much for presenting a united front to the staff of Copeland Marine, Letty thought ruefully.

Before she could come up with a graceful way to extricate herself from the awkward situation, Joel moved.

He came away from the doorway, took his right hand out of his back pocket, and extended it to Keith. He even managed a wry smile.

"What the hell," Joel murmured as he and Keith stiffly shook hands. "She is the president of the company. That's a real beauty of a black eye you've got there, Escott."

Keith winced. "Damned nose bled for an hour last night. The only good thing I can say about the situation is that you don't look much better than I do today."

"Letty's right. We're both a little the worse for wear."

Keith hesitated and then shrugged. "Hell, it was my fault. I thought something went on between you and Diana yesterday morning. You know how rumors fly in this town."

"Yeah, I know."

Keith grimaced. "Certain people made sure I heard those rumors yesterday afternoon. Diana and I have been having a few problems lately, so I guess I was more than ready to half believe what I'd heard. I stayed late at the office and then went over to the Anchor and proceeded to get smashed. Then you walked in. I saw red."

"Forget it," Joel said. "Bad timing. I can't say I wouldn't have done the same if things had been reversed.

Keith smiled bleakly. "I totally misunderstood the situation. Thought you'd come back to town because you were still carrying a torch for Diana. Copeland encouraged me to think that. But last night after Echler took you away, Letty explained how it was between you and her."

"Did she?" Joel's brows rose in mockingly polite inquiry.

Keith rubbed the back of his neck. "She told me that the two of you were involved. Told me about the connecting door in this room. Said she'd been in on the meeting between you and Diana and that it was pure business."

"Ah," said Joel very softly. His eyes went to Letty. "So she told you we were involved. Interesting."

"I know I accused you of sleeping with the boss last night," Keith said. "But I didn't realize you actually were, if you see what I mean."

"Excuse me," Letty said in a choked voice.

"What I'm trying to say," Keith continued, clearly floundering, "is that I didn't realize the two of you were, you know, really involved."

"I think that's enough," Letty gasped.

Keith smiled reassuringly. "Don't worry, I won't spread it around."

Joel nodded seriously. "Yeah, when you're sleeping with the boss, you've got to exercise a little discretion."

Letty glared at him furiously. "*Joel.* Must you be so crude?"

"Sorry, boss."

The taunting amusement in Joel's gaze filled Letty with a strong desire to wrap her fingers around his throat. "I think that is enough on that topic," she said forcefully. "The only reason I said anything at all to Keith was to reassure him that there was no longer anything of a personal nature between you and Diana. Which there isn't, is there, Joel?"

"Nope. Just business. Hasn't been anything personal between Diana and me for fifteen years. Wasn't all that much at the time, when you get right down to it."

Letty did not trust the expression in Joel's eyes. "All right.

Now that that's settled, I would very much appreciate it if you two gentlemen would get out of my room. I would like to finish packing."

Keith turned to her with a worried frown. "I know I've overstayed my welcome. But can you at least give me your word you'll look at that five-year plan?"

"I'll look at it," Letty said. "But you know I can't promise any more than that."

"It's a start." Keith relaxed visibly. "Thanks. I appreciate it more than I can say. There's a lot riding on this. More than you know, in fact. Call me if you have any questions when you get back to Seattle."

Letty followed him to the door. "I will."

She closed the door behind him and leaned back against it. Mentally she braced herself for the scene with Joel. There was bound to be one, she thought. The man did not have the sense to let it drop.

Joel ambled over to stand directly in front of her. He planted his hands against the door on either side of her head and loomed over her.

"Don't ever," he said, "do that again."

She licked her lips. "Do what?"

"Don't ever give me a direct order like that in front of someone, especially someone from Copeland Marine. I told you before, if you have something to say, wait until we're alone."

"Are you talking about that handshake?" Letty's eyes widened in surprise. She had assumed he was going to challenge her on the issue of making their relationship public.

"Yes, I am talking about that handshake."

"Damn it, Joel, you do work for me, you know. I realize that's hard for you to remember most of the time, but it doesn't change the facts."

"This is your final warning, Letty. I let you off easy this time. I shook Escott's hand like a good little boy. But if you ever try a trick like that again in front of someone from our staff or Copeland's staff, I won't be responsible for the consequences. Got it?"

Letty's temper flared. "Let's get something straight here. The only reason I made that request—"

"It was an order, not a request."

"All right, I gave you that order only because you were behaving in an extremely uncivilized fashion. You were way out of line. Furthermore, you are not to threaten me. I am the president of the company. I do not take orders from you; you take them from me. Has it occurred to you that I might fire you if you push me too far?"

Joel's mouth dropped open in astonishment. "Fire me?"

"I can do it, Joel. We both know it."

"Bullshit. You're not going to fire me. You need me to run Thornquist Gear. You know that as well as I do. If you don't know it, you're not nearly as bright as I've been assuming you are. Now listen up, Letty. As your devoted mentor, I am going to give you your management tip for the day."

She lifted her chin defiantly. "And just what would that be?"

"Don't make threats you can't carry out, *boss.*" He leaned in closer. A slow, wicked grin slashed across his face. "Did you really tell Escott we were sleeping together?"

"No. No, I most definitely did not say that." Letty ducked under his imprisoning arm. "Not exactly."

"Not exactly? This gets better and better."

"I felt sorry for Keith last night."

"Sorry for him? Are you nuts? He's the one who started that fight."

Letty began to pace back and forth across the room. "That fight would not have happened if you had not entertained Diana Escott in your room yesterday."

"I did not entertain her."

Letty ignored the interruption. "Nor would it have occurred if you had not decided to get real macho and go out drinking to relieve your frustrations last night. I'm not saying the fight was your fault, but you must admit you showed poor judgment."

"Damn it, what about Escott's judgment?"

"He was hurting because he thought you'd come back to Echo Cove to take Diana away. To make him feel better, I sort of implied that was not likely because you were sort of involved with me."

"Sort of." Joel folded his arms across his chest and leaned against the door. His expression was one of complete fascination. "I guess that sort of explains why he thinks we're sleeping together."

"I didn't exactly spell it out. I just allowed him to make certain assumptions." Letty stomped into the bathroom and scooped up an armful of toiletries. "I mentioned the connecting door between our rooms, and I also told him I was with you while you were having your *business* meeting with Diana. That's all there was to it."

Joel moved into the bathroom doorway, trapping her in the small room. "Well, well, well. I guess it sort of doesn't matter how it happened, does it? It's sort of the truth."

She clutched the toiletries and scowled at him. "What are you talking about?"

"We're sleeping together." Joel smiled coolly. "We're involved. Wasn't that how Escott put it?"

"Now, Joel . . ."

"Admit it, Letty. We've started an affair." Joel took a step into the bathroom. He leaned over Letty's armful of toiletries and kissed her soundly. When he raised his head, his eyes were gleaming. "We're involved. Say it, Letty."

She stared up at him and licked her lips. "I guess we are. Sort of."

"Damn, I love it when you use that assertive lady-executive tone." He grinned. "Come on, Letty, you can do better than that. Say it right out loud: 'I am having an affair with Joel Blackstone.'"

Letty could hardly breathe. The excitement was rushing through her like a river at high flood. The words came out in a rush, too. She said them before she could give herself a chance to think.

"I am having an affair with Joel Blackstone." *Omigod, omigod, omigod.* She'd never actually had an affair before.

Yes, she'd been engaged to Philip, and before Philip she'd thought herself in love once or twice, but in each instance there had been the understanding that the relationship was headed toward marriage. There had been a real sense of commitment. At least until both parties involved had realized there was something wrong with her.

An affair was such an open-ended thing, Letty realized. No promises. No guarantees. No commitments. *No future.*

"Yeah, an affair. I like the sound of that." Joel brushed his mouth lightly across hers. He looked extremely satisfied. "Come on, boss. Let's finish packing and get the hell out of Dodge City. We've been here too long already." He turned on his heel and walked out of the bathroom.

Letty managed to unstick herself from the floor. "Joel. Joel, wait. There's something we have to talk about."

"What's that?" Joel was in his room, throwing the last of his things into his carryall.

Letty halted in the doorway, her arms still full of cosmetics and her blow dryer. "Well, the thing is, I don't think we should flaunt our personal lives back at the office, if you see what I mean."

"Flaunt?" He arched a brow as he zipped up the bag.

"You know what I'm talking about." She scowled anxiously. "We should maintain a businesslike relationship in front of the staff of Thornquist Gear. We will have to maintain a certain decorum, if you see what I mean."

"Are you trying to tell me you don't want me strolling into your office during coffee break every afternoon and tossing you over your desk?"

Letty flushed. "There is no need to be crude about it. You know perfectly well what I'm trying to say. I want your promise that you will behave yourself at the office. You said yourself that management must have the respect of the staff.

We don't want everyone speculating about us and making off-color jokes. Very bad for the image."

"Ah, yes. The image." Joel picked up the carryall and walked toward the outside door. "Mustn't forget the corporate image. Lucky I've got you around to remind me of my duty to Thornquist Gear, Letty. Don't know how I've gotten by for the past ten years without you."

Letty slumped against the door frame as Joel went out of the room. Her whole world had been turned upside down and sent into a spin lately. Everything felt dangerous, precarious, and just slightly out of control. It was an unsettling sensation.

It was also very exciting.

The sense of being in a tightening spiral of potentially disastrous proportions intensified significantly late that afternoon when Letty walked into her office. Arthur Bigley was blinking at an even faster rate than usual.

"Ms. Thornquist. Thank God you're back." Arthur leaped to his feet. "I didn't know what to do. He just sort of barged in as if he owned the place. I called Mrs. Sedgewick, and she said Mr. Blackstone was going to be furious. She sounded very happy about that."

Letty sighed inwardly. "What seems to be the problem, Arthur?"

"That man is in there. The one who kept trying to call you. I tried to stop him, like I said, but he just took over."

"A man? In my office?"

"He arrived a couple of hours ago." Arthur's voice dropped to a soft hiss of warning. "Ms. Thornquist, he says he's your fiancé."

"My fiancé?" Letty felt as if she'd been dropped off a high cliff. "Philip is here? He's inside my office?"

Arthur blinked frantically. "He said his name was Professor Philip Dixon and that he was engaged to you. I didn't know what to do, Ms. Thornquist. I've been so worried. And Mrs. Sedgewick has been no help at all. If you ask me, she's gloating over this whole situation. I think she wants Mr. Blackstone to get annoyed. And if he does, he'll fire me."

"He will not fire you, Arthur. You work for me."

"But he'll blame me for letting Professor Dixon get into your office. I know he will."

"Stop worrying, Arthur," Letty said firmly. "I will handle Mr. Blackstone. Now, then, let's see what this is all about." She pushed open the door of her office.

Philip was sitting behind her desk. Letty was stunned by the gall of the man. He was sitting behind her desk just as if he owned the place! She was vaguely surprised to realize how territorial she had become about Thornquist Gear.

"Letty my dear." Philip got to his feet and came around the desk. He held out his arms. "I was told you were out of town. I've been wondering when you'd get back. We have so much to talk about."

He was smiling, Letty noticed. It was a classic Philip Dixon smile, graciously condescending, yet imbued with a certain patronizing charm. Philip had perfected that smile for use at faculty teas. It also worked very well, apparently, with graduate students.

The fact that Philip Dixon was extremely good looking in a very patrician style helped.

He was wearing a tweed jacket with flannel trousers, a blue button-down oxford-cloth shirt, and a maroon striped old-school tie, which Letty happened to know was a fake. Philip had graduated from a large California public university, not a private East Coast Ivy League school. One would never know that, however, unless one happened to inquire.

"What on earth are you doing in my office, Philip?" She evaded his outstretched arms and brushed past him to reclaim her chair. She sat down quickly and tossed Keith Escott's five-year plan down onto her desk. Back in control of her own office, she folded her hands in front of her. "For that matter, what are you doing here in Seattle?"

"Letty my dear, what a silly question." Philip sauntered over to the chair on the other side of the desk, hitched up his neatly pressed trousers, and sat down. He crossed his legs and regarded her with gentle concern. "I'm here to see you, of course."

"Why?"

Philip shook his head, looking saddened as well as concerned. "So much hostility, Letty. I was hoping you would have recovered your sense of perspective by now. I told you the other morning when I talked to you on the phone that we really must consider counseling for you. A good cognitive therapist will do wonders, I'm sure."

With an enormous effort of will, Letty hung on to her temper. "I thought you said I needed sex therapy."

Philip frowned thoughtfully. "I wouldn't be surprised if the hostility factor is part of the problem behind your inability to respond sexually. Again, a strong cognitive approach should get to the bottom of things in a relatively short time. But we can discuss that later."

"Really? And just what is it you wish to discuss now, Philip?"

He smiled. "Why, Thornquist Gear, of course. Don't worry, Letty. I realize you're in way over your head here." He chuckled kindly. "Let's face it, how many librarians would be equipped to take on the management of a company the size of Thornquist? But as your fiancé, I am fully prepared to deal with the business for you."

Letty nearly choked. "Is that right?"

"After all, who better to take over the reins than me? This is my area of expertise, as you well know. As a member of the faculty at Vellacott, I have acted as a management consultant to businesses of this size and scope for some time now. As your future husband I see it as my responsibility as well as my pleasure to take the burden of Thornquist Gear off your shoulders."

Letty struggled for breath. "Philip, I don't think you're seeing the big picture here. Thornquist is my company. I don't need anyone to help me run it."

"Now, darling, I know it all seems like great fun at the

moment, but the fact is, running a firm of this size takes considerable experience and training. If you want to dabble in it for a while, I don't see why we can't create a special title for you. Even let you have an office of your own."

"I *have* an office of my own." Letty shot to her feet. "And you're in it. I would like you to get out. Now."

"Letty, you're becoming emotional, darling." Philip said soothingly. "That's not like you."

The office door slammed open, and Joel walked into the room. His eyes swept Letty's tense features and then swung to Philip. "Your secretary apparently called mine earlier about a problem here, Ms. Thornquist. Who is this?"

Letty took a deep breath. "Allow me to make introductions. Philip, meet Joel Blackstone. He's my CEO. Joel, this is Philip Dixon."

"Professor Philip Dixon. On leave of absence from Vellacott College." Philip smiled and got to his feet. He stuck out his hand. "I'm pleased to meet you, Blackstone. I gather you've been holding things together around here since the death of Letty's great-uncle?"

"You could say that." Joel's voice was devoid of inflection. He ignored Philip's outstretched hand. "What's going on here, Ms. Thornquist?"

"Philip seems to think I need help running Thornquist Gear," Letty said tightly. She recalled Joel saying much the same thing to her just a few hours earlier: *"You need me to run Thornquist Gear and we both know it."*

Philip chuckled benignly. "Now, Letty, there's no need to get defensive. You know as well as I do that you cannot possibly run Thornquist by yourself. You need an expert. You also need someone you can trust to look after your best interests. Who better than the man you're going to marry?"

"There seems to be a slight misunderstanding here," Joel said softly.

Philip gave Joel a reassuring smile. "Don't worry, Blackstone. I'm sure we're going to work very well together. We'll schedule a meeting sometime during the next few days for you to give me a full report on the status of Thornquist Gear. Make sure it's complete, because I intend to use it as the basis of my new operating plan."

Letty saw the grim menace in Joel's eyes, and she panicked. At this rate there would soon be blood all over her office. "Mr. Blackstone, please, let me handle this. I'll talk to you later."

Joel turned to look at her. Letty held her breath as she saw the anger seething in him. She was sure he was going to tell her to go to hell. But at the last instant his expression altered slightly. She realized he had himself back under control.

"Right, Ms. Thornquist," Joel said with a civility that grated on every nerve ending Letty possessed. "I'll be in my office when you need me."

12

"Good Lord," Morgan Thornquist said in amazement that evening when Letty told him the story. "What happened next?"

Letty wrinkled her nose and adjusted her glasses. She was sitting on the sofa in her father's living room, waiting for Stephanie to appear from the bedroom. They were due at Stephanie's infant nutrition class in half an hour.

"Joel left. Philip told me he wanted to take me out to dinner tonight and talk about our future. I told him I had other plans for the evening, which was the perfect truth. But you know Philip. He just said we'd arrange something for tomorrow evening. I finally got him to leave. He's staying at a hotel downtown."

"What about Joel? How did you explain things to him?"

"I didn't," Letty admitted. "I was a total and complete coward about the whole thing. I waited until the coast was clear, and then I made a dash down the hall to the elevator."

"You just disappeared?" Morgan looked surprised. "That's not like you, Letty."

"I couldn't help it. I just had to get out of there. I left the building for the rest of the day. I haven't seen either Joel or Philip since that scene in my office. I have to be blunt, Dad. I'm not exactly accustomed to handling this kind of thing."

Stephanie walked into the room wearing a stunning red maternity dress that had a row of crisp, full-length pleats across the front. "What aren't you accustomed to handling, Letty?"

"Two men squabbling over me."

Stephanie gave her a surprised look. "But they're not squabbling over you, are they, Letty? They're fighting over Thornquist Gear."

Letty's stomach clenched as the full impact of that statement sank in. Of course. Trust Stephanie to get straight to the heart of the matter. "Good point, Stephanie. I hadn't looked at it in quite that light."

Morgan frowned. "It does seem highly probable that Dixon's insistence on renewing the engagement may stem from the fact that you are now something of an heiress, Letty."

"Thornquist Gear is a sizable inheritance by anyone's standards," Stephanie added. "No wonder you suddenly find yourself trapped between two ambitious suitors, Letty."

Letty felt a little ill. There was no denying that Joel's apparent eagerness to start an affair with her might be motivated by his interest in controlling Thornquist Gear. She had to keep that possibility in focus at all times. "You know something? The fast lane has a few potholes. And when you hit them fast, you hit them hard."

* * *

An hour later Letty dutifully teamed up with Stephanie when the instructor in the infant nutrition class announced that it was time to learn the fine art of making vegetable purees.

The clatter of utensils and the rise and fall of the voices of the other students filled the classroom. The instructor, a short, energetic woman named Dr. Humphries, was a noted expert in early childhood nutrition. She began moving from station to station giving advice and encouragement in a raspy, high-pitched voice.

Stephanie was, as usual, concentrating intently on the task at hand. She wore an apron over her red smock, and her short hair was covered with a net. She bent over the cookbook that lay open on the classroom counter.

"First peel and chop the carrots," Stephanie read.

"I guess I can handle that." Letty picked up a carrot from the small pile on the counter and started to wield the peeler with swift, efficient strokes.

Stephanie watched in horror. "No, not like that. Be careful, Letty. You mustn't take off so much of the skin. You're removing the most important nutrients."

"I don't think so. I read an article once that said the nutrients in vegetables lie just under the skin, not on the surface," Letty said patiently.

"I don't care what you read. It's obvious you're stripping off far too much of the carrot. Here, let me do that." Stephanie grabbed the carrot and peeler from Letty and went to work.

Letty stepped back out of the way and wondered why she was feeling irritated. It was not as though she actually wanted to peel the stupid carrot. "How did your appointment with the doctor go today?"

"It went very well, thank you." Stephanie worked intently on the carrot. "She says everything is right on schedule."

"You don't sound convinced."

"Well, it's just that there are so many unknowns, aren't there? Everything can look perfectly normal at this stage, but something could go dreadfully wrong at the last minute."

"Not likely, Stephanie." Letty watched as her stepmother finished peeling the carrot and began chopping it up into perfect disks. "I'm sure everything is fine. Just as the doctor says."

"She is one of the finest obstetricians in the city. Board certified in two specialties."

"So you've said."

"She's written several papers on the special problems of women who get pregnant after thirty-five."

"You gave them to me to read," Letty reminded her.

Stephanie examined the precision-cut carrot. "I wonder if the slices are thin enough."

"They're going into a blender, Steph. It won't matter if one is slightly larger than the others. They'll all be turned into mush."

Stephanie's mouth tightened. "I'm sorry if you're bored. You don't have to come with me to these classes, you know."

"Yes, I do. Dad would be hurt if I didn't. We're doing this for his sake, remember."

"Yes. Yes, I do remember."

Letty closed her eyes briefly. "Stephanie, I'm sorry. I didn't mean to sound rude. I'm not bored, really. Your classes are very interesting. It's just that I'm exhausted from that trip to Echo Cove, and it was upsetting to find Philip in my office this afternoon. I think I need a good night's rest."

"You needn't apologize. I realize you're still having difficulty handling the fact that your father has remarried and is starting a second family. If you feel you can't overcome your hostility, you may have to consider counseling."

Letty gritted her teeth. Everyone was suggesting therapy lately. "I am not hostile."

"Denial is never a helpful approach." Stephanie spooned

197

the carrots into the small steamer. "How long does it say to cook them?"

Letty glanced at the cookbook. "It says twelve minutes. Personally I never cook carrots that long. Why don't you try five or six minutes and then check them?"

"This is for an infant," Stephanie said. "The food needs to be thoroughly softened."

"If you say so."

"Watch the time." Stephanie turned on the heat under the carrots. "Twelve minutes, exactly."

While the carrots cooked, Dr. Humphries gave a short lecture on the nutritional value of homemade baby food. When the twelve minutes had passed, Stephanie jerked the lid off the steamer and ladled the cooked carrots into the blender.

"They're well done, all right," Letty observed.

Stephanie shot her a chilling glance. "How long does it say to blend them?"

"One minute. Then stop, stir, and blend for another minute."

"Time me."

"I don't think you have to be that precise about it. Just start blending and stop when it turns into carrot soup."

"I would prefer to follow the recipe, if you don't mind."

Letty raised her eyes ceilingward. It was hard to believe this was Stephanie, the gourmet cook who normally could whip up the most exotic creations with cool expertise and a casual flair. She obediently glanced at the minute hand on her watch. "All right. Go."

The roar of the blender cut off conversation for one blissful minute.

"Stop," Letty called.

Stephanie lifted the lid and glanced inside. "I don't see any big pieces left."

"It looks like carrot soup, all right," Letty said. "Maybe we should stop now."

"No, the directions said to stir and blend one more minute." Stephanie stirred the carrot mixture and lowered the blender lid. "All right. Ready?

"Ready." Letty watched the second hand creep past. "Stop."

Dr. Humphries strolled up at that moment and peeked inquiringly into the blender. "Oh, dear. We took it a little too far, didn't we?"

Clearly alarmed, Stephanie grabbed the cookbook off the counter. "But it says blend for a total of two minutes."

"It depends on the number of carrots you use," Dr. Humphries explained. "We're only making a small portion tonight. Next time try it for one minute."

"Yes. All right. One minute." Stephanie stared at the blender full of liquid carrots as the instructor moved on to the next station.

Letty realized her stepmother was on the verge of tears. "Stephanie?"

Stephanie snatched the blender off its mount and rinsed out the orange mixture under the faucet. "Read the next recipe to me."

"Stephanie, it's only a bunch of carrots," Letty said gently. Awkwardly she put her arm around Stephanie's trembling shoulders.

"Don't you think I know that?" Stephanie pulled away and wiped her eyes with the hem of her apron. "Just start reading, will you?"

Letty picked up the cookbook and slowly read the next recipe aloud. Stephanie engaged in a flurry of precision slicing and dicing. When she was finished, she appeared to have herself back under control.

Letty timed the next batch of pureed vegetables with great care. Stephanie looked enormously relieved when the instructor pronounced the finished product perfect.

"Excellent, Mrs. Thornquist. Just the right texture for baby's delicate taste buds. Now, then, back to our seats, everyone. We will discuss fruit juices next." Dr. Humphries sailed to the front of the classroom. The students trickled back to their chairs.

Stephanie whipped out her notebook and prepared to take down each and every pearl of wisdom that dropped from Dr. Humphries's mouth.

"Stephanie?" Letty sat down slowly beside her.

"Yes?"

"You know what you said earlier about Joel and Philip fighting over Thornquist Gear, not over me?"

"What about it?"

"I think you were right. It was a very good insight. Not exactly flattering, but probably accurate."

Stephanie shrugged. "It seemed obvious. Everyone wants something. Once you know what that something is, you can understand their motivation."

"I don't suppose it's very likely that Philip has come chasing out here to Seattle because of undying love, is it?" Letty tried to keep her voice light.

"No, but is that really a major problem? A mutual interest in a business like Thornquist Gear can unite a couple even more firmly than a baby or physical passion."

"I hadn't thought of that."

Stephanie clicked her ballpoint pen into the ready position as Dr. Humphries stepped to the lectern. "You know, Letty, Philip must have been genuinely fond of you in the beginning or he would never have asked you to marry him. If that affection is combined with a strong business bond, marriage to him might be very stable and satisfying."

"Provided I got into therapy," Letty muttered.

Fortunately Dr. Humphries was already holding forth on the virtues of homemade fruit juices for infants. Stephanie did not hear Letty's remark.

Half an hour later they left the class and walked out into the cool night. Stephanie got behind the wheel of the

Porsche. "It was a good session. Dr. Humphries has her doctorate in infant and childhood nutrition."

"So you mentioned."

"She's a noted authority on the subject."

"Gee, I don't know, Steph. A hundred bucks to learn how to pulverize vegetables into mush seems a bit steep. If you ask me, Dr. Humphries has a nice racket going. I could have shown you how to do that for fifty."

Stephanie stared, tight-lipped, at the street ahead. "You don't understand."

"There are a lot of things lately that I don't seem to understand."

Life was definitely simpler back in Indiana, Letty thought.

Joel leaned on Morgan Thornquist's doorbell until Morgan finally responded. He took his thumb off the bell when the door opened.

"Is Letty here?"

Morgan removed his reading glasses and studied his uninvited guest. "She's out with Stephanie. They're attending a class on infant nutrition. They should be back in a few minutes. Want to come in and wait?"

"Damn right. If I don't, she'll probably try to sneak past me again. Slippery as an eel."

Morgan raised his bushy brows as he led the way into the living room. "My daughter?"

"Yeah. She knew damn well I wanted to talk to her this afternoon, but she ducked out of the office." Joel dropped into an easy chair near the hearth and held his hands out to the pleasant blaze. "She tell you that dipshit ex-fiancé of hers is in town?"

"Drawn by the lure of Thornquist Gear, or so my wife believes."

Morgan settled himself into the chair across from Joel's. He set aside a book he had apparently been reading. Joel glanced automatically at the title: *Applications of Medieval Logic to Computer Analysis* by Morgan Thornquist.

"Did you write that?" Joel asked, momentarily side-tracked.

"Yes. This is one of the first copies off the press. It just arrived today. I am quite pleased with it."

"Are there really any applications of Medieval logic to modern computer analysis?"

"Yes, as a matter of fact, there are. Medieval logicians developed some very impressive and sophisticated approaches to analysis."

"No kidding?"

"Tell me what happened with Dixon today."

Joel drummed his fingers in a grim tattoo on the arm of the chair. "Dixon took over Letty's office while we were out of town. The bastard started giving me orders the minute I walked in the door. I nearly threw him out the window. But Letty practically begged me not to make a scene. Tells me we'll discuss it later, right? So I left like a good little CEO, and what does she do? She sneaks out on me. I've been looking for her for two hours."

"I believe Letty is a bit upset by recent events. She said she wasn't accustomed to dealing with brawling males."

Joel scowled. "She deals just fine with brawling males. Believe me, I've had firsthand experience."

"Have you, indeed?"

"She's no shrinking violet; she can handle that kind of thing. The problem here is Dixon. He's back, and he's trying to sweep her off her feet. He wants my company, goddamn it. Thinks he can just step in and run Thornquist according to all those stuffy business-school methods he teaches at Vellacott College."

Morgan laced his fingers across his stomach and studied Joel over the rims of his reading glasses. "I wouldn't be surprised. Professor Dixon has always been somewhat ambitious. He's been searching for some time for the ideal laboratory in which to test his management theories."

"Thornquist Gear is not a damned laboratory." Joel scowled. "Although I might be able to dig up some rusty vivisection equipment if he keeps pushing me."

"He no doubt sees Thornquist as a perfect opportunity to apply his precepts in a way that will generate a considerable income for him."

"Well, he's not going to get away with it," Joel muttered. "The only way he can get his hands on Thornquist Gear is by marrying Letty. And I'm not going to let him do it."

"I see. Does Letty know that?"

"She should by now." The restlessness that had been gnawing at him all evening was too much. He could not sit still.

Joel got to his feet and paced over to the window. The lights of the city gleamed through the gentle rain. Another spectacular view, he thought. And another beautiful home. The Thornquists were doing all right for themselves.

He glanced at his watch and wondered how soon Letty would walk through the front door. He could not wait to get his hands on her. She had a lot of explaining to do, and he intended to make sure she did it.

Then he would take her to bed and do some explaining of his own. Dixon could go rot somewhere.

"You seem excessively agitated over my daughter's supposed vulnerability to Philip Dixon," Morgan said.

"Dixon is nothing more than a con man."

"You're sure of that?"

"Damn sure." Joel glanced at his watch for the hundredth time.

Morgan gazed into the fire. "My daughter is no fool. I raised her to think clearly and logically. I doubt she'll be taken in by a con job."

"Letty may be smart, but she's too emotional to think clearly all the time."

"I beg your pardon?" Morgan was clearly affronted.

"Damn it, she is a highly emotional female. She's also very naive. And too trusting."

"Nonsense. If Letty decides to marry Philip Dixon it will be for good and sufficient reasons. I taught her to reason her way through highly charged situations. From the time she was five years old, she was required to present a summary of the logic behind any major decision she made. I am convinced she would not make a move as drastic as marriage without first assessing all the facts."

Joel spun around to stare at Morgan. "Are we talking about the same woman?"

"I assume so."

"No offense, Morgan, but I don't think you know your daughter as well as you think you do. As I said, Letty is a very emotional creature."

"Rubbish. She is intelligent, analytical, and rational. I saw to it that she developed those qualities at an early age."

Joel was incensed. "What the hell are you going to do if she decides to marry Philip Dixon? Are you going to sit back and say she obviously knows what she's doing?"

"Letty is twenty-nine years old. If she hasn't learned to think clearly by now, it's too late for me to worry about it. But as it happens, I believe she will ultimately make the right choice. I doubt that she will marry Philip for the simple reason that she knows she cannot trust him."

"Because he made an ass out of himself with that grad student? Get real, Morgan. A slick, fast-talking guy like Dixon isn't going to let a little thing like that stand in his way. He wants my company, and that means he's going to try to get his hands on Letty."

Morgan eyed him thoughtfully. "Have you asked Letty how she feels about that possibility?"

"I told you I haven't had an opportunity to ask Letty a damn thing because she slipped out on me after work." Joel stopped talking abruptly when he heard the key in the front door lock.

"That will be Stephanie and Letty now, I believe," Morgan observed.

"About time."

"Morgan?" Stephanie called from the hall.

"In here, my dear." Morgan pushed himself up out of the chair to greet his wife. "We have company."

"Who is it, dear?" Stephanie walked into the room. "Oh, I see. Hello, Joel. How are you this evening?"

"Fine. Where's Letty?"

Stephanie glanced over her shoulder. "Right here. It's Joel, Letty."

"I heard." Letty appeared. She was bundled up in her new Thornquist Gear down jacket. Her expression was distinctly wary. "What are you doing here, Joel?"

"Guess."

Her mouth tightened. "There was no need to bother my father."

Morgan helped Stephanie with her coat. "It was no bother at all, my dear. We were having a very interesting conversation about Dixon's possible reasons for being here in Seattle."

"I think we all know exactly what his reason is," Joel announced.

Stephanie nodded seriously. "Yes, I think it's quite obvious."

Morgan pursed his lips in thoughtful consideration. "I have to agree that Thornquist Gear would appear to be the clear motivating force in his recent actions."

Joel felt vindicated. At least everyone agreed with him. Dixon was definitely a threat. Surely Letty understood that. He looked at her to see how she was taking the united front of opinion. Letty eyed them all with a mutinous expression and seemed to huddle even deeper into her overstuffed coat.

"Thank you for your considered remarks on the subject," Letty said coldly. "Nice to know that not one of you believes there is even the remotest possibility that Philip might have come to Seattle because of me."

Morgan and Stephanie looked at each other and then at Joel. Joel wished he had handled the situation differently, but it was too late now. He stepped forward and caught hold of her arm.

"Come on, Letty," he said. "I'll take you home. Did you drive here tonight?"

"No. I took the bus."

"Then we don't have to worry about your car." He nodded brusquely at Morgan and Stephanie. "Good night."

"Good night." Morgan's gaze went to his daughter's arm, which was securely locked in Joel's. "Keep us posted."

"Sure." Joel walked Letty toward the front door.

Letty said nothing as they went out into the misty rain and got into the Jeep. Joel slanted her a quick sidelong glance as he drove out of the driveway and onto the street.

"Look," he finally said at the first stoplight, "I'm sorry if your ego got crunched back there because everyone thinks Dixon's here to get his hands on Thornquist Gear rather than on you. Don't take it personally, okay?"

"Don't take it personally?" She stared straight ahead through the windshield. "Joel, I've told you before that you lack sensitivity when it comes to dealing with women. Take some advice. Don't try to lessen the blow. The damage to my ego has already been done. You're only making it worse."

"You wouldn't want him back, even if he went down on his hands and knees," Joel argued. "You have too much pride."

"Do I?"

"Yes, damn it, you do. Now, forget the personal side of this and let's talk about the business angle."

"I don't feel like talking about business tonight."

Joel ignored that. "Did you tell Dixon to stay out of Thornquist Gear?"

"It's a little hard to tell Philip anything, Joel. Besides, this is his area of expertise. Philip has had a lot of experience with companies the size of Thornquist. He's annoying at times, but he's very good at what he does. He's quite capable of managing the firm."

"I don't give a damn how good he is at running companies like Thornquist. I won't have him using his past relationship with you to get a toehold in my business, and that's final."

"You know something, Joel? I'm a little worried about Stephanie," Letty said slowly.

"Huh?" He tried to follow the unexpected twist in the conversation. "Stephanie? What's Stephanie got to do with this? We're talking about you taking a strong stand against Dixon. And it's going to have to be a really strong stand, Letty. In fact, you're going to have to hit that pompous ass over the head with something damn heavy in order to convince him you mean business. I'll give you a hand."

"She's scared, Joel."

"Who? Stephanie?"

"Yes."

"Scared of Dixon?" Joel frowned. "I don't think she needs to be scared of him, exactly. This isn't anything you and I can't handle."

"She's scared of having this baby. Scared to death."

Joel finally realized Letty was off on another tack entirely. "What's the matter? Are there problems?"

"No. That's just it. As far as I can tell, everything is going along just fine."

Joel struggled to find something intelligent to say on the subject. "I suppose it's normal to have some apprehension. I mean, they say that labor still hurts like hell, even with all the modern advances. But women don't die in childbirth anymore, do they?"

"The statistical probability is quite low. Stephanie knows

that. And I don't think she's afraid of the pain, either."
Letty paused. "She's terribly anxious because she considers
this her one shot at having a baby, of course. But I think
there's more to it than that."

"Letty . . ."

"I sensed real fear in her tonight. I suddenly realized that
all this emphasis on getting the best doctor and the best
hospital and taking every class from the most noted experts
she can find is her way of dealing with the fear."

"Letty, everybody knows expectant mothers are neurotic
to some degree or another."

"Is that right?" Letty's voice sounded cool.

"Yeah. It's the hormones or something." He grinned
fleetingly. "Heck, I'll bet you've read an article about it
somewhere."

"As a matter of fact, I have. And I still say that Stephanie
is not experiencing the normal apprehension and mood
swings of pregnancy. She is genuinely terrified. And that
doesn't fit with her personality. She's usually very much like
my father. She intellectualizes everything. Very rational and
calm."

"I'm sure Stephanie will be okay."

Letty leaned back against the headrest. "Then again, what
do I know? I've never been pregnant. Maybe I'd go bonkers,
too."

The thought of Letty pregnant sent a jolt of sensation
through Joel. He pictured her ripe and round with child—
his child—and he felt more possessive than ever. He
stomped too hard on the brake as he slowed for the next
light. The Jeep shuddered to a halt, as if taking offense at the
maltreatment.

"Joel? Is something wrong?"

"No." He sucked in his breath. "Nothing's wrong."

Letty said nothing more for the remainder of the drive
back to her apartment. A thousand jumbled thoughts
flooded Joel's brain, but he could not put any of them into
words.

The disconcerting feelings finally subsided as Joel parked the Jeep in the underground garage of Letty's apartment building. He began to focus clearly once more.

In the elevator, Letty studied the numbers on the control panel. "I take it you plan to invite yourself in for a nightcap?"

Joel eyed her profile. He could not read the expression on her face. "I intend to invite myself into your bed for the night. We're having an affair, remember?"

"I wasn't quite certain how it was going to work." She scowled at him in alarm. "You're not going to just move in, or anything like that, are you? I never said anything about us living together. This is just an affair. That means we maintain separate households, doesn't it?"

"Jesus, Letty. There aren't a lot of rules we have to follow. Nobody's going to check to see if we're doing it right." He took the key out of her hand as they went down the hall. He wondered why he felt oddly hurt. "If you don't want me to stay over tonight, just say so."

She flushed as he opened the door. "I wasn't sure you'd want to. Not after what happened today."

"You mean Dixon showing up and you ducking out on me?" Joel opened the door. "I didn't like it, but that was business. This is personal."

"I'm not sure the two can be separated."

Joel closed the door and reached for her. "Listen to me, Letty. I will say this once and once only. You will never have to worry about me marrying you in order to get Thornquist Gear. I was accused once before of wanting to marry a woman in order to get my hands on a company. I'll be damned if anyone's going to accuse me of it again. Got that?"

She searched his face intently. "What should I worry about?"

Joel smiled slowly as he lowered the zipper of her down coat. "Tonight you don't have to worry about a single thing."

Her eyes were brilliant with excitement now. He could feel the passion rising in her like a glittering wave of energy. Her tongue touched the corner of her mouth. "Joel?"

"Look at you," he whispered against her throat. "You're already hot, and so far all I've done is take off your jacket. I told you last time that I'd do it right this time."

Letty cleared her throat hesitantly. "Yes, well, I suppose I'd better change into my nightgown. Or something." She pulled away slightly, turning as if to make for the bedroom.

"Forget the nightgown. You won't be needing it." Joel caught hold of her and tugged her down onto the carpet.

13

Joel took his time, and the results were spectacular, just as he had known they would be from the start. He had never experienced anything like Letty's fiery passion in his entire life. It swept through him, igniting his own desire and turning it into an inferno. His whole body felt tight and hard and ready to explode.

He paused to look down at Letty as he prepared to enter her. "You're beautiful," he managed hoarsely.

It was as though the contours of her body had been designed for his hands—soft, firm breasts, full, rounded buttocks, the inviting triangle of hair below her belly. Everything seemed to have been created with his personal preferences in mind.

Either that or his personal preferences had changed when he met Letty.

But in a pinch he could have resisted those lures. Hell, he was thirty-six years old. He had resisted a lot of lures in his time.

But he knew now as he drew his fingers through the wet heat between her legs that he could never have resisted the overwhelming generosity of her passion. She took whatever he gave her and magnified it a hundredfold. Then she turned it back on him.

She touched him as if he were a living treasure, cradling him in her gentle palm, stroking him until he groaned aloud.

"You're magnificent," Letty breathed. Her thumb moved across the broad tip of his shaft. "Absolutely incredible."

Hell, Joel thought, the longer he made love to her, the better it got. "You're the incredible one in this room." He leaned down to taste one taut nipple. He felt the shiver that went through her.

"Oh, God, yes." Letty grasped his bare shoulders, pulling him on top of her. "Please, Joel. I can't stand it anymore."

"I don't think I can, either. Look at me, Letty."

Her eyes were glowing with a sweet, hot fire as she watched his face. He reached down and slid his finger into her, testing her readiness one last time. She arched her hips in instant response.

"Joel, I mean it. I can't stand any more torture. Do it." Her nails bit into his shoulders.

At any other time, Joel realized he probably would have laughed in delight at her insistence. But he was too fiercely aroused himself to allow for humor. He had to have her. Now.

Joel surged into Letty's tight warmth, and it was everything he remembered, only infinitely better because she started to climax the moment he entered her.

It was too much. The soft contractions of Letty's body sent Joel over the edge. He heard her call his name, heard his own hoarse shout of satisfaction, and then collapsed on top of her.

He had never realized how good it could be until he met Letty.

A long while later he felt Letty stirring beneath him. Joel

raised his head and looked down at her. He smiled at the smug contentment on her face.

"You okay?" he asked softly.

Her fingertips traveled in a clever little path over his shoulders and down his arms. She stretched languidly. "I'm okay."

Joel realized he had been hoping for a bit more of a response than that. So much for the old ego.

"Yeah. Well, good," he said. "I'm real glad it was *okay* for you."

She giggled and pushed at his shoulders. Joel obligingly rolled to one side and then onto his back. Letty came down on his chest, eyes glittering.

"You crazy man. You know perfectly well that was an absolutely fantastic experience. Joel, I feel so free."

"Yeah?" He enjoyed the feeling of her breasts pillowed on his chest. "You didn't feel free before?"

"Not like this. I feel as if the real me has been trapped somewhere deep inside myself for years." She kissed him soundly. "How do you do it?"

He grinned. "I don't do it. You do."

"I wasn't able to do it before you."

He touched her full mouth with his fingertips. "You just didn't have the right kind of mentor before now."

Instead of laughing or poking him in the ribs as he had expected, Letty turned unexpectedly serious. "You know something? You may be right."

"Hey, that was a joke, damn it." He caught her head between his hands and forced her to focus directly on his eyes. "Don't go getting the idea it'll work like this with just any man now."

"It won't?" She gave him a look of innocent inquiry.

"No," Joel said with grave authority. "In fact, I can assure you that without my personal touch, it won't work at all."

"You're sure of that?"

"One hundred percent positive."

"Hmm."

"Letty?"

"Yes, Joel?"

"Stop wriggling. I'm exhausted and I need time to recover."

That got her attention. "How much time?"

"Why? You in a hurry?"

She slithered around a bit. "I think so. Yes. I'd like to run a little experiment."

He grinned up at her. "Let me guess. You want to be on top, right?"

"Uh-huh." She levered herself up into a sitting position and squeezed him with the insides of her thighs. "You just lie back and recover while I try a few things."

Joel groaned as he felt the beginnings of his own response. It was not possible, he thought. Not so soon. But he could hardly argue with the evidence. Letty smiled with ancient feminine wisdom as he began to stir beneath her. Then she bent her head to brush her mouth lightly across his.

"You know something, Letty?"

"What?"

"Your father doesn't understand you at all."

She raised her head, eyes curious. "What's that supposed to mean?"

"Nothing. Never mind. Forget it. Kiss me, boss."

No, Joel thought, Morgan Thornquist did not have a clue to what made Letty tick. The lady was as emotional and passionate as hell.

"It isn't going to work, you know." Joel slathered real butter on the last of the biscuits Letty had made for breakfast. He popped the morsel into his mouth and chewed with obvious pleasure.

"What isn't going to work?" Letty stacked dishes in the sink. She was still adjusting to the novelty of having a man present at breakfast. Philip had never stayed the entire night. It occurred to her that the intimacy of her relationship with Joel was already several quantum leaps ahead of what she had experienced with Philip.

"You won't be able to keep our relationship a secret at the office for long. Are you sure that was the last biscuit?"

"Yes, I'm sure."

"Too bad. They sure were good. Do people eat like this every morning back in Nebraska?"

"Indiana. And, no, they don't. Usually we eat cereal like everyone else. Joel, what did you mean about us not being able to keep our relationship secret?"

He shrugged and picked up his coffee mug. "Just what I said."

She glowered at him in warning. "I feel very strongly that it would be extremely inappropriate if the staff of Thornquist Gear found out you and I had a personal relationship outside the office."

"You mean if they found out we're sleeping together? I don't see that it would be any big deal. People would talk for a while and that would be the end of it."

"It would be embarrassing, tacky, and bad for office discipline."

Joel grinned. "You're the one who spilled the beans while we were in Echo Cove, remember? You gave Escott the distinct impression you and I were *involved*. I think that was how he put it."

"I did that in the heat of the moment and you know it. I was upset about the fight, and I wanted to assure him nothing was going on between you and Diana. I spoke in haste. Thank goodness Keith is a gentleman. I'm sure he won't say anything."

"Don't bet on it. Escott's trying to save Copeland Marine. If I were in his shoes, I'd use whatever tools I could find."

Letty leaned back against the sink. "I don't see how he could possibly use that information."

"Don't be an idiot. Escott is already trying to use it."

"How?" Letty demanded.

"He gave you that file because he's hoping you'll intercede on his behalf. He sensed you were the more vulnerable one, and he figures if you're sleeping with me, you might be able to influence me."

"Could I?" Letty held her breath.

"Not when it comes to business." Joel glanced at his watch and got to his feet. "You ready to leave for the office?"

Damn him, Letty thought. He did not have to sound so coolly certain that she could not influence him with sex. He was no iceman. She knew that for a fact.

Joel Blackstone was a deeply sensual man. And she was turning out to have unplumbed depths in that department herself. He should not be quite so certain of his own resistance.

"I'm ready," Letty said.

"Let's get going. By the way, if Dixon shows up today, tell him to get lost."

"I'll try. But to be perfectly honest, I think it's going to take some doing to discourage him. You may have noticed he's a bit pompous. Very sure of himself. He's accustomed to holding forth in the classroom, and he's used to being deferred to as an outstanding management consultant. Heck, he's used to being deferred to, period."

Joel took her coat out of the closet and held it for her. "If you can't get rid of him, have Bigley call me. I'll take care of it."

"You can't just throw him out onto the street, Joel." Letty stuck her arms into the thick down jacket and was instantly swallowed whole. "He's a highly respected authority in his field. He's written a number of very well received papers on modern business management theory, you know."

"Get rid of him, Letty." It was an order.

"Sometimes I think you forget who works for whom around here, Joel Blackstone."

"You can remind me of my rightful place later on tonight. In bed."

Letty's office was blessedly free of intruders when she walked into it a short while later. Arthur brought her a cup of coffee and hovered in the doorway, blinking.

"Mr. Manford from Marketing has the revised instructions on the new Pack Up and Go tent for you to approve. He's wondering if you intend to run another field test before signing off on the manual."

"Yes, I think that would be best. Set up a time for us to meet in the third-floor conference room. Tell him to bring the tent."

"Got it. Can I get you anything else, Ms. Thornquist?"

"No, thanks, Arthur." Letty opened her desk drawer and pulled out the file Keith Escott had asked her to read. She thought of Philip Dixon. "If Professor Dixon calls, tell him I'm busy, will you?"

"Sure thing, Ms. Thornquist." Arthur closed the door.

Letty opened Keith Escott's five-year plan for Copeland Marine and started reading.

An hour and a half later, she acknowledged she needed an expert to interpret some of the intricacies of Keith's plan, but she was convinced he deserved a full hearing. It was abundantly clear that Keith was sure he could put Copeland Marine back on its feet if he was given the freedom and the time to do it.

Letty toyed with a pen as she gazed across the room and wondered how to approach Joel on the delicate subject. He was going to come unglued if she ordered him to give the plan a fair examination.

Arthur's voice on the intercom interrupted Letty's thoughts. He sounded more anxious than usual.

"Ms. Thornquist? There are some people here to see you."

"People?"

"They say they're a delegation from Echo Cove. They want to talk to you."

Letty stared at the intercom. Her first thought was that Joel was going to be furious. But she could hardly send them home without listening to what they had to say. "Send them in, Arthur."

The door opened a few seconds later and Arthur ushered three men into the room. One of them was Stan, the bartender at the Anchor.

"Mr. Stan McBride, Mr. Ed Hartley, and Mr. Ben Jackson," Arthur said, consulting his notes.

"Thank you, Arthur." Letty rose to shake hands with the three men.

Arthur blinked rapidly. "Uh, should I notify Mr. Blackstone's office, Ms. Thornquist?"

Stan spoke up quickly. "We came to see you, ma'am. If you don't mind."

"That's right," Ben Jackson, thin and balding, put in eagerly. "We wanted to talk to you, ma'am. You're the president of this company."

Ed Hartley, a gloomy, long-faced individual, nodded sadly. "That's right, Miss Thornquist. We just wanted to have a few minutes of your time, if you don't mind. This is awful important to us."

Letty looked at Arthur. "I'll notify you if I need Mr. Blackstone's assistance."

"Yes, Ms. Thornquist." Arthur backed out of the room, looking distinctly skeptical.

It occurred to Letty that her secretary might go right ahead and call Joel's office anyway. Arthur's loyalties were definitely divided, and there was no denying it was Joel who had put him into this exalted new position. At Thornquist Gear, everyone aimed to please Joel.

"Excuse me a minute, gentlemen." Letty walked to the door and stepped into the outer office. She closed the door behind her.

"Arthur," she said quietly, "I want it understood that I meant what I said in there. Do not call Mr. Blackstone's office unless I specifically request you to do so. Is that quite clear?"

Arthur jumped and hastily tried to replace the receiver, which he had just picked up. The instrument missed the cradle and crashed on the desk top. "Yes, Ms. Thornquist."

"Good." Letty smiled coolly. "I want you to understand that, while it's true Mr. Blackstone promoted you into this position, I am the only one who can make certain you get to keep it. I would not be at all pleased to find out that you felt you owed your first loyalties to another executive down the hall."

Arthur blinked in obvious horror at the situation in which he found himself. "But Mr. Blackstone said I was to keep him completely informed of everyone who comes and goes in this office."

"I will see that Mr. Blackstone is kept informed of whatever he needs to know." Letty walked back into her office and closed the door. She smiled at the three determined-looking men from Echo Cove. "Now, then, gentlemen, why don't you tell me why you've made this trip to see me?"

They all started to talk at once, stumbling over each other's words. Ed Hartley, the glum one, finally took the lead. He passed a hand over his head in a gesture he had no doubt developed years earlier when he had hair.

"The thing is, Miss Thornquist," Ed said stiffly, "we've all realized just what's going on between Thornquist Gear and Copeland Marine. Now, none of us works for Copeland directly, but there's no doubt we're all going to get hurt if Copeland Marine is closed down. I run the main grocery store in town, and I can tell you up front that most of the people who buy food in my store get their paychecks from Copeland."

Stan McBride grimaced. "And like I told Blackstone that

night he got into it with Mr. Escott, I'm in the same boat as Ed here. I'll be plumb out of business if Copeland goes under, and that's a fact. Ninety percent of the guys who come into my place after work are coming from the yard."

Ben Jackson nodded his head. "I run the bank on Main Street. Maybe you saw it while you were in town? I can tell you for certain that if Copeland gets shut down, the financial lifeblood of Echo Cove is going to dry up. It's true some people work for the commercial fishing outfit that operates out of the marina, but that business just isn't big enough to support the place. Copeland's checks pay the bills for nearly everyone in town."

"What we're trying to tell you, Miss Thornquist, is that we don't want Copeland closed." Ed Hartley looked at her beseechingly. "We all know Victor Copeland ain't the nicest guy to come down the pike in recent memory, and we also know that he was a little rough on Blackstone a few years back. But heck, that's the way it goes, you know? Like it or not, Echo Cove needs Copeland and it needs Copeland's firm."

Letty folded her hands in front of her on the desk. "You're asking me to find a way to save Copeland Marine?"

"More like we're pleadin' with you, Miss Thornquist," Stan said. "I know there's some bad blood between Blackstone and Copeland, but we're talkin' about a whole town goin' under here."

Letty looked at him. "You do realize that what is happening to Copeland Marine would not have happened if the company had not been badly managed for the past few years, don't you?"

Stan shrugged helplessly. "I'll admit I don't know what Copeland's been doing with the firm. That's his business."

"He's run it into the ground," Letty murmured.

Hartley pinned her with an anxious glance. "But couldn't you get things sorted out? Or at least give Copeland a little more rope so's he can sort 'em out?"

"I don't know," Letty said honestly. "The only thing I can

tell you at the moment is that I'm looking into the situation. And that's all I'm free to say."

Stan immediately looked more hopeful. "That's what we came here to ask, Miss Thornquist. Just take a second look and see if you can't find a way to give Copeland another chance."

Joel took the stairs two at a time and pushed open the door that led to the fourth-floor hall. As he walked toward his office, he frowned down at a report he had picked up in Accounting. The new cost-cutting measures he had approved last quarter were starting to take effect. He was pleased. He decided to show the report to Letty. It would be educational for her to see how costs were controlled in a company the size of Thornquist Gear.

Hell, maybe he'd show them to her in bed tonight. He grinned to himself.

Joel was whistling tunelessly as he turned the corner in the hall and saw the three familiar faces clustered around the elevator. He halted abruptly as realization and anger erupted simultaneously. It did not take any great mental calculations to figure out what Stan McBride, Ed Hartley, and Ben Jackson were doing in the hall outside Letty's office.

"What the hell do you three think you're up to?" Joel asked coldly as he went toward them.

Stan shifted uneasily. "Hello, Blackstone. We just saw Miss Thornquist."

"If you're hoping she'll save Copeland Marine for you, forget it."

Ed Hartley, who looked just as woebegone as he had fifteen years ago, straightened his slumped shoulders. "We got a right to take our case to the owner of Thornquist Gear. We're fighting for our lives, Blackstone."

"No shit?" Joel smiled thinly. "And you want me to do you a favor and keep Copeland afloat for you, is that it? I seem to recall the day my old man went down to your grocery store, Hartley, and asked for a little credit. We were in a real bind trying to pay off Mom's hospital bills. We needed some time. Remember what you said that day, Hartley?"

Ed Hartley turned a mottled shade of red. "Christ Almighty, that was a long time ago, Joel. Your pa was two months behind as it was. I couldn't let him string it out any further. I had my own bills to pay. It would have been bad business to extend any more credit."

Joel nodded. "Sure, Hartley. I know just exactly what sort of position you were in. It would have been bad business to give my family a little help at a bad time. I'm sure you can understand that it would be real bad business for Thornquist Gear to give Copeland Marine any help now. Can't go around throwing good money after bad."

Ben Jackson scowled nervously. "You hold a mean grudge, Blackstone. That all happened damn near twenty years ago. Can't you let bygones be bygones?"

"Which bygones do you suggest I forget, Ben?" Joel switched his gaze to Jackson. "The five hundred dollar loan you wouldn't give my father when he went down to your bank, hat in hand? He needed that money to pay for the funeral expenses for Mom. I knew better than to go to you for a loan when I needed help paying for his funeral. I realized you'd turn me down, just as you did him."

Jackson looked affronted. "Now, see here, Blackstone. Your father was up to his eyeballs in debt when he came to see me. No way could I justify a loan to a man in his position. No smart banker would have done it. I had responsibilities to the board."

Joel punched the elevator call button for the men. "No smart executive in my position could justify keeping Copeland Marine alive any longer. I'm sure you gentlemen understand. You're all businessmen, after all."

"Come on," Stan McBride said desperately. "Think about what you're doing to your hometown, Blackstone."

The elevator arrived. Joel held the doors open politely. "I

do think about it, Stan. I think about it a lot. The same way you must have thought about what you were doing the night you swore to the cops that my father was too drunk to drive the night he left the Anchor and drove off a cliff."

"He was drunk, damn it."

"Not everyone in the Anchor thought so." Joel crowded the three into the waiting elevator. "But I'm sure that Victor Copeland made it clear he wanted your expert judgment as a bartender to prevail."

"Now, see here, Blackstone, you don't understand what's at stake," Ed Hartley sputtered.

"The hell I don't." Joel smiled.

The elevator doors closed on the indignant, outraged, and desperate-looking faces of McBride, Hartley, and Jackson. Joel stopped smiling abruptly.

The three men had come to see Letty. He had caught them on their way out. That meant they had already had their interview and a chance to make a pitch to the softhearted president of the company.

Such incidents were not supposed to occur.

That meant somebody had screwed up, and that somebody was named Arthur Bigley. Bigley had apparently forgotten his instructions. People who forgot their instructions did not work long at Thornquist Gear.

Joel strode down the hall and stalked into Letty's outer office.

Arthur started at the sight of him and began a frenzy of blinking. "Mr. Blackstone." Arthur's eyes filled with alarm.

Joel halted in front of his desk. "I just ran into three people in the hall who were on their way out from seeing Ms. Thornquist."

"Yes, sir."

"I was not informed of their presence in the building."

"Uh, no, sir. You weren't." Arthur clutched a pencil so hard it snapped in his fingers. The pieces dropped on the desk, rolled to the edge, and fell off onto the carpet.

"Such incidents are not supposed to happen, Bigley."

Bigley's eyes filled with tears. "No, sir. I know they aren't. Ms. Thornquist said—"

"Christ, Bigley," Joel interrupted in disgust. "Are you *crying?*"

"No, sir. I've been having trouble with my new contacts, sir."

Joel let that go. "It doesn't matter what Ms. Thornquist said," he continued softly. "You had direct orders from me, Bigley. You became an executive secretary because you gave me your solemn promise that you would follow the instructions I gave you. Is that not right, Bigley?"

"Yes, Mr. Blackstone," Arthur agreed sadly.

"You have failed in your duties, Bigley. That means I will have to remove you from this position and find someone else who can follow my instructions."

"Mr. Blackstone, please, I love this job."

"Then you should have done it right," Joel said.

The door of the inner office opened at that moment. Letty stood framed in the doorway. She took in the scene before her in one glance, and her eyes narrowed.

"What in the world do you think you're doing to my secretary, Mr. Blackstone? Get away from him at once."

Joel slanted her a cold glance, fully aware that Arthur was darting anxious, questioning looks back and forth between Letty and him. "I will talk to you in a moment, Ms. Thornquist."

"You will talk to me right now. And you will cease threatening my secretary this instant. I won't have it."

Joel glowered at her. "I have a few things to say to him, if you don't mind."

"I most certainly do mind," Letty said. "Arthur works for me. I will speak to him if it's necessary."

"I'm the one who put him into this position."

Letty smiled aloofly. "For which I am very grateful. He's doing an excellent job."

Arthur sent her a grateful look.

"That's a matter of opinion," Joel said.

"It is indeed. And since Arthur works for me, my opinion is the only one that counts. Is that not so, Mr. Blackstone?"

Joel was trapped. That knowledge did nothing for his bad temper. "You've been here only a short time, and there are still a few things you don't yet know about running this firm, Ms. Thornquist."

"Quite probably, Mr. Blackstone." Letty smiled sweetly. "Why don't you come into my office and explain them to me?" She stood back and held open the door.

Joel clenched his back teeth, clamping an iron grip on his raging temper. "I believe I'll do just that, Ms. Thornquist."

He went past Arthur's desk without looking down at him. He did not have to see his expression to sense his relief. Nor did he have to get a good look at his face to know that as far as Arthur was concerned, Letty had achieved the status of a minor deity in his eyes.

Joel was well aware of the ramifications of that encounter. He had just lost his spy in Letty's office. Win some, lose some, he reminded himself. A man had to pick and choose his battles. He had lost Bigley, but there was still a war to be fought.

He stalked into Letty's office and swung around to face her as she quietly closed the door. "What the hell did McBride, Hartley, and Jackson want?"

"I'm sure you know exactly what they wanted." Letty broke off, wincing slightly at the muffled sound of something large and heavy bouncing on the floor in the outer office. "The dictionary he keeps near his typewriter, no doubt."

"No doubt." Joel shoved his fingers into the back pockets of his jeans. "What a klutz."

"You hired him." Letty went around her desk and sat down.

"A miscalculation on my part."

"If you mean because I won't allow you to use him to

225

monitor every little thing that takes place in this office, yes. But that's not Arthur's fault. He tried his best. I, however, have informed him that he now reports to me, not to you. In the end we all have to choose our loyalties, don't we, Joel?"

"A brilliant observation, Ms. Thornquist. While we're on the subject, why don't you tell me just whose side you're on?"

She sat back. "Joel, stop raging and tell me the truth about something here."

"What?"

"Are you hell-bent on destroying Echo Cove or would it be enough for you if you could just bring down Victor Copeland?"

He stared at her. "What are you talking about?"

"Just answer me. I know you're not particularly fond of your hometown, but does your need for revenge demand that you destroy it?"

Joel was taken off guard by the question. He realized he had never bothered to separate his dislike for Echo Cove in general from his hatred of Victor Copeland in particular.

"I don't see that it makes much difference," he muttered. He started pacing the floor, the restlessness building rapidly in his gut.

"Look at it this way," Letty said, suddenly gentle. "If Victor Copeland had not owned Copeland Marine, would you have gone to all this trouble to bring down the company?"

That stopped him for a second. "No. But it's a moot point. Copeland Marine is his. It always has been. And those three jerks who were just in here don't deserve any pity, believe me."

"I believe you. But there are other people to consider."

"Such as?" he demanded.

"What about Angie Taylor?"

Joel stared at her. "The librarian? What about her?"

"You don't hate her, do you?"

"Of course not. Mrs. Taylor was"—he shrugged—"nice to me." More than nice, Joel realized. She had, without fuss or comment, provided a refuge for him during those dark days after his mother's death. For the first time in a long while Joel remembered the hours he had spent buried in the Echo Cove Public Library.

"A lot of innocent Angie Taylors are going to get hurt if you go through with your plans, Joel."

"Don't get sentimental, Letty. This is business." But Joel was beginning to feel uneasy. He had always liked Angie Taylor. And maybe one or two other people in town.

"If Copeland Marine were not the main industry of Echo Cove, would you have gone after the commercial fishing operation that is located there instead?"

"Hell, no."

"Then it's safe to say that your target is Victor Copeland, not the whole town."

"Damn it. What is this? An inquisition? I've already agreed with that. It's no secret. But I'm going to bring Copeland down and that's final."

Letty studied him for a long moment. "Joel, there may be a way to do that without sacrificing the whole town."

Joel stopped pacing and walked over to the desk. He planted his hands on the surface and loomed over her. "You can keep your klutzy secretary, and you can rewrite all the instruction manuals you want. Hell, I'll even let you plan the office Christmas party. But don't even think about getting between me and Copeland. I'm going to break him, Letty. I'll do whatever it takes. If you get in the way, you'll get hurt. Understand?"

"Yes, Joel. I understand."

He glowered at her, aware that something had gone out of her voice; it sounded flat and distant all of a sudden. He realized her lower lip was quivering slightly. He felt like a brute.

"For Christ's sake, Letty." He straightened away from the

desk and paced to the window. "I've told you how it is between me and Copeland."

"I know." Letty got to her feet. She picked up a file from her desk. "You've made it clear that revenge is more important than any other minor considerations in your life."

He gritted his teeth, knowing full well she was lumping herself in with the other minor considerations. "You're too emotional, Letty."

"I'm too emotional?" She gave a choked laugh. "That's a joke, coming from you. You're one of the most emotional people I've ever known."

That accusation infuriated him. "The hell I am."

"Joel, please, no more scenes. I've had enough for today. I want you to take Keith Escott's file and read it. See what you think. If you can get past your highly emotional reaction to his proposal, take a close look at the numbers. Tell me honestly if he's right about being able to save Copeland Marine."

"How many times do I have to tell you that I won't walk across the goddamn street to save Copeland Marine?" Joel roared.

Letty flinched, but she held her ground. She shoved her glasses up onto her nose. "Stop ranting and raving for one damn minute and *think*. Saving Copeland Marine does not necessarily mean saving Victor Copeland."

"Copeland *is* Copeland Marine."

"Only in your mind. It doesn't have to be that way, you moose-brained idiot. *Keith Escott could be Copeland Marine.*"

Joel stared at her dumbfounded. "What the hell . . ."

"It's true. Just read that report and think about it, Joel. We own controlling interest in Copeland Marine, right?"

"Damn right."

"Then we can kick out the old management and install a whole new bunch of managers. Starting at the top."

Joel's brain seemed to have turned to mush. He struggled

to grapple with the concept at hand. "Fire Victor Copeland?"

"Why not?" Letty smiled grimly. "Just as he fired your father, Joel. And then we'll hire Keith Escott to run Copeland Marine."

Joel shook off the cobwebs. "It won't work."

"You may be right. But you won't know that for certain until you read Keith's five-year plan summary, will you?"

"Give me one good reason why I should read this management plan, Letty."

"Because I'm asking you to read it."

He eyed her sharply. "Are you threatening me in your own unsubtle way? Are you telling me you won't sleep with me unless I read it?"

She gave him a brittle smile that did not conceal the hurt in her eyes. "Of course not, Joel. You said yourself just this morning that I would never be able to use our personal relationship to manipulate you when it came to business."

"Letty, I didn't mean—"

"You also made it quite clear a minute ago that you intend to have your revenge even if it means hurting me. I know exactly where I stand in all this. I have no illusions about being able to influence you just because we're involved in an affair."

"Damn it, Letty . . ."

"Try to read Keith's proposal with an open mind." Letty got to her feet and went to the door. "Now, if you'll excuse me, I'm going down to the third-floor conference room to pitch a tent."

Arthur looked up as she went past his desk. He blinked several times.

Letty smiled at him. "You know, Arthur, I've been thinking," she said. "I'm going to look into changing your title from executive secretary to executive assistant."

"Executive assistant." Arthur looked stunned. Tears trickled down his cheeks. "Thank you, Ms. Thornquist. You won't regret this, I swear it."

"It occurs to me," Letty continued smoothly, "that your glasses would be more suitable to the new image. They gave you a certain sophisticated—one might even say, aggressively corporate—look."

"I'll start wearing them right away," Arthur said quickly. "I've been having a lot of trouble adjusting to contacts."

14

He's a very passionate man, Dad. Very emotional." Letty lounged in the hearthside easy chair across from her father and gazed into the flames. She was waiting for Stephanie to emerge from the bedroom. They were scheduled to attend a class on infant development tonight.

"I'm surprised to hear that." Morgan frowned. "Blackstone struck me as the consummate business executive. Very cool and clear-headed."

"He is, when he's not emotionally involved."

"I must admit I did question that aspect of his character last night when he showed up at the door looking for you. The odd thing is, he seems to think you're the emotional one."

Letty shot her father a quick glance through half-lowered lashes. "He said that?"

"Yes, he did. He's concerned about your association with Dixon, you know. Thinks you're in danger of being swept off your feet."

"Oh, that." Letty switched her gaze back to the flames. "I know. He's afraid I'll turn Thornquist Gear over to Philip."

"I assured Joel that you would make the right decision regarding Dixon," Morgan said calmly. "Speaking of the good professor, where is he these days? I half expected to get a call from him. After all, we were nodding acquaintances when I was at Vellacott."

Letty frowned. "I've been wondering about that myself. I fully expected him to waltz into my office sometime today and tell me that he's got some brilliant new scheme to expand Thornquist Gear."

"Not like him to vanish like this after coming all this way to see you."

"Frankly, I hope he stays vanished." Letty leaned her head back against the chair cushion. "I've got enough problems on my hands."

"You'll handle them just fine, my dear." Morgan sounded calmly certain of that. "Just keep all the elements of the situation in a clear and logical perspective. It might help if you make up a decision matrix before you draw any conclusions."

Letty arched her brows. "How do you propose I include the fact that I'm having an affair with Joel Blackstone in my decision matrix, Dad? How do I weight the importance of that? Shall I give it a factor of two or five?"

Morgan frowned. "What's this? You're intimately involved with Blackstone?"

"Yes." Letty was curious to see how her father would react to the news.

"I had not realized that." Morgan fixed her with a serious expression. "Do you think that's wise, Letty? There are several delicate financial matters at stake here."

Letty's mouth curved wryly. "Tell me about them."

"Well," said Morgan, obviously intent on doing just that, "there is, first and foremost, the question of the ownership of Thornquist Gear. Then there is the issue of the actual control of the company. Ownership and control are not necessarily the same thing, Letty. On top of that, there's Dixon's presence on the scene—"

"Dad, stop. I didn't really want a list of all my problems. I know what's at stake."

Morgan nodded wisely. "Yes, of course. I should have realized you were well aware of the situation. Nevertheless, it's been my observation that emotional involvement does not mix well with business matters. Especially when the business at stake is as large as Thornquist Gear."

"I agree with you, Dad. But I seem to be stuck in the situation."

"I refuse to believe that you cannot control your emotions better than that, Letty. I've trained you to think clearly and logically, regardless of your personal feelings."

Letty wrinkled her nose. "That gets boring, Dad."

"Letty, this is not a joking matter."

"I know," Letty murmured. "I'm sorry. I guess I'm asking for advice."

"My advice is to do what I have trained you to do," Morgan said firmly. "Step back from the situation emotionally and make a logical decision matrix."

"I'll try that, Dad." Letty slumped in her chair, glumly aware that she was in too deep to make a rational, unemotional, logical decision about anything that involved Joel Blackstone.

"I'm ready," Stephanie said as she came down the hall. "Shall we go, Letty? It should be a very interesting class tonight. Dr. Marklethorpe is a renowned expert on infant and early childhood development. He's done some important research on psychological and motor function in the first six weeks of life."

"His own life or someone else's?" Letty asked blandly. When she saw the grimness in Stephanie's eyes, she regretted the words. As usual. "Sorry. A poor joke." She got up. "Let's go or we'll be late."

"Drive carefully," Morgan called after the pair. "Oh, and Letty?"

"Yes, Dad?"

"Don't forget to make that matrix. When you do, I think you'll discover that an emotional entanglement with Joel Blackstone is probably not the wisest move at this particular point."

"Yes, Dad." Letty stifled a sigh as she followed Stephanie out the door. *Easy for you to say,* she thought.

Outside in the car Stephanie glanced at her. "You're involved with Joel Blackstone?"

"Sort of. Yes."

"Do you think that's wise, Letty?"

"No."

"Then why are you doing it?"

"It just sort of happened," Letty said.

"Nonsense. I know your father. You've been raised with better self-control than that."

"Okay," Letty said, feeling goaded. "I wanted it to happen."

Stephanie switched on the Porsche's ignition. "Is this a physical thing?"

"Oh, very."

"I meant is it entirely physical or is the bond intellectual as well as emotional?"

"I don't think you could say there's a lot of intelligence involved," Letty admitted.

"Then it would probably be best to end the affair immediately," Stephanie advised. She eased the Porsche out of the drive.

Letty gazed out at the streetlights and wished she had never mentioned her affair to her father. So much for asking for paternal advice.

She had known ahead of time exactly what Morgan would say. It was the same thing he had been saying since she was a child: "Make a decision matrix, Letty. Weigh all the crucial factors and enter them on a grid. The appropriate conclusion will be obvious."

An hour later, midway through a set of slides showing infants in various stages of rest and activity, Letty realized Stephanie was getting increasingly tense. She leaned over and spoke softly.

"Are you all right, Steph?"

"Yes." Stephanie stared straight ahead at a slide of a six-week-old infant stretching its arms and legs.

Dr. Marklethorpe's voice droned in the darkened classroom. "As you will see, the infant is capable of communicating a great deal of information even at the age of six weeks. When accompanied by yawning, this stretching activity signals the infant is sleepy."

"Gosh, I would never have guessed," Letty murmured in an aside to Stephanie.

"Quiet," Stephanie whispered.

"Sorry." So much for trying to lighten the mood. Letty concentrated on the screen.

"You will notice in this slide," Marklethorpe said, "that the infant is alert and tracking with her eyes. This means she is in a data assimilation mode. This is an excellent time to introduce a new element into her environment. Think of this as learning time."

"Brilliant observation," Letty mumbled.

"Now, then, compare the development at six weeks with the development of the infant at birth. Here we have a slide showing a newborn with a very high APGAR rating. The APGAR system rates the strength of the baby's cry and its general physical condition at birth. It's an excellent indicator of . . ."

Letty saw Stephanie lean forward and clutch her stomach. *"Stephanie.* What is it?"

"Nothing." Stephanie's voice was a painful, strangled whisper.

"Stop saying that. Something *is* wrong. Come on, let's get out of here."

Much to Letty's surprise, Stephanie did not resist. Letty

led her along the back row of seats and out into the hall. Stephanie's face was pale in the harsh glare of the fluorescent lights.

"I'm going to call your doctor," Letty said. "I'll tell her we're on our way to the emergency room and we'll meet her there."

"No. Wait." Stephanie grabbed at her arm as Letty made to move toward a pay phone down the hall. "I'm all right. I swear it. Nothing's wrong."

"Stephanie, something is very wrong. You look as if you've seen a ghost."

Stephanie burst into tears. "Oh, God, I think I did."

Letty was stunned by the flood of emotion from the normally calm, cool, and intellectual Stephanie. Instinctively she put her arms around her stepmother and held her as great sobs racked her body.

"Steph, what is it? Tell me. I can't help you if you don't tell me."

"I lost him, Letty."

"Lost who?"

"My baby. I lost him at three months. Ten years ago this month. He was dead inside me. All that time I was preparing for him, buying baby clothes, choosing names, all that time, and he was dead."

Letty closed her eyes and tightened her grip on Stephanie. "I'm so sorry."

"I'm so afraid I'm going to lose Matthew Christopher, too. I get more afraid every day. I'm going crazy with the fear."

Letty hugged her gently. "You won't lose him. He's alive and well and kicking like mad. He'll be safe in your arms in another few weeks. You've got one of the best doctors in the state. You've got the best hospital in the city."

"I know, but so many things could go wrong."

"He's strong and healthy. He's got my father's terrific genes, remember?"

"But he's got some of mine, too. And I lost my first baby.

What if there's something wrong with me? What if I lose Matthew Christopher because there's a basic genetic flaw in me?"

"There is nothing wrong with you. It's going to be all right, Steph." Letty kept talking, saying the same, soothing things over and over again. "When the time comes, you'll have the most advanced medical technology available to you. Your doctor will be with you, watching over every detail."

Gradually Stephanie's sobs subsided.

When she finally lifted her head from Letty's shoulder, her face was blotched and red from crying. She groped for a tissue in her purse. "I'm sorry you had to witness that. I've made a fool of myself. I'm sorry. I'm not behaving very rationally these days, am I? I've got to get myself back under control."

"Stephanie, you're pregnant." Letty smiled. "Everything I've read says that being irrational is allowed."

"I don't want Morgan to see me like this."

"Like what, for heaven's sake?"

"Like this. In such an abnormal state." Stephanie blotted her eyes and blew into the tissue. "He wouldn't understand. I'm not myself."

"Have you told him about the miscarriage?"

"No, I haven't." Stephanie shoved the tissue back into her purse. "It all happened a long time ago. During the first year of my first marriage. I was never able to get pregnant again. I'd given up all hope until Morgan and I became involved. I was so thrilled when I found out. And Morgan seemed pleased."

"He is. He's looking forward to molding another generation of Thornquist brains. I think he figures he made a few mistakes with me, and he's anxious to get it right this time."

"Letty, I've been frightened all along. Right from the start. And it's been getting worse."

"You should have talked about it before now," Letty said. "I think you ought to tell Dad everything."

"He'd be appalled at my irrational behavior."

"Nonsense. My father grew up on a farm. He was a regular human being before he got that Ph.D., and he still is, once you get past that intellectual veneer he's acquired. He's really very compassionate and understanding. How the heck do you think Mom and I tolerated him?"

Stephanie shook her head. "He thinks I'm just like him. That's why he married me. And I *am* very much like him. Usually. It's only since I started worrying about losing this baby that I've gone off the deep end."

"You haven't gone off the deep end. You're just tense and worried. And I'll tell you something else. I've known my father for twenty-nine years, and he's not always cool and cerebral. I still remember how he went bonkers when I fell off my bike and had to be rushed to the emergency room with a broken wrist. You'd have thought I was at death's door. Mom spent more time calming him down than she did patting me on the head."

"Oh, Letty . . ."

Letty smiled sadly. "And when Mom died, I thought for a while I was going to lose Dad, too. My father is no iceberg, Steph."

"Well, I know he's not an iceberg. We *are* having a baby, you know." Stephanie actually turned slightly pink. "I understand that Morgan does have a passionate side to his nature."

"Just keep in mind that passion isn't the only emotion he's capable of," Letty said dryly. She took Stephanie's arm and started walking down the hall. "What you have to remember, Steph, is that this time your pregnancy is sailing along smoothly. In fact, you're in the safety zone."

"How do you know that?"

"I read an article somewhere," Letty said vaguely. "You're not much more than a month away from your due date. Heavens, even if the worst possible case occurred and you went into labor tomorrow, your baby is still old enough and strong enough to survive."

"Oh, God, don't say that," Stephanie gasped. "Premature babies have all kinds of problems."

Letty realized she had miscalculated her choice of reassuring words. "The point is, you've got everything under control, and your doctor has assured you that you're carrying a healthy, normal baby. Everything is going to be fine, Steph."

"The doctor is excellent," Stephanie whispered.

"The best."

"And so is the hospital."

"Absolutely top-notch."

"Fully equipped with state-of-the-art fetal monitors and incubators."

"Right. Able to handle anything." Letty opened the door at the end of the hall and led Stephanie out into the parking lot. "I'll drive. You need a little time to pull yourself together."

Stephanie looked momentarily dubious. "Have you ever driven a Porsche before?"

"No. But don't worry. I'm picking up new stuff every day out here on the frontier. Lucky for me, I'm a fast learner."

Letty walked into her apartment half an hour later and was startled to find Joel in the living room. He was lounging on the couch, his feet up on a hassock. He had a small glass of brandy beside him and Keith Escott's five-year management plan in his hand. He looked up when Letty came to a halt in front of him.

"Hi," Joel said. "How did the baby class go?"

"I'll tell you all about it later. First, why don't you tell me what you're doing in my apartment at ten o'clock at night?"

"We're having an affair, remember?"

"I thought you were extremely annoyed with me because of what happened at the office this morning."

"I was pissed as hell. But as you said, the business side of our relationship doesn't have anything to do with the personal side."

"You're the one who keeps saying that, not me."

"So, I'm right." Joel flipped over a page.

Letty regarded him for a long moment and then sat down on the sofa beside him. "I see you're reading Keith's management plan."

"Yeah."

"What do you think?"

"I haven't finished it."

Letty got to her feet. "Maybe I'll whip up a batch of cookies while you read."

"Hell of an idea."

Joel ate half the batch of chocolate chip cookies Letty prepared. Then he opened his briefcase, took out a hand-held calculator, and started punching in numbers. "You might as well go to bed," he told Letty. "I'm going to be at this for a while."

Letty went to bed and tried to read. She fell asleep in the middle of a chapter. A long time later she felt Joel crawling into bed beside her. She stirred.

"Joel? What did you think?"

"I don't want to talk about it tonight." His voice sounded grim.

"But, Joel—"

"Go to sleep, Letty."

"Thanks for reading it," Letty whispered.

A long time later she was awakened again. Joel's hand was between her legs.

"Joel? *Joel.*"

"You know something, Letty? You get wet for me even in your sleep." He leaned over her. "All I have to do is touch you."

"It's two o'clock in the morning," Letty grumbled.

"I can't sleep. I need to run, but there's no place to run tonight. And all my exercise equipment is back in my apartment."

"You can't sleep?" She touched his bare shoulder.

"No." His fingers moved in a tantalizing pattern.

Letty sucked in her breath. "Are you trying to tell me you think sex will help you get to sleep?"

"I'm trying to tell you that I want you very badly right now."

Letty smiled and put her arms around his neck. "All you have to do is ask."

The next morning Joel refused to give Letty any insight into what he thought of Escott's management plan.

"I'm still going over it," was all he said as he wolfed down a pile of incredibly light buttermilk pancakes.

She did not like being kept on tenterhooks, he realized, but what the hell. She deserved it. He certainly did not like the growing possibility that the red meat that was Copeland Marine might be snatched from his salivating jaws.

In any event, he could not give Letty an opinion yet, he told himself as he pored over the plan again in his office. He was still reviewing the damn report. The really annoying thing about Escott's ideas was that they just might work.

Joel had been secretly hoping to find a fatal flaw in the management plan, something he could use to show Letty that there was no hope of saving Copeland Marine. Unfortunately, Escott had done a brilliant job of outlining the potential of the company and had come up with a realistic method of fulfilling it.

It would have been so much easier, Joel thought, if he could have pointed to a simple, logical reason for shooting down Letty's suggestion of salvaging the company.

His secretary's voice on the intercom interrupted Joel just as he was starting to run another set of numbers.

"A Mrs. Diana Escott to see you, sir. Are you free?" The chilly note in Mrs. Sedgewick's voice said it all: she did not entirely approve of Joel's visitor.

Damn, Joel thought. Just what he needed. "Send her in, Mrs. Sedgewick."

Diana swept into the room in a cloud of unsubtle perfume. The whiff of aroma made Joel realize that Letty never wore perfume. He disliked strong artificial fragrances. He liked the way Letty smelled all on her own.

"Hello, Joel."

"This is a surprise." Joel got slowly to his feet. "Sit down, Diana."

"Thank you."

Diana dropped gracefully into the chair across from his desk. She was dressed in a chic black and white suit that complemented her dramatic coloring. The jacket was nipped in at the waist and flared out gently over her hips. When she crossed her long legs, Joel saw that her high heels were glossy and black. He watched her survey the office with a long, assessing glance.

"You really have done very well for yourself, haven't you, Joel?"

"It's a living. What can I do for you, Diana?"

"You know why I'm here."

Joel leaned back in his chair. "Maybe you had better spell it out."

"Keith told me he gave you his five-year plan for Copeland Marine."

"He didn't give it to me. He gave it to Letty. I mean, Ms. Thornquist."

Diana brushed that aside with a dismissive movement of her elegant hand. "We all know who runs Thornquist Gear."

"Is that right? I've been starting to wonder about that myself."

Diana's eyes blazed. "This is not a joke. Since you left Echo Cove, I've learned a great deal about the situation here. According to what I heard, this Letty Thornquist person only recently inherited the company. She's an ex-librarian, for heaven's sake. Worked at a college in the Midwest somewhere. She knows nothing about business."

"Just out of curiosity, where did you hear all that?"

"A man named Philip Dixon talked to Daddy yesterday."

"Dixon. He was in Echo Cove?" Joel sat forward abruptly. "That son of a bitch."

Diana frowned. "Do you know him?"

"I know him."

"He's telling everyone that he'll be marrying Letty Thornquist soon and that he'll be making the decisions for Thornquist Gear in the future. I think Daddy's trying to cut some sort of a deal with him."

Joel paused, letting the possibilities sink in. "Your father believes Dixon's on the level?"

"Isn't he? Joel, I can't stand this anymore. It's all getting so confused. If you're going to shut down Copeland Marine, just do it and get it over with, will you? Don't drag things out like this."

Joel started to respond, but before he could say anything, his attention was caught by a commotion in his outer office.

"Kindly stand aside, Mrs. Sedgewick. I told you I want to see Mr. Blackstone now. When I say now, I mean *now*." Letty's voice was muffled by the paneling of the door, but every word was audible.

"I cannot allow you to just barge in on Mr. Blackstone when he's in conference," Mrs. Sedgewick retorted fiercely. "I told you, he's with someone at the moment."

"I know who he's with. Arthur informed me a minute ago. Now get out of my *way*."

The door slammed open, revealing a more than normally disheveled Letty. One would never have guessed that her little blue suit had been freshly pressed that morning. Joel knew for a fact it had been, of course, because he had watched her get dressed.

Letty's militant expression was not one whit marred by the fact that her glasses were tilted and she was slightly out of breath. Nor was her triumphant entrance hampered in the least by Mrs. Sedgewick, who was clutching at the hem of Letty's suit jacket.

"I tried to stop her, Mr. Blackstone," Mrs. Sedgewick called from behind Letty.

"Thank you, Mrs. Sedgewick. I know you did your best." Joel hid a grin. He got to his feet and gazed at Letty with polite inquiry. "Was there something you wanted, Ms. Thornquist?"

"Yes, there was. I mean, yes, there is something I want." Letty turned and closed the door in Mrs. Sedgewick's outraged face. Then she summoned up a lofty smile and aimed it at Diana. "I was told you were here, Mrs. Escott. I knew you would want to speak to me as well as to Joel. After all, the entire management team should be present for this kind of meeting, don't you think?"

Diana looked from Joel to Letty and back again. "What is going on here?"

"You'd never know it," Joel said, "but we're trying to run a company." He waited until Letty sat down, and then he resumed his own seat. "You may be interested to hear, Ms. Thornquist, that Professor Philip Dixon paid a recent visit to Echo Cove."

"He *what?*"

"Yes, I was a bit surprised to hear it myself. Apparently he's telling everyone who will listen that he intends to marry you and take control of Thornquist Gear."

"Oh, my God," Letty said, dismayed. She turned to Diana. "I imagine you've come here to find out what's really going on, haven't you?"

"Yes." Diana studied her coolly. "I take it there's no truth to Dixon's claims?"

"Heavens, no," said Letty. "Now, then, I hope we've settled that issue." She drew herself up and straightened her shoulders, which did little to unrumple the blue jacket. "I suppose the next thing on your mind is the status of your husband's excellent management plan."

Diana glanced uncertainly at Joel. "Well, yes, as a matter of fact, it is. I was just telling Joel, and I may as well tell you, that it's cruel to let things drag along. It's obvious you're going to shut down Copeland Marine. Do it and get it done."

"What's your hurry, Diana?" Joel asked softly.

She shot him a grim, unreadable glance. "I want it over.

What's so hard to understand about that?" She stood up and walked stiffly to the window. "I just want it over. The uncertainty is making everything worse. Don't torture Keith by making him think his plan actually has possibilities. He doesn't deserve that."

Letty watched her. "Don't you think Keith's ideas should be examined before a decision is made?"

"No."

Joel glanced at Letty and discovered she was staring at him with a confused frown. He didn't blame her. He was feeling somewhat confused himself. "Why don't you want us to review the plan, Diana?"

"Because it's a waste of time, that's why." Diana shot him a quick glance and then turned her attention to the scene outside the window. "Daddy has never been able to use any of Keith's ideas. He says they're all garbage. Why would you find them worthwhile?"

Joel traded another glance with Letty. He was suddenly very glad she was in the room. He had the distinct impression he was missing something here. "Escott has done a lot of sound thinking. I'm not saying we're going to implement any portion of this plan, but I will say it's solid. He knows what he's doing."

Letty gave Joel an approving look, which Joel pretended to ignore. Diana, however, looked stricken.

"That's right, Diana," Letty said firmly. "We're not trying to torture anyone. Joel—I mean, Mr. Blackstone—and I are giving Keith's plan a thorough review and consideration."

"Don't," Diana murmured. "Please, don't. Go ahead and shut down Copeland Marine." She looked at Joel. "It's what you planned all along. Do it."

Joel eyed her curiously. But he said nothing, because Letty was getting to her feet and he suddenly trusted her instincts in this situation more than he did his own. He could not figure out what was going on.

"Are we to understand that you actually want us to liquidate your father's company, Diana?"

"Yes, damn it." Diana whirled around, eyes bright with unshed tears. "I told you I want you to close it down as soon as possible."

Joel leaned back in his chair. "Mind telling us why, Diana?"

But it was Letty who answered. "I think I know why," she said slowly. "You're afraid, aren't you, Diana? You're afraid that your husband can't handle whatever your father will dish out if we put Keith's plan into effect."

"Oh, God," Diana breathed, her voice tight. "Daddy will be furious if you use any of Keith's ideas. He'll take it as a personal affront. He's rejected every suggestion Keith has ever made for Copeland Marine. If you come along now and use Keith's plan to salvage the firm, I don't know what Daddy will do."

"You'd rather we shut down the entire operation, wouldn't you, Diana? Even if it means destroying the whole town of Echo Cove." Letty looked at her with deep sympathy. "You think that's the only way you can be free of your father."

Diana stared at her and then turned to Joel. "I didn't let you rescue me fifteen years ago, Joel, because I lost my nerve. I was too young to take such an enormous risk. Or maybe I wasn't desperate enough to give up everything then. But now I am. Don't you understand? Daddy's rages are getting worse."

"Now, hold on a second here, Diana." Letty studied her intently. "You're assuming that Keith doesn't have whatever it's going to take to stand up to your father if Victor turns on him, right?"

Diana knotted her hands into small fists. "Joel could have done it. He has done it. Look at how he's brought Copeland Marine to its knees. But Keith is different."

"I'm not so sure about that," Letty murmured.

Diana glared at her. "You think just because Keith managed to win a stupid brawl with Joel at the Anchor that makes him a macho guy? You think it makes Keith capable of standing up to Daddy?"

Joel cleared his throat and glowered at Letty. "I beg your pardon, Ms. Thornquist. Did you by some remote chance tell Diana that Escott won that fight?"

"Yes, I did." She gave him a frosty glance. "It's the truth, isn't it?"

"It's a matter of opinion," Joel said through set teeth.

"Well, it's only natural you would prefer to call it a draw," Letty said sympathetically. "I understand that it's unpleasant to have to admit you lost."

"Very unpleasant."

"But facts are facts," Letty continued brightly, "and we're in a tricky situation right now. We must stick to realities. And the primary thing to keep in mind is that I believe Keith Escott would be the ideal person to take over the management of Copeland Marine."

"You don't know what you're saying," Diana whispered. "You're a fool." She turned and walked out of the room.

15

A heavy silence hung over Joel's office after the door closed behind Diana. Letty waited uncomfortably for Joel to say something. When he did not, she smiled tentatively.

"Joel, you're not really upset because I told Diana that Keith pounded you into the floor during that bar fight, are you?"

"Pounded me into the floor?" Joel repeated softly. "It gets worse every time I hear the story."

"Pounded, flattened, beat to a pulp, what does it matter? It was in a good cause. I was trying to shore up their relationship a little."

"I take it you don't think my ego is a worthy cause?"

Letty grinned. "I think your ego could sustain a direct hit from a nuclear warhead without getting badly damaged."

"Thanks a lot. All the same, next time I'd appreciate it if you wouldn't have me lose quite so badly. Maybe I could at least give a good account of myself." Joel tossed a pen down on his desk and got to his feet. He stalked to the window.

Letty eyed him warily. "You're not really mad at me, are you?"

"No. If I was really mad at you, you'd know it."

Letty nodded. "That's what I figured. Now, then, tell me the truth. Were you serious when you told Diana that you're considering Keith's proposal?"

"I was serious." Joel didn't turn around. He kept his attention on the street below. "There's nothing wrong with Escott's plan. It could work."

"*Joel.* You mean you'll go for it?" Without giving him time to respond, Letty shot up out of her chair, dashed across the room, and threw her arms around Joel from behind. She hugged him fiercely. "You won't regret it, I swear it. It's the right thing to do. You'll see."

"I said I was thinking about it," Joel growled. "I didn't say I was committing myself to it. Do you mind telling me why you're so determined to save that rinky-dink town?"

Letty released him and took a step back. She was surprised at the question. "I'm doing it for your sake, of course."

"My sake?" Joel swung around to confront her. His face was rigid and his eyes were harsh. "What the hell is that supposed to mean?"

Letty cocked her head, uncertain how to explain it to him in terms he would accept. "Destroying the entire town would be too much for you to carry around on your conscience," she said gently. "Don't you see, Joel? Your plan goes beyond simple justice. It's overkill."

"I can handle my own conscience, Letty."

She touched him placatingly, willing him to think his vengeance through to the logical conclusion. "Think what will happen to all those families who depend on Copeland Marine for their livelihood. You know yourself what happens when people are thrown out of work. Look what it did to your father."

Joel's jaw clenched. "Damn it, Letty . . ."

"Joel, listen to me. I've read a number of articles on the

stress induced by unemployment. The rate of domestic violence jumps up. Crime goes up. So does divorce. Suicide rates increase." She saw him flinch at that, but she did not stop. "Yes, suicide, Joel."

"Christ, Letty, you read too damn many articles."

She kept pushing, sensing that he was listening, even though he did not like what he was hearing. "A wave of unemployment in a small community like Echo Cove will be devastating. Families will get sucked down into poverty. They'll wind up on welfare, and some of them may never get off. Do you really want that kind of thing on your conscience?"

"Stop worrying about my conscience." Joel grasped her shoulders and brought her close to his rigidly set face. "Do you hear me, Letty? I'll worry about my own goddamn conscience."

"You haven't done a very good job of it so far," she said. "You're still carrying around the burden your father stuck you with fifteen years ago. You're still feeling responsible for his death, aren't you?"

"I *was* responsible for it."

"No. No, you were not, Joel Blackstone." Letty flattened her palms against his chest. "You have carried his last words around with you for fifteen years, and you blame yourself for everything that happened. But you are not to blame, damn it. And it's time you realized it."

"If I hadn't screwed Diana Copeland, my father would be alive today. That's the bottom line here, Letty. Don't try to pretend it isn't."

"You were a young man in love, and Diana Copeland was a willing partner. You heard her a few minutes ago. She admitted she encouraged your affections because part of her wanted you to rescue her from her father's domineering grip."

"Letty, that's got nothing to do with this."

"The heck it doesn't," Letty retorted. "It has everything to do with it. You did not kill your father. By all accounts he was a very ill man. He never fully recovered from the death of your mother, and he was not equipped to handle the stress of getting fired."

"He blamed me," Joel said through his teeth.

"Well, he should have blamed Victor Copeland," Letty declared. "Copeland was the one who fired him without just cause. You're not responsible for another man's vicious or criminal behavior. Joel, listen to me. Chances are that what happened to your father that night was an accident. It's true, it might have been suicide. You'll never know the answer, and that may be hard to live with."

"Goddamn hard."

"I understand. But you must not continue to torture yourself with guilt. Go ahead and have your revenge on Victor Copeland. Copeland was grossly unfair when he punished your father for your actions. You've got a right to even the score. But let it end there."

Joel's hands dropped from her shoulders. He shoved his fingers through his hair. "I don't know if it will ever end, Letty."

"Some things don't," she admitted. "But you can contain them. You can keep them from obsessing you. And that's what this elaborate scheme to crush Copeland Marine is, when you get right down to it. An obsession. You've got better things to do with your life, Joel."

He shot her a savage glance. "Such as?"

Letty decided the moment had arrived to take the bull by the horns. "Well, for one thing, you're thirty-six years old. Isn't it time you started thinking about getting married and starting a family?"

"A *family*." He stared at her, clearly startled. "What the hell brought that up?"

"I don't know," Letty mumbled, regretting her impulsive words. "Maybe I've gone to one too many of Stephanie's baby classes." *And maybe I've fallen in love with you, Joel Blackstone,* she thought.

"Yeah, maybe you have been going to too many baby

classes. And reading too many articles." Joel gave her an odd look as he circled her to get back behind his desk. "Look, I've told you I'm giving Escott's proposal serious consideration. That's all I'm going to say now. Go pitch a tent or something. I want to do some thinking."

Letty fumbled for and found a wan smile. "That's no way to talk to the president of the company," she chided.

Joel's eyes gleamed. "You're right. Any good CEO who was properly focused on the corporate image would politely tell the president that her shirttail is hanging out in back."

Letty flushed and reached behind her to stuff the hem of her silk shirt back inside the waistband of her skirt. "It's Mrs. Sedgewick's fault. She kept grabbing at me when I was trying to get in here earlier."

"Why did you stage a knock-down, drag-out battle with Mrs. Sedgewick to interrupt Diana and me, anyway?" Joel asked softly.

Letty sniffed and started for the door. "For the sake of corporate decorum, naturally. It doesn't look good for a male CEO to be closeted alone with an attractive woman for a long time. I didn't want people to talk."

"Uh-huh. Is there just the remotest possibility that you were a touch jealous, Madam President? Perhaps feeling a tad possessive? Maybe even mildly alarmed by the thought of me being alone in here with another woman?"

Letty's hand was on the doorknob. "Nonsense. Jealousy is an irrational emotion. I'm not capable of that. Just ask my father."

"Few of us have your father's ability to rise above petty emotions," Joel drawled. "Some of us tend to wallow in them."

"Speak for yourself." Letty started to turn the doorknob and hesitated. "Joel?"

"Yeah?"

"Do you mind telling me exactly what you saw in Diana fifteen years ago?"

252

"In a nutshell?"

"Yes."

Joel shrugged. "She was the prettiest girl in town, and she was an incredible flirt. She was also spoiled rotten. When she decided she wanted a taste of walking on the wild side, which for her meant dating someone from the wrong side of the tracks, I jumped at the opportunity to accommodate her. After I got to know her a little better, I felt kind of sorry for her. I saw her as a bird in a gilded cage, I guess."

"But in the end you fell helplessly, mindlessly, passionately in love with her, didn't you?"

Joel's mouth quirked. "I'll tell you something, Letty. The phrase 'helplessly, mindlessly, passionately in love' has a slightly different meaning for a twenty-one-year-old male than it does for a thirty-six-year-old male."

Letty licked her lips. "So you would probably not feel that way about her today? If you were to meet her for the first time without all the past emotional baggage attached, say?"

"No. I wouldn't feel like that at all."

Letty's heart lifted at that. "Because you realize she's not really your type?"

Joel looked thoughtful. "I think it would be mostly because she looks too damn neat in a suit. I seem to be turned on by the rumpled look these days."

Letty slammed the door on her way out of the office. Mrs. Sedgewick glowered.

The following morning, ensconced behind her own desk and deep into a description of the new ad campaign for Pack Up and Go tents, Letty realized she was still stewing over what Joel had said after Diana left the office the previous day. Or, rather, over his startled surprise when she mentioned marriage and a family.

Okay, so he had obviously not been thinking a whole lot lately about getting married and starting a family.

One could attribute that to general male obtuseness.

Maybe he just needed a little prodding in the right direction. Letty brightened briefly at the thought that she had at least planted the notion in his brain. Now all she could do was wait and see if it took root.

On a more positive note, she felt reasonably secure now about his lack of romantic interest in Diana Escott. She had not sensed any deep undercurrents of romantic passion flowing between Joel and Diana. They definitely shared a past, and both were carrying scars from that past, but Letty was almost certain Joel was no longer attracted to the other woman.

Letty turned the page in the report on the ad campaign and frowned over a photo of a male model in the process of pitching one of the new tents.

The model appeared to have been taking steroids; he certainly had the biggest biceps Letty had ever seen. Everything else on him was rather large also. He could obviously have erected the new lightweight tent with one hand.

This was not the right image, Letty decided. The new line was being targeted at families who were not experienced campers. The ads needed to focus on ordinary people discovering how easy it was to handle the new line of Thornquist Gear.

Letty reached out to punch the intercom. Before she could activate it, Arthur's voice squawked anxiously. "Professor Dixon is on his way in to see you, Ms. Thornquist. Is that all right?"

Letty stifled a groan. "It's fine, Arthur."

A second later the office door swung open and Philip strode into the room. The first thing Letty noticed was that he was not wearing his usual tweed jacket and oxford-cloth shirt. Instead, he looked riveting in a silver-gray suit, pale pink silk shirt, and discreetly striped tie. There was a dark pink handkerchief in his breast pocket. He was wearing highly polished wingtips and carrying an expensive leather briefcase.

It was clear Philip had made the shift from respected professor to captain of industry.

"Good morning, Letty my dear." Philip smiled benignly down upon her. "How are you today?"

"Just fine, Philip." Letty eyed him warily. "May I ask what you thought you were doing in Echo Cove?"

"Got word of that did you?" Philip put down his briefcase and settled into the chair across from Letty. "I came across a reference to the takeover while I was going through some papers on your desk the other day. Thought I'd better check out the situation firsthand."

"I see." Letty put as much ice into her words as possible. "Philip, I don't think you understand how much I resent your high-handed actions. This is my company."

"Yes, yes, I know, my dear." Philip was apparently willing to be indulgent. "But, as we discussed, you definitely don't have the background to handle the cut and thrust of the business world." He chuckled. "This is hardly the reference desk at the Vellacott Library, is it?"

"I think I'm doing all right," Letty said. "Mr. Blackstone is quite capable of guiding me through the maze of the modern business environment. He has kindly agreed to act as my mentor."

Philip frowned. "That brings up a topic I think we should discuss immediately. My trip to Echo Cove revealed to me a great deal of information about our current CEO. I'm afraid the long and the short of it is that we shall have to dismiss Joel Blackstone."

Letty blinked. "I can assure you that will be easier said than done."

"Nonsense. Simply a matter of terminating his employment, just as one would do with any other incompetent manager. We can arrange a nice little bonus for him, if you like."

"I would hardly call Mr. Blackstone incompetent. He has single-handedly turned Thornquist Gear into a major northwestern corporation."

Philip made a tut-tutting sound. "Unfortunately, I feel that he is destined to be a victim of his own success. Frankly, he's risen above the level of his own competence. To put it bluntly, Letty, Thornquist Gear needs stronger, more dynamic, more modern leadership."

"No kidding."

"Thornquist requires a man of vision at the helm." Philip gave her a sober man-of-vision look. "It needs someone who can mix and mingle with the major players who occupy the upper strata of today's business world. It needs a man with a solid grounding in the intricacies of modern economics and finance. It needs a leader who knows how to network with other leaders in the industry."

"And that man is you?" Letty hazarded a guess.

Philip gave her an approving smile. "I knew you would understand that eventually. You're really quite bright in some ways, Letty."

A loud commotion in the outer office interrupted Letty before she could think of a suitable rejoinder to that comment.

"Where the hell is he?" Joel's voice was a muffled growl.

"Mr. Blackstone, wait, you can't go in there until I announce you." A heavy object, possibly Arthur's heavily laden in-basket, crashed to the floor. "Just a minute, sir."

"Out of my way, Bigley."

"You are not going to barge in there, Mr. Blackstone."

"The hell I'm not," Joel roared.

There was another thump, and then Arthur's voice rose to a defiant snarl. "Over my dead body, sir."

"Your choice, Bigley."

Letty jumped to her feet and rushed to the door. She flung it open and was confronted by Arthur's back. Her secretary had apparently thrown himself into the breach. He was braced, hands and feet spread out, blocking the doorway. When the door opened behind him, he nearly fell into the inner office.

"Ms. Thornquist," Arthur managed grimly, "everything's under control." He was not blinking because he had switched back to his glasses.

Joel bared his teeth at Letty. "Get him out of my way before I do something serious."

Letty sighed. "Thank you, Arthur. I will see Mr. Blackstone now."

Arthur scowled at Joel. "Are you sure, Ms. Thornquist? He definitely does not have an appointment."

"As it happens, I want to talk to him," Letty said smoothly. "Thank you for handling matters so forcefully, Arthur. You did an excellent job."

Arthur glowed. "Thank you, Ms. Thornquist."

Letty smiled politely at Joel. "Won't you come in, Mr. Blackstone?"

"Thank you, Ms. Thornquist." The sarcasm was as sharp as any blade. Joel threw Arthur a victorious smile. "And thank you for your gracious assistance, Bigley."

Arthur inclined his head coolly, sat down, and turned his back to him.

Joel walked past Letty and pinned Philip with a grim look. "What the hell did you think you were doing screwing around with Thornquist Gear business in Echo Cove?"

Philip was unruffled by the challenge. "Hello, Blackstone. Letty and I were just discussing your future employment status with this company."

"You were *what?*" Joel shot a scathing glance at Letty.

"It's okay," Letty assured him as she closed the door and resumed her seat. "I told him I didn't think we could fire you. Why don't you sit down, Joel?"

He ignored that. "Letty, I've had about enough of visiting professors. And I will not allow this idiot to interfere in what's going on between Thornquist Gear and Copeland Marine." He turned back to Philip. "Got that, Dixon?"

Philip twitched the crease of his silver-gray trousers with an unperturbed air. "As I was just starting to explain to Letty, I've had a few thoughts on the Copeland Marine maneuver."

"Spare me," Joel said. "I don't give a damn about your thoughts on it."

"Initially, I was displeased to see that you had engineered a venture as sophisticated as the buyout and takeover of Copeland Marine on your own, Joel."

"Letty, you'd better get him out of here before I throttle him."

Philip continued as if no one had spoken. "After all, you have no appropriate formal education and no practical experience in corporate management. As far as I have been able to determine, you lack an M.B.A. or any other suitable degree. Nor have you spent time working in management in any corporation other than Thornquist."

"Letty, I'm warning you . . ."

Philip nodded, as if to himself. "I am happy to say, however, that on the whole the takeover approach was fundamentally sound. Whether by luck or by instinct, you made all the right moves, Joel."

Joel sprawled in a chair looking thoroughly disgusted. Letty smiled sympathetically and shrugged to indicate there was no stopping Philip until he wound down.

"I must point out, though, that had I been running Thornquist at the time, I would not have picked Copeland Marine as a target. Doubtless the sell-off and liquidation of the machinery and facilities will yield a reasonable profit. But there really are not enough assets to make the project worthwhile."

Joel ceased listening. He turned to Letty and began to talk to her as if they were alone in the room. "I called Escott. Told him I want to talk to him."

Letty smiled happily. "You did?"

Philip frowned vaguely but continued holding forth. "Your choice of a target company appears to have been influenced by some emotional motivation on your part, Blackstone. One does not survive in the business world if one makes too many decisions based on gut-level emotion."

Joel kept his gaze on Letty. "I told Escott we'd have dinner with him and Diana tonight. I'll lay all my cards on the table then. Can you make it?"

"Yes, yes, of course," Letty said quickly before he could change his mind. She glanced at her calendar. "I don't have any class to attend with Stephanie tonight."

"Good. I want you there," Joel said. "You're better at reading these people than I am."

"Why, thank you." Letty was thrilled at the compliment. He was beginning to appreciate her business talents, she thought.

Philip leaned forward in a bid for attention. "Are we by any chance discussing dinner with Mr. and Mrs. Keith Escott?"

"Letty and I were discussing it," Joel informed him. "You were not involved in the conversation, as far as I can recall."

Philip looked at Letty with an expression of disapproval. "I'm not so sure it's a good idea to meet with Escott, Letty. Matters are at a rather touchy stage right now. Best leave this sort of thing in my hands."

Joel stood up. "Speaking of touchy matters, Professor."

Philip glanced at him. "Yes?"

"I wonder if I might have your expert opinion on something that I have been debating for some time now."

"Certainly, certainly."

Letty stared at Joel, immediately alarmed by the smooth, deferential tone. "Uh, Joel . . . I mean, Mr. Blackstone—"

"This is an executive matter, Letty," Joel told her in an authoritative tone. "A little over your head." He smiled thinly at Philip. "What do you say we go down the hall to the elevator, Professor Dixon? I want you to look at an item in our new product line."

"Be glad to take a look." Philip got to his feet and picked up his briefcase. "I'll be in touch with you later, my dear."

"Good-bye, Philip."

Letty watched with increasing dread as Joel guided Philip

out of the office. She waited until she heard them walk out into the hall, and then she scurried after them.

"Ms. Thornquist?" Arthur looked up in concern. "Did you want something?"

"Shush." Letty waved him to silence and peeked cautiously around the edge of the outer door.

Joel had his finger on the elevator call button, his head bent in respectful consideration of whatever Philip was saying. Letty watched as the elevator arrived and the doors opened.

Philip stepped inside, still pontificating. Joel nodded sagely then reached inside to the control panel and punched a button. He hovered between the elevator doors until the last possible second. Then he stepped back into the hall and let them close on Philip, who was still holding forth.

The elevator descended minus one occupant.

Joel turned to see Letty watching the show. His brows rose with mocking innocence. "He's on his way to the basement. You see? It's simple to get rid of a pompous ass."

Letty walked down the hall to where he was standing. "I'll keep that trick in mind next time you become annoying."

Joel leaned one arm against the wall and looked down at her with gleaming eyes. "Mind telling me what you ever saw in him?"

"I don't know," Letty said thoughtfully. "Maybe it's the way he looks in a suit. Kind of dashing, don't you think?" She surveyed Joel's unbuttoned collar. "I've always been a sucker for a guy with a tie."

Morgan called at three-thirty, right after his last class of the day. Letty finished making a note regarding the over-developed male model in the tent ad and picked up the phone.

"Hi, Dad. What's up?"

"Normally I wouldn't bother you with this sort of thing, Letty. But I am a bit concerned."

Letty put down her pen. "About Stephanie?"

"You know?"

"About her earlier miscarriage? Yes, she told me last night. I'm glad she finally talked to you."

"She says you persuaded her to confide in me. I can't believe she's been holding all that anxiety inside all these months. She should have told me about her fears back at the beginning."

"She didn't want you to think she was behaving irrationally."

Morgan paused. "Yes. I hadn't realized. I told her I knew what she was going through and that I understood only too well. Mary was pregnant once before you were born. She had a miscarriage, too."

"Mother had one? I didn't know that."

"No reason you should. It happened years ago, but I still remember the shock. And I also recall how nervous Mary was when she first realized she was pregnant again with you. She was afraid of history repeating itself. We sweated out the first months of the second pregnancy together."

"Did you tell all that to Stephanie?" Letty asked.

"Of course. It seemed to help somewhat. She's still anxious, but at least now she feels free to talk about it." Morgan hesitated. "I wanted to thank you, Letty."

Letty smiled into the phone. "For telling her it was okay to tell you the whole story? No problem. I explained that beneath that overeducated exterior, there still beats the heart of a nice midwestern farm boy."

Morgan chuckled. "You and Mary were always good at that kind of thing, Letty."

"What kind of thing?"

"Understanding the emotional side of people. Figuring out what made them tick."

"Mother was terrific at it. I'm not so sure about me. As proof positive that I make major mistakes when it comes to judging people, there's the infamous example of my engagement to Professor Philip Dixon. Earlier today Joel asked me what I ever saw in Philip. It was a good question. I didn't have a good answer."

Morgan coughed slightly to clear his throat. "That brings up another subject. I've been thinking about your announcement the other evening, Letty."

"What announcement?"

"The one in which you stated you are, shall we say, involved in a romantic liaison with Joel Blackstone."

"It's more than a romantic liaison on my part. I'm in love with the man, Dad."

"I see." Morgan sighed. "I was afraid of that. How does he feel?"

Letty considered the question. "Right now he's too wrapped up in this Copeland Marine business to stop and analyze his own feelings."

"Translated, does that mean his feelings for you are not as strong as yours for him?" Morgan asked dryly.

A small chill went down Letty's spine. She scowled at the receiver. "He just needs a little time."

"Letty, you misjudged Philip Dixon. Don't make a second error in judgment. Have you drawn up that decision matrix yet?"

"No," Letty admitted.

"Do it, Letty. A woman in your position must think with her head, not her heart. The owner of Thornquist Gear cannot afford to allow herself to be carried away by uncontrolled passion. I don't want to see you hurt."

Letty said good-bye and hung up the phone. Her father was right about one thing. She had better start facing reality. The bottom line was that she did not really want an affair with Joel Blackstone.

True, it had been exciting at first. And it was still exciting, the most exciting thing she had ever done. She could hardly deny that. But deep down she had a strong feeling that she was not really cut out for an affair.

The day she started sleeping with Joel Blackstone, a part of her had begun planning on marriage.

She did not really understand affairs. When you got right down to it, they were pointless. She had been raised to think in terms of commitment and love and family.

Back where she came from, people got married when they fell in love.

16

That's the offer, Escott," Joel said that evening. "Eighteen months to prove you can pull Copeland Marine out of the red and that's all. Take it or leave it."

Letty held her breath as she and everyone else at the table waited for Keith's response. Around them the restaurant in the downtown hotel where the Escotts were staying hummed with muted conversation and the clink of glassware and cutlery. The tension at the table had been thick as Joel spelled out the terms of the deal. But there had also been a palpable aura of excitement and enthusiasm around Keith. And he responded to Joel's offer in a heartbeat.

"I'll take it," Keith said.

Joel nodded. "Okay, it's a deal. For the moment, I want absolute secrecy on this. I'll tell Copeland myself—when we're ready. Understood?"

"Sure." Keith smiled faintly. "You've got a right, although I'll have to admit it would have given me a great deal of pleasure to hand the old man an early retirement."

Letty saw Diana's lips tighten. Across the table, the women's eyes met. There was anger and something else in Diana's gaze. Letty suddenly realized the other ingredient was fear.

But Diana said nothing as her husband and Joel fell into an intense discussion of just how the five-year plan would be implemented during the first few months. Letty kept quiet as she, too, listened to Joel's cool, logical, and well-organized comments.

He really was good at this sort of thing, Letty thought. He had a flair for business, and he appeared to thrive on it. It was obvious he was in his element.

For his part, Keith was showing an ambitious and aggressively enthusiastic side that was clearly taking Diana by surprise. Head slightly bent, she toyed with her food and sipped continually at her wine. After a few minutes she looked up and met Letty's eyes again.

"I'm going to go upstairs to our room for a minute. Would you mind coming with me?" Diana asked bluntly.

Letty slid a quick glance at Joel, but he was concentrating on something Keith was saying. She reluctantly placed her napkin on the table. "All right."

Diana stood up quickly. "Please excuse us," she murmured to the men. "We'll be back in a minute."

Keith broke off a comment about finding new suppliers and smiled at his wife. "Sure, honey."

Joel raised an inquiring brow at Letty, who gave him a small silent shrug. He turned back to Keith as she left the table with Diana.

Diana said nothing as Letty accompanied her out of the restaurant and into the large lobby. They walked in silence to the bank of elevators. Letty could feel Diana's stiff, angry tension all the way up to the twentieth floor, where they got out and started down the hall. She was wondering if she ought to say something to break the charged silence when Diana finally spoke.

"I know you're wondering what this is all about."

Diana inserted her key into the lock and moved into the room.

"I think I have a good idea." Letty followed her into the room and closed the door. "You're opposed to Keith taking over the reins of Copeland Marine, aren't you?"

"Opposed to it?" Diana whirled around to confront Letty. Her face was tight and drawn. "I'm scared to death. I'm terrified. I'd give anything to stop it. The whole thing is going to be a disaster and yes, *yes,* I'm opposed to it. My God, that's putting it mildly."

Letty eyed her thoughtfully. "Are you that certain Keith can't pull it off?"

"I have no idea if Keith can save the company or not. How would I know what he's capable of doing? He's never had a chance to prove what he can handle in the three years we've been married. That's not the point."

Letty sat down in one of the chairs near the window. "What is the point, Diana?"

"Daddy." The single word was spoken in a stark, desperate tone.

Letty watched her. "Are you telling me you're really afraid of your father? Of what he'll do when he finds out that control of Copeland Marine has been taken away from him?"

"Yes." Diana's hands clenched and unclenched. "I'm scared to death of what he'll do. Keith won't listen to me, and I know Joel doesn't give a damn."

Letty was silent for a moment, unsure of how to probe further. Then she decided to be blunt. "Do you think your father's capable of violence?"

Diana's eyes snapped to hers and then away again. "I don't know," she whispered. "That's the worst part. I'm not sure if I'm right to be this frightened. But I have seen Daddy get very angry. He loses control, gets almost wild. Lately I've had the feeling he's closer to the edge than ever before."

Letty frowned. "How often has this happened?"

"Not often, thank God. I think he beat my mother a few times. She lied about it. Told me she'd fallen or something, and God help me, I wanted to believe her. It was only when I got older that I realized Daddy had hit her. She never would admit it, though. Until the day she died, she denied it. I think she was trying to protect me from the truth."

"How often has he gotten violent since your mother's death?"

"The worst time was fifteen years ago when he caught me in that barn with Joel." Diana's breathing seemed labored. "I thought he was going to kill him. Daddy had a length of wood, and he kept swinging it, kept trying to crush Joel. If Joel hadn't been as quick and as strong as he was, I know Daddy would have killed him. I know it."

Letty shivered as her imagination painted a vivid picture of the scene in the barn. "Any other instances?"

"Nothing I'm sure of. I think he punched one of his employees during an argument a few years ago, but it was hushed up. No one said anything about it, and the man left the yard soon afterward. I'm sure that wasn't the only time that sort of thing occurred."

"Diana . . ."

Diana massaged her temples. "You have to understand, it isn't what's happened so far that has me frightened; it's what *could* happen. I know Daddy is getting worse. I can feel it."

"Are you telling me you think he'll come after Joel once he hears what's happening with Copeland Marine?"

Diana got to her feet, her eyes tortured. "It's Keith I'm worried about. Don't you see? Daddy has spent three years telling me that he wishes he'd never encouraged me to marry Keith. He treats Keith like dirt. He ignores him half the time, and the other half of the time he taunts him. I'm terrified of what he'll do when he discovers Keith will be the one giving the orders around Copeland Marine."

"I see," Letty whispered, absorbing the implications.

"If Joel walked into Daddy's office and took charge

directly, that would be one thing." Diana moved to the dressing table and picked up a brush. She stared at it as if wondering what it was and then set it back down again. "Joel is tough. Strong. He could handle Daddy. But Keith is different."

"What you're really saying is that you don't think Keith can handle your father."

Diana's eyes widened in frustration. "He hasn't been able to handle him for the past three years. Why should he be able to do it now?"

"I don't know. Why don't you ask him why he's so determined to take over Copeland Marine and save it?" Letty suggested softly.

"I know why he wants to save it." Diana snatched up a tissue and carefully blotted her eyes. "It was part of the deal. He married me because Daddy dangled the lure of Copeland Marine in front of him."

"Why did you marry him?"

"Because Daddy handpicked him for me, and I thought that because Daddy approved of him, he was the one man in the world I could safely marry."

Letty took a deep breath. "I see. You were afraid to marry anyone else because of what your father might do?"

"Yes. I thought I was playing it safe. But the joke was on me. I fell in love with Keith in spite of everything."

Letty thought about that. "I don't think Keith would have stuck around to be treated like dirt by your father for three years just because he hoped eventually to get his hands on the firm. Keith's very smart. That's obvious from the five-year plan he put together. He would have seen the writing on the wall back at the beginning and cut his losses, unless he had another reason for sticking around."

Diana stared at her. "What other reason could there have been?"

"Well, it sure wasn't the prospect of taking over a failing company like Copeland Marine. Why on earth would he want that mess?" Letty smiled. "Has it occurred to you that Keith married you and has tolerated your father all this time simply because he loves you?"

Diana wadded up the tissue in one hand. "It's not that simple. It's never that simple when you're Victor Copeland's daughter. God, I thought it would be all right when I married Keith. Now I'm more vulnerable than ever. Keith has been talking about having children, but I can't even bear the thought. A baby would be one more hostage for Daddy to use to control us."

Letty shivered. "Diana, has your father ever been violent with you? Ever hurt you?"

She shook her head. "No. Not physically." Her smile was grim and tremulous. "I was his little golden girl for years. And as long as I played that role, I got anything I wanted. But whenever I tried to do anything on my own or make my own decisions, he got so *angry.*"

"And his anger frightened you?"

Diana nodded. "I finally told him I didn't care if he cut me off without a cent. I was tired of being a bird in a gilded cage, as Joel used to call me. But after that scene in the barn I realized Daddy might do something a lot worse than just take away my inheritance if I made him too angry."

"So you've been living with what amounts to emotional blackmail for fifteen years?" Letty concluded, incredulous.

Diana bit her lip and looked away. "In a sense. And, heaven help me, I've had to blackmail others in order to keep them safe. Every time Keith talked about leaving Echo Cove and starting over somewhere else, I told him I didn't want to leave. I told him I wanted him to stay at Copeland Marine. But the truth is, I was afraid of what Daddy would do if we defied him."

Letty got to her feet and walked over to Diana. "When Joel showed up again after all these years, you really did think he was going to rescue you, didn't you?"

"I thought that if he closed down Copeland Marine once

and for all, Keith and I would be free. We could go somewhere else. We'd have an excuse to leave town. Yes, I thought he was going to rescue me at last." Diana burst into tears. "But it's turning out all wrong. Now Keith is in danger."

"Have you talked to Keith about this?" Letty asked.

"I tried, but he won't listen. He says he can handle it."

Letty hesitated. "I'll talk to Joel. I'll make sure he takes the possibility of violence into account when he makes his plans. But I think that's all we can do. You saw Keith and Joel downstairs. They're really into this new plan. Neither of them is going to back off just because of some vague fears on our part."

"I know," Diana said. "I feel like Cassandra. I'm trying to warn everyone, but no one will listen."

"What did you and Diana talk about when you left the table this evening?" Joel asked an hour later when he opened the door of Letty's apartment.

"Her father." Letty walked into the hall and let her coat slide from her shoulders. She tossed it over the back of the couch and sat down. "She's afraid of him, Joel."

"Bull. He's always given her everything she wanted." He went into the kitchen and started opening cupboards. "She's not afraid of him; she's afraid of what things are going to be like when he's no longer in charge in Echo Cove."

Letty slid her feet out of her high heels. "No, that's not it. She's genuinely afraid of him. Afraid he might hurt Keith. She says she's been afraid of the potential violence in her father since that day he found you and her together in the barn." Letty met Joel's eyes as he walked back into the living room carrying two snifters of brandy. "Did Copeland try to kill you that afternoon?"

Joel shrugged. "If that teak board he was swinging had connected with my skull, he probably would have killed me, yeah."

"Oh, my God," Letty whispered.

"Hey, don't look so panicked. It was fifteen years ago, and you've got to remember he hated my guts for daring to touch his precious darling daughter. He doesn't hate Escott. Hell, Keith told me this evening that Copeland actually introduced him to Diana. Encouraged the marriage."

Letty sighed. "I don't know, Joel. I'm starting to get really worried. I hope this is all going to work out."

Joel looked at her and smiled dangerously. "It better. It was all your idea, remember?"

Letty's eyes widened. Joel was right. The entire plan to save Copeland Marine was going forward because she had pushed it from the beginning. "Oh, my God."

"Welcome to the real world, Madam Librarian. I warned you that you weren't sitting in your ivory tower back in Iowa any longer."

"Indiana," she corrected automatically.

But there was no real heat in her response. Her mind was too busily occupied with the potential ramifications of what was happening and with the realization that she would be responsible if disaster struck.

That night it was Letty who found herself awake at two o'clock in the morning. She lay in bed, gazing up into the shadows and wondering if she was coming down with the flu. She felt somewhat nauseated.

Joel scowled at the brief memo from Marketing that he found on his desk the next morning.

TO: Joel Blackstone
FROM: C. Manford
RE: Ad campaign for Pack Up and Go camping equipment.

Thought you ought to know that Ms. Thornquist has told us she does not like the male model used in the ads. She suggests we scrap the photos and shoot a new sequence featuring people who look like novices rather than experts.

Okay to rework thrust of campaign?

Joel swore softly. It irritated him to have to admit it, but Letty did have a point. She had hit on what was wrong with the entire campaign. The problem was that time was running out. The new line of camping gear would be in the stores in a few weeks. Decisions had to be made.

"The hell with it," Joel muttered. Letty's instincts on some things seemed to be better than his. He had been unsure of the beefcake campaign right from the start. He picked up a pen and scrawled a message to Manford telling him to go ahead and reshoot the photos using plenty of kids and moms.

Letty was achieving one victory after another around the offices of Thornquist Gear, Joel reflected as he shoved the approval memo into his out-basket. Arthur Bigley was now one hundred percent loyal to her. The ad campaign was virtually under Letty's guidance. The manuals for the new tents were being rewritten. Copeland Marine was not going to be liquidated.

It was enough to make a man shiver in his boots. One of these days, if he was not extremely careful, Joel told himself ruefully, he was going to wake up and discover that Letty was actually running things around here.

Half an hour later Mrs. Sedgewick's voice droned on the intercom. "Ms. Thornquist to see you, sir."

Joel started to tell her to send Letty in, but before he could say anything, the door flew open and Letty burst into the room. Her eyes were very bright and she was laughing with delight. She waved a copy of the memo he had signed off on half an hour earlier.

"Thank you, Mr. Blackstone. I knew you'd approve it. You did the right thing." She hurriedly closed the door on Mrs. Sedgewick and then she dashed across the room.

She leaned down and kissed Joel full on the mouth. "Do you know what I really like about you, Joel Blackstone?"

"I'm good in bed?"

"That's beside the point." Her eyes gleamed happily. "What I really like about you is that you listen to me. Even when you're annoyed with me, you pay attention to what I have to say. I can't wait to get started on this new campaign."

She whirled around and raced back out of the office, shirttail flying.

Joel smiled to himself and went back to work.

At eleven-thirty Mrs. Sedgewick's voice on the intercom again interrupted his thoughts. "A Mr. Victor Copeland to see you, sir."

Adrenaline pumped into Joel's veins. He had been expecting this. He had known that sooner or later Copeland would approach him directly and try to make a deal. It was the only option left for him.

This was it. After fifteen years, Joel knew he was about to deliver the coup de grace.

"Send him in, Mrs. Sedgewick."

Victor Copeland strode into the office, looking oddly out of his element. Back in Echo Cove, he was a tin god. Here in Seattle, he was just one more aging fat man in a business suit. The flesh of his short, massive neck rolled over the edge of his too-tight collar. His jowly face was heavily lined with suppressed anger and an element of desperation. His small eyes gleamed malevolently.

"Looks like you've done all right for yourself, Blackstone." Victor scanned the office furnishings as he lowered himself into a chair. "Never would have thought you could get this far."

"I know what you thought of me, Copeland," Joel said. "but that's ancient history, isn't it? Why are you here today?"

Copeland narrowed his eyes. "I'll lay it on the line for you.

273

I'll admit I made a mistake fifteen years ago. Should have let you marry my girl. You've got guts. You could have handled Copeland Marine."

"It's a little late to come to that conclusion, isn't it?"

"Don't see why," Victor said smoothly. "No reason we can't all take up right where we left off fifteen years ago."

Joel eyed him, barely concealing his amazement. "What the hell is that supposed to mean?"

"Just what it sounds like. I'm ready to make a deal, Blackstone. You back off on the takeover of Copeland Marine and I'll let you have Diana."

"Jesus." Joel could hardly believe what he was hearing. "You'll let me have her?"

"Sure, why not? You always did want her, ain't that right? Couldn't keep your goddamn hands off of her."

"That was a long time ago, Copeland. Things have changed. In case you've forgotten, Diana is married to someone else at the moment."

Copeland snorted. "Escott's no problem. Diana can get a divorce. Fact is, I'll be glad to get rid of Escott. He's always hounding me, trying to get me to try something new, telling me we need to alter the contracts we've been usin' for years and get new suppliers. Damn fool. I made a mistake when I picked him out for Diana. I'll admit that."

"You've made a lot of mistakes over the years, haven't you, Copeland?" Joel smiled grimly. "But the biggest one you made was firing Dad because of what I'd done."

Copeland flinched, and then his face began turning purple. "It was your fault, you son of a bitch. If you hadn't touched my Diana, I never would have fired your pa."

All your fault. Joel tried to push aside the nightmare image of his father screaming silently through the window of the sinking car. *All your fault.*

He breathed deeply, just as he did when he was running. It was going to be finished very soon, he reminded himself.

"You had a right to go after me." Joel sat forward, his

hands flat on the desk. "But you had no right to punish Dad for what I'd done."

"Shit, that happened fifteen years ago. I was pissed off. Everyone in Echo Cove knows better than to get me pissed off. Everyone except you."

Joel shrugged. "I'm sure you'll be pleased to know that the management of Thornquist Gear has decided to give Copeland Marine another eighteen months to pull itself out of the red."

Relief appeared first in Copeland's eyes. It was followed by an expression of triumph. "I knew it. Knew you'd back off in the end. It was that little Thornquist gal, wasn't it? She wouldn't let you shut Copeland down because she knew what it would do to the town."

This was it. This was the moment he had been waiting for, Joel thought. He searched himself for some powerful sense of satisfaction, but all he seemed to be experiencing was a cold, distant curiosity. It was as if he were an observer rather than the one taking revenge.

"Don't get too excited, Copeland. Your company has been given an eighteen-month extension, but you haven't."

"What the hell are you talking about? Nobody can run that company except me and you damn well know it. Copeland Marine is mine."

"Not anymore. As of today, you are no longer president of Copeland Marine. In fact, as the owner of the controlling interest in the firm, I am ordering you not to set foot on Copeland Marine property unless and until I give approval."

Copeland's jaw dropped. "What are you tryin' to say, you bastard? You think you can run my company from here?"

"No. I'm putting your son-in-law in charge. Escott assumes the reins officially this afternoon. You're out of the picture as of right now."

"*Escott.* That gutless pansy? You can't turn it over to him. Copeland Marine is my company! It's always been my

275

company." Copeland surged to his feet. His hands balled up into massive fists at his sides. "Nobody takes Copeland Marine away from me. You hear me, Blackstone? Nobody."

"I hear you." Sensing the violence in Copeland, Joel stood up slowly. He realized he was hoping the man would take a swing.

"Nobody." Copeland swept his arm over the surface of Joel's desk, knocking the wire basket, calendar, lamp, and a sheaf of files onto the carpet. "You can't do this to me."

Joel smiled savagely. "What are you so upset about, Copeland? I'm only doing to you what you did to my father. I'm firing you. No big deal. You can always go look for another job, can't you?"

"You goddamn bastard." Copeland reached down and scooped up the fallen lamp. He started to swing it at Joel the same way he had once swung a length of solid teak.

"Just like old times, isn't it, Copeland?" Joel taunted softly. "Come on. Let's see you try it. Give me the excuse I've been looking for to take you apart."

Copeland raised his huge arm. *"Fucking bastard."*

The office door opened.

"Excuse me," Philip Dixon said with astonishing calm. "Am I interrupting anything?" He looked from Joel to Copeland, a slight frown furrowing his elegant brow. "Hello, Copeland. Here to make a last-minute pitch to save Copeland Marine? Afraid there's not much point. Blackstone is quite correct when he says that the only realistic alternative is liquidation. I've consulted on any number of similar situations, and one has to face facts."

Copeland stared at Philip for an instant. Then he hurled the lamp down onto the carpet in a gesture of frustrated fury.

He stormed out of the office without another word.

Joel watched him go, and then he turned to Philip. "Nice timing, Dixon."

"Copeland appeared rather upset."

"Yeah, he did, didn't he?" Joel looked at Mrs. Sedgewick,

who was hovering uncertainly in the doorway. "Call Escott at his hotel. Tell him I want to talk to him immediately. And then get someone in here to clean up this mess."

"Yes, sir." Mrs. Sedgewick, looking unusually subdued, vanished.

Philip cleared his throat to get attention. "I stopped by to talk to you about the details of the Copeland Marine liquidation. As it happens, I have a few thoughts on the matter."

Joel planted his hands on his desk and leaned forward. "Dixon, I am not in a good mood. The last thing I want to do right now is listen to you pontificate about my business. Get the hell out of here. Now."

Something in Joel's icy tone must have finally penetrated Philip's pompous arrogance. He drew himself up with an affronted expression. "Well, if you feel that way about it, I'll come back later."

"Don't bother."

Philip did not deign to respond to that. He took himself off and politely closed the door behind him. Joel stood at his desk, breathing slowly and deeply for a couple of minutes before he sat down.

It was done. After all these years, it was finally done.

Joel still could not identify what he was feeling. There should have been a sense of release. A sensation of triumph. Something powerful.

But all he seemed to be able to think about now was the more practical matter of the safety of the Copeland Marine yard. Victor Copeland had looked dangerous.

Mrs. Sedgewick buzzed the intercom. "Mr. Escott on line two."

Joel grabbed the phone. "Escott?"

"What's up? Something wrong?"

"Copeland was just here. I gave him the news."

"How did he take it?" Keith asked tensely.

"He's mad as hell, and he's looking for trouble."

"That figures. Any idea what he might do?"

277

"My chief concern is that he'll decide if he can't have Copeland Marine, nobody else can have it, either," Joel said. He stared unseeingly out the window, trying to think of all the possibilities and how to cover them.

"You think he might try to torch the yard or something?" Keith asked.

"I don't know. I don't think so, because in his mind, Copeland Marine is his and it will always be his. He would be destroying his own creation. But I've seen Copeland like this once before. He's unpredictable until he calms down."

"I know what you mean. I've seen him in a rage once or twice. He went after one of his employees once. Took three of us to pull him off. It takes him a while to come out of it."

"I know. All right, Escott, as of right now you are one hundred percent responsible for the Copeland Marine facilities."

"I understand," Keith said coolly. "Guess I'd better get my ass down to Echo Cove and make sure Copeland doesn't take the place apart."

"Yeah, you'd better do that." Joel rubbed the back of his neck, thinking quickly. "And I think you'd better organize a twenty-four-hour security guard on the yard for a while. No point in taking any chances."

There was a pause on the other end of the line. "I'll take care of it."

"I'll have my secretary give you the name of a security agency here in Seattle. I used them a couple of times when I was having some loading-dock theft problems. Contact them immediately and get as many men as you'll need to guard the Copeland yard."

"Got it. Listen, Blackstone . . ."

"Yeah?"

"I'm leaving Diana here at the hotel," Keith said quietly. "Her father doesn't know where she is. I didn't tell anyone where we're staying. I don't want her anywhere near Echo Cove until things have cooled down. And I don't want her to know all the details of what's going on right now. She'll panic."

"She's your wife, Escott. Tell her whatever you want to tell her. Just make sure Copeland doesn't torch that yard."

"I'm on my way." Beneath the cool, efficient tone, Keith's voice was filled with exultant determination. "Hey, Blackstone?"

"Yeah?"

"Thanks. You won't regret this."

"Make sure I don't."

Joel hung up the phone, aware that in Keith's mind Copeland Marine already belonged to him.

Joel drummed his fingers rapidly on the desk. Things could get nasty, as he had warned Letty last night. But he had known that was a possibility from the beginning. Victor Copeland was not going to surrender control of Copeland Marine and all that went with it very easily.

Joel had taken that reality into account when he was planning to liquidate the firm. But he had always assumed that if Copeland lost control and went for someone's throat, it would be his.

Now there were other forces involved. Maybe too many other forces. Too many other people.

Joel's restlessness grew. He usually felt this way only in the middle of the night when he was unable to sleep.

He thought about changing into his sweats and going for a run along the waterfront. Then he realized that what he really needed was to talk to Letty.

Letty had a way of helping him see things more clearly at times. She would understand the new elements in the equation, the emotional and human elements that he sometimes misunderstood or simply ignored.

Joel leaned forward and punched his intercom button. "Mrs. Sedgewick, put me through to Ms. Thornquist's office."

"Yes, sir."

A moment later Bigley came on the line, his voice infused with new self-confidence and an awesome aura of competence.

"This is Ms. Thornquist's executive assistant, sir. I regret to inform you that Ms. Thornquist is unavailable. She has just left for lunch with Professor Dixon."

17

Now, then, Letty, I've already contacted Dr. Sweetley and told her the nature of your problems. We've made an appointment for you on Monday afternoon. I think you'll like her. She seems quite competent." Philip surveyed the grilled salmon the waiter had placed in front of him. "We were lucky she could work you into her schedule so quickly."

Letty ignored her pan-fried oysters and fries. She rested her elbows on the table and propped her chin on the back of her laced fingers. "Philip, you really are something else, you know that? Absolutely incredible."

He smiled. "Thank you, my dear. It's good to hear you sounding more like yourself. Although I do understand why you've been avoiding me lately."

"You do?"

"Certainly. When I discussed your attitude with Dr. Sweetley, she explained that you were naturally somewhat ambivalent about a return to the status quo of our relationship."

Letty shook her head. "'Ambivalent' is a rather ambivalent term for what I feel. I can give you a much more precise description, if you like."

"No need." Philip dissected his salmon with a knife and fork, searching cautiously for bones. "According to Dr. Sweetley you suffered from low-self esteem during our relationship due to your inability to experience orgasm."

"For heaven's sake, Philip. Not so loud." Letty felt herself growing hot with embarrassment and irritation. She glanced around quickly to make certain Philip had not been overheard.

She had agreed to have lunch with him on the spur of the moment. He had walked into her office claiming that they really needed to talk. Letty had decided it was time to try to make him understand that she had absolutely no intention of ever renewing the engagement.

She also had to evict Philip from Thornquist Gear in a peaceable manner before Joel lost his patience entirely. Letty was afraid the little scene she had witnessed at the elevators yesterday was only the beginning. There was no telling what Joel would do the next time Philip annoyed him.

Philip was sparing no expense on lunch, Letty acknowledged. The restaurant, stylishly decorated in Art Deco tones of pink and green with accents of black, was located near the Pike Place Market. It was packed with tourists and local business people who were "doing lunch." Letty wondered how Philip had discovered the place. Perhaps Dr. Sweetley had recommended it.

"Dr. Sweetley has also suggested that you are no doubt experiencing some generalized anxiety about our relationship and that you are in a state of denial regarding your inability to fully satisfy your sexual partner."

"Is that right?"

"Yes. She says you are probably projecting, and it is also

very likely that you are practicing some form of sublimation. Personally, I suspect running Thornquist Gear has become a substitute for sex for you."

"Philip, what would you say if I told you that I don't have to substitute anything for sex? That I'm getting plenty of the real thing?"

Philip gave her a concerned look. "Dr. Sweetley explained that you might insist that you were happy in a new relationship. Trying to convince me that you are sexually involved with another man is a way of venting your hostility, as I'm sure you're well aware. It's all right, my dear. There is no need to invent another relationship."

Letty gritted her teeth. "Let's try this again from the top, Philip. I will spell this out for you in short, easily understood sentences. Our engagement is over. I have no desire to start it up again. I do not want to marry you. I do not want your help managing Thornquist Gear. I have a CEO to help me do that. Furthermore—"

Philip held up a hand. "That brings up an interesting point." He frowned thoughtfully as he put down his fork. "We really must arrange to terminate Blackstone immediately. I told you I do not care for the way he is handling this takeover and liquidation of Copeland Marine."

"Joel stays," Letty said.

"I really don't think we can allow that. I must tell you, Letty, that I have come to the conclusion that Blackstone wields too much influence over you."

With that, Letty lost her temper entirely. There was no point in trying to talk to Philip. She got to her feet and leaned forward, hands flat on the table. "I said he stays. He works for me. I own Thornquist Gear. *He stays.*"

Philip's expression turned to one of reproach. "I can see that the stress you've been under lately has taken its toll. It's a good thing I scheduled that appointment with Dr. Sweetley for you."

Letty stared at him. "You haven't heard a single thing I've said, have you? You've never heard a word I said unless it agreed with something you said. At least Joel talks to me. Even when he's mad at me, he hears what I'm saying. I cannot believe I was ever stupid enough to get engaged to you."

Philip began to look alarmed. "Letty, you must get control of yourself, my dear."

"I am in complete control of myself." Letty glanced down at her plate of pan-fried oysters and fries. She scooped it up and dumped the contents over Philip's head before he realized her intention.

"Letty, have you lost your mind?" Philip brushed frantically at the french fries and oysters that were cascading down his face onto his gray-vested suit. He shot to his feet, grabbing up a napkin and using it to brush at the grease that was soaking into his jacket.

"I have only one other thing to say to you, Philip Dixon. Thank God for Gloria the grad student and her scarlet-tinted lips. If it hadn't been for her, it might have taken me a lot longer to realize what an insufferable ass you are."

Letty snatched up her purse, whirled and strode toward the door.

She collided with Joel, who had just walked into the restaurant. His arms went around her, steadying her.

"Something wrong with your lunch?" he inquired politely. "Or is that the way people eat their oysters back in Illinois?"

"Indiana," Letty muttered, her face buried against his chest. "What are you doing here?"

"I came looking for you, Madam President. In case you aren't aware of it, we've got a slight management crisis on our hands back at the office. You ready to leave?"

"Yes," she hissed, raising her head. She did not look back to see what was happening at the table. Letty could hear the commotion as waiters bustled to clean up the mess. "Let's get out of here."

"Spoken like a true executive."

Joel took her arm and steered her out of the restaurant

and onto the sidewalk. They forged their way through the noontime crowds thronging the red brick-paved street that ran through the heart of the Pike Place Market.

It was not easy, but Joel navigated with expert precision. They circled the crowd hovering around a fishmonger's stand, evaded two panhandlers and a mime, and managed to get past the long row of busy vegetable stalls.

Letty was still fuming silently when she realized Joel had come to a halt beside a tiny eatery selling walkaway food through a window that opened directly onto the sidewalk. "What are you doing?"

"Getting us some lunch. I take it you didn't have a chance to eat much of yours."

"No. I'm not hungry anymore."

"Nonsense," Joel said bracingly. "An executive has to keep up her energy." He looked at the young woman waiting on the other side of the counter. "Two hummus and pita bread sandwiches, please. With cucumber and yogurt sauce."

"You got it." The young woman went to work filling two large, round pitas with the mixture. A moment later she handed the two plump sandwiches wrapped in wax paper through the window to Joel.

"Here you go. Eat up." Joel put one of the pitas into Letty's hand.

"He made an appointment for me," Letty said tightly. She took a whopping bite out of the sandwich. "Can you imagine?"

"An appointment for what?"

"Therapy. To help me work through my sex problems."

Joel chewed a mouthful of hummus. His eyes gleamed. "You don't have any sex problems."

Letty flushed. "I know. I tried to tell him that. But he didn't hear a word I said. I realize now he never did hear anything I said."

"Did you dump your oysters and fries all over him because he had the nerve to make the appointment?"

"No. I did that because he told me to fire you. He said he felt you were having too much influence on me."

"No kidding? Too much influence, huh?"

"You needn't look so thrilled with yourself." Letty glowered up at him through her glasses. "I happen to be very upset."

"You are? Because you ditched Dixon? I wouldn't let it worry me, if I were you."

"No, you wouldn't, would you?" Letty retorted. "But it just so happens that what I am ditching is the only genuine proposal of marriage I've had in recent memory. That isn't something one throws away lightly, you know."

Joel nearly choked on a mouthful of sandwich. "Marriage?" He started coughing and sputtering. His eyes watered. "Marriage?" he got out a second time as he gasped for air.

Letty experienced a hollow feeling in the pit of her stomach. "I can see the idea is utterly foreign to you," she said stiffly. "But back where I come from marriage is still considered the normal and proper method of formalizing a romantic relationship."

"Look, honey, I didn't mean the idea seemed weird or anything," Joel said quickly. He swallowed the remainder of his hummus sandwich in one gulp. "It's just that if you're implying that you and I should start thinking of marriage, you need to understand something up front."

"What's that?" she demanded.

"There's no way in hell I can marry you as long as you own Thornquist Gear."

She stopped on the sidewalk, heedless of the tide of people eddying around her. "Why not?"

"Damn it. Don't you understand? Because everyone, including you, would think I was marrying you to get Thornquist, that's why. I told you that back at the beginning."

Letty scowled thoughtfully. "I wouldn't think that."

"Come off it, Letty. You'd be bound to wonder about it

sooner or later." Joel tossed his sandwich wrapper into a trash can and started striding swiftly along the sidewalk.

Letty saw the futility of arguing with him. At least he was not telling her he couldn't marry her because he didn't love her, she reassured herself. "Okay, we'll let that slide for now."

"Damn right we will. The last time I wanted to marry a woman everyone thought I was after her father's company. I sure as hell am not going to have people saying that about me a second time."

"I see." Diana again, Letty thought sadly. She hurried to catch up with Joel, aware that the hollow feeling in her stomach was filling with ice. So much about Joel had been shaped by what happened to him fifteen years ago, she thought. She wondered how many more stone walls like this one she was fated to run into because of those events.

They walked in silence down First Avenue, passing an eclectic mix of pawnshops, adult theaters, restaurants, boutiques, and galleries. The sky overhead was a uniform steel gray, but the rain had not yet started to fall. It was cold.

"Joel?"

"Yeah?"

"What was the management crisis you mentioned back in the restaurant?" Letty asked finally.

He threw her a sidelong glance. "I had a visit from Copeland this morning."

Letty was startled. "I didn't know he was in the building."

"Bigley must be falling down on the job," Joel remarked coolly.

"Well? What happened? Did you tell him Keith is in charge now?"

"I told him."

"Joel, what happened?"

"He flew into a rage. Picked up a lamp and started destroying my office. The day was saved by Professor Dixon, who happened to walk in at the appropriate moment and alter the course of events."

"Oh, my God."

"I then got Escott on the phone, told him what had happened, and he and I both agreed he had better get back to Echo Cove. We're putting a twenty-four-hour security guard on the Copeland Marine yard for a while. There's no telling what Copeland might do before he cools down."

"Did Diana go home with Keith?"

"No. He wanted her to stay in Seattle. He thinks she'll panic if she finds out what's going on with her father."

"Oh, my God," Letty whispered again. She halted in the middle of the sidewalk a second time. "We'd better go check on her, Joel. She'll be very upset. I told you she's been scared all along that something awful will happen."

Joel looked disgusted. "Letty, the last thing I want to do right now is talk to Diana."

"Well, I'm going to go see her. Her hotel is only a few blocks from here. I'll see you back at the office." Letty turned and started to cross the street.

"Damn it, hold on." Joel stepped into the crosswalk with her. "If that's the way you're going to be about it, I'll go with you."

Ten minutes later Letty knocked on Diana's hotel room door. She opened it at once. Her eyes looked bloodshot from a recent crying jag, and her lovely face was pinched and drawn. She glanced from Joel to Letty and back.

"What do you want? Haven't you interfered enough with my life?"

"It's all right," Letty said quietly as she stepped into the room. "I know you're scared. But Keith is going to be all right. He and Joel have everything under control, don't you, Joel?"

"Right. Sure. Things are under control." Joel sounded bored. He followed Letty reluctantly into the hotel room and remained standing near the door after Letty closed it. It was obvious he was more than ready to leave as soon as possible.

"Keith says Daddy has been told he's no longer running

Copeland Marine." Diana looked at Joel. "Are you the one who told him?"

"Yeah."

"Dear God." Diana sat down in the chair near the window. She folded her hands tightly in her lap and gazed silently out over the Seattle skyline. "You don't know what you've done, Joel. But I will tell you this: when it's all over, I will never, ever forgive you. I realize that probably doesn't seem like much of a threat, but I promise you I will hate you to my dying day."

Letty's sympathy dissolved. A wave of anger took its place. "Stop it, Diana. This is not Joel's doing, and you know it. Keith came to us with his proposal to run Copeland Marine. Your husband is the one who instigated this whole thing, and don't you ever forget it."

Joel shrugged. "Escott's doing it for you, Diana. He's willing to fight for Copeland Marine. Why don't you give him a chance?"

Diana swung her head around. Her eyes were brilliant with fury and pain. "Have you forgotten the past so soon, Joel Blackstone? The last time a man tried to do something for me that went against Daddy's wishes, *somebody died.*"

A sudden stillness descended. Letty glanced at Joel's face and saw that it was set in stark lines.

"What are you saying, Diana?" Joel came away from the door, took two steps across the room, and grabbed her by the shoulders. He yanked her to her feet. "What are you trying to tell me?"

"Nothing," she gasped, looking terrified of his cold fury. "I just wanted you to remember what happened the last time, damn you."

"I have never forgotten what happened," Joel said with deadly softness. "My father was killed when he drove his car off a cliff. Or so they said. Do you know something about that so-called accident, Diana? Because if you do, you'd better tell me right now."

"I don't know anything about it." Diana's mouth was

trembling uncontrollably. "All I know is that your father died at least partly because of what happened between us."

Letty stepped between them. "Stop it, both of you. I don't want to hear another word on the subject. Joel, I have told you before that you are not responsible for your father's death. He died in a terrible accident, but you were not driving and that's the bottom line."

Joel's eyes locked with hers for a moment. She watched him regain his self-control. Then he turned away without a word and went back to stand by the door.

Letty faced Diana. "As for you, Diana, you've got a choice to make. The same one you had to make fifteen years ago. You're a lucky woman. Few of us get a second chance to make the right choice."

Diana's eyes flew to hers. "What are you talking about?"

"It's very simple. For the second time in your life you've found a man who is willing to rescue you from your father. Are you going to let Keith do it or are you going to cave in to your own fears the way you did when Joel tried to save you? Think about it."

Without waiting for a response, Letty went to the door. She pushed her glasses higher up on her nose as she looked at Joel. "Are you ready to go?"

"I was ready ten minutes ago." Joel jerked open the door. He glanced back at Diana before he followed Letty out of the room. "You might try having a little faith in Escott. He could use the support. I think Letty's right. He can handle your daddy for you."

Letty heard Diana's sobs start as soon as Joel had closed the door. She said nothing as they walked to the elevators.

"Letty?"

"Yes?" She stabbed the call button and studied the signal lights on the panel.

"I want you to know I'm glad Diana didn't let me rescue her fifteen years ago."

Letty felt her mood lighten slightly. She nodded brusquely, saying nothing.

Joel held the elevator doors for her when they slid open. "You know what I like about you?"

"What?"

"You wouldn't have sat around hoping to be rescued all your life and then chucked your big chance because of cold feet. You've got more guts than that. I guess they build 'em real sturdy back in Indiana, don't they?"

Letty blinked. "Did you say Indiana?"

"Yeah."

"That's what I thought you said." Some of the coldness in the pit of Letty's stomach started to thaw. "Yes. They build 'em sturdy back there."

Two hours later Letty ducked into the ladies' room on the third floor. She was on her way back from a meeting with Cal Manford in the marketing department, and she had been delighted to learn that her suggestions for the new ad campaign were being carried out swiftly.

She was ensconced in a stall, thinking about the recent scene in the hotel room with Diana, when she heard the outer door of the rest room swing open. Two young women entered.

One of them giggled. "Are you sure?"

"Beth says she's seen them coming into work together every morning for the past few days," said the other woman. Letty could see that she was wearing red heels. "She says they walk down First Avenue from the same direction, which probably means they're coming from her place. Beth says she heard someone mention that Ms. Thornquist has an apartment on First."

"I'll bet it's true, then. They are sleeping together. Who would have believed it? She doesn't exactly look like his type, you know? I mean, she was a librarian, for heaven's sake."

"Oh, I don't know. Roger in Accounting said he thinks she's kind of cute," Red Shoes said. "And Arthur Bigley thinks she walks on water."

"Still, Blackstone has never messed around with any of his employees. And I can tell you there are a few women in this building who wouldn't mind helping him pitch a tent somewhere."

"Ms. Thornquist is hardly an employee," Red Shoes murmured.

"You're right. Just think, the CEO is sleeping with the president of the company. That's got to be a first."

"Maybe that's how Blackstone is planning to maintain control of Thornquist," Red Shoes mused.

Letty did not dare emerge from the stall until the two women had left. Then, still reeling with shock and embarrassment, she darted out, washed her hands with amazing speed, and opened the outer door. A quick glance both ways revealed that the hall was deserted.

Fearful of getting on one of the elevators, where someone might notice her flaming face and inquire about it, she dashed into the stairwell and raced up the steps to the fourth floor.

She was panting for breath by the time she stepped out into the hall. She nearly died when a clerk hovering near the elevators glanced her way and nodded respectfully.

She knows, Letty thought. They all know.

She waited until the elevator had arrived and taken away the all-seeing clerk. Then Letty hurried down the hall to Joel's office. She saw with relief that his secretary was away from her desk.

Joel's door was closed. Letty knocked once and went straight in without waiting for a reply.

Joel looked up with a frown as she closed the door and sagged back against it.

"What the hell is wrong with you? Are you all right?" he asked.

"No," Letty gasped. "Something terrible has happened."

Joel finally began to look genuinely concerned. "What?"

"Joel, they know. The whole staff knows. I just heard it in the rest room, for God's sake."

"That's probably the best place to get up-to-date information about this place," Joel observed. "What exactly did you hear?"

"They've all guessed about us." Letty gave a high-pitched little shriek of dismay. "They know we're having an affair. Secretaries are talking about it in the rest room, for crying out loud."

"Oh, that." Joel relaxed and went back to studying a report that lay in front of him. "I told you that you wouldn't be able to keep it secret for long."

Letty was incensed. She stared at his bent head. "Joel, for heaven's sake, this is not a joke." She hurried over to his desk, went around behind it, and grabbed his shoulder. "Listen to me. This is a moment of enormous humiliation and embarrassment for me."

Joel raised his head, his eyes thoughtful. "It is?"

"Well, of course it is. We don't do things like this back where I come from. And if we do, we do them discreetly."

"We've been discreet, Ms. Thornquist." Joel smiled faintly. He pushed his chair back from his desk. His fingers closed around Letty's wrist, and he drew her down onto his lap. "Look on the bright side. We don't have to be so damn discreet anymore."

Letty's eyes widened as she sat down abruptly on his knee. "Joel, I don't think you realize the gravity of the situation. There's a question of office morale here."

"Morale, huh?" Joel started to nuzzle her throat.

"Absolutely. This sort of romantic liaison is frowned upon."

"Who frowns on it?" His hand closed around her hip. His fingers squeezed gently. "I sure don't have any problem with it."

"Joel, stop that." She batted ineffectually at his hands. "I'm trying to have a serious conversation here."

"Keep talking." He slid his hand down her thigh and started to move his fingers up under the hem of her skirt.

His mouth was warm and persuasive on the curve of her neck.

Letty tried to keep herself focused on the main issue, but a sense of excitement was already unfurling within her. It was always like this when Joel touched her. She felt his fingers high up on her inner thigh and she shivered. "This is another management crisis. We need to decide how we're going to handle this, Joel."

"You don't like the way I'm handling it?" His fingers had reached her panties. They began moving in lazy patterns. "I'm sorry to hear that, Ms. Thornquist. As your chief executive officer, I know it's my duty to handle these upper management problems for you, and I certainly want you to be satisfied with my performance."

"Joel, you are impossible." Letty could feel herself growing damp at his touch. She stirred against him, parting her legs a little in spite of her ambivalent emotions.

"I ask you to have faith in me, Madam President."

She wriggled on his knee, and somehow his fingers slipped under the leg band of her panties. "Oh, my God."

"My sentiments, exactly. You feel so good, honey." He nuzzled her ear. "I'm so hot for you right now that I'm seriously contemplating taking you here on my desk."

"Joel."

"In fact, I think that as your CEO it is my duty to recommend that course of action." His arms curved around her, and he started to rise up out of the chair.

A scene flickered into Letty's mind, a scene she would never forget. It had haunted her for weeks. All of a sudden she knew how to exorcise the ghost.

"Wait," Letty said urgently.

Joel slowly lowered himself back into the chair. His eyes were filled with a lively combination of laughter and passion. "Losing your nerve, Ms. Thornquist? Pity. But later tonight I suppose we can always carry on where we just left off."

"No, I'm not losing my nerve." She licked her lips as she

glanced toward the closed door. "It's just that I think I've got a more interesting idea."

His eyes narrowed speculatively. "And what would that be?"

"Well, I was just thinking. There's something I've been wanting to try lately."

"You've been reading articles again, I take it?"

"No, not exactly. This is something else." Letty blushed. Her eyes met his and then slid quickly away. Her pulse was pounding with the excitement of the outrageous and the forbidden. She eased herself down off Joel's knee and knelt between his legs.

"Well, damn," Joel murmured when she fumbled with his belt buckle. He looked down at the top of her head. "Ms. Thornquist, you amaze me."

"I'm amazing myself." She touched the heavy bulge in his jeans with light, tentative fingers. "Do you like it like this?"

"I'll be honest with you, Ms. Thornquist." Joel's voice was suddenly very husky. "I have never before done anything quite this exotic in my office. Professional decorum and the company image, you know."

Letty was afraid she might burst into nervous giggles as she slowly and cautiously lowered his zipper. There was a rasping, metallic sound and then she was cradling him in her palm. Her fingers were full of the fierce, hard length of him, and she was no longer poised on the brink of laughter.

"You really are beautiful," Letty whispered as she leaned forward to touch him with the tip of her tongue.

Joel sucked in his breath. His fingers tightened in her hair. "God, Letty, that feels so good. Yes, baby. Just like that. *Yes.*"

Growing bolder by the second, Letty leaned closer, tasting the essence of him. She could feel Joel's intense reaction and the knowledge thrilled her.

Joel made her feel like the most sensual woman on the face of the earth.

Joel made her feel beautiful.

With Joel she had learned the extent of her power as a woman, and the feeling was glorious.

She leaned closer to him, determined to give him the kind of pleasure he had so often given her.

At that moment the office door swung open without warning. Letty froze. She knew with sudden icy clarity that she was fully visible from the doorway.

"Oh, there you are, Blackstone," Philip said. "Your secretary isn't at her desk, but I thought I'd pop in anyway. I've got a couple of things to discuss." There was a brief, shocked pause. When Philip spoke again he sounded as if he was strangling. "My God. *Letty.*"

Joel's fingers stayed clenched in Letty's hair. "Good news, Dixon," he said thickly. "She doesn't need therapy."

18

"You know something?" Letty asked as she methodically worked her way through a pile of spicy rice noodles with peanuts and chili peppers, "I have decided that if I can survive what happened today in your office, I can survive anything."

It was the first time she had mentioned the incident.

Joel grinned. He could not help it. Every time he thought of the expression on Philip Dixon's face that afternoon, he wanted to laugh. He knew he would still be chuckling about it forty years from now.

Basic male instinct assured Joel that there probably would not be a whole lot of trouble from Dixon in the future. In fact, Joel fully expected the man to be on the next plane back to Indiana.

Good riddance.

Dixon had fled the scene in ignominious retreat the moment he had fully grasped just what was going on before his very eyes. Joel had felt a satisfying surge of triumph as he had watched his thoroughly vanquished rival make a chaotic withdrawal from the scene.

The rush he had gotten from knowing he no longer had to worry about Philip Dixon had been almost as good as the feel of Letty's mouth on him.

Unfortunately, he had not been able to continue savoring either the victory or Letty's gentle tongue. Letty had promptly succumbed to shock.

Regretfully Joel had zipped his jeans and assisted his boss back to her own office. There he had explained in grave tones to an extremely concerned Arthur Bigley that the president of Thornquist Gear was not feeling well that afternoon.

Arthur had immediately started fixing a pot of tea. Joel left him to the task of reviving Letty and sauntered back down the hall feeling more cheerful than he had in some time.

At five-thirty when Joel went back down the hall a second time to see if Letty had recovered, he found her hard at work on the new ad campaign. She had refused to meet his eye, studiously not mentioned the incident, and appeared oblivious of the fact that it was time to go home.

Joel had guided her out of the building and into the din of a nearby after-work bar where he had ordered a glass of white wine for her. He had specified the inexpensive bar wine because there was obviously no sense wasting money on a respectable label. Letty was in no condition to appreciate it.

After the drink he had shepherded her into the Thai restaurant next door for dinner. She seemed unaware that he had ordered her Phud Thai four-star hot.

"Next time remember to lock the door before you seduce me in my office," Joel advised.

"There definitely will not be a next time in your office." Letty adjusted her glasses and gave him a disapproving look. "However, I am beginning to believe that, having gotten through the experience of being discovered in a compromising position, I can now cope a little better with the idea of having an affair."

Joel scowled at her, not liking the expression of thoughtful speculation in her eyes. "Is that right? I got the impression earlier today that you were starting to have problems with the idea of a long-term affair. You were starting to use the M-word."

Letty lifted one shoulder in an elaborate shrug and concentrated on her highly spiced rice noodles. "Well, you have to understand that it does require a drastic adjustment in my old-fashioned midwestern notions of propriety. Back where I come from it's still considered appropriate to get married before one starts a family."

"A *family*." It was Joel's turn to go into shock. "Are you telling me you're pregnant? You couldn't possibly be pregnant. We've been careful." He thought about that first time in the barn and winced.

"I'm not pregnant." She smiled. "Yet."

"Don't go making wild statements like that. It's not good for my heart."

"Don't you want a family, Joel?"

He thought about Letty having his baby, pictured her pregnant, imagined her holding an infant. It was not the first time the image had danced fleetingly through his mind, and each time it appeared, it did odd things to him. It made him want to use the M-word himself, for example.

But he could not marry Letty so long as she owned Thornquist Gear and that was that.

"Eventually," Joel said. "Yeah, sure. Eventually I want kids."

"You shouldn't wait too much longer, you know. Maybe we should start working on it. What do you think? I mean, now that I'm getting the hang of having an affair and am able to be totally blasé about it, maybe there's no need to get married at all. This isn't the Heartland. This is the West Coast. The fast lane."

Irritation flared in him. "We're not having kids until we're married, and we're not getting married as long as you own Thornquist Gear. That's final, Letty. Absolutely final."

She studied him coolly. "You want me to give up my inheritance before you'll consider marriage?"

"I never asked you to give up a damn thing. I'm asking you to sell it to me. I'll give you a fair price. Hell, you'll make more off the sale of Thornquist Gear than you'd make in twenty years of working as a librarian."

Letty considered that with a dark frown. "That sounds suspiciously like buying myself a husband."

"Damn it, you wouldn't be buying me. You'd be selling Thornquist to me. There's a big difference."

She chewed reflectively on her lower lip. "What if you changed your mind after the sale?"

"Jesus. What are you talking about now?"

"What if you decided you didn't want to marry me after I sold Thornquist to you? There wouldn't be any way I could force you to keep up your end of the bargain." Letty shook her head. "No, I think it's too big a risk. Let's just continue with the affair. I'm getting accustomed to it. There are certainly some exciting moments."

He stared at her. "You're in a weird mood, aren't you?"

"It's been a weird day. First I dump a plate of oysters and fries over the one man who has actually made me an honorable proposal of marriage. Next I find myself trying to offer aid and comfort to your ex-girlfriend. Then I get caught in an extremely inappropriate position in your office, and now I'm eating food that's hot enough to set fire to the plate."

"As I said back at the beginning, you're not in Kansas anymore."

"Indiana."

Joel fell into a brooding silence after that exchange. He had to admit he had counted on Letty finding the affair uncomfortable after a while. He had suspected from the start that her quest for wild, illicit passion and pizzazz would not last long. Old virtues and values would quickly reassert themselves. When that happened, Joel had reasoned, she would start talking about marriage.

Once he knew he had her hooked, he could negotiate. He fully intended to marry Letty. He was not quite certain when that decision had crystallized in his brain, but it was rock solid now. However, he intended to do so on his own terms.

No one was going to accuse him of marrying her in order to get his hands on Thornquist Gear.

He had not counted on Letty coming to the conclusion that a permanent affair would be acceptable. Nor had he anticipated that 'she would actually start talking about having children without marriage. Things were getting out of hand.

Letty seemed in a far more upbeat mood by the time she had finished her noodles. Joel got to his feet, paid the bill, and led her out onto the street. A thought struck him as they turned to start up First Avenue to her apartment.

"Clean shirts," Joel said abruptly.

"What about them?"

"I don't have any more at your place. We'll have to drop by my apartment."

"Okay," Letty agreed. "Actually, that brings up an interesting point. We're going to have to decide if it's economically worthwhile to maintain two apartments. Maybe we should just move into one. What do you think?"

Joel squashed his irritation. "You were the one who said we should keep our own apartments."

"That was before I realized that I could handle a real, full-fledged affair."

"Your father isn't going to approve of our having a perpetual affair, Letty. He'll expect some sign of commitment fairly soon."

"He'll just have to get used to the affair, won't he?"

"He's kind of an old-fashioned guy," Joel reminded her. "I can tell. And you're his only daughter. Sooner or later he'll expect you to get married."

"Who knows? Maybe I will get married. Sooner or later."

They caught a bus up to the First Hill neighborhood where Joel lived. It was faster and easier than going back to Letty's place to get the Jeep out of her garage.

It occurred to Joel as they walked into the small lobby that he had not been spending a lot of time at his own apartment lately. It was Letty's place that felt like home now. Maybe he should consider getting rid of his apartment.

But that would only encourage Letty's new notion of having all the benefits of marriage without the license.

Things were getting complicated.

"This won't take long," he said as they got out of the elevator and started down the hall. He dug his keys out of his jeans. "Maybe I'd better check the refrigerator while I'm here. I think I left some milk in there."

"It's probably gone sour by now," Letty said. "It's a good thing you don't have any plants to worry about. You know, Joel, you really should consider moving in with me. It's a waste of money to maintain this place. And I've got a better view."

"I'll think about it," Joel muttered.

Then he shoved his key into the lock of his front door and realized instantly that something was very wrong.

"Damn it to hell."

Letty glanced at him in alarm. "What is it?"

Joel eased the key back out of the lock and pushed the door open. It swung inwardly very easily. Too easily.

"Somebody busted the lock," Joel said. "Ten to one the place has been cleaned out. Goddamn it. I'll bet they got the new speakers I bought two months ago. And the computer. And Lord knows what else."

He strode furiously into the apartment and went down the short hall to the living room. He realized at once that what had taken place had been more than a quick, efficient burglary.

The apartment looked as if a bomb had exploded in the middle of it. Furniture had been overturned, the cushions ripped open with a knife. Lamps had been smashed. Books had been dumped from the shelves.

Everything of value was still there, but it had all been systematically destroyed, not stolen. The new stereo speakers looked like gutted fish. They had been slashed open and the innards torn out.

"Oh, my God," Letty whispered. She moved closer to Joel.

Wordlessly, Joel toured the apartment with Letty at his heels. The clothes in his closet had been doused with varnish. The smell reminded Joel of a boatyard. The food in the refrigerator had been dumped all over the kitchen floor and left to rot. Joel grimaced at the odor of sour milk.

"Vandals?" Letty asked softly.

"No," Joel said, thinking of the varnish that had been flung on everything in his closet. "Victor Copeland. He must have come here right after he left my office this morning."

"How did he know where you lived?"

Joel shook his head. "I don't know, but it probably wasn't all that difficult to find out."

"Joel, this looks sick."

"I know." Joel recalled the wildness in Copeland's eyes that night fifteen years ago in the abandoned barn. He had known then that if it had been possible to do so, Copeland would have willingly killed in that moment.

Joel walked over to where the phone was lying on the carpet. He picked it up and saw that the clip on the end of the cord was still intact. He plugged it into the jack. He had the number for Copeland Marine in his pocket. He dialed it quickly.

The phone was answered almost at once by Keith Escott.

"Figured you'd be spending the night there," Joel said. "This is Blackstone."

"What's up?" Keith asked, apparently sensing the grimness in Joel's voice.

"It looks as if Copeland went on a rampage through my apartment this afternoon. He destroyed the place."

"Christ. The man's gone over the edge."

"Yeah, I think that's a real possibility."

Keith sighed. "I've suspected he was getting worse for some months now."

"Letty thinks Diana's afraid of him, and I do, too," Joel said. "Diana is frightened of what he might do if he gets too angry."

"And afraid I won't be able to protect her or myself if that happens. I know." Keith sounded weary, as if he had been fighting that battle for a long time.

"If it's any consolation, she didn't have any faith in me, either, fifteen years ago," Joel said quietly. "Her daddy is very scary. But now it looks as if the two of us are going to have to do something about him. I'm going to call the police after we hang up. I'll tell them what's going on and who we think is behind this vandalism. But don't count on them being able to do much at this point. We don't have any proof."

"You think he's on his way down here?"

"I think it's a real good possibility. Everything under control there?"

"Yes," said Keith. "I've got two men doing sentry duty shifts twenty-four hours a day. And I'm here in the office all the time. I've moved in for a while."

Joel went over to the window and lowered his voice. "You armed?"

"Are you kidding?" Keith said equally softly. "I've got an automatic. Bought it three years ago right after I married Diana and began to realize just how close to the edge my new father-in-law was."

"Right. I'll talk to you in the morning. If anything happens tonight you can reach me at my office."

"Got it." Keith hesitated. "I'm going to call Diana. Tell her to stay in the hotel room. I don't think she's in any real danger. Copeland has never hurt her, as far as I know, but apparently he used to beat her mother. She let that much information slip once."

Joel slid a glance at Letty, who was watching him intently. She had her arms folded tightly under her breasts. "Look, I'm going to send Letty over to her father's place. You want Diana to go there with her?"

"Thanks," Keith said, sounding relieved. "I'd feel a lot better if I knew she wasn't alone."

"I'll take care of it." Joel started to hang up the phone.

"Blackstone?"

"Yeah?"

"If I manage to keep Copeland from torching this yard and if I pull it out of the red, you and I are going to have to do a deal. Fair enough?"

Joel smiled humorlessly. "Fair enough. Save Copeland Marine and I'll sell it to you. Real cheap."

Keith chuckled. "I'll call you if anything happens."

Joel hung up and turned to Letty. "Let's go, honey. We have to stop at the hotel and pick up Diana."

She looked mutinous. "I don't want to be tucked away somewhere while you're trying to protect yourself and Thornquist Gear from some crazy man. This is my company, Joel. I've got a right to help defend it."

"Not a chance. I'm the one who dragged Thornquist Gear into this situation. I'll take care of the cleanup." Joel took her arm and drew her out of the devastated apartment and into the hall. "You're not going to be anywhere near Thornquist Gear or me tonight."

She gave him an anxious look. "Are you saying he might come after you personally?"

"He hit my apartment. I don't know where he'll go next. I

still have a hunch he's on his way to Echo Cove. But who knows for certain? As Escott said, the man's gone over the edge."

"Joel, please let me stay with you," Letty begged.

"No."

"Damn it, I own the company. I am ordering you to let me stay with you."

"The answer is no, Letty."

"But why?"

"You know why." He got her into the elevator and punched the lobby button. "This entire situation exists because I set up the takeover of Copeland Marine. It has nothing to do with you, and that's the way I intend to keep it."

She touched his arm, her eyes pleading. "Joel, this is not your fault."

Anger washed through him. "It is my fault, goddamn it, and I am not going to risk your neck. Escott and I will deal with Copeland, and that's final."

"But, Joel . . ."

"What's the matter?" he bit out. "Don't you think I can handle this? You told Diana she should have more faith in Escott. Well, where's your faith in me?"

Letty looked at him in shocked silence for several long seconds. "All right," she finally said very quietly. "I'll go to Dad's house."

Joel heaved an inner sigh of relief. That particular tactic was definitely a case of hitting below the belt. He told himself he would apologize later. The important thing now was to make certain Letty was not in the vicinity if Victor Copeland came calling tonight.

Letty was still in an unnaturally quiet mood when they reached the hotel where Diana was staying. But when Diana opened the door, her eyes full of anxious questions, Letty made an obvious effort to pull herself together.

She took charge of dealing with Diana, for which Joel was

profoundly grateful. He would thank her later, he told himself. Right after he apologized for virtually blackmailing her into following orders.

"Keith called," Diana said to Letty. "He wants me to spend the night with you at your father's house. I argued with him, but he was very insistent. I've already packed."

Letty grimaced wryly. "I'm afraid we women are being sent off to hide in the wagons while the men deal with the bad guys."

Diana glanced uneasily at Joel and then away. "I'm afraid my father is not well, mentally. I don't know what to say. I'm sorry. I'm so sorry for everything."

"It's hardly your fault, Diana," Letty said firmly. "Come on, we'd better get going." She put her arm around Diana's shoulders and guided her out of the hotel room.

Joel picked up Diana's elegant leather suitcase and followed the two women out the door.

Twenty minutes later they all stood in Morgan and Stephanie's living room. Joel ran through the explanations and was relieved when Morgan agreed immediately with his decision.

"Letty and Diana can stay here with Stephanie tonight," Morgan announced. "I'll come down to Thornquist Gear and keep the midnight vigil with you, Joel."

Joel started to protest but changed his mind when he saw the stubborn expression in Morgan's eyes. Something told him there was no point in arguing with an Indiana farmer once he had made up his mind. All the logic in the world would not alter Morgan's decision.

What the hell, the man was going to be his father-in-law someday, Joel thought.

"All right," he said.

Joel was profoundly grateful when nobody put up any more arguments. Letty walked out to the Jeep with him while they waited for Morgan to throw a few items into a duffel bag. Her expression was serious and intent.

"Joel, there's something I want to tell you."

He leaned back against the Jeep and smiled. "More orders for your CEO, Madam President?"

Her eyes were huge and solemn with concern. "I want you to be very careful tonight."

"I will," he promised.

"Joel, I love you. You know that, don't you?"

For an instant he was stunned at the admission. Then elation soared in him. For the moment, at least, it blotted out all the other things he had been feeling since he'd walked into his apartment and seen the evidence of Victor Copeland's ungovernable rage. He reached for Letty.

"Damn, Letty," he muttered thickly, "you've picked a fine time to tell me." He pulled her into his arms, fumbling for the feel of her through the plump layers of her Thornquist Gear down coat. "You know I love you, too, don't you?"

"Well, you hadn't actually said so," she reminded him. The comment was tart, but her eyes were brimming with delight. "However, I have been extremely optimistic."

"Don't ever forget it." He kissed her mouth, the only part of her that was not swallowed up by her voluminous jacket. Her lips were warm in spite of the cold air. Joel groaned and pulled her closer.

"I'm ready," Morgan called as he came down the steps.

Letty stepped back and smiled at Joel. "Remember what I said. Be careful."

"Letty . . ." Joel broke off. This was not the time to say all the things he wanted to say. He smiled wryly. "Sure, boss."

Within the hour Joel and Morgan were camped out in Joel's office. Joel had a cordless telephone at hand. A security guard had been posted at the building entrance downstairs and the state-of-the-art security system that had been installed last year had been activated and double-checked.

"Now we wait," Morgan said calmly.

Joel lounged back in his chair and stacked his feet on the desk. "Now we wait."

"Do you play chess, by any chance?" Morgan asked.

Joel eyed him warily. "Some."

"Excellent." Morgan beamed. "I just happen to have brought along a small set. Can I interest you in a game?"

"I am not, by any chance, being hustled, am I?"

Morgan gave him a reproachful look. "What a suspicious mind you have. I was just thinking of a friendly little game to pass the time."

"How friendly?"

"Well," Morgan said with an air of grave consideration, "I suppose a small wager might liven things up a bit, eh?"

"What kind of wager did you have in mind?" Joel asked as he watched Morgan open his duffel bag and remove a miniature chess set.

"We'll think of something." Morgan opened the board and set out the pieces. "In the meantime we might as well have a little chat."

"About what?"

"This affair you're having with my daughter," Morgan said bluntly. "I want to know when you're going to marry her."

Joel groaned. "I knew you were going to start with that. Dammit, Morgan, stay out of this."

"Can't do that. I'm opposed, on philosophical grounds, to the idea of you having an open-ended affair with Letty."

"The hell you are." Joel smiled faintly. "You're opposed to it because you were brought up on a bunch of old-fashioned midwestern small-town notions. And all the lofty education you've had hasn't changed those notions one bit, has it?"

"Afraid not." Morgan surveyed the chess pieces and then leaned back in his chair. "Her mother would never have approved and neither do I."

"Don't worry about it, Morgan. I was brought up in a small town, too, remember?"

Morgan cocked a bushy brow. "Meaning?"

"Meaning I'm going to marry her. Eventually." Joel considered his first move.

"Mind if I ask why you're waiting?"

Joel glanced up. "There's the little matter of Thornquist Gear to be cleared up first."

"Ah." Morgan looked satisfied. "Afraid folks will think you married her for the company, is that it?"

"That's it. When Letty decides to go through with the deal I had worked out with Charlie, I'll marry her." He moved his first pawn.

Morgan nodded. "A standoff. Should be interesting to see what happens next." He leaned forward and moved a pawn. "About that wager of ours."

"What about it?"

"What do you say we specify that one way or another you and Letty will be married by next spring?"

Joel was not all that sorry when he lost the match an hour and a half later. What the hell, he thought. One way or another he did plan to be married to Letty by the spring.

At midnight Morgan crawled into one of the Thornquist Gear sleeping bags that Joel had commandeered for the night. He eyed Joel, who was still sitting at his desk. "You going to get some sleep?"

"Maybe. Later. I think I'll take another walk around the building. Check in with the security guard."

"You just heard from him fifteen minutes ago. Everything's quiet. Everything's probably going to remain quiet. And if anything does happen, your high-tech security system will wake you up and tell you about it."

"I know. But I don't feel like sleeping." Joel stood up and opened his desk drawer. He removed the revolver he had put there earlier. "I'll be back in a little while."

"You be careful with that thing," Morgan advised. "Don't go shooting yourself in the foot."

Joel went out into the hall and shut the door behind him.

He headed for the stairwell to start another floor-by-floor tour of Thornquist Gear.

He had built this place, he thought as he walked past the silent, empty offices. He was responsible for every square inch of it, from the display cases on the first floor to the sizable payroll the company met every month. He had made the decision to get into catalog sales, and he had supervised the installation of the expensive new mainframe computers that were needed. He had pored over the designers' plans every time the sales floor had been expanded. He had selected the security system. He had established the management hierarchy that made the company function so effectively.

And now Thornquist Gear stood like a stone wall between him and the future he wanted with Letty. Somehow he had to find a way to climb that wall.

The call from Echo Cove came at six in the morning. Joel was brewing coffee and watching for the first hint of dawn over the city when the phone warbled. He grabbed it halfway through the first ring.

"Blackstone here."

"It's Escott." Keith sounded out of breath but triumphant. "Damned if the son of a bitch didn't try to torch the place, after all. Showed up about twenty minutes ago. I saw him myself."

"What happened?"

"The guards and I managed to stop him, but he got away. The bastard left two cans of gasoline behind. Can you believe it? He was going to burn the whole damn place down. He didn't care what it would do to this town. You were right when you said he's decided that if he can't have Copeland Marine, nobody can have it."

"Did you notify the cops?"

"Sure. They're on their way. But, Blackstone?"

"Yeah?"

"I wouldn't count on them holding him for long, even if

they do stop him. He's still Victor Copeland, and you know what that means in this town."

"I know."

"There's something else," Keith said slowly. "The guy has really flipped this time. I've never seen him like this. I don't know what he'll do if he gets out of Echo Cove. Are you absolutely certain Diana and Letty are safe?"

Joel looked across the room at Morgan who was levering himself up out of the sleeping bag. "I'll make sure of it, Escott."

"All right. I'll call you if I get any more news."

"Right." Joel hung up slowly, his gaze still on Morgan. "He tried to destroy Copeland Marine. Escott and the guards stopped him, but he got away. Keith's worried about Diana."

"And you're worried about Letty?"

Joel nodded. "I think I'd better stash both of them someplace where Copeland would never think to look."

"What about the cabin?" Morgan asked. "They could be there in an hour and a half or so. And there's no way in hell Copeland could know about that place."

Joel drummed his fingers rapidly on the desk. "The question is, how long can I persuade Letty to stay there?"

"Probably not for long. You'd better catch Copeland fast."

19

I'm not so sure you should have come with us, Stephanie." Letty turned her father's BMW off the main road and started along the winding blacktop path that bordered the river gorge.

"I wanted to come with you," Stephanie insisted firmly. "Morgan has obviously decided to play cops and robbers with Joel, and I would have been sitting around the house, bored to death. I wouldn't even have had you to go to any classes with me, Letty."

Letty glanced at her in surprise. "I thought you only wanted me to go with you to your classes because Dad wanted it."

Stephanie smiled wryly. "I'll admit that at first I did it to please Morgan. But I went to one entitled Looking Forward to Successful Potty Training all by myself yesterday afternoon, and I have to admit it wasn't nearly as interesting without you. I kept thinking about all the amusing comments you would have made. Especially when the instructor

313

demonstrated the proper position of the toddler on the seat."

"Why would I have found that funny?"

"Because he used himself as a model."

Letty chuckled. "Okay, so I probably would have found that worth a wisecrack or two. But are you sure you feel comfortable about leaving the city for a couple of days in your condition?"

"I've decided to stop being a wimp about this baby." Stephanie adjusted the seat belt for the hundredth time. "I'm perfectly healthy, the baby is perfectly healthy, and my due date is three weeks away. Besides, we're only an hour and a half away from Seattle."

"I've heard first babies are often late," Diana volunteered quietly from the back seat. They were the first words she had spoken for over half an hour.

Not that any of them had been particularly chatty, Letty thought as she slowed the car to navigate the narrow, twisting road. None of them had wanted to be shipped off to the wilderness while the men engaged in a demonstration of modern machismo.

But Joel and Morgan had presented a united front that had been backed up with an urgent phone call from Keith.

With all three men pleading, threatening, and cajoling, Letty and Diana had reluctantly thrown in the towel. That was when Stephanie had volunteered to keep them company during their exile.

"Actually, my doctor has been wondering lately if the dates might be a little off," Stephanie said in response to Diana's remark.

"Keith has been talking about having a baby lately." Diana stared out the window of the car. "I told Letty I've been afraid."

Stephanie glanced back at Diana. "Afraid of your father?"

"Yes. I knew if he had a grandchild, Daddy would be very possessive of it. Perhaps even more so than he is of me. And his rages have been getting more frequent lately. I was terrified of the possibilities."

Stephanie looked shocked. "My God, you've been living with your fear of your father for a long time, haven't you, Diana?"

Diana's face tightened. "Too long. I'm glad it's going to end. One way or another, I'm glad. Looking back on it, I feel as if I've been living under the thumb of a terrorist."

"And every person who's come into your life has become a hostage," Letty concluded softly. "No wonder you were afraid to have children."

"Yes. Maybe after this is all over . . ." Diana's words trailed off.

"We all carry some kind of secret fear with us, don't we?" Letty brought the car to a halt in front of the Thornquist mountain home. "Sooner or later we all need someone to help us work through the fears."

Stephanie's brows rose. "No offense, Letty, but I can't imagine you being afraid of anything."

Diana gave a small exclamation as she reached for the door handle. "That's for certain. What in the world have you ever been afraid of, Letty?"

Letty turned in the seat. "Do you really want to know?"

Stephanie and Diana stared at her in surprise.

"Well, yes," said Stephanie, her eyes curious.

Diana cocked her head. "Yes, I would, too. Frankly, I've had the impression you were something of an Amazon."

Letty smiled ruefully. "Not quite. I've been afraid for a long time. Afraid that there was something missing in my life. Maybe missing in me. I seemed to be an observer, instead of a participant. Do you understand?"

Stephanie turned thoughtful. "I think so."

"Great-Uncle Charlie rescued me from that by leaving me Thornquist Gear. All of a sudden at Thornquist I'm an actor, not a member of the audience."

"You've certainly been involved," Diana agreed dryly.

Letty ignored her. Now that she had started, it was hard to stop. "There's more. You two were afraid to have children. Well, I was afraid I wouldn't be able to."

Stephanie was startled. "Why?"

"I was afraid I'd never find the kind of man I wanted to be the father of my children. And if I did find him, I was afraid I wouldn't be able to hold on to him because I wouldn't be able to respond satisfactorily in bed."

"For heaven's sake, Letty," Stephanie began.

"It's true." Letty looked at her. "I couldn't even hold on to Philip Dixon. Five weeks into our engagement he had to find Gloria the grad student to satisfy his ego because I couldn't have an orgasm."

Stephanie's eyes widened in sympathy. "Oh, Letty, didn't you know you can get professional help for that kind of problem?"

Letty stared at her. Then she started to laugh. She laughed so hard she nearly fell out of the car when she finally got the door open.

"You'll be glad to know," she told Stephanie as she wiped her eyes, "that I won't be needing therapy after all."

Hours later Letty lifted the lid off the pot of soup that was simmering on the stove. She stirred carefully, taking a quiet pleasure in watching the plump beans and colorful vegetables swirl through the rich broth. She had offered to make the soup from scratch, and much to her surprise, Stephanie had not objected.

"Smells good," Stephanie observed from the doorway. "I'd forgotten how good homemade soup can taste on a cold day."

Letty frowned and glanced out the window. "It is cold, isn't it? And it's starting to get cloudy outside. Back home we'd say it's fixing to snow."

"It's too early in the season for anything more than a few light flurries." Stephanie went over to the refrigerator and opened the door. "In any event Morgan checked the weather reports before he and Joel packed us off. He said there was no snow predicted. Just rain. Shall I make a salad?"

Letty smiled. "Sounds good. Provided you don't practice one of your infant recipes on us."

Stephanie grimaced as she removed lettuce from the refrigerator. "Don't worry. I'm helpless without my blender."

Diana appeared in the doorway. "Smells like dinner in here."

Letty glanced at her. "I thought you were taking a nap?"

"I couldn't sleep." Diana glanced out the window. "Do you think it's going to rain?"

"Looks like it." Stephanie started washing lettuce under the faucet.

Diana surveyed the pot of simmering soup. "I can make dumplings if anyone's interested," she offered hesitantly.

Letty was surprised. Diana had seemed listless all day. "I didn't think anyone out here on the West Coast would know how to make dumplings."

Diana shrugged, not returning Letty's smile. "My mother taught me how a long time ago. I haven't made them for years." She went to the counter and opened the small sack of flour Letty had purchased when they stopped for groceries earlier.

A curious harmony settled over the kitchen as the three of them went to work. It occurred to Letty that there was nothing like cooking a meal with other women to create an elemental bond. There was something primitive and female about the ritual. Or maybe that was just the old-fashioned Heartland pioneer woman in her, she decided wryly.

"I was thinking about something you said in the car this morning, Letty." Stephanie used a fork to combine vinegar and olive oil in a small bowl. "About each of us needing someone else to help us work through our private fears. It's been bothering me."

It was Diana who responded to that. She glanced up, her eyes intense. "Why?"

Stephanie's mouth thinned. "I suppose because I have a hard time accepting that I might be the weak one in my relationship with Morgan. I've always taken care of myself. I'm incredibly grateful that he's helped me create this baby, but a part of me is nervous about having to be rescued from my infertility. It's made me realize that things aren't really equal between us. I suppose what it really comes down to is that I wish he needed me as badly as I need him."

"You've got to be kidding." Letty glanced at her in astonishment. "You don't think my father needs you just as much as you need him?"

Stephanie whipped the oil and vinegar fiercely. "I know he cares for me. But I doubt that he actually needs me."

"You're wrong, you know." Letty smiled. "You and the baby have given him a whole new lease on life. After Mother's death, my father started turning into an old man before my very eyes. I was powerless to stop the process. You've made him young again, Steph. He told me so himself."

Stephanie stopped beating the salad dressing. Her eyes were very bright and a little anxious. "Did he really?"

"Really." Letty chuckled. "And even if he hadn't said it aloud, I would have known it. I noticed the difference in him the minute I got off the plane. Your relationship is definitely working both ways."

"I wish mine were," Diana said. "All I've done for Keith is make his life a living hell."

"Nonsense." Letty removed the lid from the soup pot and stirred the contents again. "Keith is a born knight-errant. He needs a beautiful maiden to save and an opportunity to slay a couple of dragons. You've provided him with both. He's just been waiting for his big chance, and now he's got it."

Diana set down the measuring cup and stared at her. "Is that how you see him?"

"Absolutely."

"Are you saying that because he took on Joel in that awful bar brawl?"

Letty laughed. "Not only because of that. I'm also thinking about how quickly he produced that five-year plan to salvage Copeland Marine. He didn't come up with that detailed scenario overnight. He had been working on it for a long time. Which means that he had just been waiting for his opportunity."

Diana grew thoughtful. "I remember how excited he was the night he came home and told me that Copeland Marine was in danger of a takeover."

"What Keith needs now is for you to believe in him, and you're giving him that kind of backing. He's on his way to saving the world. Or at least Echo Cove." Letty stood aside while Diana ladled the dumpling batter onto the surface of the bubbling broth.

"I hope so," Diana said fervently. "God, I hope someone can control Daddy before it's too late."

"They'll find him and stop him," Stephanie said soothingly. "He's a very sick man. He needs treatment."

Diana put the lid on the pot and stared sightlessly at it. "I don't think he's sick. I think he's evil. I've always wondered what really happened to Joel's father. For years I've secretly wondered if Daddy had something to do with Hank Blackstone's death."

Letty felt a chill go down her spine. She exchanged a worried glance with Stephanie, but neither of them said another word on the subject of Victor Copeland.

The phone rang at nine o'clock that evening. It was Joel. He was in his office, preparing for another night of camping out with Morgan.

"There's been no sign of Copeland," Joel told Letty quietly. "The Echo Cove cops didn't find him. No telling what he's up to now. How are things going up there?"

"We're all right." Letty sat on the arm of an overstuffed chair, one leg crossed over the other. She swung her foot tensely, aware of all the things she wanted to say to him. "Joel, you know you can't keep us up here indefinitely."

"I know. Just a day or two, I promise." There was a pause. "Letty?"

"Yes?"

"I love you."

Letty smiled happily. "Good. Are you going to do the right thing and marry me real quick?"

"Give you an inch and you take a mile, don't you? Men don't like pushy women."

"I know. I read an article about that. But I've decided it's only wimpy men who object to forceful women."

"I see." Joel's chair squeaked. Letty knew he was lounging back in it. She could almost see the faint smile on his face and the amusement in his eyes. "I guess that means I have to put up with your demanding ways or risk being called a wimp."

"Right. Joel?"

"Yeah?"

"I love you."

"I know," he said gently. "You'd better put Stephanie on the phone. Morgan is leaning over the desk, demanding to talk to her."

Stephanie took the phone. "Hello, Morgan. Yes, I'm fine. My back is bothering me a little, but that's normal these days." As she spoke, Stephanie idly massaged her lower back. "Yes, I'm going to go to bed early. Good night, dear. I'll talk to you in the morning."

Keith called a few minutes later and talked to Diana for a long time. "Be careful, darling," Diana said just before she hung up. "The only thing I really care about in Echo Cove is you."

Letty opened a pack of cards as silence fell on the beautiful house. Outside, the wind was howling restlessly through the trees. "Anyone for a game of gin?" she asked.

They were all in bed by ten-thirty.

Letty was the first one up the next morning. She awoke shortly before dawn and emerged from the bathroom with some vague notion of making pancakes. She realized the wind was still shrieking through the trees.

Then she looked out the window and saw the gray and white world that had engulfed the cabin overnight. Letty could see only a yard or two beyond the window because of the thick, swirling snow. She had no difficulty ascertaining that the blanket of white on the ground was already very thick and growing thicker by the minute.

Diana came into the front room, tying the sash of her robe. Her eyes widened in dismay. "My God, look at that blizzard. I guess that settles it. The men can all relax. Looks as if we're going to be stuck here for a while."

Stephanie came out of the bathroom. She looked pale and shaken.

Letty frowned. "What's wrong, Steph?"

"My water just broke."

Letty met her eyes and saw the fear in them. The finest obstetrician in Seattle and the most sophisticated neonatal facilities in the state were only seventy miles away. But they might as well have been seventy thousand miles.

No one in her right mind would risk driving even seven miles in the blinding snowstorm that had gripped the mountains.

Diana put her hand to her throat as she glanced from Stephanie's stricken face to Letty's. "If her water has broken she's about to go into labor. What are we going to do?"

Letty took a deep breath and managed a smile. "Isn't it lucky that I recently read some articles on the joys of having a baby at home?"

When the phone on Joel's desk rang he grabbed it up instantly. Mrs. Sedgewick was not at her desk yet. It was far too early for a business call.

"Blackstone," he said, expecting to hear Keith Escott's

voice on the other end of the line. Across the room Morgan sipped a cup of coffee and watched him.

"Last time it was your father," Victor Copeland snarled. "This time it's going to be your whore. I know where she is. I'm going to get her. Just like I got your father. This is how it works, Blackstone. You took something of mine. Now I'm going to take something of yours. Dead simple, isn't it?"

"Copeland, wait, you bastard." Joel's fingers locked around the phone as if he could somehow grab Copeland through the line.

But it was too late. Copeland had slammed down the receiver on his end.

Joel kept his death grip on the phone and started to dial the number of the Thornquist cabin. The fury was burning in him. *"Last time it was your father."* There was no longer any doubt. Copeland was a killer.

"What is it? Was that Copeland?" Morgan put down his coffee.

"It was Copeland, all right. He says he knows where Letty is and he's going after her." Joel listened to the telephone company recording that had come on the line. "Shit."

"What?"

Joel dropped the receiver into its cradle and looked at Morgan. "I can't get through to the cabin."

Morgan narrowed his eyes and gazed out the window. "This rain we're seeing here may be coming down as snow in the mountains. The phones are always going down during a snowstorm up there."

"Christ." Joel forced himself to think. "I've got to get to her."

"You got chains for the Jeep?"

"Sure." Joel stood up, shrugged into a blue down jacket, and pocketed his revolver. "Keep trying the phones. See if you can get through to the cops up there. Tell them what's going on."

"No," Morgan said. "You're not leaving me here. I'm

going with you. My daughter and my wife are up there. Escott can stand by the phones. I'll call him and let him know what's happening."

Joel nodded once. "All right. Move."

They both moved. Fortunately the morning rush hour traffic was light leaving the city. Most of the commuters were headed into downtown Seattle, not out to the suburban east side. Nevertheless, it took time. Too much time.

Once free of the city, Joel was able to move more quickly. It was raining heavily on Interstate 90 as they started climbing into the heavily forested terrain east of Seattle.

The rain turned to sleet and then to snow in the space of half a mile. By the time they turned off the freeway onto the back road cut into the mountain above the river, visibility was down to a few yards.

"We're going to have to stop to put on the chains," Morgan said.

"I know. I'll pull over up ahead."

Morgan shot him a quick glance. "It won't take long. I'm an old hand at this. I've been putting on chains since I was seven."

"Figures. I keep telling Letty you midwesterners are a hardy bunch."

"You better believe it. Joel, she's going to be all right. Diana is with them. Copeland won't hurt his own daughter. She can handle him until we get there."

"I wish I could believe that. How the hell did he learn about the cabin?"

"That," said Morgan, "is a very good question."

Joel was about to respond when some sixth sense made him glance into the rearview mirror. "Damn. There's someone right behind us."

"Give him plenty of warning before you try to pull over in this muck."

"I will."

The big car behind the Jeep was following far too closely

for the treacherous conditions. The snow-covered road was slick, and braking action would be almost nonexistent without four-wheel drive or chains.

Joel was suddenly very conscious of the sheer drop to the right of the narrow road. It was a long way down to the river.

Morgan turned around in his seat. He squinted through the rear window. "What the hell's the matter with that idiot?"

"Damned if I know." Joel started to ease the Jeep to the side of the road.

At that moment the big car—a Chrysler, Joel noticed—surged forward and swung out as if intending to pass.

"I don't believe it," Morgan said disgustedly. "You West Coast folks are never going to learn how to drive in snow."

Joel glanced to his left and saw the outline of Victor Copeland's massively overweight body behind the wheel of the big car.

"Damn it to hell," he said softly as realization dawned. "Copeland didn't know where Letty was. He waited until we left the office, and then he followed us. It's me he wants."

Joel remembered all too clearly how his father had died. He suddenly knew Copeland intended the same fate for him. The narrow river gorge yawned at the edge of the slick road, invisible because of the driving snow.

Copeland had followed them all the way from Seattle, waiting for his opportunity. There had been no chance on the busy interstate, but now the two cars were alone on a narrow road.

Joel waited, sensing what was coming. He reacted just as the nose of the big car edged toward the Jeep's fender.

He jerked the steering wheel to the left and took his foot off the accelerator. The Jeep immediately started to fall back, slowing rapidly in the thickening snow. Its left front fender struck the rear fender of Copeland's car.

The big Chrysler went into a ponderous skid as Copeland lost control of the rear wheels.

Through the constantly shifting veil of snow Joel and

Morgan watched the Chrysler spin halfway around and come to a halt blocking the narrow road.

Joel put the Jeep into reverse. Then, through the thick mist of white, he saw the door of the Chrysler open. Copeland was reaching for something in the back seat.

"He's got a gun," Joel said. He eased his foot down on the accelerator and backed the Jeep up as quickly as he could. All he needed was thirty more feet, he realized. That would put the Jeep out of sight around a bend in the road.

Fifteen more feet. He could hardly see the roadway at all now. The only consolation was that he knew Copeland's visibility was just as bad.

Ten feet. Or was it five? Maybe the road had already started curving and he was in the process of backing the Jeep straight over the cliff into the river. He turned the wheel cautiously.

"That's far enough," Morgan said. "We're on the blind side of the curve."

"Out." Joel yanked at the clasp of his seat belt. "He'll find the Jeep in another couple of minutes. All he has to do is keep walking down the road and he'll blunder straight into it. Head up that slope toward the trees."

"Don't worry. I'm not hanging around here." Morgan opened the door on his side and got out of the vehicle.

Joel and Morgan scrambled through the driving snow into the shelter of the trees. The blowing storm was still swirling furiously around them, providing a cloak of invisibility that would dissolve the instant the wind died down.

From the shelter of a heavily branched fir, Joel tried to watch the road. He could barely make out the shape of the Jeep sitting in the middle of it.

Then the boiling snow cleared like fog for an instant, and he saw the big figure lumbering around the bend. Copeland had a gun in his left hand. He found his way to the Jeep's front window and pointed the gun into the interior.

"*Blackstone.* You son of a bitch. Blackstone, where are you? You want to know why I ran your pa off the road that night? 'Cause I thought it was you, that's why. It was supposed to be you, goddamn it."

Copeland's cry of rage was carried on the shrieking wind. It was the enraged howl of a beast deprived of its prey.

An instant later Joel lost sight of him and the Jeep altogether in a renewed burst of wild wind.

"If we get any farther away from the Jeep, we'll run the risk of getting lost out here," Morgan said quietly. "This could turn into a whiteout at the rate it's going."

"Copeland can't see us any better than we can see him." Joel edged back behind the tree. "My guess is he'll stay near the Jeep until he can see clearly. This may be the only chance we'll have."

"You're going to try to get to him?"

"Yeah." Joel took the revolver out of his jacket pocket. "I'm going down there. Watch for him. You may spot him before I do. If you do, yell."

"I don't like this."

"Neither do I," said Joel. He took his glove off his right hand so that he could get a better grip on the revolver. His fingers immediately began to get cold.

He started cautiously down the slope, moving through the trees to where he thought the edge of the road should be. Around him the snow continued to eddy and whirl, occasionally clearing just enough to allow him to get his bearings. He thought about how stupid it would be to get lost out here just a few feet from the Jeep.

The wind lessened for a few seconds, and the veil of snow cleared. Joel saw Victor Copeland at the same instant that Copeland saw him. They were separated by the width of the road.

"Bastard. I'll teach you to mess with Victor Copeland. Who the hell do you think you are?" Copeland raised the gun in his fist and fired.

Joel dived into the thick snow. Copeland's shot crackled over his head. Joel raised his gun, but the wind picked up speed again, drawing a white curtain between the two men.

Joel started crawling forward on his belly through the snow. When he got home he was going to be able to testify personally to the effectiveness of Thornquist Gear boots and down jackets, he thought. He was in no danger of freezing yet, thanks to them.

Except for his right hand. It wouldn't be long before his fingers were numb. He had to finish this quickly.

"Joel. On your right. Look right." Morgan's warning roared through the blowing snow.

Joel obeyed instantly. He swung the revolver and his gaze simultaneously to the right just as the deadly white shroud lifted once more.

Copeland was less than two yards away, flailing about as he struggled to orient himself to Morgan's voice. He stumbled and fired wildly into the woods.

Joel pushed himself to his feet and launched himself at Copeland, knocking him off balance.

They went down heavily into the bank of snow at the edge of the road that overlooked the river. The revolver fell from Joel's numbed fingers. He landed on top of Copeland's huge frame.

Copeland convulsed as he tried to bring his gun up to aim at Joel.

Joel slammed a fist into Copeland's thick midsection and then grabbed the wrist of his gun hand. He held on with both hands and twisted desperately.

Copeland screamed with rage and pain. The gun fell into the snow. Joel tried to leap back out of the way of a huge fist. His booted foot skidded in the snow, and he lost his balance.

Copeland's blow found its target. The strength behind it was incredible. Joel's entire left arm went numb. He glanced down and saw the gun disappearing into the snow. He grabbed it with cold fingers.

Copeland was already on his feet, charging like a bull elephant. Joel sidestepped him at the last instant.

"Don't make me pull the trigger, you son of a bitch," Joel yelled as Copeland staggered and turned for another charge.

"You won't pull it. You haven't got the guts to pull it. I followed you all this way, and I'm going to kill you. Should have killed you fifteen years ago."

Copeland's savage grin was visible through the falling snow. The sound of his heavy wheezing was louder than the wind.

"I said stop," Joel repeated. "I meant it." It was like talking to a wild animal intent on charging. The man was beyond reason. Copeland had death in his eyes as he closed in for the kill.

Joel leveled the gun, pointing it at Copeland's midsection. In another two seconds he would have no choice. Copeland's eyes promised death.

Just as Copeland started to charge again, a wild burst of wind blew a blinding eddy of snow around the two men. Copeland roared. Joel realized the man was still charging despite the lack of visibility—but he was no longer moving toward Joel. He was heading toward the gorge.

Copeland never saw the low, metal guardrail. He struck it with his knee, tripped, and fell forward over the edge.

There was a scream and then a shocking silence as the big man fell down the side of the gorge into the river below.

Joel stood looking over the guardrail for a long moment. He realized he could see the river clearly. The fury of the storm was starting to lessen. Then he remembered his numb fingers. He slowly put on his glove.

Morgan came up beside him. He looked down at the still figure lying face down in the water at the edge of the river. "We'll have to push his car out of the way before we can go on to the cabin. But there's no rush now. They're all safe."

Joel felt something that had been coiled very tightly within him start to relax. He thought of Letty waiting at the cabin. "Yes," he said. "They're safe."

"Are you okay?" Morgan asked.

"I'm okay. Let's put the chains on and get going."

It took nearly an hour to drive the rest of the way to the cabin. By the time they arrived, the intensity of the storm had diminished. In the wake of the howling wind, a deep stillness cloaked the forest.

Joel parked the Jeep in front of the house and climbed out. He felt drained and exhausted. He realized that the only thing he really wanted in the whole world in that moment was Letty. The door on the other side of the Jeep opened and Morgan emerged.

"Hell of a trip," Morgan said, stretching.

A woman's keening cry of anguish ripped through the white silence.

Joel and Morgan lunged toward the front door of the house.

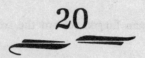

20

Stephanie screamed. "Too fast. It's all happening too fast," she gasped. And then she cried out again.

"It's okay, Steph. You're doing just great," Letty told her from the foot of the bed. She glanced at Diana, who was holding Stephanie's hand and putting cool compresses on her forehead.

"The contractions are right on top of each other as far as I can tell," Diana said tensely. She squeezed Stephanie's fingers.

"Something's wrong," Stephanie managed before another wave of pain robbed her of her voice.

"Nothing's wrong. Everything you've gone through so far fits with the description in the book. It's just happening on a very fast schedule, that's all." Letty braced herself as more water and some blood gushed forth from between Stephanie's bent knees.

She had propped Stephanie up in a semireclining position

because she had read it was a more natural one for childbirth than lying flat on one's back.

Beside her, neatly arranged on a clean white cloth, was a piece of string to tie off the cord and several kitchen towels that Diana had scrupulously washed and disinfected. Letty's secret fear was uncontrollable bleeding that she would not be able to stop with the aid of a few dish towels.

But she had not mentioned that fear to Stephanie. Nor had she reminded Stephanie of all the other things that could go wrong. She knew Stephanie was all too well aware of them. She had gone over and over the terrible list as her labor had set in.

When Stephanie had begun fretting over the lack of sophisticated fetal monitors, Letty had told her about an article she had recently read. It had claimed that fetal monitoring was not really necessary in healthy, normal deliveries.

When Stephanie had worked herself up into a state of near hysteria over the possibility that the baby was in the wrong position in the womb, Letty cited a statistic that said over ninety-five percent of all babies got into the head-down position on schedule.

And so it went. Every time Stephanie thought of something new to worry about, Letty tried to calm her by citing something reassuring she had read on the subject. Diana picked up the idea immediately and repeated the same facts over and over to Stephanie. Together they concentrated on reminding Stephanie that women had been having babies at home for aeons.

The labor had gone very swiftly, and it had been hard on all of them. All three women were bathed in sweat. Stephanie was soaking wet. Diana mopped her brow. Letty wished she had someone to mop her brow. This business of giving birth was very messy. The articles she'd read had failed to mention just how messy. They had glossed over that part, just as they had glossed over the level of pain the mother endured.

"I think I hear a car," Diana said suddenly.

Letty ignored her. She was too busy watching Matthew Christopher's tiny head appear. "He's almost here, Steph. Push. Help her push, Diana."

Diana gripped Stephanie's hand as Stephanie screamed again.

Her awareness of Stephanie's pain was the worst part of this whole thing, Letty thought. The only solution was to try to step back from it emotionally and concentrate instead on Matthew Christopher.

"His head is clear," Letty said triumphantly. She reached out to cradle the infant as he barged head first into the world. "I've got one shoulder. Both. Stephanie, he's beautiful. And he *is* a boy. On the APGAR scale of one to ten, I'd say he's a twenty."

"My baby," Stephanie breathed, sounding dazed. "Let me see my baby."

Matthew Christopher whimpered loudly, expressing his extreme displeasure with the entire procedure just as the front door of the house flew open.

"What the hell's going on in here?" Joel shouted from the living room. "Letty? Letty, are you okay?"

"Stephanie?" Morgan's voice sounded frantic. "Where are you?"

"Morgan?" Stephanie called weakly. "Morgan, our baby is here."

Letty quickly wrapped Matthew Christopher in clean towels and laid him in Stephanie's arms. Then she turned toward the door of the bedroom and saw Joel and Morgan standing there looking stunned.

She smiled at her father. "Come and meet your son, Dad."

"Good God Almighty." Morgan's awed gaze went from Matthew Christopher to Stephanie. His eyes lit with a loving tenderness and concern. He took a step forward. "Stephie my dear, are you all right?"

"I'm fine," she whispered, obviously dazzled by the infant

in her arms. "We're all fine. It was a piece of cake, as they say. Letty had read several articles on the subject, you see."

Letty went with Joel when he told her he had to talk to Diana. They found her alone in the kitchen. She was methodically rinsing coffee mugs at the sink. She glanced over her shoulder when they walked slowly into the room.

"It's about Daddy, isn't it?"

"He's dead, Diana."

"I know." She put a clean mug on the drainboard. "I think I knew it when you arrived."

Joel looked at her, his gaze somber. "I don't know how to tell you this. But I'm sorry for all you've been through."

Diana stood quietly at the sink, gazing out the window at the afternoon sun on the snow. "Do you want to know what I feel, Joel? I feel a sense of relief. I'm not happy or sad. Just relieved. It's over at last. I feel as if I'm emerging from hell, thanks to you and Keith."

Matthew Christopher cried out from the vicinity of the bedroom, a lusty, demanding little cry signifying new life and new hope. Diana's head turned toward the sound.

Letty smiled and went forward to put her arms around her. "Now you and Keith can have your own baby."

Tears streaked Diana's face as she hugged Letty, but she was smiling. "Yes. It's safe now, isn't it? Thank, God. Now it's finally safe to have Keith's baby."

"I wasn't sure how she'd take it," Joel said later that night as he lay in bed with Letty.

"Diana's going to be all right." Letty curved herself into his warmth, grateful that he was there beside her and that he was safe. Outside, the storm had long since ceased. "How are you taking it?"

"I'm all right." Joel's arm tightened around her. "He murdered my father, Letty. He thought it was me in the car that night, and he forced it off the road."

Letty touched him gently. "At least you know for certain

what really happened that night. As bad as they are, you finally have the answers."

"Yeah." Joel was quiet for a moment. "Knowing for sure what happened makes it easier to handle, for some reason. It was not knowing the truth that had been eating at me all those years."

"Your father's death has been avenged. And you know he didn't kill himself because of you. Can you let go of the past now?"

Joel looked at her. "I think I started to let go of the past the day I met you."

Letty smiled tremulously. "Fair enough. I did the same with a lot of my own past when I met you."

"In any event," Joel continued softly, "I don't have much choice but to put it all behind me, do I? I'm going to be too busy with my future to worry about my past. Speaking of which, you looked very interesting with a baby in your arms, Madam President."

"Interesting?"

"Yeah. Interesting. I liked it. I can see you in our new ad campaign already. We'll photograph you holding a baby in one arm and pitching a Pack Up and Go tent with the other. Real hardy pioneer stuff, you know?"

"Forget it. That ad campaign has to be finished in three weeks, and it takes nine months to have a baby."

"Well," Joel said, "I guess maybe we'd better get started right away." He rolled over on top of her, covering her body with his own and crushing her deep into the thick mattress.

"Hold it," Letty said, already breathless. "Where I come from, we don't start planning babies until we've planned the wedding."

"Don't worry about it, one way or another there's going to be a wedding before next spring." Joel kissed her throat.

"You're sure?"

"I'm sure." He kissed her mouth.

"I don't know, Joel," Letty said with a tiny considering

frown. "I was just starting to get used to the idea of an affair."

"I told you, you're not really cut out for an affair, Letty."

"I thought I was handling it very well," she said.

"You're not the type."

"I'm not so sure about that. I mean any woman who can do what I did to you in your office is the type who can handle anything."

"Trust me. You were not cut out to have an affair." He ran his hand down over her thigh, found the hem of her nightgown, and tugged it upward.

"What about all the passion and pizzazz?" Letty smiled up at him, her hands moving on his shoulders. "I'm really enjoying that part, Joel."

Joel laughed softly in the shadows. "Passion and pizzazz are our middle names, Letty my love. We've got enough to last us for the rest of our lives."

Her smile turned quizzical. "And what about Thornquist Gear?"

Joel shrugged. "Everyone's going to say I married you to get my hands on the company. I can deal with it. I didn't think I could before today, but things have changed. I feel differently now. I think I've put a few things into perspective."

"No." Letty cradled his face between her palms. She looked up at him, knowing what she wanted to do. "No one's going to say you married me to get your hands on the company. Joel, you built Thornquist Gear. You put everything you had into it. You've fought for it and you've nourished it and you've protected it. Thornquist is your baby, and I have no moral right to it."

"Letty, it's just a business. Don't get emotional about it."

She grinned. "You're a fine one to talk. You're the most emotional man I know."

"The hell I am," he muttered. "I have a lot more self-control than you do, Madam President."

"Let's not argue about that," Letty said. "I have a deal to offer you."

Joel went still. "A deal?"

Letty took a deep breath. "I'll sell Thornquist to you before the wedding. Same terms Great-Uncle Charlie was going to give you."

"It's all right, Letty. You don't need to do that."

She touched his cheek. "You don't understand. I didn't really understand myself until now. I thought I needed the company in order to give me the fresh start I wanted in life. And maybe I did need it at first. But I don't need it any longer. New beginnings, the kind that last, come from within. We make them for ourselves."

"And now you think you no longer need Thornquist Gear to add excitement and adventure to your life?"

"No. I've got everything I need."

"What if I told you I no longer need the company, either?"

"I'd say we have a problem on our hands."

Joel chuckled. "I didn't say I didn't want it; I just said I could live without it. But as it happens, neither of us has to prove we don't need Thornquist Gear. You are not going to sell the company to me, Letty."

"I'm not?"

Joel rolled off of her and onto his back. He pulled her down on top of him. "No."

Letty stiffened. "But, Joel . . ."

"I am not a hotshot CEO for nothing, Madam President. I've got a counterproposal."

"I'm listening."

He smiled with satisfaction. "We'll split the company fifty-fifty. I'll buy out half of Thornquist Gear. You keep the other half. We'll own it jointly."

"But, Joel . . ."

He put his fingers firmly over her mouth. "That's my offer. Take it or leave it. But don't try giving me all of Thornquist, because I don't want it. I intend to share it with you, Letty."

She laughed softly. "Will I still get to be president?"

Joel grinned. "You bet. And I'm going to remain CEO. Deal?"

"Deal."

He pulled her face down to his and kissed her with a thoroughness that was more binding than any contract.

Joel awoke a few hours later. He glanced at the clock and saw that it was nearly one. Letty stirred beside him.

The dream?" she asked softly.

He searched his mind for the remnants of the old nightmare. Then he waited for the rush of adrenaline.

Nothing.

"No," Joel said. "I just woke up. But I don't think I was dreaming."

She pressed herself against him. "It's over," she whispered.

"Yes."

Joel cuddled her close and went back to sleep.

Two months later Joel loped down the stairs to the third floor and strode along the hall to the conference room. He walked through the door and stopped short at the sight of Letty held high in the arms of a huge blond Adonis.

Muscles bulged and rippled beneath the male model's bronzed skin. The leather shorts he was wearing were strained across thighs the size of tree trunks. His dazzling blue eyes and sparkling white teeth flashed in the fluorescent lighting.

Letty looked very small and fragile cradled against the bodybuilder's massive chest. One of her black pumps had fallen to the floor, and Joel was outraged at the sight of her pretty little bare foot being exposed to all and sundry.

"Would you mind putting the president of Thornquist Gear back on her feet?" Joel said coldly.

The Adonis blinked and looked immediately alarmed. "Sure. Sorry about that." He hastily set Letty back on the floor.

"Hello, Mr. Blackstone." Letty smiled cheerfully as she struggled to tuck in her blouse and straighten her rumpled jacket.

"Good afternoon, Mrs. Blackstone. Who the hell is this and what does he think he's doing carting you around like a sack of potatoes?"

"This is Mark," Letty said. "He's going to be the model for our new ad campaign. You know, the one aimed at the experienced high-country backpacker and rock climber."

"I trust he's not going to try to pack you into the high country?"

"Heavens, no. He was just proving to me that he could lift a hundred and twenty pounds of camping and climbing gear, weren't you, Mark?"

"Yes, ma'am." Mark flashed another perfect smile.

Letty examined him with professional admiration. "I think he's going to look just great climbing a glacier or something with lots of Thornquist Gear on his back. This new campaign is going to be smashing."

"Speaking of the new campaign, I have a few things to discuss with you concerning it, Mrs. Blackstone." Joel braced one elbow against the door frame and glowered at her. He lowered the file he was holding in one hand and tapped it against his leg.

Letty's brows rose behind her glasses. "Is there a problem?"

"There is one hell of a problem," Joel bit out. "The campaign is apparently fifty thousand dollars over budget."

"Oh, that."

"Yes, that. Would you care to explain where the money is going, Madam President?"

Letty laughed up at him with warm, loving eyes. "Certainly, Mr. Blackstone. Do you want to hear the explanation before or after I tell you that I have every reason to believe I'm pregnant?"

That very morning Joel had decided that it was probably

not possible for him to be any happier than he was already. Now he realized he was wrong. He forgot about the little matter of a fifty thousand dollar cost overrun and started to grin like an idiot.

"You're pregnant?" Joel ignored the embarrassed expression on the face of the blond Adonis. "You're going to have our baby?"

"It would appear so." Letty pushed her glasses up onto her nose and smiled demurely. "What do you say to that, Mr. Blackstone?"

Joel tossed the file over his left shoulder. The data on the ad budget was sent flying into the air.

Eyes gleaming, he walked over to Letty and lifted her carefully into his arms. "I say the hell with the fifty thousand dollars. What's a few bucks between a president and her CEO?"

"I knew you'd be reasonable about it, Joel."

Joel carried her out the door and down the hall. "Let's go back to my office, Mrs. Blackstone, and discuss something far more important than ad budget overruns."

"Yes, of course, Mr. Blackstone." Letty glowed up at him. "And this time we must remember to lock the door before we start our discussions."

Joel's laughter echoed down the halls of Thornquist Gear. Life was very good.

Also available from

New York Times bestselling author

JAYNE ANN KRENTZ

Absolutely, Positively

Deep Waters

Eye of the Beholder

Family Man

Flash

The Golden Chance

Grand Passion

Hidden Talents

Perfect Partners

Sharp Edges

Silver Linings

Sweet Fortune

Trust Me

Wildest Hearts

and writing as Jayne Castle:

Zinnia

Orchid

Amaryllis

POCKET BOOKS
A VIACOM COMPANY

2365.01

Visit
❖ Pocket Books ❖
online at

··

www.SimonSays.com

··

Keep up on the latest new
releases from your favorite
authors, as well as author
appearances, news, chats,
special offers and more.

SIMON & SCHUSTER
A VIACOM COMPANY
www.SimonSays.com

Pocket
Books

2381-01

Jayne Ann Krentz writing as
Jayne Castle

Amaryllis Lark is undeniable beautiful.
She's also one of the best psychic detectives on St.
Helen's, the earth colony recently cut off from the
mother planet, yet not so very different from
home—a place where love still defies the most
incredible odds. Lucas Trent, the rugged head of
Lodestar Exploration, isn't keen on the prim and
proper type, and Amaryllis is *excruciatingly* proper.

Amaryllis

Amaryllis may have psychic powers, but she can't
read minds—least of all her own. When a wild
murder investigation leads to a red-hot love affair,
Amaryllis is shocked, Lucas is delighted—and no
power on heaven, earth, or St. Helen's can keep
them apart!

Available from Pocket Books

POCKET
B O O K S

1238-01

New York Times bestselling author

JAYNE ANN KRENTZ

DEEP WATERS

"There is no finer exponent of
contemporary romance than the
immensely poplar Jayne Ann Krentz."
—*Romantic Times*

Available from Pocket Books

POCKET
B O O K S

1266-02

POCKET BOOKS
PROUDLY PRESENTS

FLASH

JAYNE ANN KRENTZ

Available in paperback from
Pocket Books

Turn the page for a preview of
Flash. . . .

Eight years earlier

Jasper Sloan sat in front of the fire, a half-finished glass of whiskey on the arm of the chair beside him, a thick file of papers in his hand. Page by page he fed the incriminating contents of the folder to the ravenous flames.

It was midnight. Outside a steady Northwest rain fell, cloaking the woods in a melancholy mist. The lights of Seattle were a distant blur across the waters of Puget Sound.

In the past his Bainbridge Island home had been a retreat and a refuge for Jasper. Tonight it was a place to bury the past.

"Watcha doin', Uncle Jasper?"

Jasper tossed another sheet to the flames. Then he looked at the ten-year-old pajama-clad boy in the doorway. He smiled slightly.

"I'm cleaning out some old files," he said. "What's the matter, Kirby? Couldn't you get to sleep?"

"I had another bad dream." There were shadows in Kirby's intelligent, too-somber eyes.

"It will fade in a few minutes." Jasper closed the half-empty file and set it on the wide arm of the chair. "I'll get you a cup of warm milk."

The dozen books on parenting that Jasper had consulted during the past several months had given conflicting advice on the subject of warm milk. But the stuff seemed to be effective on Kirby's bad dreams. At least there had been fewer of them lately.

"Okay." Kirby padded, barefoot, across the oak floor and sat down on the thick wool rug in front of the hearth. "It's still raining."

"Yes." Jasper walked into the kitchen and opened the refrigerator. He took out the carton of milk. "Probably stop by morning, though."

"If it does, can we set up the targets and do some more archery practice?"

"Sure." Jasper poured milk into a cup and stuck it into the microwave. He punched a couple of buttons. "We can do a little fishing, too. Maybe we'll get lucky and catch dinner."

Paul appeared in the doorway, yawning hugely. He glanced at the file on the chair. "What's goin' on out here?"

"Uncle Jasper's getting rid of some old papers he doesn't want anymore," Kirby explained.

Jasper looked at his other nephew. Paul was a year and a half older than Kirby. Instead of the overly serious expression that was Kirby's trademark, Paul's young gaze mirrored a hint of his father's reckless, aggressive approach to life.

Fletcher Sloan had bequeathed his deep, engaging blue eyes and his light brown hair to both of his sons. In the years ahead, when the softness of youth would give way to the harsher planes and angles of manhood, Jasper knew that Paul and Kirby would become living images of the dashing, charismatic man who had fathered them.

He also had a hunch that, given the strong forces of their two very different personalities, there would be problems as both boys entered their teens. He could only hope that the parenting books he was buying by the palette-load these days would guide him through the tricky years.

Jasper was relying on the books because he was only too well aware of his inadequacies in the field of parenting. His own father, Harry Sloan, had not been what anyone could call a strong role model.

Harry had been a devout workaholic all of his life who had had very little time for his sons or anyone else. Although ostensibly retired, he still went into the office every day. Jasper sensed that the day Harry stopped working would be the day he died.

Jasper poured a second cup of milk for Paul. He would have to take things as they came and do the best he could. It wasn't like there was much choice, he reminded himself. Fortunately, there were a lot of books on parenting.

He watched the digital readout on the microwave as it ticked off the time. For a disorienting moment, the numbers on the clock wavered and became years. He counted backward to the day, two decades earlier, when Fletcher had entered his life.

Flamboyant, charming, and slightly larger-than-life, Fletcher had become Jasper's stepbrother when Jasper's widowed father had remarried.

Jasper had few memories of his mother, who had died in a car crash when he was four. But his stepmother, Caroline, had been kind enough in a reserved fashion. Her great talent lay in managing the social side of Harry's life. She was very good at hosting dinner parties at the country club for Harry's business associates.

It had always seemed to Jasper that his father and stepmother lived in two separate universes. Harry lived for his work. Caroline lived for her country club activities. There did not appear to be any great bond of love between them, but both seemed content.

Caroline's only real fault was that she had doted on Fletcher. In her eyes her son could do no wrong. Instead of helping him learn to curtail his tendencies toward reckless irresponsibility and careless arrogance, she had indulged and encouraged them.

Caroline was not the only one who had turned a blind eye to Fletcher's less admirable traits. Six years younger than his new brother and eager for a hero to take the place of a father who was always at work, Jasper had been willing to overlook a lot, also.

Too much, as it turned out.

Fletcher was gone now. He and his wife, Brenda, had been killed nearly a year ago in a skiing disaster in the Alps.

Caroline had been stunned by the news of her son's death. But she had quickly, tearfully explained to Jasper and everyone else involved that she could not possibly be expected to assume the task of raising Paul and Kirby.

Her age and the social demands of her busy life made it impossible to start all over again as a mother to her grandsons. The boys needed someone younger, she said. Someone who had the patience and energy to handle children.

Jasper had taken Paul and Kirby to live with him. There had been no one else. He had committed himself to the role of substitute father with the same focused, well-organized, highly disciplined determination that he applied to every other aspect of his life.

The past eleven months had not been easy.

The first casualty had been his marriage. The divorce had become final six months ago. He did not blame Andrea for leaving him. After all, the job of playing mother to two young boys who were not even related to her had not been part of the business arrangement that had constituted the foundation of their marriage.

The microwave pinged. Jasper snapped back to the present. He opened the door and took out the mugs.

"Did you have a nightmare, too, Paul?" he asked.

"No." Paul wandered over to the fire and sat down, tailor-fashion, beside Kirby. "I woke up when I heard you guys talking out here."

"Uncle Jasper says we can do some more archery and maybe go fishing tomorrow," Kirby announced.

"Cool."

Jasper carried the two cups to where the boys sat in front of the fire. "That's assuming the rain stops."

"If it doesn't, we can always play Acid Man on the computer," Kirby said cheerfully.

Jasper winced at the thought of being cooped up in the house all weekend while his nephews entertained themselves with the loud sound effects of the new game.

"I'm pretty sure the rain will stop," he said, mentally crossing his fingers.

Paul looked at the closed file on the arm of the chair. "How come you're burning those papers?"

Jasper sat down and picked up the folder. "Old business. Just some stuff that's no longer important."

Paul nodded, satisfied. "Too bad you don't have a shredder here, huh?"

Jasper opened the file and resumed feeding the contents to the eager flames. "The fire works just as well."

In his opinion, the blaze worked even better than a mechanical shredder. Nothing was as effective as fire when it came to destroying damning evidence.

Five years later

Olivia Chantry poured herself a glass of dark red zinfandel wine and carried it down the hall toward the bedroom that had been converted into an office. She still had on the high-necked, long-sleeved black dress she had worn to her husband's funeral that afternoon.

Logan would have been her ex-husband if he had lived. She had been preparing to file for a divorce when he had suddenly jetted off to Pamplona, Spain. There he had gotten very drunk and had run with the bulls. The bulls won. Logan had been trampled to death.

Trust him to go out in a blaze of glory, Olivia thought. And to think she had once believed that a marriage based on friendship and mutual business interests would have a solid, enduring foundation. Uncle Rollie had been right, she decided. Logan had needed her, but he had not loved her.

Halfway down the hall she paused briefly at the thermostat to adjust the temperature. She had been feeling cold all day. The accusing expressions on the faces of the Dane family, especially the look in the eyes of Logan's younger brother, Sean, had done nothing to warm her. They knew she had seen a lawyer. They blamed her for Logan's spectacular demise.

Her cousin Nina's anguished, tearful eyes had only deepened the chill inside Olivia.

Uncle Rollie, the one member of Olivia's family who understood her best, had leaned close to whisper beneath the cover of the organ music.

"Give 'em time," Rollie said with the wisdom of eighty years. "They're all hurting now, but they'll get past it eventually."

Olivia was not so certain of that. In her heart she knew that her relationships with the Danes and with Nina would never be the same again.

When she reached the small, cluttered office, she took a sip of the zinfandel to fortify herself. Then she put down the glass and went to the black metal file cabinet in the corner. She spun the combination lock and pulled open a drawer. A row of folders appeared, most crammed to overflowing with business correspondence, tax forms, and assorted papers. One of these days she really would have to get serious about her filing.

She reached inside the drawer and removed the journal. For a moment she gazed at the leather-bound volume and considered the damning contents.

After a while she sat down at her cluttered desk, kicked off her black, low-heeled pumps, and switched on the small shredder. The machine whirred and hummed to life, a mechanical shark eager for prey.

The small bedroom-cum-office with its narrow windows was oppressive, she thought as she opened the journal. In fact, she hated the place where she and Logan had lived since their marriage six months ago.

She promised herself that first thing in the morning she would start looking for a bigger apartment. Her business was starting to take off. She could afford to buy herself a condo. One with lots of windows.

One by one, Olivia ripped the pages from the journal and fed them into the steel jaws. She would have preferred to burn the incriminating evidence, but she did not have a fireplace.

The zinfandel was gone by the time the last entry in the journal had been rendered into tiny scraps. Olivia sealed the plastic shredder bag and carried it downstairs to the basement of the apartment building. There she dumped the contents into the large bin marked *Clean Paper Only*.

When the blizzard of shredded journal pages finally ceased Olivia closed the lid of the bin. In the morning a large truck would come to haul away the contents. The discarded paper, including the shredded pages of the journal, would soon be transformed into something useful. Newsprint, maybe. Or toilet tissue.

Like almost everyone else who lived in Seattle, Olivia was a great believer in recycling.

The present

Jasper knew that he was in trouble because he had reached the point where he was giving serious consideration to the idea of getting married again.

His attention was deflected from the dangerous subject less than a moment later when he realized that someone was trying very hard to kill him.

At least, he *thought* someone was attempting to murder him.

Either way, as a distraction, the prospect was dazzlingly effective. Jasper immediately stopped thinking about finding a wife.

It was the blinding glare of hot, tropical sunlight on metal reflected in the rearview mirror that got Jasper's attention. He glanced up. The battered green Ford that had followed him from the tiny village on the island's north shore was suddenly much closer. In another few seconds the vehicle would be right on top of the Jeep's bumper.

The Ford shot out of the last narrow curve and bore down on the Jeep. The car's heavily tinted windows, common enough here in the South Pacific, made it impossible to see the face of the person at the wheel. Whoever he was, he was either very drunk or very high.

A tourist, Jasper thought. The Ford looked like one of the rusty rentals he had seen at the small agency in the village where he had selected the Jeep.

There was little room to maneuver on the tiny, two-lane road that encircled tiny Pelapili Island. Steep cliffs shot straight up on the left. On Jasper's right the terrain fell sharply away to the turquoise sea.

He had never wanted to take this vacation in paradise, Jasper thought. He should have listened to his own instincts instead of the urgings of his nephews and his friend, Al.

This was what came of allowing other people to push you into doing what they thought was best for you.

Jasper assessed the slim shoulder on the side of the pavement. There was almost no margin for driving error on this stretch of the road. One wrong move and a driver could expect to end up forty feet below on the lava- and boulder-encrusted beach.

He should have had his midlife crisis in the peace and comfort of his own home on Bainbridge Island. At least he could have been more certain of surviving it there.

But he'd made the extremely rare mistake of allowing others to talk him into doing something he really did not want to do.

"You've got to get away, Uncle Jasper," Kirby had declared with the shining confidence of a college freshman who has just finished his first course in psychology. "If you won't talk to a therapist, the least you can do is give yourself a complete change of scene."

"I hate to say it, but I think Kirby's right," Paul said. "You haven't been yourself lately. All this talk about selling Sloan & Associates, it's not like you, Uncle Jasper. Take a vacation. Get wild and crazy. Do something off-the-wall."

Jasper had eyed his nephews from the other side of his broad desk. Paul and Kirby were both enrolled for the summer quarter at the University of Washington. In addition, both had part-time jobs this year. They had their own apartment near the campus now, and they led very active lives. He did not believe for one moment that both just happened, by purest coincidence, to find themselves downtown this afternoon.

He did not believe both had been struck simultaneously by a whim to drop by his office, either. Jasper was fairly certain that he was the target of a planned ambush.

"I appreciate your concern," he said. "But I do not need or want a vacation. As far as selling the firm is concerned, trust me, I know what I'm doing."

"But Uncle Jasper," Paul protested. "You and Dad built this company from scratch. It's a part of you. It's in your blood."

"Let's not go overboard with the dramatics," Jasper said. "Hell, even my fiercest competitors will tell you that my timing is damn near perfect when it comes to business. I'm telling you that it's time for me to do something else."

Kirby frowned, his dark blue eyes grave with concern. "How is your sleep pattern, Uncle Jasper?"

"What's my sleep pattern got to do with anything?"

"We're studying clinical depression in my Psych class. Sleep disturbance is a major warning sign."

"My sleep habits have been just fine."

Jasper decided not to mention the fact that for the past

month he had been waking up frequently at four in the morning. Unable to get back to sleep, he had gotten into the habit of going into the office very early to spend a couple of hours with the contents of his business files.

His excuse was that he wanted to go over every detail of the extensive operations of Sloan & Associates before he sold the firm to Al. But he knew the truth. He had a passion for order and routine. He found it soothing to sort through his elegantly arranged files. He knew few other people who could instantly retrieve decade-old corporate income tax records or an insurance policy that had been canceled five years earlier.

Maybe he could not control every aspect of his life, he thought, but he could damn sure handle the paperwork related to it.

"Well, what about your appetite?" Kirby surveyed him with a worried look. "Are you losing weight?"

Jasper wrapped his hands around the arms of his chair and glowered at Kirby. "If I want a professional psychological opinion, I'll call a real shrink, not someone who just got out of Psych 101."

An hour later, over lunch at a small Italian restaurant near the Pike Place Market, Al Okamoto stunned Jasper by agreeing with Paul's and Kirby's verdict.

"They're right." Al forked up a swirl of his spaghetti puttanesca. "You need to get away for a while. Take a vacation. When you come back we'll talk about whether or not you still want to sell Sloan & Associates to me."

"Hell, you too?" Jasper shoved aside his unfinished plate of Dungeness crab-filled ravioli. He had not been about to admit it to Kirby that afternoon, but lately his normally healthy appetite had been a little off. "What is it with everyone today? So what if I've put in a few extra hours on the Slater project? I'm just trying to get everything in order for the sale."

Al's gaze narrowed. "It's not the Slater deal. That's routine, and you know it. You could have handled it in your sleep. If you were getting any sleep, that is, which I doubt."

Jasper folded his arms on the table. "Now you're telling me I look tired? Damn it, Al—"

"I'm telling you that you need a break, that's all. A weekend off isn't going to do the trick. Take a month. Go veg out on some remote, tropical island. Swim in the ocean, sit under a palm tree. Drink a few margaritas."

"I'm warning you, pal, if you're about to tell me that I'm depressed . . ."

"You're not depressed, you're having a midlife crisis."

Jasper stared at him. "Are you crazy? I am not having any such thing."

"You know what one looks like, do you?"

"Everyone knows what a midlife crisis looks like. Affairs with very young women. Flashy red sports cars. A divorce."

"So?"

"In case you've forgotten, my divorce took place nearly eight years ago. I am not interested in buying a Ferrari that would probably get stolen and sent to a chop shop the first week I owned it. And I haven't had an affair in—" Jasper broke off suddenly. "In a while."

"A *long* while." Al aimed his fork at Jasper. "You don't get out enough. That's one of your problems. You lack a normal social life."

"So I'm not a party animal. So sue me."

Al sighed. "I've known you for over five years. I can tell you that you never do anything the usual way. Stands to reason that you wouldn't have a typical, run-of-the-mill midlife crisis. Instead of an explosion, you're going through a controlled meltdown."

"For which you recommend a tropical island vacation?"

"Why not? It's worth a try. Pick one of those incredibly expensive luxury resorts located on some undiscovered island. The kind of place that specializes in unstressing seriously overworked executives."

"How do they manage the unstressing part?" Jasper asked.

Al forked up another bite of pasta. "They give you a room with no phone, no fax, no television, no air conditioner and no clocks."

"We used to call that kind of hotel a flophouse."

"It's the latest thing in upscale, high-end vacations," Al assured him around a mouthful of spaghetti. "Costs a fortune. What have you got to lose?"

"I dunno. A fortune maybe?"

"You can afford it. Look, Paul and Kirby and I have already picked out an ideal spot. An island called Pelapili. It's at the far end of the Hawaiian chain. We made the reservations for you."

"You did *what?*"

"You're going to stay there for a full month."

"The hell I am, I've got a business to run."

"I'm the vice president, second largest shareholder, and the chief associate in Sloan & Associates, remember? You say you want to sell out to me. If you can't trust me to hold the company together for a mere month, who can you trust?"

In the end, Jasper had run out of excuses. A week later he had found himself on a plane to Pelapili Island.

For the past three and a half weeks he had dutifully followed the agenda that Al, Kirby, and Paul had outlined for him.

Every morning he swam in the pristine, clear waters of the bay that was only a few steps from his high-priced, low-tech cottage. He spent a lot of time reading boring thrillers in the shade of a palm tree, and he drank a few salt-rimmed margaritas in the evenings.

On days when he could not stand the enforced tranquillity for another minute, he used the rented Jeep to sneak into the village to buy a copy of the *Wall Street Journal*.

The newspapers were always at least three days old by the time they reached Pelapili, but he treasured each one. Like some demented alchemist, he examined every inch of print for occult secrets related to the world of business.

Jasper thrived on information. As far as he was concerned, it was not just power, it was magic. It was the life-blood of his work as a venture capitalist. He collected information, organized it, and filed it.

Cutting himself off from the flow of daily business information in the name of relaxation had been a serious mistake. He knew that now.

He still did not know if he was in the midst of a midlife crisis, but he had come to one definite conclusion: He was bored. He was a goal-oriented person, and the only goal he'd had until now on Pelapili was to get off the island.

Things had changed in the last sixty seconds, however. He had a new goal. A very clear one. He wanted to avoid going over the edge of the cliff into the jeweled sea.

The car was almost on top of him. On the off-chance that the driver was simply incredibly impatient, Jasper tried easing cautiously toward the shoulder. The Ford now had room to pass, if that was the objective.

For a few seconds Jasper thought that was what would happen. The nose of the Ford pulled out into the other lane.

But instead of accelerating on past, it nipped at the fender of Jasper's Jeep.

Metal screamed against metal. A shudder went through the Jeep. Jasper fought the instinct to swerve away from the Ford. There was no room left on the right-hand shoulder. Another foot and he would be airborne out over the rocky cove.

The reality of what was happening slammed through him. The Ford really was trying to force the Jeep over the edge of the cliff. Jasper knew that he would die an unpleasant but probably very speedy death if he did not act quickly.

He was intensely aware of the physical dimensions of the space around him. He gauged the distance to the upcoming curve and the speed of his own vehicle. He sensed the driver of the Ford had nerved himself for another strike.

Jasper turned the wheel, aiming the Jeep's bumper at the Ford's side. There was a shudder and another grating shriek of metal-on-metal. Jasper edged closer.

The Ford swerved to avoid the second impact. It went into the next curve in the wrong lane. The driver, apparently panicked by the thought of meeting an oncoming vehicle, overcorrected wildly.

For an instant Jasper thought the Ford would go straight over the edge of the cliff. Somehow, it managed to cling to the road.

Jasper slowed quickly and went cautiously into the turn. When he came out of it he caught a fleeting glimpse of the Ford. It was already several hundred feet ahead. As he watched, it disappeared around another curve.

The driver of the Ford had obviously decided to abandon the assault on the Jeep. Jasper wondered if the other man, assuming it was a man, had lost his nerve or simply sobered up very quickly after the near-death experience on the curve.

Drunken driving or maybe an incident of road rage, Jasper told himself. That was the only logical explanation.

To entertain for even a moment the possibility that someone had deliberately tried to kill him would constitute a sure sign of incipient paranoia. Kirby would have a field day. Probably drag Jasper off to his psychology class for show-and-tell.

Damn. He hadn't even gotten the license number.

Jasper tried to summon up an image of the rear of the green car. He was very good with numbers.

But when he replayed the discrete mental pictures he had of the Ford he realized he did not remember seeing a license plate.

A near accident. That was the only explanation.

Don't go paranoid on me here, Sloan.

He spent most of the warm, tropical night brooding on the veranda of his overpriced, amenity-free cottage. For a long time he sat in the wicker chair and watched the silver moonlight slide across the surface of the sea. He could not explain why the uneasiness within him increased with every passing hour.

He had put the incident on the island road firmly in perspective. He knew that it was illogical to think for one moment that anyone here on Pelapili had any reason to try to murder him. No, it was not the brush with disaster that afternoon that was creating the disturbing sensation.

But the restlessness would not be banished. He wondered if he was suffering from an overdose of papaya, sand and margaritas. The problem with paradise was that it held no challenge.

A two in the morning he realized that it was time to go back to Seattle.